MORE
TWISTED

Also by Jeffery Deaver

Mistress of Justice
The Lesson of Her Death
Praying for Sleep
Speaking in Tongues
A Maiden's Grave
The Devil's Teardrop
The Blue Nowhere
Garden of Beasts

The Rune Series

Manhattan is my Beat
Death of a Blue Movie Star
Hard News

The Location Scout series

Shallow Graves
Bloody River Blues
Hell's Kitchen

The Lincoln Rhyme thrillers

The Bone Collector
The Coffin Dancer
The Empty Chair
The Stone Monkey
The Vanished Man
The Twelfth Card
The Cold Moon
The Sleeping Doll

Short stories

Twisted

Jeffery DEAVER

MORE TWISTED

HODDER &
STOUGHTON

Copyright © 2006 by Jeffery Deaver

First published in the United States of America in 2006
by Simon & Schuster, Inc.
First published in Great Britain in 2006 by Hodder and Stoughton
A division of Hodder Headline

The right of Jeffery Deaver to be identified as the Author of the
Work has been asserted by him in accordance with the Copyright,
Designs and Patents Act 1988.

A Hodder and Stoughton Book

3

A CIP catalogue record for this title is available from the British
Library

Hardback ISBN 978 0 340 93385 5

Trade Paperback ISBN 978 0 340 93386 2

Printed and bound by Clays Ltd, St Ives plc

Hodder Headline's policy is to use papers that are natural,
renewable and recyclable products and made from wood grown in
sustainable forests. The logging and manufacturing processes are
expected to conform to the environmental regulations of the
country of origin.

Hodder and Stoughton
A division of Hodder Headline
338 Euston Road
London NW1 3BH

To John Gilstrap

Contents

Preface 1

Chapter and Verse 5

Commuter 24

The Westphalian Ring 41

Surveillance 69

Born bad 95

Interrogation 116

Afraid 136

Double Jeopardy 152

Tunnel Girl 182

Locard's Principle 204

A Dish Served Cold 254

Copycat 294

The Voycur 328

The Poker Lesson 345

Ninety-eight Point Six 374

A Nice Place to Visit 397

Afterword to "Afraid" 431

Preface

From time to time I do something even more terrifying than write sick and twisted novels and stories; I grab a microphone and get up in front of a roomful of people.

No, I'm not talking *American Idol*; I'm referring to teaching writing.

One of the most often asked questions when I'm playing professor is this: Should I start writing short stories and then work my way up to novels? My answer is no. It's not like starting to ride a tricycle and then graduating to a bike. Forgive my clumsy mixing of metaphors, but short stories and novels aren't even apples and oranges; they're apples and potatoes.

Novels seek to emotionally engage readers on all levels, and, to achieve that goal, authors must develop characters in depth, create realistic settings, do extensive research and come up with a structured pacing that alternates between the thoughtful and the rip-roaring.

A short story's different. As I said in the introduction to my first collection of stories,

> The payoff in the case of short stories isn't a roller coaster of plot reversals involving characters they've spent lots of time learning about and loving or hating, set in places with atmosphere carefully described. Short stories are like a sniper's bullet. Fast and shocking. In a story, I can make good bad and bad badder and, the most fun of all, really bad seem good.

The title of my anthologies (*Twisted* was the first) is no coincidence. To me, that big oh-my-God surprise is what short stories are all about. A few years ago I wrote a book about a psychotic illusionist and I realized that the novel was, in some ways, about me (as a writer, let me add quickly, not as a psycho or a magician). In researching the book I learned a lot about sleight of hand, misdirection, diversion and illusion, and I understood that those tricks are exactly what I've been doing for years to lull my readers into complacency and then, bang, zing 'em when they least expect it.

While they're watching my left hand, my right is getting ready to strike.

Since that first collection was published in 2003, I've kept up my guilty pleasure of taking off a day or two here and there and writing more stories, all of which adhere to the philosophy I mention above: throw morality and sentiment out the window, and go for the gut-wrenching twist.

In this collection, like my previous one, you'll find a wide variety of stories, which incorporate my favorite themes: revenge, lust, psychosis, betrayal and greed, along with a healthy (so to speak) dose of family dysfunction. There's one story set in Italy and one in Victorian England. One features a slick lawyer in a small town and another finds gullible tourists in a big one. You'll see Peeping Toms, remorseless murderers, my own take on *The Da Vinci Code* and even a story about—who'd've thought?—an author who writes suspense.

And for those who'd like an insight into tricks of the trade, I've included in an afterword a short piece about one of the stories here ("Afraid"), which I wrote as an illustration of how I incorporate the concept of fear into my fiction. I've placed it at the end, so as not to give away any susprises.

Finally, a word of thanks to those who've encouraged me to write these stories, particularly Janet Hutchins and her inestimable *Ellery Queen's Mystery Magazine,* Marty Greenburg, Otto Penzler, Deborah Schneider, David Rosenthal, Marysue Rucci and, as always, Madelyn Warcholik.

So, sit back and enjoy—and see if you can outguess me. Keep your eye on my right hand.

Or do I mean left?

—*J.W.D.*

Chapter and Verse

Reverend . . . can I call you 'Reverend'?"

The round, middle-aged man in the clerical collar smiled. "That works for me."

"I'm Detective Mike Silverman with the County Sheriff's Department."

Reverend Stanley Lansing nodded and examined the ID and badge that the nervously slim, salt-and-pepper–haired detective offered.

"Is something wrong?"

"Nothing involving you, sir. Not directly, I mean. Just hoping you might be able to help us with a situation we have."

"Situation. Hmm. Well, come on inside, please, Officer . . ."

The men walked into the office connected to the First Presbyterian Church of Bedford, a quaint, white house of worship that Silverman had passed a thousand times on his route between office and home and never really thought about.

That is, not until the murder this morning.

Reverend Lansing's office was musty and a gauze of dust covered most of the furniture. He seemed embarrassed. "Have to apologize. My wife and I've been away on vacation for the past week. She's still up at the lake. I came back to write my sermon—and to deliver it to my flock this Sunday, of course." He gave a wry laugh. "*If* there's anybody in the pews. Funny how religious commitment seems to go up around Christmas and then dip around vacation time." Then the man of the cloth looked around the office with a frown. "And I'm afraid I don't have anything to offer you. The church secretary's off too. Although between you and me, you're better off not sampling her coffee."

"No, I'm fine," Silverman said.

"So, what can I do for you, Officer?"

"I won't keep you long. I need some religious expertise on a case we're running. I would've gone to my father's rabbi but my question's got to do with the New Testament. That's your bailiwick, right? More than ours."

"Well," the friendly, gray-haired reverend said, wiping his glasses on his jacket lapel and replacing them, "I'm just a small-town pastor, hardly an expert. But I probably know Matthew, Mark, Luke and John better than your average rabbi, I suspect. Now, tell me how I can help."

"You've heard about the witness protection program, right?"

"Like *Goodfellas*, that sort of thing? *The Sopranos*."

"More or less, yep. The U.S. Marshals run the federal program but we have our own state witness protection system."

"Really? I didn't know that. But I guess it makes sense."

"I'm in charge of the program in the county here and one of the people we're protecting is about to appear as a witness in a trial in Hamilton. It's our job to keep him safe through the trial and after we get a conviction—we hope—then we'll get him a new identity and move him out of the state."

"A Mafia trial?"

"Something like that."

Silverman couldn't go into the exact details of the case—how the witness, Randall Pease, a minder for drug dealer Tommy Doyle, had seen his boss put a bullet into the brain of a rival. Despite Doyle's reputation for ruthlessly murdering anyone who was a threat to him, Pease agreed to testify for a reduced sentence on assault, drug and gun charges. The state prosecutor shipped Pease off to Silverman's jurisdiction, a hundred miles from Hamilton, to keep him safe; rumor was that Doyle would do anything, pay any money, to kill his former underling—since

Pease's testimony could get him the death penalty or put him away for life. Silverman had stashed the witness in a safe house near the Sheriff's Department and put a round-the-clock guard on him. The detective gave the reverend a generic description of what had happened, not mentioning names, and then said, "But there's been a setback. We had a CI—a confidential informant—"

"That's a snitch, right?"

Silverman laughed.

"I learned that from *Law and Order.* I watch it every chance I get. *CSI* too. I love cop shows." He frowned. "You mind if I say 'cop'?"

"Works for me. . . . Anyway, the informant got solid information that a professional killer's been hired to murder our witness before the trial next week."

"A hit man?"

"Yep."

"Oh, my." The reverend frowned as he touched his neck and rubbed it near the stiff white clerical collar, where it seemed to chafe.

"But the bad guys made the snitch—found out about him, I mean—and had him killed before he could give us the details about who the hit man is and how he planned to kill my witness."

"Oh, I'm so sorry," the reverend said sympathetically. "I'll say a prayer for the man."

Silverman grunted anemic thanks but his true thoughts were that the scurvy little snitch deserved an express-lane ride to hell—not only for being a loser punk addict, but for dying before he could give the detective the particulars about the potential hit on Pease. Detective Mike Silverman didn't share with the minister that he himself had been in trouble lately in the Sheriff's Department and had been shipped off to Siberia—witness protection—because he hadn't closed any major cases in a while. He needed to make sure this assignment went smoothly, and he absolutely could not let Pease get killed.

The detective continued, "Here's where you come in—I hope. When the informant was stabbed, he didn't die right away. He managed to write a note—about a Bible passage. We think it was a clue as to how the hit man was going to kill our witness. But it's like a puzzle. We can't figure it out."

The reverend seemed intrigued. "Something from the New Testament, you said?"

"Yep," Silverman said. He opened his notebook. "The note said, 'He's on his way. Look out.' Then he wrote a chapter and verse from the Bible. We think he was going to write something else but he didn't get a chance. He was Catholic so we figure he knew the bible pretty well—and knew something in particular in that passage that'd tell us how the hit man's going to come after our witness."

The reverend turned around and looked for a Bible on his shelf. Finally he located one and flipped it open. "What verse?"

"Luke, twelve, fifteen."

The minister found the passage and read. "'Then to the people he said, 'Beware! Be on your guard against greed of every kind, for even when someone has more than enough, his possessions do not give him life.'"

"My partner brought a Bible from home. He's Christian, but he's not real religious, not a Bible-thumper. . . . Oh, hey, no offense."

"None taken. We're Presbyterians. We don't thump."

Silverman smiled. "He didn't have any idea of what that might mean. I got to thinking about your church—it's the closest one to the station house—so I thought I'd stop by and see if you can help us out. Is there anything in there you can see that'd suggest how the defendant might try to kill our witness?"

The reverend read some more from the tissue-thin pages. "This section is in one of the Gospels—where different disciples tell the story of Jesus. In chapter twelve of Luke, Jesus is warning the people about the Pharisees, urging them not to live a sinful life."

"Who were they exactly, the Pharisees?"

"They were a religious sect. In essence they believed that God existed to serve them, not the other way around. They felt they were better than everyone else and put people down. Well, that was the story back then—you never know, of course, if it's accurate. People did just as much political spinning then as they do now." Reverend Lansing tried to turn on the desk lamp but it didn't work. He fiddled with the curtains, finally opening them and letting more light into the murky office. He read the passage several times more, squinting in concentration, nodding. Silverman looked around the dim place. Books mostly. It seemed more like a professor's study than a church office. No pictures or anything else personal. You'd think even a minister would have pictures of family on his desk or walls.

Finally the man looked up. "So far, nothing really jumps out at me." He seemed frustrated.

Silverman felt the same way. Ever since the CI had been found stabbed to death that morning, the detective had been wrestling with the words from the gospel according to Luke, trying to decipher the meaning.

Beware! . . .

Reverend Lansing continued, "But I have to say, I'm fascinated with the idea. It's just like *The Da Vinci Code*. You read it?"

"No."

"It was great fun. All about secret codes and hidden messages. Say, if it's okay with you, Detective, I'd like to spend some time researching, doing some thinking about this. I love puzzles."

"I'd appreciate it, Reverend."

"I'll do what I can. You have that man under pretty good guard, I assume?"

"Oh, you bet, but it'll be risky getting him to court. We've got to figure out how the hit man's going to come at him."

"And the sooner the better, I assume."

"Yessir."

"I'll get right to it."

Grateful for the man's willingness to help, but discouraged he had no quick answers, Silverman walked out through the silent, deserted church. He climbed into his car and drove to the safe house, checked on Ray Pease. The witness was his typical obnoxious self, complaining constantly, but the officer babysitting him reported that there'd been no sign of any threats around the safe house. The detective then returned to the department.

In his office Silverman made a few calls to see if any of his other CIs had heard about the hired killer; they hadn't. His eyes kept returning to the passage, taped up on the wall in front of his desk.

Beware! Be on your guard against greed of every kind, for even when someone has more than enough, his possessions do not give him life.

A voice startled him. "Wanta get some lunch?"

He looked up to find his partner, Steve Noveski, standing in the doorway. The junior detective, with a pleasant, round baby face, was staring obviously at his watch.

Silverman, still lost in the mysterious Bible passage, just stared at him.

"Lunch, dude," Noveski repeated. "I'm starving."

"Naw, I've gotta get this figured out." He tapped the Bible. "I'm kind of obsessed with it."

"Like, you think?" the other detective said, packing as much sarcasm into his voice as would fit.

■

That night Silverman returned home and sat distractedly through dinner with his family. His widower father had joined them, and the old man wasn't pleased that his son was so preoccupied.

"And what's that you're reading that's so important? The New Testament?" The man nodded toward the Bible he'd seen his son poring over before dinner. He shook his head and turned to his daughter-in-law. "The boy hasn't been to temple in years and he couldn't find the Pentateuch his mother and I gave him if his life depended on it. Now look, he's reading about Jesus Christ. What a son."

"It's for a case, Dad," Silverman said. "Listen, I've got some work to do. I'll see you guys later. Sorry."

"See you later sorry?" the man muttered. "And you say 'you guys' to your wife? Don't you have any respect—"

Silverman closed the door to his den, sat down at his desk and checked messages. The forensic scientist testing the murdered CI's note about the Bible passage had called to report there was no significant evidence to be found on the sheet and neither the paper nor the ink were traceable. A handwriting comparison suggested that it had been written by the victim but he couldn't be one hundred percent certain.

And, as the hours passed, there was still no word from Reverend Lansing. Sighing, Silverman stretched and stared at the words once again.

"Beware! Be on your guard against greed of every kind, for even when someone has more than enough, his possessions do not give him life."

He grew angry. A man died leaving these words to warn them. What was he trying to say?

Silverman had a vague memory of his father saying good-bye that night and later still an even more vague memory of his wife saying good night, the den door closing abruptly. She was mad. But Michael Silverman didn't care. All that mattered at the moment was finding the meaning to the message.

Something the reverend had said that afternoon came back to him. *The Da Vinci Code.* A code . . . Silverman thought about the snitch: The man hadn't been a college grad but he was smart in his own way. Maybe he had more in mind than the literal meaning of the passage; could it be that the specifics of his warning were somehow encoded in the letters themselves?

It was close to four a.m. but Silverman ignored his exhaustion and went online. He found a website about word games and puzzles. In one game you made as many words as you could out of the first letters from a saying or quotation. Okay, this could be it, Silverman thought excitedly. He wrote down the first letters of each of the words from Luke 12:15 and began rearranging them.

He got several names: *Bob, Tom, Don* . . . and dozens of words: *Gone, pen, gap* . . .

Well, *Tom* could refer to Tommy Doyle. But he could find no other clear meaning in the words or any combination of them.

What other codes were there he might try?

He tried an obvious one: assigning numbers to the letters, A equaled 1, B 2 and so on. But when he applied the formula all he ended up with were sheets of hundreds of random digits. Hopeless, he thought. Like trying to guess a computer password.

Then he thought of anagrams—where the letters of a word or phrase are rearranged to make other words. After a brief search on the web he found a site with an anagram generator, a software program that let you type in a word and a few seconds later spit out all the anagrams that could be made from it.

For hours he typed in every word and combination of words in the passage and studied the results. At six a.m., utterly exhausted, Silverman was about to give up and fall into bed. But as he was arranging the printouts of the anagrams he'd downloaded, he happened to glance at one—the anagrams that the word *possessions* had yielded: *open, spies, session, nose, sepsis* . . .

Something rang a bell.

"Sepsis?" he wondered out loud. It sounded familiar. He looked the word up. It meant infection. Like blood poisoning.

He was confident that he was on to something and, excited, he riffled through the other sheets. He saw that "greed" incorporated "Dr."

Yes!

And the word "guard" produced "drug."

Okay, he thought in triumph. Got it!

Detective Mike Silverman celebrated his success by falling asleep in his chair.

∎

He awoke an hour later, angry at the loud engine rattling nearby—until he realized the noise was his own snoring.

The detective closed his dry mouth, winced at the pain in his back and sat up. Massaging his stiff neck, he staggered upstairs to the bedroom, blinded by the sunlight pouring through the French doors.

"Are you up already?" his wife asked blearily from bed, looking at his slacks and shirt. "It's early."

"Go back to sleep," he said.

After a fast shower he dressed and sped to the office. At eight a.m. he was in his captain's office, with his partner, Steve Noveski, beside him.

"I've figured it out."

"What?" his balding, joweled superior officer asked.

Noveski glanced at his partner with a lifted eyebrow; he'd just arrived and hadn't heard Silverman's theory yet.

"The message we got from the dead CI—how Doyle's going to kill Pease."

The captain had heard about the biblical passage but hadn't put much stock in it. "So how?" he asked skeptically.

"Doctors," Silverman announced.

"Huh?"

"I think he's going to use a doctor to try to get to Pease."

"Keep going."

Silverman told him about the anagrams.

"Like crossword puzzles?"

"Sort of."

Noveski said nothing but he too seemed skeptical of the idea.

The captain screwed up his long face. "Hold on here. You're saying that here's our CI and he's got a severed jugular and he's playing *word* games?"

"Funny how the mind works, what it sees, what it can figure out."

"Funny," the senior cop muttered. "Sounds a little, whatsa word, contrived, you know what I mean?"

"He had to get us the message and he had to make sure that Doyle didn't tip to the fact he'd alerted us. He had to make it, you know, subtle enough so Doyle's boys wouldn't figure out what he knew, but not so subtle that we couldn't guess it."

"I don't know."

Silverman shook his head. "I think it works." He explained that Tommy Doyle had often paid huge fees to brilliant, ruthless hit men who'd masquerade as somebody else to get close to their unsuspecting victims. Silverman speculated that the killer would buy or steal a doctor's white jacket and get a fake ID card and a stethoscope or whatever doctors carried around with them nowadays. Then a couple of Doyle's cronies would make a halfhearted attempt on Pease's life—they couldn't get close enough to kill him in the safe house, but causing injury was a possibility. "Maybe food poisoning." Silverman explained about the sepsis anagram. "Or maybe they'd arrange for a fire or gas leak or something. The hit man, disguised as a med tech, would be allowed inside and kill Pease there. Or maybe the witness would be rushed to the hospital and the man'd cap him in the emergency room."

The captain shrugged. "Well, you can check it out—provided you don't ignore the grunt work. We can't afford to screw this one up. We lose Pease and it's our ass."

The pronouns in those sentences may have been first person plural but all Silverman heard was a very singular "you" and "your."

"Fair enough."

In the hallway on their way back to his office Silverman asked his partner, "Who do we have on call for medical attention at the safe house?"

"I don't know, a team from Forest Hills Hospital, I'd guess."

"We don't know who?" Silverman snapped.

"I don't, no."

"Well, find out! Then get on the horn to the safe house and tell the babysitter if Pease gets sick for any reason, needs any medicine, needs a goddamn bandage, to call me right away. Do *not* let any medical people see him unless we have a positive ID and I give my personal okay."

"Right."

"Then call the supervisor at Forest Hills and tell him to let me know stat if any doctors or ambulance attendants or nurses—*anybody*—don't show up for work or call in sick or if there're some doctors around that he doesn't recognize."

The young man peeled off into his office to do what Silverman had ordered and the senior detective returned to his own desk. He called a counterpart at the county sheriff's office in Hamilton and told him what he suspected and added that they had to be on the lookout for any medical people who were close to Pease.

The detective then sat back in his chair, rubbing his eyes and massaging his neck. He was more and more convinced he was right, that the secret message left by the dying informant was pointing toward a killer masquerading as a health care worker. He picked up the phone again. For several hours, he nagged hospitals and ambulance services around the county to find out if all of their people and vehicles were accounted for.

As the hour neared lunchtime, his phone rang.

"Hello?"

"Silverman." The captain's abrupt voice instantly killed the detective's sleep-deprivation haze; he was instantly alert. "We just had an attempt on Pease."

Silverman's heart thudded. He sat forward. "He okay?"

"Yeah. Somebody in an SUV fired thirty, forty shots through the front windows of the safe house. Steel-jacketed rounds, so they got through the armored glass. Pease and his guard got hit with some splinters, but nothing serious. Normally we'd send 'em to the hospital but I was thinking about what you said, about the killer pretending to be a tech or doctor, so I thought it was better to bring Pease straight here, to Detention. I'll have our sawbones look 'em both over."

"Good."

"We'll keep him here for a day or two and then send him up to the federal WP facility in Ronanka Falls."

"And have somebody head over to the Forest Hills emergency room and check out the doctors. Doyle's hired gun might be thinking we'd send him there and be waiting."

"Already ordered," the captain said.

"When'll Pease get here?"

"Anytime now."

"I'll have the lockup cleared." He hung up, rubbed his eyes again. How the hell had Doyle found out the location of the safe house? It was the best-kept secret in the department. Still, since no one had been seriously injured in the attack, he allowed himself another figurative pat of self-congratulations. His theory was being borne out. The shooter hadn't tried to kill Pease at all, just shake him up and cause enough carnage to have him dive to the floor and scrape an elbow or get cut by flying glass. Then off to the ER—and straight into the arms of Doyle's hit man.

He called the Detention supervisor at the jail and arranged to have the existing prisoners in the holding cell moved temporarily to the town police station, then told the man to brief the guards and warn them to make absolutely certain they recognized the doctor who was going to look over Pease and his bodyguard.

"I already did. 'Causa what the captain said, you know."

Silverman was about to hang up when he glanced at the

clock. It was noon, the start of second guard shift. "Did you tell the afternoon-shift personnel about the situation?"

"Oh. Forgot. I'll do it now."

Silverman hung up angrily. Did he have to think of everything himself?

He was walking to his door, headed for the Detention Center intake area to meet Pease and his guard, when his phone buzzed. The desk sergeant told him he had a visitor. "It's a Reverend Lansing. He said it's urgent that he sees you. He said to tell you that he's figured out the message. You'd know what he means."

"I'll be right there."

Silverman grimaced. As soon as he'd figured out what the passage meant that morning the detective had planned to call the minister and tell him they didn't need his help any longer. But he'd forgotten all about it. Shit. . . . Well, he'd do something nice for the guy—maybe donate some money to the church or take the reverend out to lunch to thank him. Yeah, lunch would be good. They could talk about TV cop shows.

The detective met Reverend Lansing at the front desk. Silverman greeted him with a wince, noticing how exhausted he looked. "You get any sleep last night?"

The minister laughed. "Nope. Just like you, looks like."

"Come on with me, Reverend. Tell me what you came up with." He led the man down the corridor toward intake. He decided he'd hear what the man had to say. Couldn't hurt.

"I think I've got the answer to the message."

"Go on."

"Well, I was thinking that we shouldn't limit ourselves just to the verse fifteen itself. That one's just a sort of introduction to the parable that follows. I think that's the answer."

Silverman nodded, recalling what he'd read in Noveski's Bible. "The parable about the farmer?"

"Exactly. Jesus tells about a rich farmer who has a good harvest. He doesn't know what to do with the excess grain. He thinks he'll build bigger barns and figures he'll spend the rest of his life enjoying what he's done. But what happens is that God strikes him down because he's greedy. He's materially rich but spiritually impoverished."

"Okay," Silverman said. He didn't see any obvious message yet.

The reverend sensed the cop's confusion. "The point of the passage is greed. And I think that might be the key to what that poor man was trying to tell you."

They got to the intake dock and joined an armed guard who was awaiting the arrival of the armored van carrying Pease. The existing prisoners in the lockup, Silverman learned, weren't all in the transport bus yet for the transfer to the city jail.

"Tell 'em to step on it," Silverman ordered and turned back to the minister, who continued his explanation.

"So I asked myself, what's greed nowadays? And I figured it was Enron, Tyco, CEOs, internet moguls. . . . And Cahill Industries."

Silverman nodded slowly. Robert Cahill was the former head of a huge agri-business complex. After selling that company he'd turned to real estate and had put up dozens of buildings in the county. The man had just been indicted for tax evasion and insider trading.

"Successful farmer," Silverman mused. "Has a big windfall and gets in trouble. Sure. Just like the parable."

"It gets better," the minister said excitedly. "There was an editorial in the paper a few weeks ago—I tried to find it but couldn't— about Cahill. I think the editor cited a couple of Bible passages about greed. I can't remember which but I'll bet one of them was Luke twelve, fifteen."

Standing on the intake loading dock, Silverman watched the van carrying Randy Pease arrive. The detective and the guard looked around them carefully for any signs of threats as the armored vehicle backed in. Everything seemed clear. The detective knocked on the back door, and the witness and his body-guard hurried out onto the intake loading dock. The van pulled away.

Pease started complaining immediately. He had a small cut on his forehead and a bruise on his cheek from the attack at the safe house but he moaned as if he'd fallen down a two-story flight of stairs. "I want a doctor. Look at this cut. It's already infected, I can tell. And my shoulder is killing me. What's a man gotta do to get treated right around here?"

Cops grow very talented at ignoring difficult suspects and witnesses, and Silverman hardly heard a word of the man's whiny voice.

"Cahill," Silverman said, turning back to the minister. "And what do you think that means for us?"

"Cahill owns high-rises all over town. I was wondering if the way you're going to drive your witness to the courthouse would go past any of them."

"Could be."

"So a sniper could be on top of one of them." The reverend smiled. "I didn't actually think that up on my own. I saw it in a TV show once."

A chill went through Silverman's spine.

Sniper?

He lifted his eyes from the alley. A hundred yards away was a high-rise from whose roof a sniper would have a perfect shot into the intake loading dock where Silverman, the minister, Pease and the two guards now stood. It could very well be a Cahill building.

"Inside!" he shouted. "Now."

They all hurried into the corridor that led to the lockup and Pease's babysitter slammed the door behind them. Heart pounding from the possible near miss, Silverman picked up a phone at the desk and called the captain. He told the man the reverend's theory. The captain said, "Sure, I get it. They shoot up the safe house to flush Pease, figuring they'd bring him here and then put a shooter on the high-rise. I'll send a tactical team to scour it. Hey, bring that minister by when you've got Pease locked down. Whether he's right or not, I want to thank him."

"Will do." The detective was miffed that the brass seemed to like this idea better than the anagrams, but Silverman'd accept any theory as long as it meant keeping Pease alive.

As they waited in the dim corridor for the lockup to empty out, skinny, stringy-haired Pease began complaining again, droning on and on. "You mean there was a shooter out there and you didn't fucking know about it, for Christ's sake, oh, sorry about the language, Father. Listen, you assholes, I'm not a suspect, I'm the *star* of this show, without me—"

"Shut the hell up," Silverman snarled.

"You can't talk to me—"

Silverman's cell phone rang and he stepped away from the others to take the call. "'Lo?"

"Thank God you picked up." Steve Noveski's voice was breathless. "Where's Pease?"

"He's right in front of me," Silverman told his partner. "He's okay. There's a tac team looking for shooters in the building up the street. What's up?"

"Where's that reverend?" Noveski said. "The desk log doesn't show him signing out."

"Here, with me."

"Listen, Mike, I was thinking—what if the CI didn't leave that message from the Bible."

"Then who did?"

"What if it was the hit man himself? The one Doyle hired."

"The killer? Why would he leave a clue?"

"It's not a clue. Think about it. He wrote the biblical stuff himself and left it near the body, as *if* the CI had left it. The killer'd figure we'd try to find a minister to help us figure it out—

but not just any minister, the one at the church that's closest to the police station."

Silverman's thoughts raced to a logical conclusion. Doyle's hit man kills the minister and his wife at their summer place on the lake and masquerades as the reverend. The detective recalled that the church office had nothing in it that might identify the minister. In fact, he seemed to remember that the man had trouble even finding a Bible and didn't seem to know his desk lamp bulb was burned out. In fact, the whole church was deserted and dusty.

He continued the logical progression of events: Doyle's boys shoot up the safe house and we bring Pease here for safekeeping at the same time the reverend shows up with some story about greed and a real estate developer and a sniper—just to get close to Silverman . . . and to Pease!

He understood suddenly: There *was* no secret message. *He's on his way. Look out—Luke 12:15*. It was meaningless. The killer could've written *any* biblical passage on the note. The whole point was to have the police contact the phony reverend and give the man access to the lockup at the same time that Pease was there.

And *I* led him right to his victim!

Dropping the phone and pulling his gun from its holster, Silverman raced up the hall and tackled the reverend. The man cried out in pain and gasped as the fall knocked the wind from his lungs. The detective pushed his gun into the hit man's neck. "Don't move a muscle."

"What're you doing?"

"What's wrong?" Pease's guard asked.

"He's the killer! He's one of Doyle's men!"

"No, I'm not. This is crazy!"

Silverman cuffed the fake minister roughly and holstered his gun. He frisked him and didn't find any weapons but figured he'd probably intended to grab one of the cops' own guns to kill Pease—and the rest of them.

The detective yanked the minister to his feet and handed him off to the intake guard. He ordered, "Take him to an interrogation room. I'll be there in ten minutes. Make sure he's shackled."

"Yessir."

"You can't do this!" the reverend shouted as he was led away roughly. "You're making a big mistake."

"Get him out of here," Silverman snapped.

Pease eyed the detective contemptuously. "He coulda killed me, you asshole."

Another guard ran up the corridor from intake. "Problem, Detective?"

"We've got everything under control. But see if the lockup's empty yet. I want that man inside ASAP!" Nodding toward Pease.

"Yessir," the guard said and hurried to the intercom beside the security door leading to the cells.

Silverman looked back down the corridor, watching the minister and his escort disappear through a doorway. The detective's hands were shaking. Man, that was a close one. But at least the witness is safe.

And so is my job.

Still have to answer a hell of a lot of questions, sure, but—

"No!" a voice cried behind him.

A sharp sound, like an axe in a tree trunk, resounded in the corridor, then a second, accompanied by the acrid smell of burnt gunpowder.

The detective spun around, gasping. He found himself staring in shock at the intake guard who'd just joined them. The young man held an automatic pistol mounted with a silencer and he was standing over the bodies of the men he'd just killed: Ray Pease and the cop who'd been beside him.

Silverman reached for his own gun.

But Doyle's hit man, wearing a perfect replica of a Detention Center guard's uniform, turned his pistol on the detective and shook his head. In despair Silverman realized that he'd been partly right. Doyle's people had shot up the safe house to flush out Pease—but not to send him to the hospital; they knew the cops would bring him to the jail for safekeeping.

The hit man looked up the corridor. None of the other guards had heard or otherwise noticed the killings. The man pulled a radio from his pocket with his left hand, pushed a button and said, "It's done. Ready for the pickup."

"Good," came the tinny reply. "Right on schedule. We'll meet you in front of the station."

"Got it." He put the radio away.

Silverman opened his mouth to plead with the killer to spare his life.

But he fell silent, then gave a faint, despairing laugh as he glanced at the killer's name badge and he realized the truth—that the dead snitch's message hadn't been so mysterious after all. The CI was simply telling them to look out for a hit man masquerading as a guard whose first name was what Silverman now gaped at on the man's plastic name plate: "Luke."

And, as for the chapter and verse, well, that was pretty simple too. The CI's note meant that the killer was planning the hit shortly after the start of the second shift, to give himself fifteen minutes to find where the prisoner was being held.

Right on schedule . . .

The time on the wall clock was exactly 12:15.

The Commuter

Monday started out bad.

Charles Monroe was on the 8:11 out of Greenwich, his usual train. He was juggling his briefcase and coffee—today tepid and burnt tasting—as he pulled his cell phone out of his pocket to get a head start on his morning calls. It brayed loudly. The sound startled him and he spilled a large comma of coffee on his tan suit slacks.

"God damn," he whispered, flipping open the phone. Monroe grumbled, "'Lo?"

"Honey."

His wife. He'd told her never to call on the cell phone unless it was an emergency.

"What is it?" he asked, rubbing the stain furiously as if the anger alone would make it vanish.

"Thank God I got you, Charlie."

Hell, did he have another pair of trousers at the office? No. But he knew where he could get one. The slacks slipped from his mind as he realized his wife had started crying.

"Hey, Cath, settle down. What is it?" She irritated him in a lot of ways—her incessant volunteering for charities and schools, her buying bargain-basement clothes for herself, her nagging about his coming home for dinner—but crying wasn't one of her usual vices.

"They found another one," Cathy said, sniffling.

She did, however, often start talking as if he were supposed to know exactly what she meant.

"*Who* found another what?"

"Another body."

Oh, that. In the past several months, two local residents had been murdered. The South Shore Killer, as one of the local rags had dubbed him, stabbed his victims to death and then eviscerated them with hunting knives. They were murdered for virtually no reason. One, following what seemed to be a minor traffic dispute. The other was killed, police speculated, because his dog wouldn't stop barking.

"So?" Monroe asked.

"Honey," Cathy said, catching her breath, "it was in Loudon."

"That's miles from us."

His voice was dismissing but Monroe in fact felt a faint chill. He drove through Loudon every morning on his way to the train station in Greenwich. Maybe he'd driven right past the corpse.

"But that makes three now!"

I can count too, he thought. But said calmly, "Cath, honey, the odds're a million to one he's going to come after you. Just forget about it. I don't see what you're worried about."

"You don't see what I'm worried about?" she asked.

Apparently he didn't. When Monroe didn't respond she continued, "*You*. What do you think?"

"Me?"

"The victims have all been men in their thirties. And they all lived near Greenwich."

"I can take care of myself," he said absently, gazing out the window at a line of schoolchildren waiting on a train platform. They were sullen. He wondered why they weren't looking forward to their outing in the city.

"You've been getting home so late, honey. I worry about you walking from the station to the car. I—"

"Cath, I'm really busy. Look at it this way: He seems to pick a victim once a month, right?"

"What? . . ."

Monroe continued, "And he's just killed somebody. So we can relax for a while."

"Is that . . . Are you making a joke, Charlie?"

His voice rose. "Cathy, I really have to go. I don't have time for this."

A businesswoman in the seat in front of him turned and gave him an angry glance.

What's her problem?

Then he heard a voice. "Excuse me, sir?"

The businessman sitting next to him—an accountant or lawyer, Monroe guessed—was smiling ruefully at him.

"Yes?" Monroe asked.

"I'm sorry," he said, "but you're speaking pretty loud. Some of us are trying to read."

Monroe glanced at several other commuters. Their irritated faces told him they felt the same.

He was in no mood for lectures. Everybody used cell phones on the train. When one would ring, a dozen hands went for their own phones.

"Yeah, well," Monroe grumbled, "I was here first. You saw me on the phone and you sat down. Now, if you don't mind . . ."

The man blinked in surprise. "Well, I didn't mean anything. I was just wondering if you could speak a little more softly."

Monroe exhaled a frustrated sigh and turned back to his conversation. "Cath, just don't worry about it, okay? Now, listen, I need my monogrammed shirt for tomorrow."

The man gave him a piqued glance, sighed and gathered up his newspaper and briefcase. He moved to the seat behind Monroe. Good riddance.

"Tomorrow?" Cathy asked.

Monroe didn't actually need the shirt but he was irritated at Cathy for calling and he was irritated at the man next to him for being so rude. So he said, more loudly than he needed to, "I just said I have to have it for tomorrow."

"It's just kind of busy today. If you'd said something last night . . ."

Silence.

"Okay," she continued, "I'll do it. But, Charlie, promise you'll be careful tonight coming home."

"Yeah. Okay. Gotta go."

"'Bye—"

He hit disconnect.

Great way to start the day, he thought. And punched in another number.

"Carmen Foret, please," he told the young woman who answered.

More commuters were getting on the train. Monroe tossed his briefcase on the seat next to him to discourage anybody else's sitting there.

A moment later the woman's voice answered.

"Hello?"

"Hey, baby, it's me."

A moment of silence.

"You were going to call me last night," the woman said coolly.

He'd known Carmen for eight months. She was, he'd heard, a talented real estate broker and was also, he supposed, a wonderful, generous woman in many ways. But what he *knew* about her—all he really cared to know—was that she had a soft, buoyant body and long, cinnamon-colored hair that spread out on pillows like warm satin.

"I'm sorry, sweetheart, the meeting went a lot later than I thought."

"Your secretary didn't think it went all that late."

Hell. She'd called his office. She hardly ever did. Why last night?

"We went out for drinks after we revised the deal letter. Then we ended up at the Four Seasons. You know."

"I know," she said sourly.

He asked, "What're you doing at lunch today?"

"I'm doing a tuna salad sandwich, Charlie. What're *you* doing?"

"Meet me at your place."

"No, Charlie. Not today. I'm mad at you."

"Mad at me? 'Cause I missed one phone call?"

"No, 'cause you've missed about three hundred phone calls since we've been dating."

Dating? Where did she get *that*? She was his mistress. They slept together. They didn't date, they didn't go out, they didn't court and spark.

"You know how much money I can make on this deal. I couldn't mess up, honey."

Hell. Mistake.

Carmen knew he called Cathy "honey." She didn't like it when he used the endearment with her.

"Well," she said frostily, "I'm busy at lunch. I may be busy for a lot of lunches. Maybe all the lunches for the rest of my life."

"Come on, babe."

Her laugh said: Nice try. But he wasn't pardoned for the "honey" glitch.

"Well, you mind if I come over and just pick up something?"

"Pick up something?" Carmen asked.

"A pair of slacks."

"You mean, you called me just now because you wanted to pick up some laundry?"

"No, no, babe. I wanted to see you. I really did. I just spilled some coffee on my slacks. While we were talking."

"Gotta go, Charlie."

"Babe—"

Click.

Damn.

Mondays, Monroe was thinking. I hate Mondays.

He called directory assistance and asked for the number of a jewelry store near Carmen's office. He charged a five-hundred-dollar pair of diamond earrings and arranged to have them delivered to her as soon as possible. The note he dictated read, "To my grade-A lover: A little something to go with your tuna salad. Charlie."

Eyes out the window. The train was close to the city now. The big mansions and the little wannabe mansions had given way to row houses and squat bungalows painted in hopeful pastels. Blue and red plastic toys and parts of toys sat in the balding backyards. A heavyset woman hanging laundry paused and, frowning, watched the train speed past as if she were watching an air show disaster clip on CNN.

He made another call.

"Let me speak to Hank Shapiro."

A moment later a gruff voice came on the line. "Yeah?"

"Hey, Hank. It's Charlie. Monroe."

"Charlie, how the hell're we coming with our project?"

Monroe wasn't expecting the question quite this soon in the conversation. "Great," he said after a moment. "We're doing great."

"But?"

"But what?"

Shapiro said, "It sounds like you're trying to tell me something."

"No. . . . It's just things're going a little slower than I thought. I wanted to—"

"Slower?" Shapiro asked.

"They're putting some of the information on a new computer system. It's a little harder to find than it used to be." He tried to joke, "You know, those old-style floppy disks? They called them file folders?"

Shapiro barked, "I'm hearing 'little slower.' I'm hearing 'little harder.' That's not my problem. I need that information and I need it soon."

The morning's irritations caught up with Monroe and he whispered fiercely, "Listen, Hank, I've been at Johnson, Levine for years. Nobody has the insider information I do except Foxworth himself. So just back off, okay? I'll get you what I promised."

Shapiro sighed. After a moment he asked, "You're sure he doesn't have any idea?"

"Who, Foxworth? He's completely in the dark."

A fast, irritating image of his boss flickered in Monroe's thoughts. Todd Foxworth was a large, quirky man. He'd built a huge ad agency from a small graphic design firm in SoHo. Monroe was a senior account executive and vice president. He'd risen about as far as he could in the company doing account work but Foxworth had resisted Monroe's repeated suggestions that the agency create a special title for him. Tension sat between the men like a rotting plum and over the past year Monroe had come to believe that Foxworth was persecuting him—continually complaining about his expense account, his sloppy record keeping, his unexplained absences from the office. Finally, when he'd gotten only a seven percent raise after his annual review, Monroe'd decided to retaliate. He'd gone to Hunter, Shapiro, Stein & Arthur and offered to sell them insider client information. The idea troubled him at first but then he figured it was just another way of collecting the twenty percent raise that he thought he was due.

Shapiro said, "I can't wait much longer, Charlie. I don't see something soon, I may have to cut bait."

Crazy wives, rude commuters. . . . Now this. Jesus. What a morning.

"This info'll be grade-A gold, Hank."

"Better be. I sure as hell am paying for gold."

"I'll have some good stuff by this weekend. How 'bout you come up to my country place and you can look it over. It'll be nice and private."

"You got a country place?"

"I don't broadcast it. Fact is, well, Cathy doesn't know. A friend and I go up there sometimes . . ."

"A friend."

"Yeah. A friend. And she's got a girlfriend or two she could invite up if you wanted to come."

"Or two?"

Or three, Monroe thought but let it go.

A long silence. Then Shapiro chuckled. "I think she oughta bring just one friend, Charlie. I'm not a young man anymore. Where is this place?"

Monroe gave him directions. Then he said, "How 'bout dinner tonight? I'll take you to Chez Antibes."

Another chuckle. "I could live with that."

"Good. About eightish."

Monroe was tempted to ask Shapiro to bring Jill, a young assistant account exec who worked at Shapiro's agency—and who also happened to be the woman he'd spent the evening with at the Holiday Inn last night when Carmen had been trying to track him down. But he thought: Don't push your luck. He and Shapiro hung up.

Monroe closed his eyes and started to doze off, hoping to catch a few minutes' sleep. But the train lurched sideway and he was jostled awake. He stared out the window. There were no houses to look at anymore. Only sooty, brick apartments. Monroe crossed his arms and rode the rest of the way to Grand Central Station in agitated silence.

■

The day improved quickly.

Carmen loved the earrings and she came close to forgiving him (though he knew full restitution would involve an expensive dinner and a night at the Sherry-Netherland).

In the office, Foxworth was in a surprisingly cheerful mood. Monroe had worried that the old man was going to grill him about a recent, highly padded expense account. But not only did Foxworth approve it, he complimented Monroe for the fine job he'd done on the Brady Pharmaceutical pitch. He even offered him an afternoon of golf at Foxworth's exclusive country club on Long Island next weekend. Monroe had contempt for golf and particular contempt for North Shore country clubs. But he liked the idea of taking Hank Shapiro golfing on Foxworth's tab. He dismissed the idea as too risky though the thought amused him for much of the afternoon.

At seven o'clock—nearly time to leave to meet Shapiro—he suddenly remembered Cathy. He called home. No answer. Then he dialed the school where she'd been volunteering recently and found that she hadn't come in today. He called home once more. Still she didn't pick up.

He was troubled for a moment. Not that he was worried about the South Shore Killer; he just felt instinctively uneasy when his wife wasn't home—afraid that she might find him with Carmen, or whoever. He was also reluctant for her to find out about his deal with Shapiro. The more money she knew he made the more she'd want. He called once more and got their machine.

But then it was time to leave for dinner and, since Foxworth had left for the night, Monroe ordered a limo and put the expense down to general office charges. He cruised downtown, sipping wine, and had a good dinner with Hank Shapiro. At eleven p.m. he dropped Shapiro off at Penn Station then took the limo to Grand Central. He caught the 11:30 to Greenwich, made it to his car without being stabbed by any knife-wielding crazy men and drove home to peace and quiet. Cathy'd had two martinis and was fast asleep. Monroe watched a little TV, fell asleep on the couch and slept late the next morning; he made the 8:11 with thirty seconds to spare.

■

At nine-thirty, Charlie Monroe strode into the office, thinking: Monday's over with, it's a new day. Let's get life moving again. He decided to spend the morning getting into the new computer system and printing out prospective client lists for Shapiro. Then he'd have a romantic lunch with Carmen. He'd also give Jill a call and charm her into drinks tonight.

Monroe'd just stepped into his office when Todd Foxworth, even more cheerful than yesterday, waved to him and asked him if they could have a chat. An ironic thought occurred to Monroe—that Foxworth had changed his mind and was going to give him a good raise after all. Would he still sell the confidential info? This was a dilemma. But he decided, hell, yes, he would. It'd make up for *last* year's insulting five percent raise.

Monroe sat down in Foxworth's cluttered office.

It was a joke in the agency that Foxworth didn't exactly carry on a coherent conversation. He'd ramble, he'd digress, he'd even make up words. Clients found it charming. Monroe had no patience for the man's scattered persona. But today he was in a generous mood and smiled politely as the rumpled old man chattered like a jay.

"Charlie, a couple things. I'm afraid something's come up and that invite for golf this weekend? I know you'd probably like to hit some balls, were looking forward to it, but I'm afraid I've got to renege on the offer. Sorry, sorry."

"That's okay. I—"

"Good club, Hunter's is. You ever play there? No? They don't have a pool, no tennis courts. You go there to play golf. Period. End of story. You don't play golf, it's a waste of time. Of course there's that dogleg on the seventeenth . . . nasty, nasty, nasty. Never near par. Impossible. How long you been playing?"

"Since college. I really appreciate—"

"Here's the other thing, Charlie. Patty Kline and Sam Eggleston, from our legal department, you know 'em, they were at Chez Antibes last night. Having dinner. Worked late and went to dinner."

Monroe froze.

"Now I've never been there but I hear it's funny the way the place's designed. They have these dividers, sort of like those screens in Japanese restaurants, only not Japanese of course because it's a French restaurant but they look sort of Japanese. Anyhoo, to make a long story short they heard every word you and Hank Shapiro said. So. There you have it. Security's cleaning out your desk right now and there're a couple guards on their way here to escort you off the property and you better get yourself a good lawyer because theft of trade secrets—Patty and Sam tell me this; what do I know? I'm just a lowly wordsmith—is pretty damn serious. So. Guess I won't say good luck to you, Charlie. But I will say get the hell out of my agency. Oh, and by the way, I'm going to do everything I can to make sure you never work on Madison Avenue again. 'Bye."

Five minutes later he was on the street, briefcase in one hand, cell phone in the other. Watching boxes of his personal effects being loaded into a delivery truck destined for Connecticut.

He couldn't understand how it'd happened. Nobody from the agency *ever* went to Chez Antibes—it was owned by a corporation that competed with one of Foxworth's big clients and so it was off limits. Patty and Sam wouldn't have gone there unless Foxworth had told them to—to check up on Monroe. Somebody must've blown the whistle. His secretary? Monroe decided if it was Eileen, he'd get even with her in a big way.

He walked for several blocks trying to decide what to do and when nothing occurred to him he took a cab to Grand Central.

Bundled in the train as it clacked north, speeding away from the gray city, Monroe sipped gin from the tiny bottle he'd bought in the club car. Numb, he stared at the grimy apartments then at the pale bungalows then mini estates then the grand estates as the train sped north and east. Well, he'd pull something out of the situation. He was good at that. He was the best. A hustler, a salesman. . . . He was grade-A.

He cracked the cap on the second bottle, and then the thought came to him: Cathy'd go back to work. She wouldn't want to. But he'd talk her into it. The more he thought about it the more the idea appealed to him. Damn it, she'd hung out around the house for years. It was *his* turn. Let her deal with the pressure of a nine-to-five job for a change. Why should he have to put up with all the crap?

Monroe parked in the driveway, paused, took several deep breaths, then walked into the house.

His wife was in the living room, sitting in a rocking chair, holding a cup of tea.

"You're home early."

"Well, I've got to tell you something," he began, leaning against the mantel. He paused to let her get nervous, to rouse her sympathies. "There's been a big layoff at the agency. Foxworth wanted me to stay but they just don't have the money. Most of the other senior people are going too. I don't want you to be scared, honey. We'll get through this together. It's really a good opportunity for both of us. It'll give you a chance to start teaching again. Just for a little while. I was thinking—"

"Sit down, Charles."

Charles? His mother called him Charles.

"I was saying, a chance—"

"Sit down. And be quiet."

He sat.

She sipped her tea with a steady hand, eyes scanning his face like searchlights. "I had a talk with Carmen this morning."

His neck hairs danced. He put a smart smile on his face and asked, "Carmen?"

"Your girlfriend."

"I—"

"You what?" Cathy snapped.

"Nothing."

"She seemed nice. It was a shame to upset her."

Monroe kneaded the arm of his Naugahyde chair.

Cathy continued, "I didn't plan to. Upset her, I mean. It's just that she'd somehow she got the idea we were in the process of getting divorced." She gave a brief laugh. "Getting divorced because I'd fallen in love with the pool boy. Where'd she get an idea like that, I wonder?"

"I can explain—"

"We don't have a pool, Charles. Didn't it occur to you that that was a pretty stupid lie?"

Monroe's hands slipped together and he began worrying a fingernail. He'd almost told Carmen that Cathy was having an affair with a neighbor or with a contractor. Pool boy was the first thing that came to mind. And, yes, afterwards he did think it was pretty stupid.

"Oh, if you're wondering," Cathy continued, "what happened was someone from the jewelry store called. They wanted to know whether to send the receipt here or to Carmen's apartment. By the way, she said the earrings were really tacky. She's going to keep them anyway. I told her she ought to."

Why the hell had the clerk done that? When he'd placed the order he'd very explicitly said to send the receipt to the office.

"It's not what you think," he said.

"You're right, Charlie. I think it's probably a lot worse."

Monroe walked to the bar and poured himself another gin. His head ached and he felt stuffy from too much liquor. He swallowed a mouthful and set the glass down. He remembered when they'd bought this set of crystal. A sale at Saks. He'd wanted to ask for the clerk's phone number but Cathy had been standing nearby.

His wife took a deep breath. "I've been on the phone with a lawyer for three hours. He seemed to think it won't take much longer than that to make you a very poor man. Well, Charlie, we don't have much more to talk about. So you should pack a suitcase and go stay somewhere else."

"Cath . . . This is a real bad time for me—"

"No, Charles, it *will* be bad. But it's not bad yet. Good-bye."

A half hour later he was finished packing. As he trudged down the stairs with a large suitcase Cathy studied him carefully. It was the way she examined aphids when she spritzed them with bug spray and watched them curl into tiny dead balls.

"I—"

"Good bye, Charles."

Monroe was halfway to the front hall when the doorbell rang.

He set the suitcase down and opened the door. He found two large sheriff's deputies standing in front of him. There were two squad cars in the driveway and two more deputies on the lawn. Their hands were very close to their pistols.

Oh, no. Foxworth was pressing charges! Jesus. What a nightmare.

"Mr. Monroe?" the largest of the deputies asked, eyeing his suitcase. "Charles Monroe?"

"Yes. What is it?"

"I wonder if we could talk to you for a moment."

"Sure. I—What's the matter?"

"Can we come in?"

"I, well, sure."

"Where you going, sir?"

He suddenly realized that he didn't have a clue.

"I . . . I don't know."

"You're leaving but you don't know where?"

"Little domestic problem. . . . You know how it is."

They stared at him, stone-faced.

Monroe continued. "I guess I'm going to the city. Manhattan."

Why not? It was as good a place as any.

"I see," the smaller deputy said and then glanced at his towering partner. "Out of state," he said significantly.

What did he mean by that?

The second deputy asked, "Is this your MasterCard number, Mr. Monroe?"

He looked at the slip the officer was holding out. "Uhm, yes it is. What's this all about?"

"Did you place a mail order yesterday with Great Northern Outdoor Supplies in Vermont?"

Great Northern? Monroe had never heard of them. He told the officers this.

"I see," said the large cop, not believing him.

"You do own a house on Harguson Lake outside of Hartford, don't you?"

Again he felt the sizzling chill in his spine. Cathy was looking at him—with a look that said nothing would surprise her any longer.

"I—"

"It's easy enough to check, sir. You may as well be honest."

"Yes, I do."

"When did you get it, Charles?" Cathy asked in a weary voice.

It was going to be a surprise . . . Our anniversary . . . I was just about to tell you . . .

"Three years ago," he said.

The shorter of the deputies persisted, "And you didn't have an order sent by Great Northern via overnight delivery to the house on that property?"

"An order? No. What order?"

"A hunting knife."

"A knife? No, of course not."

"Mr. Monroe, the knife you ordered—"

"I didn't order any knives."

"—the knife ordered by someone *claiming* to be Charles Monroe and using your credit card and sent to your property was similar to the knives that've been used in those murders in the area."

The South Shore Killer . . .

"Charlie!" Cathy gasped.

"I don't know anything about any knives!" he cried. "I *don't*!"

"The state police got an anonymous tip about some bloody clothes on the shore of Harguson Lake. Turned out to be your property. A T-shirt from the victim two days ago. We also found another knife hidden near the T-shirt. Blood on it matches blood from the victim killed two months ago near Route fifteen."

God, what was going on?

"No! This is a mistake! I've never killed anyone."

"Oh, Charlie, how could you?"

"Mr. Monroe, you have the right to remain silent." The large deputy continued with the rest of the Miranda warning, while the other slipped the cuffs on him.

They took his wallet from his pocket. His cell phone too.

"No, no, let me have the phone! I get to make a call. I know I do."

"Yeah, but you have to use our phone, sir. Not yours."

They led him outside, fierce grips on his biceps. Struggling, panicky. As they approached the squad car Monroe happened to look up. Across the street was a slightly built man with sandy hair. A pleasant smile on his face, he leaned against a tree as he watched the excitement.

He seemed very familiar . . .

"Wait," Monroe cried. "Wait."

But the sheriff's deputies didn't wait. They firmly shepherded Monroe into the back of their car and drove out of the driveway.

It was as they passed the man and Monroe glanced at him from a different angle that he recognized him. It was the commuter—the one who'd sat next to him on the train yesterday morning. The rude one who'd asked him to be quiet.

Wait . . . Oh, no. No!

Monroe began to understand. The man had heard all of his conversations—with Shapiro, with Carmen, the jewelry store.

He'd taken down the names of everyone Monroe'd been talking to, taken down his MasterCard number, the name and address of his mistress and the details of his meeting with Hank Shapiro . . . and the location of his house in the country! He'd called Foxworth, he'd called Cathy, he'd ordered the hunting knife. . . .

And he'd called the police too.

Because he was the South Shore Killer . . .

The man who murders because of the least affront—a fender bender, a barking dog.

With a wrenching gesture, Monroe twisted around and saw the man gazing at the receding squad car.

"We have to go back!" Monroe shouted. "We have to! He's back there! The killer's back there!"

"Yessir, now if you'll just shut up, we'd appreciate it. We'll be at the station house in no time."

"No!" he wailed. "No, no, no!"

As he looked back one last time he saw the man lift his hand to his head. What was he doing? Waving? Monroe squinted. No, he was . . . He was mimicking the gesture of holding a telephone to his ear.

"Stop! He's there! He's back there!"

"Sir, that'll be enough outta you," the large deputy said.

A block behind them, the commuter finally lowered his hand, turned away from the street and started down the sidewalk, walking briskly in a contented lope.

The Westphalian Ring

The Charing Cross burglary had been the most successful of his career.

And, as he was now learning, it would perhaps be the one that would permanently end this vocation.

As well as earn him a trip to a fetid cell in Newgate prison.

Sitting in his chockablock shop off Great Portland Street, wiry Peter Goodcastle tugged at the tuft of wispy hair above his ear and below his bald head and nodded grimly at his visitor's words, just audible amid the sound of Her Majesty's Public Works' grimy steam hammer breaking up the brick road to repair a water main.

"The man you robbed," his uneasy companion continued, "was the benefactor to the Earl of Devon. And has connections of his own throughout Parliament and Whitehall Street. The queen speaks highly of him."

The forty-four-year-old Goodcastle knew this, and considerably more, about Lord Robert Mayhew, as he did all his burglary victims. He always learned as much as he could about them; good intelligence was yet one more skill that had kept him free from Scotland Yard's scrutiny in the twelve years since he'd returned from the war and begun plying his trade as a thief. He'd sought as much data as he could about Mayhew and learned that he was indeed well regarded in the upper circles of London society and among the royals, including Queen Victoria herself; still, because of the man's massive wealth and obsession for amassing and hoarding rare jewelry and valuables, Goodcastle assessed, the rewards would be worth the risk.

But in this estimate he'd clearly been wrong.

"It's the ring he's upset about. Not the other pieces, certainly not the sovereigns. No, the ring. He's using all his resources to find it. Apparently it was handed down to him by his father, who received it from *his* father. It's of great personal value to him."

It was, of course, always wiser to filch items to which the owners had no sentimental attachment, and Goodcastle had decided that the ring fell into such a category because he'd found it sitting in a cheap, unlocked box on Mayhew's dressing counter, covered by a dozen pieces of worthless costume jewelry and cuff links.

But the thief now concluded that the casual treatment was merely a clever ruse to better protect the precious item—though only from thieves less skilled than Goodcastle, of course; he had inherited the family antiquities business ten years ago and of necessity had become an expert in valuing such items as music boxes, silver, furniture . . . and old jewelry. Standing masked in Mayhew's dressing chamber, he'd frozen in shock as he uncovered the treasure.

Crafted by the famed goldsmith Wilhelm Schroeder of Westphalia early in the century, the ring featured bands of gold, alternating with those of silver. Upon the gold were set diamonds, upon the silver, deep-blue sapphires. So astonished and delighted was Goodcastle at this find that he took only it, a diamond cravat pin, a modest broach and fifty gold guineas, eschewing the many other objets d'art, pieces of jewelry and gold and silver coin cluttering Mayhew's boudoir (another rule of thievery: the more modest the take, the more likely that weeks or months will pass before the victim discovers his loss, if indeed he ever does).

This was what he had hoped had occurred in the Charing Cross burglary. The incident had occurred last Thursday and Goodcastle had seen no reports of the theft in the *Daily Telegraph*, the *Times* or other papers.

But sadly such was not the case, his informant—a man well placed within Scotland Yard itself—was now explaining.

"What's more," the man whispered, fiddling with the brim of his Hamburg and looking out over the cool, gray April sky of London, "I've heard that the inspectors have reason to believe that the thief has a connection to the furniture or antiquities trade."

Alarmed, Goodcastle whispered, "How on earth can they have found that? An informant?"

"No, the coppers discovered in Sir Mayhew's apartment certain clues that led them to that conclusion."

"Clues? What clues?" As always, Goodcastle had been meticulous not to leave anything of his own behind. He'd taken all his tools and articles of clothing with him. And he never carried a single document or other token that would lead the police to him or to Goodcastle Antiquities.

But his confederate now chilled the burglar's blood further with the explanation. "The inspectors found bits of various substances on the ladder and in the bedroom and dressing room. I understand one was a bit of cut and desiccated horsehair, of the sort used in stuffing upholstered divans, sofas and settees, though Mayhew has none of that kind. Also, they located some wax unique to furniture polishing and of a type frequently bought in bulk by craftsmen who repair, refurbish or sell wooden pieces. . . . Oh, and they discovered some red brick dust too. It was on the rungs of the ladder. And the constables could find no similar dust on any of the streets nearby. They think its source was the thief's boots." The man glanced outside the shop, at the reddish dust from the pulverized brick covering the sidewalk.

Goodcastle sighed angrily at his own foolishness. He'd replaced the ladder exactly as he'd found it in Mayhew's carriage house but had not thought to wipe off any materials transferred from his shoes.

The year was 1892 and, as the world hurtled toward the start of a new millennia, one could see astonishing scientific advances everywhere. Electric lighting, petroleum-driven vehicles replacing horse-drawn landaus and carriages, magic lantern moving pictures . . . It was only natural that Scotland Yard too would seek out the latest techniques of science in their pursuit of criminals.

Had he known before the job that the Yarders were adopting this approach, he could've taken precautions: washing his hands and scrubbing his boots, for instance.

"Do you know anything more?" he asked his informant.

"No, sir. I'm still in the debtors' crimes department of the Yard. What I know about this case is only as I have overheard in random conversation. I fear I can't inquire further without arousing suspicion."

"Of course, I understand. Thank you for this."

"You've been very generous to me, sir. What are you going to do?"

"I honestly don't know, my friend. Perhaps I'll have to leave the country for the Continent—France, most likely." He looked his informant over and frowned. "It occurs to me that you should depart. From what you've told me, the authorities might very well be on their way here."

"But London is a massive city, sir. Don't you think it's unlikely they will beat a path to your door?"

"I would have believed so if they hadn't displayed such diligence in their examination of Mayhew's apartment. Thinking as we now know they do, if I were a Yard inspector, I would simply get a list of the queen's public works currently under way or ascertain the location of any brick buildings being demolished and compare that with lists of furniture and antiquities dealers in the vicinity. That would indeed lead very near to my door."

"Yes, that would make sense. . . . Frightful business, this." The man rose, putting his hat on his head. "And what will happen to you if they arrive here, Mr. Goodcastle?"

Arrested and imprisoned, of course, the shopkeeper thought. But he said, "I will hope for the best. Now, you should leave and I think it wiser if we don't see each other again. There is no reason for you to go to the dock at criminal court as well."

The nervous man leapt up. He shook Goodcastle's hand. "If you do leave the country, sir, I wish you the best of luck."

The burglar gave the informant a handful of sovereigns, a bonus well above what he'd already paid him.

"God bless, sir."

"I could most assuredly use His assistance in this matter."

The man left quickly. Goodcastle looked after him, half expecting to see a dozen constables and inspectors surrounding his shop, but all he observed were the public works laborers in their grimy overalls, carting away the shattered brick from the powerful chisel of the steam hammer, and a few passersby, their black brollies unfurled to fend off the sporadic spring rain.

The shop deserted at the moment and his chief craftsman, Markham, in the back, at work, the shopkeeper slipped into his office and opened the safe hidden behind a Turkish rug he'd mounted on the wall and further concealed behind a panel of oak constructed to resemble part of the wall.

He extracted a cloth bag, containing several pieces from recent burglaries, including the cravat stickpin, the broach, the guineas and the magnificent Westphalian ring from Mayhew's apartment.

The other items paled in comparison to the German ring. The light from the gas lamp hit the gems and fired a fusillade of beams, white and blue, into the room. The Frenchman to whom Goodcastle had arranged to sell it would pay him three thousand pounds, which meant of course that it was worth many times that. Yet Peter Goodcastle reflected that as marvelous as this creation was it had no particular appeal to him personally. Indeed, once he'd successfully executed a burglary of an abode or museum or shop he cared little for the object he'd made off with, except as it provided income and thus the means to continue his felonious vocation, though even regarding his recompense, he was far from greedy. Why, receiving three thousand sovereigns for the ring, or its true value of perhaps thirty thousand, or merely a handful of crowns wasn't the point. No, the allure to Goodcastle was the act of the theft and the perfection of its execution.

One might wonder how exactly he had chosen this curious line of work. Goodcastle's history revealed some privilege and a fine education. Nor had he rubbed shoulders with any particularly rough crowds at any point in his life. His parents, both long deceased, had been loving, and his brother was, of all things, a parish priest in Yorkshire. He supposed much of the motivation propelling him to steal could be traced to his terrible experiences during the Second Afghan War. Goodcastle had been a gunner with the famed Royal Horse Artillery, which was among the detachments ordered to stop an enemy force of Ghazis intent on attacking the British garrison at Kandahar. On the searingly hot, dusty day of 27 July 1880 the force of 2,500 British and Indian infantry, light cavalry and artillery met the enemy at Maiwand. What they did not realize until the engagement began, however, was that the Afghans outnumbered them ten to one. From the very beginning the battle went badly, for in addition to overwhelming numbers of fanatical troops the enemy had not only smoothbores, but Krupp guns as well. The Ghazis pinpointed their weapons with deadly accuracy and the shells and the blizzard of musket balls and repeater rounds ravaged the British forces.

Manning gun number 3, Goodcastle's crew suffered terribly but managed to fire over one hundred rounds that day, the barrel of the weapon hot enough to cook flesh—as was proven by the severe burns on his men's arms and hands. Finally, though, the overwhelming force of the enemy prevailed. With a pincer maneuver they closed in. The Afghans seized the English cannon, which the British had no time to spike and destroy, as well as the unit's colors—the first time in the history of the British army such a horror had occurred.

As Goodcastle and the others fled in a terrible rout, the Ghazis turned the British guns around and augmented the carnage, with the Afghans using the flagpoles from the regiment's own flags as ramming rods for the shot!

A horrific experience, yes—twenty percent of the Horse Artillery was lost, as was sixty percent of the 66th Foot Regiment—but in some ways the worst was visited upon the surviving soldiers only after their return to England. Goodcastle found himself and his comrades treated as pariahs, branded cowards. The disdain mystified as much as it devastated their souls. But Goodcastle soon learned the reason for it. Prime Minister Disraeli, backed by a number of lords and the wealthy upper class, had been the prime movers in the military intervention in Afghanistan, which served no purpose whatsoever except to rattle sabers at Russia, then making incursions into the area. The loss at Maiwand made many people question the wisdom of such involvement and was an instant political embarrassment. Scapegoats were needed and who better than the line troops who were present at one of the worst defeats in British history?

One particular nobleman infuriated Goodcastle by certain remarks made to the press, cruelly bemoaning the shame the troops had brought to the nation and offering not a word of sympathy for those who lost life or limb. The shopkeeper was so livid that he vowed revenge. But he'd had enough of death and violence at Maiwand and would never, in any case, injure an unarmed opponent, so he decided to punish the man in a subtler way. He found his residence and a month after the improvident remarks the gentleman discovered that a cache of sovereigns—hidden, not very cleverly, in a vase in his office—was considerably diminished.

Not long after this a factory owner reneged on promises of employment to a half dozen veterans of the Afghan campaign.

The industrialist too paid dearly—with a painting, which Good-castle stole from his summer house in Kent and sold, the proceeds divvied up among those who'd been denied work. (Goodcastle's experience in his father's antiquities business stood him in good stead; despite the veterans' concern about the questionable quality of the canvas, done by some Frenchman named Claude Monet, the thief was able to convince an American dealer to pay dearly for the blurred landscape.)

The vindication these thefts represented certainly cheered him—but Goodcastle finally came to admit that what appealed most deeply wasn't revenge or the exacting of justice but the exhilaration of the experience itself. . . . Why, a well-executed burglary could be a thing of beauty, as much so as any hand-carved armoire or Fragonard painting or William Tessler gold broach. He tamed his guilt and began pursuing his new calling with as much vigor and cunning as was displayed by all men, in whatever profession, who were counted successful.

Once he inherited the familial shop on Great Portland Street he found that he and his workers had unique access to the finest homes in metropolitan London, as they collected and delivered furniture—perfect hunting grounds for a refined burglar. He was too clever to rob his own clients, of course, but he would listen and observe, learning what he might about these customers' neighbors or acquaintances—any recent valuables they'd purchased, sums of money they'd come into, where they might secrete their most precious objects, when they regularly traveled out of London, the number and nature of grooms and waiting-servants and guard hounds.

A brilliant idea, and perfectly executed on many occasions. As on Thursday last in the apartment of Sir Robert Mayhew.

But it is often not the plan itself that goes awry, but an entirely unforseen occurrence that derails a venture. In this case, the unexpected cleverness of Scotland Yard inspectors.

Goodcastle now replaced the Westphalian ring and the other items in the safe and counted the cash inside. Five hundred pounds. At his home in London he had another three thousand sovereigns, plus other valuable items he'd stolen recently but hadn't yet found buyers for. In his country house was another five thousand quid. That would set him up easily in the southern provinces of France, where he spent time with Lydia, the raven-haired beauty from Manchester he often traveled with. She could join him there permanently when she'd settled her own business affairs.

But living forever in France? His heart sank at the thought. Peter Goodcastle was an Englishman through and through. For all its sooty air from the dark engines of industry, its snobbish elite, its Victorian imperialism, his shabby treatment after Maiwand, he still loved England.

But he would not love ten years in Newgate.

He swung the safe door shut and closed the secret panel, letting the tapestry fall back over it. Caught in furious debate about what he might do, he wandered out into his shop once again, finding comfort in the many fine objects offered for sale.

An hour later, having come to no decision as to a course of action, he was wondering if perhaps he'd been wrong about the prowess of the police. Maybe they had hit on some lucky initial conclusions, but the investigation had perhaps stalled and he would escape unscathed. But it was then that a customer walked into the shop and began to browse. The shopkeeper smiled a greeting then bent over a ledger in concentration but he continued to keep an eye on the customer, a tall, slim man in a black greatcoat over a similarly shaded morning suit and white shirt. He was carefully examining the clocks and music boxes and walking sticks with the eye of someone intent on buying something and getting good value for his money.

As a thief, Peter Goodcastle had learned to be observant of detail; as a shopkeeper he had come to know customers. He was now struck by a curious fact: The man perused only the *wooden* items on display, while the inventory consisted of much porcelain, ivory, mother of pearl, pewter, brass and silver. It had been Goodcastle's experience that a customer desirous of buying a music box, say, would look at all varieties of such items, to assess their value and quality in general, even if his intent was to acquire a wooden one.

Goodcastle then noted something else. The man was subtly running his finger along a crevice in the seam of a music box. So, his interest wasn't in the wood itself but in the wax covering it, a sample of which he captured under his nail.

The "customer" was not that at all, the shopkeeper understood with dismay; he was one of the Yarders his informant had told him about earlier.

Well, all is not lost yet, Goodcastle reasoned. The wax he used was somewhat rare, due to its price and availability only in commercial quantities, but it was hardly unique; many other furniture and antiquity dealers bought the same substance. This was not by any means conclusive evidence of his guilt.

But then the policeman took a fancy to a red overstuffed chair. He sat on it and patted the sides, as if getting a feel for its construction. He sat back and closed his eyes. In horror Goodcastle noted the man's right hand disappeared out of sight momentarily and subtly plucked a piece of the stuffing out of the cushion.

The substance was desiccated horsehair, which surely would match the piece found in Robert Mayhew's apartment.

The inspector rose and prowled up and down the aisles for some moments longer. Finally he glanced toward the counter. "You are Mr. Goodcastle?"

"I am indeed," the shopkeeper said, for to deny it would merely arouse suspicion at a later time. He wondered if he was about to be arrested on the spot. His heart beat fiercely.

"You have a fine shop here." The inspector was attempting to be amiable but Goodcastle detected the coldness of an inquisitor in the eyes.

"Thank you, sir. I should be most glad to assist you." His palms began to sweat and he felt ill within the belly.

"No, thank you. In fact, I must be going."

"Good day. Do return."

"I shall," he said and walked outside into the brisk spring air.

Goodcastle stepped back into the shadows between two armoires and looked out.

No!

His worst fears were realized. The man had started across the street, glanced back into the store and, not seeing the proprietor, knelt, presumably to tie his shoelace. But the lace was perfectly secured already; the point of this gesture was to pinch up some of the brick dust from the construction currently being undertaken—to match against similar dust Goodcastle had left on the rungs of the ladder or inside the apartment in Charing Cross, he thought in agony. The policeman deposited the dust in a small envelope and then continued on his way, with the jaunty step of a man who has just found a wad of banknotes on the street.

Panic fluttered within Goodcastle. He understood his arrest was imminent. So, it's to be a race to escape the clutch of the law. Every second counted.

He strode to the back door of the shop and opened it. "Markham," he called into the back room, where the round, bearded craftsman was putting a coat of lacquer on a Chinese-style bureau. "Mind the shop for an hour or two. I have an urgent errand. "

■

Bill Sloat was hunched over his cluttered, ale-stained table at the Green Man Pub, surrounded by a half dozen of his cronies, all of them dirty and dim, half-baked Falstaffs, their only earthly reason for being here that they did Sloat's bidding as quickly and as ruthlessly as he ordered.

The gang-man, dressed in an unwashed old sack suit, looked up as Peter Goodcastle approached and pierced a bit of apple with his sharp toad-sticker, eating the mealy fruit slowly. He didn't know much about Goodcastle except that he was one of the few merchants on Great Portland Street who coughed up his weekly ten quid—which he called a "business fee"—and didn't need a good kick in the arse or slash with a razor to be reminded of it.

The shopkeeper stopped at the table and nodded at the fat man, who muttered, "What's brought you 'ere, m'lord?"

The title was ironic, of course. Goodcastle didn't have a drop of noble blood in his limp veins. But in a city where class was the main yardstick by which to measure a man, more so even than money, Goodcastle swam in a very different stream than Sloat. The gang-man's East End upbringing had been grim and he'd never gotten a lick of boost, unlike Goodcastle, whose parents had come from a pleasant part of Surrey. Which was reason enough for Sloat to dislike him, despite the fact he coughed up his quid on time.

"I need to speak to you."

"Do you now? Speak away, mate. Me ear's yours."

"Alone."

Sloat harpooned another piece of apple and chewed it down then muttered, "Leave us, boys." He grunted toward the ruffians around the table, and, snickering or grumbling, they moved away with their pints.

He looked Goodcastle over carefully. The man was trying his hardest to be a carefree bloke but the man clearly had a desperate air about him. Ah, this was tidy! Desperation and its cousin fear were far better motivators than greed for getting men to do what you wanted. Sloat pointed toward Goodcastle with a blunt finger that ended in a nail darkened from the soot that fell in this part of town like black snow. "You'll come a cropper if you're 'ere to say you don't 'ave me crust this week."

"No, no, no. I'll have your money. It's not that." A whisper: "Hear me out, Sloat. I'm in trouble. I need to get out of the country quickly, without anybody knowing. I'll pay you handsomely if you can arrange it."

"Oh, me dear friend, *whatever* I do for you you'll pay 'and-somely," he said, laughing. "Rest assured of that. What'd you do, mate, to need a 'oliday so quick like?"

"I can't tell you."

"Ey, too shy to share the story with your friend Bill? You cuckold some poor bloke? You owe a sack of lolly to a gambler? . . ." Then Sloat squinted and laughed harshly. "But no, m'lord. You're too bald and too skinny to get a married bird to shag. And your cobblers ain't big enough for you to go wagering more'n a farthing. So, who's after you, mate?"

"I can't say," he whispered.

Sloat sipped more of his bitters. "No matter. Get on with it. It's me dinnertime and I 'ave a 'unger."

Goodcastle looked around and his voice lowered even further. "I need to get into France. Nobody can know. And I need to leave tonight."

"Tonight?" The ruffian shook his head. "Lord love me."

"I heard you have connections all over the docks."

"Bill's got 'is connections. That 'e does."

"Can you get me onto a cargo ship bound for Marseille?"

"That's a bleedin' tall order, mate."

"I don't have any choice."

"Well, now, I might be able to." He thought for a moment. "It'll cost you a thousand quid."

"*What?*"

"It's bloody noon, mate. Look at the clock. It ain't easy, what you're asking, you know. I'll 'ave to run around all day like a chicken without its 'ead. Blimey. Not to mention the risk. The docks're lousy with guards, customs agents, sergeants at arms—thick as fleas they are. . . . So there you 'ave it, guv'nor. A thousand." He skewered another brown apple wedge and chewed it down.

"All right," Goodcastle said, scowling. The men shook hands.

"I need something up front. 'Ave to paint some palms, understand."

Goodcastle pulled out his money purse and counted out some coin.

"Crikey, guv'nor." Bill laughed. The massive hand reached out and snatched the whole purse. "Thank'ee much. . . . Now, when do I get the rest?"

Goodcastle glanced at his pocket watch. "I can have it by four. Can you make the arrangements by then?"

"Rest assured I can," Sloat said, waving for the barmaid.

"Come by the shop."

Sloat squinted and looked the man over warily. "Maybe you won't own up to what you done, but tell me, mate, just 'ow safe is it to be meetin' you?"

The shopkeeper gave a grim laugh. "You've heard the expression 'giving somebody a taste of their own medicine'?"

"I 'ave, sure."

"Well, that's what I'm going to do. Don't worry. I know how to make sure we're alone."

Goodcastle sighed once more and then left the Green Man.

Sloat watched him leave, thinking, A thousand quid for a few hours' work.

Desperation, he thought, is just plain bloody beautiful.

■

At five minutes to four that afternoon, Peter Goodcastle was uneasily awaiting Bill Sloat's arrival.

While he'd made his arrangements to evade the law, Goodcastle had kept up the appearance of going through his business as usual. But he'd continued to observe the street outside. Sure enough, he'd noted several plain-clothed detectives standing well back in the shadows. They pretended to be watching the construction work on the street but in fact it was obvious that their attention was mostly on Goodcastle and the store.

The shopkeeper now put his plan into action. He summoned the craftsman, Markham, and one of the men he regularly used for transporting furniture to and from clients' houses. Purposely acting suspicious, like an actor in a one-shilling melodrama, Goodcastle slipped the young deliveryman a paper-wrapped package, which contained a music box. He gave instructions to take it to Goodcastle's own house as quickly as possible. Witnessing the apparently furtive mission, and probably assuming that the box contained loot or damning evidence, one of the detectives started after the young man as soon as he left the shop.

Goodcastle then dismissed Markham for the day and gave him a similar package, with instructions to take it home with him and make sure the music box mechanism was dependable. The remaining detective observed the craftsman leave the shop, clutching the parcel, and, after a moment of debate, appeared to decided it was better to pursue this potential source of evidence rather than remain at his station.

Goodcastle carefully perused the street and saw no more detectives. The workers had left and the avenue was deserted except for a married couple, who paused at the front window, then stepped inside. As they looked over the armoires, Goodcastle told them he would return in a moment and, with another glance outside into the empty street, stole into the office, closing the door behind him.

He sat at his desk, lifted aside the Turkish rug and opened the secret panel then the safe. He was just reaching inside when he was aware of a breeze wafting on his face, and he knew the door to the office had been opened.

Goodcastle leapt up, crying, "No!" He was staring at the husband of the couple who'd just walked into the shop. He was holding a large Webley pistol.

"Lord in heaven!" Goodcastle said, gasping. "You've come to rob me!"

"No, sir, I'm here to arrest you," he said calmly. "Pray don't move. I don't wish to harm you. But I will if you give me no choice." He then blew into a police whistle, which uttered a shrill tone.

A moment later, beyond him, Goodcastle could see the door burst open, and in ran two Scotland Yard inspectors in plain clothes, as well as two uniformed constables. The woman—who'd obviously been posing as the first inspector's wife—waved them toward the office. "The safe is back there," she called.

"Capital!" called one inspector—the lean, dark man who'd been in the store earlier, masquerading as a customer. His fellow officer, wearing a bowler, was dressed similarly, a greatcoat over a morning suit, though this man differed in his physique, being taller and quite pale, with a shock of flaxen hair. Both policemen took the shopkeeper by the arms and led him out into the store proper.

"What's the meaning of this?" Goodcastle blustered.

The white-faced inspector chuckled. "I warrant you know right well."

They searched him and, finding no weapons, unhanded him. The inspector who'd entered with the woman on his arm replaced his Webley with a notebook, in which he began taking down evidence. They dismissed the woman with effusive thanks and she explained that she'd be back at the police precinct station house if they needed her further.

"What is this about?" Goodcastle demanded.

The pale officer deferred to the lean one, apparently a chief inspector, who looked Goodcastle over carefully. "So you're the man who burglarized Robert Mayhew's apartment."

"Who? I swear I don't know what you're speaking of."

"Please, Mr. Goodcastle, don't malign our intelligence. You saw me in your shop earlier, did you not?"

"Yes."

"During that visit here I managed to collect a sample of furniture wax from several wooden pieces. The substance is identical to the wax we found traces of in Lord Mayhew's dressing chamber—a material that neither he nor his servants had ever been in contact with. We found too a horse hair that matched one that I extracted from your chair."

"I'm at a loss—"

"And what do you have to say about the fact that the brick dust in front of your store is the same as that which we found on the rungs of the ladder used to break into Lord Mayhew's first floor? Don't deny you are the thief."

"Of course I deny it. This is absurd!"

"Go search the safe," the chief inspector said to a constable, nodding toward the back office. He then explained, "When I was here earlier I tried to ascertain where you might have a hiding place for your ill-gotten gains. But your shop boasts far too much inventory and too many nooks and crannies to locate what we are seeking without searching for a week. So we stationed those two detectives outside on the street to make you believe we were about to arrest you. As we had anticipated, you led them off . . . I assume in pursuit of two parcels of no evidentiary value whatsoever."

"Those deliveries a moment ago?" Goodcastle protested. "I sent one music box home for myself to work on tonight. Another, my man was taking with him to do the same."

"So you say. But I suspect you're prevaricating."

"This is most uncalled for. I—"

"Please, allow me to finish. When you sent our men on a goose chase, that told us that your flight was imminent, so my colleague here and a typist from the precinct house came in as customers, as they'd been waiting to do for several hours." He turned to the policeman who'd played the husband and added, "Capital job, by the way."

"Most kind of you."

The chief inspector turned back to Goodcastle. "You were lulled to incaution by the domestic couple and, prodded by the urgency of escape, you were kind enough to lead us directly to the safe."

"I am, I swear, merely an antiques merchant and craftsman."

The pale detective chuckled again, while the "husband" continued to take everything down in his notebook.

"Sir," the constable said as he stepped from the office. "A problem."

"Is the safe locked?"

"No, sir. The door was open. The trouble is that ring is not inside."

"Ring?" Goodcastle asked.

"What *is* inside?" the lean officer asked, ignoring the shopkeeper.

"Money, sir. That's all. About five hundred pounds."

"Are they guineas?"

"No, sir. Varied currency but notes mostly. No gold."

"It's the receptacle for my receipts, sirs. Most merchants have one."

Frowning, the head detective looked into the office beyond them and started to speak. But at that moment the door opened again and in strode Bill Sloat. The ruffian took one look at the constables and inspectors and started to flee. He was seized by the two coppers and dragged back inside.

"Ah, look who we have here, Mad Bill Sloat," said the bowlered inspector, lifting an eyebrow in his pale forehead. "We know about you, oh, yes. So you're in cahoots with Goodcastle, are you?"

"I am not, copper.

"Keep a respectable tone in your mouth."

Goodcastle said uneasily, "By the queen, sir, Mr. Sloat has done nothing wrong. He comes in sometimes to view my wares. I'm sure that's all he's doing here today."

The chief inspector turned to him. "I sense you're holding back, Goodcastle. Tell us what is on your mind."

"Nothing, truly."

"You'll be in the dock sooner than we have planned for you, sir, if you do not tell us all."

"Keep your flamin' gob shut," Sloat muttered.

"Quiet, you," a constable growled.

"Go on, Goodcastle. Tell us."

The shopkeeper swallowed. He looked away from Sloat. "That man is the terror of Great Portland Street! He extorts money and goods from us and threatens to sic his scoundrels from the Green Man on us if we don't pay. He comes in every Saturday and demands his tithe."

"We've heard rumors of such," the flaxen-haired detective said.

The chief inspector looked closely at Goodcastle. "Yet today is Monday, not Saturday. Why is his here now?"

The villain shouted at the shopkeeper, "I'm warning you—"

"One more word and it'll be the Black Maria for you, Sloat."

Goodcastle took a breath and continued. "Last Thursday he surprised me in my shop at eight a.m. I hadn't opened the doors yet, but had come in early because I had finished work on several pieces late the night before and I wanted to wax and polish them before I admitted any customers."

The chief detective nodded, considering this. To his colleagues he said, "The day of the burglary. And not long before it. Pray continue, Goodcastle."

"He made me open the door. He browsed among the music boxes and looked them over carefully. He selected that one right there." He pointed to a rosewood box sitting on the counter. "And he said that in addition to his extortion sterling, this week he was taking that box. But more, I was to build a false compartment in the bottom. It had to be so clever that no one examining the box, however carefully, could find what he'd hidden in there." He showed them the box and the compartment—which he'd just finished crafting a half hour before.

"Did he say what he intended to hide?" the senior Yarder asked.

"He said some items of jewelry and gold coins."

The villain roared, "'E's a flamin' liar and a brigand and when—"

"Quiet, you," the constable said and pushed the big man down roughly into a chair.

"Did he say where he'd acquired them?"

"No, sir."

The detectives eyed one another. "So Sloat came here," the senior man offered, "selected the box and got wax on his fingers. The horsehair and brick dust attached themselves to him as well. The timing would allow for his proceeding directly to Lord Mayhew's apartment, where he left those substances."

"It makes sense," the third offered, looking up from his notebook.

The pale detective asked, "And you have no criminal past, Goodcastle? Don't lie. It's easily verified."

"No, sir. I swear. I'm a simple merchant—if I've done anything wrong, it was in not reporting Sloat's extortion. But none of us along Great Portland Street dared. We're too frightened of him. . . . Forgive me, sirs, it's true—I did send the police across the street on a merry chase. I had no idea why they were present but they seemed like detectives to me. I had to get them away from here. Mr. Sloat was due momentarily and I knew that if he noticed the law when he arrived he would think I'd summoned them and might beat me. Or worse."

"Search him," the pale-visaged detective ordered, nodding toward Sloat.

They pulled some coins, a cigar and a cosh from his pockets, as well as the money purse. The white-faced detective looked inside. "Guineas! Just like the sort that Lord Mayhew lost."

The Royal Mint had stopped producing gold guineas, worth a pound and a shilling, in 1813. They were still legal tender, of course, but were rare. This was why Goodcastle had not taken many from Lord Mayhew's; spending them could draw attention to you.

"That purse is not mine!" Sloat raged. "It's 'is!"

"That's a lie!" Goodcastle cried. "Why, if it were mine, why would *you* have it? I have mine right here." He displayed a cheap leather pouch containing a few quid, crowns and pence.

The constable holding the pouch then frowned. "Sir, something else is inside—hidden in a pocket in the bottom." He extracted two items and displayed them. "The cravat pin, like the one Sir Mayhew reported missing. Most surely the same one. And the ruby broach, also taken!"

"I'm innocent, I tell you! Goodcastle 'ere come to me with a story of 'aving to get his arse to France tonight."

"And what was the motive for this hasty retreat?" the inscribing detective asked.

"'E didn't say," Sloat admitted.

"Convenient," the pale detective said wryly. It was clear that they didn't believe the ruffian.

Goodcastle tried to keep a curious and cautious expression on his face. In fact, he was wracked by anxiety, wondering if he could pull off this little theater. He'd had to act fast to save himself. As he'd told Sloat he was going to treat Scotland Yard to a taste of their own medicine—but not to forsake his homeland and flee to France, which he'd decided he could never do. No, he'd use evidence to connect *Sloat* to the burglary—through a fabricated story about the music box with the hidden compartment on the one hand and, on the other, making certain Sloat took the incriminating money purse from Goodcastle at the Green Man.

But would the police accept the theory?

It seemed for a moment that they would. But just as Goodcastle began to breathe somewhat easier, the chief inspector turned quickly to him. "Please, sir. Your hands?"

"I beg your pardon?"

"I will examine your hands. One final test in this curious case. I am not yet completely convinced the facts are as they seem."

"Well, yes, of course."

Goodcastle held his palms out, struggling to keep them steady. The detective looked them over. Then he looked up, frowning. After a moment he lowered his head again and smelled Goodcastle's palm. He said to Sloat, "Now yours."

"Listen 'ere, coppers, you bloody well ain't—"

But the constables grabbed the man's beefy hands and lifted them for the chief inspector, who again examined and sniffed. He nodded and then turned slowly to Goodcastle. "You see, the Westphalian ring is of a unique design—silver *and* gold, unusual in metal craft. Gold, as you know, needs no polishing to prevent tarnish. But silver does. Mayhew told us that the ring had been recently cleaned with a particular type of silver polish that is scented with perfume derived from the lily flower. It is quite expensive but well within Mayhew's means to buy liberally for his staff to use." Then he turned toward Sloat. "Your hands emit a marked scent of lily and display some small traces of the off-white cream that is the base for the polish, while Mr. Goodcastle's do not. There's no doubt, sir. You are the thief."

"No, no, I am wronged!"

"You may make your case before the judges, sir," the light-haired policeman said, "from the dock."

Goodcastle's heart pounded fiercely from this final matter—about the polish. He'd nearly overlooked it but had decided that if the detectives were now so diligent in their use of these minuscule clues to link people to the sites of crimes, Goodcastle needed to be just as conscientious. If a burglar could leave evidence during the commission of a felony, he might also pick up something there that might prove equally damning. He thought back to the ring and Mayhew's dressing chamber. He recalled that he'd recognized the scent of Covey's Tarnish-Preventing Cream in the velvet-lined boxes. On the way to the Green Man, he'd bought some, slathered it liberally on his palm. Shaking Sloat's hand to seal their agreement had transferred some to the ruffian's skin. Before returning to his shop, Goodcastle had scrubbed his own hands clean with lye soap and discarded the remaining polish.

"Cooperate, sir, and it will go easier on you," the hatted detective said to Sloat.

"I'm the victim of a plot!"

"Yes, yes, do you think you're the first brigand ever to suggest that? Where is the ring?"

"I don't know anything of any ring."

"Perhaps we'll find it when we search your house."

No, Goodcastle thought, they wouldn't find the ring. But they *would* find a half dozen other pieces stolen by Goodcastle in various burglaries over the past year. Just as they'd find a crude diagram of Robert Mayhew's apartment—drawn with Sloat's own pencil on a sheet of Sloat's own paper. The burglar had planted them there this afternoon after he'd met with the ruffian at the Green Man (taking exemplary care this time to leave no traces that would link him to *that* incursion).

"Put him in darbies and take him to the jail," the pale officer ordered.

The constables slapped irons on the man's wrists and took him away, struggling.

Goodcastle shook his head. "Do they always protest their innocence so vehemently?"

"Usually. It's only in court they turn sorrowful. And that's when the judge is about to pass sentence," said the pale officer. He added, "Forgive us, Mr. Goodcastle, you've been most patient. But you can understand the confusion."

"Of course. I'm pleased that that fellow is finally off the streets. I regret that I didn't have the courage to come forward before."

"A respectable gentleman such as yourself," offered the detective with the notebook, "can be easily excused on such a count, being alien to the world of crime and ruffians."

"Well, my thanks to you and all the rest at Scotland Yard," he said to the chief inspector.

But the man gave a laugh and turned toward the pale detective, who said, "Oh, you're under a misapprehension, Mr. Goodcastle. Only I am with the Yard. My companions here are private consultants retained by Sir Robert Mayhew. I am Inspector Gregson." He then nodded toward the dark, slim man Goodcastle had taken to be the chief detective. "And this is the consulting detective Sherlock Holmes."

"A pleasure," Goodcastle said. "I believe I've heard of you."

"Indeed," Holmes replied, as if shopkeeper should most certainly have heard of him. The man seemed like a don at King's College, brilliant but constantly distracted by complex thoughts.

Gregson nodded toward the man who had portrayed the husband and introduced Dr. John Watson, who shook Goodcastle's hand cordially and asked a few more questions about Bill Sloat, the answers to which he jotted into his notebook. He explained that he often wrote accounts of the more interesting cases he and Holmes were involved in.

"Yes, of course. That's where I've heard of you both. The accounts are often published in the newspapers. So that is you! An honor."

"Ah," said Holmes, managing to summon a look simultaneously prideful and modest.

Goodcastle asked, "Will this be one adventure you write about?"

"No, it will not," Holmes said. He seemed piqued—perhaps because, even though a villain was under arrest, his reading of the clues had led to the wrong suspect, at least in his perception of the affair.

"But where, Holmes, is the ring?" Gregson asked.

"I suspect that that Sloat has already disposed of it."

"Why do you think so?" Watson asked.

"Elementary," Holmes said. "He had the other ill-gotten gains on his person. Why not the ring too? I deduced from his clothing that the blackguard lives in the company of a woman; both the jacket and trousers of his sack suit had been darned with identical stitching, though in places that wear through at different rates—the elbow and the inseam—suggesting that they were repaired by the same person though at different times. The conclusion must be that a wife or female companion did the work. His request of Mr. Goodcastle here regarding the secret compartment makes clear that he does not trust people, so he would be loathe to leave the ring in an abode where another person dwells and would have kept it on him until the special music box was ready. Since he *doesn't* have the ring on him any longer, we can conclude that he has disposed of it. And since he has no significant sums of cash with him, other than Lord Mayhew's guineas, we can conclude that he used the ring to settle an old debt."

"Where did he dispose of it, do you think?"

"Alas, I'm afraid that the piece is on its way overseas."

When the others glanced at each other quizzically, Holmes continued, "You of course observed the fish scales on Sloat's cuffs?"

"Well," said Gregson, "I'm afraid I for one did not."

"Nor I," Watson said.

"They were scales unique to saltwater fish."

"You *knew* that, Holmes?" the Yarder asked.

"Data, data, data," the man replied petulantly. "In this line of work, Gregson, you must fill your mind with every fact it is possible to retain. Now, the scales could mean nothing more than that he'd walked past a fishmonger. But you certainly observed the streaks of pitch on his shoes, did you not?" When the others merely shook their heads, Holmes sighed, his visage filled with exasperation. He continued. "You gentlemen know the expression, 'devil to pay.'"

"Of course."

"The figurative meaning is to suffer consequences. But most people don't know its literal derivation. The phrase has nothing to do with handing money over to fallen angels. The 'devil' is that portion of a sailing vessel between the inner and outer hulls. To 'pay' it is to paint the outer seams with hot pitch to make them watertight. Obviously climbing between the hulls is an unpleasant and dangerous job, usually meted out as punishment to errant sailors. The pitch used is unique and found only around the waterfront. Because of the fish scales and the tar, I knew that Sloat had been to the docks within the past several hours. The most logical conclusion is that he owed the captain of a smuggling vessel some significant sum of money and traded the ring to him in exchange for the extinguishing of the debt." Holmes shook his head. "The ring could be on any one of dozens of ships and all of them out of our jurisdiction. I'm afraid Lord Mayhew will have to look to Lloyd's to make himself whole in this matter. In the future, let us hope, he will use better locks upon his windows and doors."

"Brilliant deductions," said Gregson of the white face and flaxen hair.

Indeed it was, Goodcastle noted, despite the fact that it was completely incorrect.

Holmes pulled a cherrywood pipe from his pocket, lit it and started for the door. He paused, glanced around the shop and turned back to Goodcastle, his eyebrow cocked. "Sir, perhaps you can help me in another matter. Since you deal in music boxes. . . . I have been on the lookout for a particular box a client of mine once expressed interest in. It is in the shape of an octagon on a gold base. It plays a melody from *The Magic Flute* by

Mozart and was made by Edward Gastwold in York in 1856. The box is rosewood and is inlaid with ivory."

Goodcastle thought for a moment. "I'm sorry to say that I'm not familiar with that particular piece. I've never been fortunate enough to come upon any of Gastwold's creations, though I hear they're marvelous. I certainly can make inquiries. If they bear fruit, shall I contact you?"

"Please." Holmes handed the shopkeeper a card. "My client would pay dearly for the box itself or would offer a handsome finder's charge to anyone who could direct him toward the owner."

Goodcastle put the card in a small box next to his till. Reflecting: What a clever man this Holmes is. The Gastwold music box was not well known; for years it had been in the possession of the man who owned the massive Southland Metalworks Ltd. in Sussex. In doing his research into Sir Mayhew's life in preparation for the burglary, he'd learned that Mayhew was a major stockholder in Southland.

Holmes had asked a simple, seemingly innocent question, in hopes that Goodcastle would blurt out that, indeed, he knew of the box and its owner.

Which would have suggested that he might have delved, however subtly, into Mayhew's affairs.

Surely Holmes had no such client. Yet still he knew of the box. Apparently he'd taught himself about music boxes just in case facts about such items came in useful—exactly as Goodcastle did when preparing for his burglaries. ("Data, data, data," Holmes had said; how true!)

Goodcastle said to them, "Well, good day, gentlemen."

"And to you, sir. Our apologies." It was the amiable Dr. Watson who offered this.

"Not at all," Goodcastle assured them. "I would rather have an aggressive constabulary protecting us from the likes of Bill Sloat than one that is remiss and allows us to fall prey to such blackguards."

And, he added to himself, I would most *certainly* have a constabulary that is candid in how they pursue wrongdoers, allowing me the chance to improve the means of practicing my own craft.

After the men had left, Goodcastle went to the cupboard, poured a glass of sherry. He paused at one of the jewelry cases in the front of the store and glanced at a bowl containing cheap cuff links and shirt studs. Beside it was a sign that said, *Any Two Items for £1*. He checked to make certain the Westphalian ring was discreetly hidden beneath the tin and copper jewelry, where it would remain until he met with his French buyer tomorrow.

Goodcastle then counted his daily receipts and, as he did every night, carefully ordered and dusted the counter so that it was ready for his customers in the morning.

Surveillance

The knocking on the door not only woke Jake Muller from an afternoon nap but it told him immediately who his visitor was.

Not a polite single rap, not a friendly Morse code but a repeated slamming of the brass knocker. Three times, four, six . . .

Oh, man, not again.

Rolling his solid body from the couch, Muller paused for a moment to slip into a slightly higher level of wakefulness. It was five p.m. and he'd been gardening all day—until about an hour ago when a Dutch beer and the warmth of a May afternoon had lulled him to sleep. He now flicked on the pole lamp and walked unsteadily to the door, pulled it open.

The slim man in a blue suit and sporting thick, well-crafted politician's hair brushed past Muller and strode into the living room. Behind him was an older, burlier man in tweedy brown.

"Detective," Muller muttered to the man in blue.

Lieutenant William Carnegie didn't reply. He sat on the couch as if he'd just stepped away from it for a trip to the bathroom.

"Who're you?" Muller asked the other one bluntly.

"Sergeant Hager."

"You don't need to see his ID, Jake, do you?" Carnegie said.

Muller yawned. He'd wanted the couch but the cop was sitting stiffly in the middle of it so he took the uncomfortable chair instead. Hager didn't sit down. He crossed his arms and looked around the dim room then let his vision settle on Muller's faded blue jeans, dusty white socks and a T-shirt advertising a local clam dive. His gardening clothes.

Yawning again and brushing his short, sandy hair into place, Muller asked, "You're not here to arrest me, right? Because you would've done that already. So, what do you want?"

Carnegie's trim hand disappeared into his trim suit jacket and returned with a notebook, which he consulted. "Just wanted to let you know, Jake—we found out about your bank accounts at West Coast Federal in Portland."

"And how'd you do that? You have a court order?"

"You don't need a court order for some things."

Sitting back, Muller wondered if they'd put some kind of tap on his computer—that was how he'd set up the accounts last week. Annandale's Major Crimes Division, he'd learned, was very high tech; he'd been under intense surveillance in the past several months.

Living in a fishbowl. . . .

He noticed that the tweedy cop was surveying the inside of Muller's modest bungalow.

"No, Sergeant Haver—"

"Hager."

"—I don't look like I'm living in luxury, if that's what you were observing. Because I'm not. Tell me, did you work the Anco case?"

The sergeant didn't need the glance from his boss to know to keep mum.

Muller continued, "But you *do* know that the burglar netted five hundred thousand and change. Now if—like Detective Carnegie here thinks—I was the one who stole the money, wouldn't I be living in something a little nicer than this?"

"Not if you were smart," the sergeant muttered and decided to sit down.

"Not if I were smart," Muller repeated and laughed.

Detective Carnegie looked around the dim living room and added, "This, we figure, is sort of a safe house. You probably have some real nice places overseas."

"I wish."

"Well, don't we all agree that you're not your typical Annandale resident?"

In fact Jake Muller *was* a bit of an oddball in this wealthy Southern California town. He'd suddenly appeared here about six months ago to oversee some businesses deals in the area. He was single, traveled a lot, had a vague career (he owned companies that bought and sold other companies was how he explained it). He made good money but had picked for his residence this modest house, which, as they'd just established, was nowhere close to luxurious.

So when Detective William Carnegie's clever police computer compiled a list of everyone who'd moved to town not long before the Anco Armored Delivery heist four months ago, Muller earned suspect status. And as the cop began to look more closely at Muller, the evidence got better and better. He had no alibi for the hours of the heist. The tire treads on the getaway car were similar to those on Muller's Lexus. Carnegie also found that Muller had a degree in electrical engineering; the burglar in the Anco case had dismantled a sophisticated alarm system to get into the cash storage room.

Even better, though, from Carnegie's point of view, was the fact that Muller had a record: a juvenile conviction for grand theft auto and an arrest ten years ago on some complicated money laundering scheme at a company he was doing business with. Though the charges against Muller were dropped, Carnegie believed he was let go only on a technicality. Oh, he knew in his heart that Muller was behind the Anco theft and he went after the businessman zealously—with the same energy that had made him a celebrity among the citizens of Annandale. Since Carnegie had been appointed head of Major Crimes, two years ago, robberies, drug sales and gang activities had dropped by half. Annandale had the lowest crime rate of any town in the area. He was also well liked among prosecutors—he made airtight cases against his suspects.

But on the Anco case he stumbled. Just after he'd arrested Jake Muller last month a witness came forward and said the man seen leaving the Anco grounds just after the robbery didn't look at all like Muller. Carnegie asserted that a smart perp like Muller would use a disguise for the getaway. But a state's attorney decided there was no case against him and ordered the businessman released.

Carnegie fumed at the embarrassment and the blot on his record. So when no other leads panned out the detective returned to Muller with renewed fervor. He kept digging into the businessman's life and slowly began shoring up the case with circumstantial evidence: Muller frequently played golf on a course next to Anco headquarters—the perfect place for staking out the company—and he owned an acetylene torch that was powerful enough to cut through the loading dock door at Anco. The detective used this information to bully his captain into beefing up surveillance on Muller.

Hence, the interrupted nap today with the stop-the-presses information about Muller's accounts.

"So what about the Portland money, Jake?"

"What about it?"

"Where'd the money come from?"

"I stole the crown jewels. No, wait, it was the Great Northfield Train Robbery. Okay, I lied. I knocked over a casino in Vegas."

William Carnegie sighed and momentarily lowered his lids, which ended with perfect, delicate lashes.

The businessman asked, "What about that other suspect? The highway worker? You were going to check him out."

Around the time of the heist a man in a public works jumpsuit was seen pulling a suitcase from some bushes near the Anco main gate. A passing driver thought this looked suspicious and noted the license plate of the public works truck, relaying the information to the Highway Patrol. The truck, which had been stolen a week before in Bakersfield, was later found abandoned at Orange County's John Wayne Airport.

Muller's lawyer had contended that this man was the robber and that Carnegie should pursue him.

"Didn't have any luck finding him," the Annandale detective said.

"You mean," Muller grumbled, "that it was a long shot, he's out of the jurisdiction and it's a hell of a lot easier to roust me than it is to find the real thief." He snapped, "Goddamn it, Carnegie, the only thing I've ever done wrong in my life was listening to a couple of buddies I shouldn't have when I was seventeen. We borrowed—"

"'Borrowed'?"

"—a car for two hours and we paid the price. I just don't get why you're riding me like this."

But in truth Muller knew the answer to that perfectly well. In his long and varied career, he'd met a number of men and women like self-disciplined William Carnegie. They were machines powered by mindless ambition to take down whoever they believed was their competitor or enemy. They were different from people like Muller himself, who are ambitious, yes, but whose excitement comes from the game itself. The Carnegies of the world were ruled solely by their need to win; the process was nothing to them.

"Can you prove the funds came from a legitimate source?" the sergeant asked formally.

Muller looked at Carnegie. "What happened to your other assistant, Detective? What was his name? Carl? I liked him. He didn't last too long."

Carnegie had gone through two assistants in the time he'd been after Jake Muller. He supposed that though the citizenry and the reporters were impressed with the obsessive-compulsive cop he'd make his coworkers' lives miserable.

"Okay," the detective said. "If you're not going to talk that's just the way it is. Oh, but I should let you know: We've got some information we're looking at right now. It's very interesting."

"Ah, more of your surveillance?"

"Maybe."

"And what exactly did you find?"

"Let's just call it interesting."

Muller said, "'Interesting.' You said that twice. Hey, you want a beer? You, Sergeant?"

Carnegie answered for both of them. "No."

Muller fetched a Heineken from the kitchen. He continued. "So what you're saying is that after you've gone over this interesting information you'll have enough evidence to arrest me for real this time. But if I confess it'll go a lot easier. Right?"

"Come on, Jake. Nobody was hurt at Anco. You'll do, what, five years. You're a young guy. It'd be a church social for you."

Muller nodded for a moment, drank a good bit of beer. Then said seriously, "But if I confessed, then I'd have to give the money back, right?"

Carnegie froze for a moment. Then he smiled. "I'm not going to stop until I nail you, Jake. You know that." He said to the sergeant, "Let's go. This's a waste of time."

"At last there's something we agree on," Muller offered and closed the door after them.

■

The next day, William Carnegie, wearing a perfectly pressed gray suit, white shirt and striped red tie, strode into the watch room of the Annandale police station, Hager behind him.

He nodded at the eight officers sitting in the cheap fiberglass chairs. The men and women fell silent as the detective surveyed his troops.

Coffee was sipped, pencils tapped, pads doodled upon.

Watches glanced at.

"We're going to make a push on the case. I went to see Muller yesterday. I lit a fire under him and it had an effect: Last night I was monitoring his email and he made a wire transfer of fifty thousand dollars from a bank in Portland to a bank in Lyon, France. I'm convinced he's getting ready to flee the jurisdiction."

Carnegie had managed to get level-two surveillance on Muller. This high-tech approach to investigations involved establishing real-time links to his online service provider and the computers at Muller's credit card companies, banks, cell phone service and the like. Anytime that Muller made a purchase, went online, made a call, withdrew cash and so on, the officers on the Anco team would know almost instantly.

"Big Brother's going to be watching everything our boy's doing."

"Who?" asked one of the younger cops.

"*1984*?" Carnegie responded, astonished that the man hadn't heard of the novel. "The book?" he asked sarcastically. When the officer continued to stare blankly he added, "Big Brother was the government. It watched everything the citizens did." He nodded at a nearby dusty computer terminal and then turned back to the officers. "You, me, and Big Brother—we're closing the net on Muller." Noting the stifled grins, he wished he'd been a bit less dramatic. But, damn it, didn't they realize that Annandale had become the laughingstock of Southern California law enforcers for not closing the Anco case? The CHP, LAPD and even the cops in small towns nearby couldn't believe that Annandale Police, despite having the biggest per capita budget of any town in Orange County, hadn't collared a single perp in the heist.

Carnegie divided the group into three teams and assigned them to shifts at the computer workstations, with orders to relay to him instantly everything that Muller did.

As he was walking back to his office to look further at Muller's wire transfer to France he heard a voice. "Hey, Dad?"

He turned to see his son striding down the corridor toward him, dressed in his typical seventeen-year-old's uniform: earrings, shabby Tomb Raider T-shirt and pants so baggy they looked like they'd fall off at any moment. And the hair: spiked up and dyed a garish yellow. Still, Billy was an above-average student and nothing like the troublemakers that Carnegie dealt with in an official capacity.

"What're you doing here?" he asked. It was early May. School should be in session, shouldn't it?

"It's parent-teacher day, remember? You and Mom're supposed to meet Mr. Gibson at ten. I came by to make sure you'd be there."

Damn . . . Carnegie'd forgotten about the meeting. And he was supposed to have a conference call with two investigators in France about Muller's wire transfer. That was set for nine-forty-five. If he postponed it, the French policemen wouldn't be available later because of the time difference and the call would have to be delayed until tomorrow.

"I've got it on my calendar," the detective said absently; something had begun to nag at his thoughts. What was it? He added to his son, "I just might be a little late."

"Dad, it's important," Billy said.

"I'll be there."

Then the thought that been buzzing around Carnegie's consciousness settled. "Billy, are you still taking French?"

His son blinked. "Yeah, you signed my report card, don't you remember?"

"Who's your teacher?"

"Mrs. Vandell."

"Is she at school now?"

"I guess. Yeah, probably. Why?"

"I need her to help me with a conference call. You go on home now. Tell your mother I'll be at the meeting as soon as I can."

Carnegie left the boy standing in the middle of the hallway and jogged to his office, so excited about the brainstorm of using the French teacher to help him translate that he nearly collided with a workman hunched over one of the potted plants in the corridor, trimming leaves.

"Sorry," he called and hurried into his office. He phoned Billy's French teacher and—when he told her how important the case was—she reluctantly agreed to help him translate. The conference call went off as scheduled and the woman's translation efforts were a huge help; without his brainstorm to use the woman he couldn't have communicated with the two officers at all. Still, the investigators in France reported that they'd found no impropriety in Muller's investments or financial dealings. He paid taxes and had never run into any trouble with the gendarmes.

Carnegie asked if they had tapped his phone and were monitoring his online and banking activities.

There was a pause and then one of the officers responded. Billy's French teacher translated, "They say, 'We are not so high tech as you. We prefer to catch criminals the old-fashioned way.'" They did agree to alert their customs agents to check Muller's luggage carefully the next time he was in the country.

Carnegie thanked the two men and the teacher then hung up

We prefer to catch criminals the old-fashioned way. . . .

Which is why we'll get him and you won't, thought the detective as he spun around in his chair and began staring intently at Big Brother's computer monitor once again.

■

Jake Muller stepped out of the department store in downtown Annandale, following the young man he'd noticed in the jewelry department.

The boy kept his head down and walked quickly away from the store.

When they were passing an alleyway Muller suddenly jogged forward, grabbed the skinny kid by the arm and pulled him into the shadows.

"Jesus," he whispered in shock.

Muller pinned him up against the wall. "Don't think about running." A glance toward the boy's pockets. "And don't think about anything else."

"I don't—" the boy said with a quivering voice, "I don't have a gun or anything."

"What's your name?"

"I—"

"Name?" Muller barked.

"Sam. Sam Phillips. Like, whatta you want?"

"Give me the watch."

The boy sighed and rolled his eyes.

"Give it to me. You don't want me to have to take it off you." Muller outweighed the boy by fifty pounds.

The kid reached into his pocket and handed him the Seiko that Muller had seen him lift off the counter at the store. Muller took it.

"Who're you? Security? A cop?"

Muller eyed him carefully and then pocketed the watch. "You were clumsy. If the guard hadn't been taking a leak he would've caught you."

"What guard?"

"That's my point. The little guy in the ratty jacket and dirty jeans."

"He was a security guard?"

"Yeah."

"How'd you spot him?"

Muller said grimly, "Let's say I've had my share of run-ins with guys like that."

The boy looked up for a moment, examined Muller then resumed his study of the asphalt in the alley. "How'd you spot *me*?"

"Wasn't hard. You were skulking around the store like you'd already been busted."

"You gonna shake me down or something?"

Muller looked up and down the street cautiously. Then he said, "I need somebody to help me with this thing I've got going tomorrow."

"Why me?" the boy asked.

"There're some people who'd like to set me up."

"Cops?"

"Just . . . some people." Muller nodded at the watch. "But since *I* spotted *you* boost that, I know you're not working for anybody."

"Whatta I have to do?"

"It's easy. I need a driver. A half hour's work."

Part scared, part excited. "Like, how much?"

"I'll pay you five hundred."

Another examination of the scenery. "For a half hour?"

Muller nodded.

"Damn. Five hundred?"

"That's right."

"What're we doing?" he asked, a little cautious now. "I mean, exactly."

"I've got to . . . pick up a few things at this place—a house on Tremont. I need you to park in the alley behind the house while I go inside for a few minutes."

The kid grinned. "So, you going to 'jack some stuff? This's a heist, right?"

Muller shushed him. "Even if it was, you think I'd say it out loud?"

"Sorry. I wasn't thinking." The boy squinted then said, "Hey, there's this friend of mine? And we've got a connection. He's getting us some good stuff. I mean, way sweet. We can turn it around in a week. You come in with a thousand or two, he'll give us a better discount. You can double your money. You interested?"

"Drugs?"

"Yeah."

"I don't ever go near 'em. And you shouldn't either. They'll screw up your life. Remember that. . . . Meet me tomorrow, okay?"

"When?"

"Noon. The corner of Seventh and Maple. Starbucks."

"I guess."

"Don't guess. Be there." Muller started to walk away.

"If this works out you think maybe there'd be some more work for me?"

"I might be away for a while. But, yeah, maybe. If you handle it right."

"I do a good job, mister. Hey, what's *your* name?"

"You don't need to know that."

The kid nodded. "That's cool. Sure. . . . One other thing? What about the watch?"

"I'll dispose of the evidence for you."

After the kid was gone Muller walked slowly to the mouth of the alley and peeked out. No sign of Carnegie's surveillance team. He'd been careful to lose them but they had this almost magical ability to appear from nowhere and nail him with their Big Ear mikes and telephoto lenses.

Pulling on his Oakland baseball cap and lowering his head, he stepped out of the alley and walked down the sidewalk fast, as if satellites were tracking his position from ten thousand miles in space.

■

The next morning William Carnegie was late coming into the office.

Since he'd screwed up by missing the parent-teacher meeting yesterday he'd forced himself to have breakfast with his wife and Billy.

When he walked into the police station at nine-thirty Sergeant Hager told him, "Muller's been doing some shopping you ought to know about."

"What?"

"He left his house an hour ago. Our boys tailed him to the mall. They lost him but not long after that we got a charge notice from one of his credit card companies. At Books 'N' Java he bought six books. We don't know exactly what they were but the product code from the store listed them as travel books. Then he left the mall and spent thirty-eight dollars for two boxes of nine-millimeter ammunition at Tyler's Gun Shop."

"Jesus. I always figured him for a shooter. The guards at Anco're lucky they didn't hear him breaking in; he would've taken them out. I know it. . . . Did the surveillance team pick him up again?"

"Nope. They went back to his house to wait."

"Got something else," called a young policewoman nearby. "He charged forty-four dollars' worth of tools at Home Depot."

Carnegie mused, "So, he's armed and sounds like he's planning another heist. Then he's going to flee the state." Gazing at one of the computer screens, he asked absently, "What're you going after this time, Muller? A business, a house?"

Hager's phone rang. He answered and listened. "That was the babysitter in front of Muller's. He's back home. Only something funny. He was on foot. He must've parked up the street someplace." He listened some more. "They say there's a painting truck in his driveway. Maybe that's why."

"No. He's up to something. I don't trust anything that man does."

"Got another notice!" one officer called. "He just went online. . . ." The police had no court order allowing them to view the content of what Muller downloaded, though they could observe the sites he was connected to. "Okay. He's on the Anderson & Cross website."

"The burglar alarm company?" Carnegie asked, his heart pounding with excitement.

"Yep."

A few minutes later the officer called, "Now he's checking out Travel-Central dot com."

A service that lets you make airline reservations online.

"Tell surveillance we'll let them know as soon as he goes off-line. They should be ready to move. I've got a feeling this's going to happen fast."

We've got you now, Carnegie thought. Then he laughed and looked at the computers affectionately.

Big Brother Is Watching You. . . .

■

In the passenger seat of his car Jake Muller nodded toward a high fence in an alleyway behind Tremont Street. "Sam, pull over there."

The car braked slowly to a stop.

"That's it, huh?" the nervous kid asked.

Nodding toward a white house on the other side of the fence.

"Yep. Now, listen. If a cop comes by just drive off slow. Go around the block but turn left at the street. Got that? Stay off Tremont, whatever you do."

The boy asked uneasily, "You think somebody'll come by?"

"Let's hope not." Muller took the tools he'd just bought that morning out of the trunk, looked up and down the alley then walked through the gate in the fence and disappeared around the side of the house.

Muller returned ten minutes later. He hurried through the gate, carrying a heavy box and a small shopping bag. He disappeared again and returned with several more boxes. He loaded everything in the back of the car and wiped sweat from his forehead. He dropped hard into the passenger's seat. "Let's get outta here."

"Where're the tools?"

"I left 'em back there. What're you waiting for? Go."

The kid hit the accelerator and the car jumped into the middle of the alley.

Soon they were on the freeway and Muller gave directions to a cheap motel on the far side of town, the Starlight Lodge. There Muller climbed out. He walked into the lobby and registered for two nights. He returned to the car. "Room 129. He said it's around the side in the back."

They found the spot, parked and climbed out. Muller handed the boy the room key. He opened the door and together they carried the boxes and the shopping bag inside.

"Kinda lame," the kid said, looking around.

"I won't be here that long."

Muller turned his back and opened the grocery bag. He extracted five one-hundred-dollar bills and handed them over. He added another twenty. "You'll have to take a cab back downtown."

"Man, looks like a good haul." Nodding at the bag of money.

Muller said nothing. He stuffed the bag into a suitcase, locked it and slipped it under the bed.

The kid pocketed the bills.

"You did a good job today, Sam. Thanks."

"How'll I find you, mister? I mean, if you want to hire me again?"

"I'll leave a message at the Starbucks."

"Yeah. Good."

Muller glanced at his watch. He emptied his pockets on the dresser. "Now I gotta shower and go meet some people."

They shook hands. The boy left and Muller swung the door shut after him.

In the bathroom he turned the shower on full, the water hot. He leaned against the wobbly basin and watched the steam roll out of the stall like stormy clouds and wondered where his life was about to go.

■

"There's something screwy," Sergeant Hager called out.

"What?"

"A glitch of some kind." He nodded at one computer. "Muller's still online at his house. See? Only we just got an advisory from National Bank's credit card computer. Somebody using Muller's card got a room at the Starlight Lodge on Simpson about forty-five minutes ago. There's gotta be a mistake. He—"

"Oh, Christ," Carnegie spat out. "There's no mistake. Muller left his computer on so we'd think he was home. *That's* why he parked the car around the corner. So our men wouldn't see him leave. He snuck through a side yard or out the back." Carnegie grabbed the phone and raged at the surveillance team that their subject had gotten away from him. He ordered them to check to make sure. He slammed the receiver down and a moment later a sheepish officer called back to confirm that the painters said Muller had left over an hour ago.

The detective sighed. "So while we were napping he knocked over the next target. I don't believe it. I just—"

"He just made another charge," a cop called. "Eighteen gallons of gas at the Mobil Station on Lorenzo and Principale."

"Tanked it up." Carnegie nodded, considering this. "Maybe he's going to drive up to San Francisco to catch a flight. Or Arizona or Las Vegas, for that matter." Walking to the wall map, the detective stuck pins in the locations Hager had mentioned. He was calmer now. Muller may have guessed they'd be monitoring his online activity but obviously didn't know the extent of their surveillance.

"Get a county unmarked to tail him."

"Detective, just got a report from the speed pass main computer," one of the officers across the room called. "Muller turned onto the four-oh-eight at Stanton Road four minutes ago. He entered at the northbound tollboth."

The little box on your windshield that automatically paid tolls on highways, bridges and tunnels could report exactly when and where you used it.

Another pin was stabbed into the map.

Hager directed the pursuing officers to that interchange.

Fifteen minutes later, the cop monitoring the speed pass computer called out once again, "He just turned off the tollway. At Markham Road. The eastbound tollbooth."

Eastbound into the Markham neighborhood? Carnegie reflected. Well, that made sense. This was a tough part of town, populated by rednecks and bikers living in ramshackle bungalows and trailers. If Muller had an accomplice Markham would be a good source for that sort of muscle. And nearby was the desert, with thousands of square miles to hide the Anco loot.

"Still no visual yet," Hager said, listening on his phone to the pursuing officers.

"Damn. We're going to lose him."

But then another officer called, "I just got a ping from Muller's cell phone company—he's turned on the phone and's making a call. They're tracing it . . . ." A moment later he called out, "Okay. He's headed northbound on La Ciena."

Another blue-tipped pin in the map.

Hager relayed this information to the county cops. Then he listened and gave a laugh. "They've got the car! . . . Muller's pulling into the Desert Rose trailer park. . . . Okay. . . . He's parking at one of the trailers. . . . Getting out . . . . He's talking to a white male, thirties, shaved head, tattoos. . . . The male's nodding toward a shed on the back of the property. . . . They're walking back there together. . . . They're getting a package out of the shed. . . . Now they're going inside."

"That's good enough for me," Carnegie announced. "Tell 'em to stay out of sight. We'll be there in twenty minutes. Advise us if the suspect starts to leave."

As he started for the door, he said a silent prayer, thanking both the Lord—and Big Brother—for their help.

The drive took closer to forty minutes but Jake Muller's car was still parked in front of the rusty, lopsided trailer.

The officers on the scene reported that the robber and his bald accomplice were still inside, presumably planning their escape from the jurisdiction.

The four police cars from headquarters were parked several trailers away and nine Annandale cops, three armed with shotguns, were crouching behind sheds and weeds and rusty autos. Everybody kept low, mindful that Muller was armed.

Carnegie and Hager eased forward toward the trailer. They had to handle the situation carefully. Unless they could catch a glimpse of the Anco payroll money through the door or window, or unless Muller carried it outside in plain view, they had no probable cause to arrest him. They circled the place but couldn't see in; the door was closed and the curtains drawn.

Hell, Carnegie thought, discouraged. Maybe they could—

But then fate intervened.

"Smell that?" Carnegie asked in a whisper.

Hager frowned. "What?"

"Coming from inside."

The sergeant inhaled deeply. "Pot or hash," he said, nodding.

This would give them probable cause to enter.

"Let's do it," Hager whispered. And he gestured for the other officers to join him.

One of the tactical cops asked if he should do the kick-in but Carnegie shook his head. "Nope. He's mine." He took off his suit jacket and strapped on a bulletproof vest then drew his automatic pistol.

Gazing at the other officers, he mouthed, Ready?

They nodded.

The detective held up three fingers, then bent them down one at a time.

One . . . two . . .

"Go!"

He shouldered open the door and rushed into the trailer, the other officers right behind him.

"Freeze, freeze, police!" he shouted, looking around, squinting to see better in the dim light.

The first thing he noticed was a large plastic bag of pot sitting by the doorway.

The second thing was that the tattooed man's visitor wasn't Jake Muller at all; it was Carnegie's own son, Billy.

■

The detective stormed into the Annandale police station, flanked by Sergeant Hager. Behind them was another officer, escorting the sullen, handcuffed boy.

The owner of the trailer—a biker with a history of drug offenses—had been taken down the hall to Narcotics and the kilo of weed booked into evidence.

Carnegie had ordered Billy to tell them what was going on but he'd clammed up and refused to say a word. A search of the property and of Muller's car had yielded no evidence of the Anco loot. He'd gotten a frosty reaction from the Orange County troopers who'd been tailing Muller's car when Carnegie had raged at them about misidentifying his son as the businessman. ("Don't recall you ever bothered to put his picture out on the wire, Detective," one of them reminded.)

Carnegie now barked to one of the officers sitting at a computer screen, "Get me Jake Muller."

"You don't have to," an officer said. "He's right over there."

Muller was sitting across from the desk sergeant. He rose and looked in astonishment at Carnegie and his son. He pointed to the boy and said sourly, "So they got you already, Sam. That was fast. I just filled out the complaint five minutes ago."

"Sam?" Carnegie asked.

"Yeah, Sam Phillips," Muller said.

"His name's Billy. He's my son," Carnegie muttered. The boy's middle name was Samuel, and Phillips was the maiden name of the detective's wife.

"Your son?" Muller asked, eyes wide in disbelief. He then glanced at what one officer was carrying—an evidence box containing the suitcase, wallet, keys and cell phone that had been found in Muller's car. "You recovered everything," he said. "How's my car? Did he wreck it?"

Hager started to tell him that his car was fine but Carnegie waved his hand to silence the big cop. "Okay, what the hell is going on?" he asked Muller. "What'd you have to do with my boy?"

Angry, Muller said, "Hey, this kid robbed *me*. I was just trying to do him a favor. I had no idea he was your son."

"Favor?"

Muller eyed the boy up and down. "Yesterday I saw him steal a watch from Maxwell's, over on Harrison Street."

Carnegie turned a cold eye on his son, who continued to keep his head down.

"I followed him and made him give me the watch. I felt bad for him. He seemed like he was having a tough time of it. I hired him to help me out for an hour or so. I just wanted to show him there were people out there who'd pay good money for legitimate work."

"What'd you do with the watch?" Carnegie asked.

Muller looked indignant. "Returned it to the shop. What'd you think? I'd keep stolen merchandise?"

The detective glanced at his son and demanded, "What did he hire you to do?"

When the boy said nothing Muller explained. "I paid him to watch my car while I moved a few things out of my house."

"*Your* house?" the boy asked in shock. "On Tremont?"

To his father Muller said, "That's right. I moved into a motel for a few days—I'm having my house painted and I can't sleep with the paint fumes."

The truck in Muller's driveway, Carnegie recalled.

"I couldn't use the front door," Muller added angrily, "because I'm sick of those goons of yours tailing me every time I leave the house. I hired your son to stay with the car in the alley; it's a tow zone back there. You can't leave your car unattended even for five minutes. I dropped off some tools I bought this morning and picked up a few things I needed and we drove to the motel." Muller shook his head. "I gave him the key to open the door and I forgot to get it when he left. He came back when I was in the shower and ripped me off. My car, my cell phone, money, wallet, the suitcase." In disgust he added, "Hell, and here I gave him all that money. And practically begged him to get his act together and stay clear of drugs."

"He told you that?" Carnegie asked.

The boy nodded reluctantly.

His father sighed and nodded at the suitcase. "What's in there?"

Muller shrugged, picked up his keys and unlocked and opened the case.

Carnegie supposed that the businessman wouldn't be so cooperative if it contained the Anco loot but he still felt a burst of delight when he noticed that the paper bag inside was filled with cash.

His excitement faded, though, when he saw it held only about three or four hundred dollars, mostly wadded-up ones and fives.

"Household money," Muller explained. "I didn't want to leave it in the house. Not with the painters there."

Carnegie contemptuously tossed the bag into the case and angrily slammed the lid. "Jesus."

"You thought it was the Anco money?"

Carnegie looked at the computer terminals around them, cursors blinking passively.

Goddamn Big Brother. . . . The best surveillance money can buy. And look what had happened.

The detective's voice cracked with emotion as he said, "You followed my son! You hired the painters so you could get away without being seen, you bought the bullets, the tools. . . . And what the hell were you doing looking at burglar alarm websites?"

"Comparative shopping," Muller answered reasonably. "I'm buying an alarm system for the house."

"This is all a setup! You—"

The businessman silenced him by glancing at Carnegie's fellow officers, who were looking at their boss with mixed expressions of concern and distaste over his paranoid ranting. Muller nodded toward Carnegie's office. "How 'bout you and I go in there? Have a chat."

Inside, Muller swung the door shut and turned to face the glowering detective. "Here's the situation, Detective. I'm the only prosecuting witness in the larceny and auto theft case against your son. That's a felony and if I decide to press charges he'll do some serious time, particularly since I suspect you found him in the company of some not-so-savory friends when he was busted. Then there's also the little matter of Dad's career trajectory after his son's arrest hits the papers."

"You want a deal?"

"Yeah, I want a deal. I'm sick of this delusion crap of yours, Carnegie. I'm a legitimate businessman. I didn't steal the Anco payroll. I'm not a thief and never have been."

He eyed the detective carefully then reached into his pocket and handed Carnegie a slip of paper.

"What's this?"

"The number of a Coastal Air flight six months ago—the afternoon of the Anco robbery."

"How'd you get this?"

"My companies do some business with the airlines. I pulled some strings and the head of security at Coastal got me that number. One of the passengers in first class on that flight paid cash for a one-way ticket from John Wayne Airport to Chicago four hours after the Anco robbery. He had no checked baggage. Only carry-on. They wouldn't give me the passenger's name but that shouldn't be too tough for a hardworking cop like you to track down."

Carnegie stared at the paper. "The guy from the Department of Public Works? The one the witness saw with that suitcase near Anco?"

"Maybe it's a coincidence, Detective. But I know I didn't steal the money. Maybe *he* did."

The paper disappeared into Carnegie's pocket. "What do you want?"

"Drop me as a suspect. Cut out all the surveillance. I want my life back. And I want a letter signed by you stating that the evidence proves I'm not guilty."

"That won't mean anything in court."

"But it'll look pretty bad if anybody decides to come after me again."

"Bad for my job, you mean."

"That's exactly what I mean."

After a moment Carnegie muttered, "How long've you been planning this out?"

Muller said nothing. But he reflected: Not that long, actually. He'd started thinking about it just after the two cops had interrupted his nap the other day.

He'd wire-transferred some money to one of his banks in France from an investment account to fuel the cops' belief that he was getting ready to flee the country (the French accounts were completely legit; only a fool would hide loot in Europe).

Then he'd done some surveillance of his own, low-tech though it was. He'd pulled on overalls, glasses and a hat and snuck into police headquarters, armed with a watering can and clippers to tend to the plants he'd noticed inside the station the first time he was arrested. He'd spent a half hour on his knees, his head down, clipping and watering, in the hallway outside the watch room, where he'd learned the extent of the police's electronic invasion of his life. He'd heard too the exchange between Billy Carnegie and the detective—a classic example of an uninvolved father and a troubled, angry son.

Muller smiled to himself now, recalling that after the meeting Carnegie had been so focused on the case that, when he nearly tripped over Muller in the corridor, the cop had never noticed who the gardener was.

He'd then followed Billy for a few hours until he caught him palming the watch. Then he tricked the boy into helping him. He'd hired the painters to do some interior touch-up—to give him the excuse to park his car elsewhere and to check into the motel. Then, using their surveillance against them, he'd fooled the cops into believing he was indeed the Anco burglar and was getting ready to do one last heist and flee the state by buying the travel books, the bullets and the tools and logging on to the alarm and travel agency websites. At the motel he'd tempted Billy Carnegie into stealing the suitcase, credit cards, phone and car—everything that would let the cops track the kid and nail him red-handed.

He now said to Carnegie, "I'm sorry, Detective. But you didn't leave me any choice. You just weren't ever going to believe that I'm innocent."

"You used my son."

Muller shrugged. "No harm done. Look on the good side—his first bust and he picked a victim who's willing to drop the charges. Anybody else, he wouldn't've been so lucky."

Carnegie glanced through the blinds at his son, standing forlorn by Hager's desk.

"He's savable, Detective," Muller said. "If you want to save him. . . . So, do we have a deal?"

A disgusted sigh was followed by a disgusted nod.

Outside the police station, Muller tossed the suitcase into the back of his car, which had been towed to the station by a police truck.

He drove back to his house and walked inside. The workmen had apparently just finished and the smell of paint was strong. He went through the ground floor, opening windows to air the place out.

Strolling into his garden, he surveyed the huge pile of mulch, whose spreading had been postponed because of his interrupted nap. The businessman glanced at his watch. He had some phone calls to make but decided to put them off for another day; he was in the mood to garden. He changed clothes, went into the garage and picked up a glistening new shovel, part of his purchases that morning at Home Depot. He began meticulously spreading the black and brown mulch throughout the large garden.

After an hour of work he paused for a beer. Sitting under a maple tree, sipping the Heineken, he surveyed the empty street in front of his house—where Carnegie had stationed the surveillance team for the past few months. Man, it felt good not to be spied on any longer.

His eyes then slid to a small rock sitting halfway between a row of corn stalks and some tomato vines. Three feet beneath it was a bag containing the $543,300 from Anco Security, which he'd buried there the afternoon of the robbery just before he'd ditched the public works uniform and driven the stolen truck to Orange County Airport for the flight to Chicago under a false name—a precautionary trip, in case he needed to lead investigators off on a false trail, as it turned out he'd had to do, thanks to compulsive Detective Carnegie.

Jake Muller planned all of his heists out to the finest of details; this was why he'd never been caught after nearly fifteen years as a thief.

He'd wanted to send the cash to his bagman in Miami for months—Muller hated it when heist money wasn't earning interest—but with Carnegie breathing down his neck he hadn't dared. Should he dig it up now and send it off?

No, he decided; it was best to wait till dark.

Besides, the weather was warm, the sky was clear and there was nothing like gardening on a beautiful spring day. Muller finished his beer, picked up the shovel and returned to the pile of pungent mulch.

Born Bad

Sleep, *my child and peace attend thee, all through the night. . . .*

The words of the lullaby looped relentlessly through her mind, as persistent as the clattering Oregon rain on the roof and window.

The song that she'd sung to Beth Anne when the girl was three or four seated itself in her head and wouldn't stop echoing. Twenty-five years ago, the two of them: mother and daughter, sitting in the kitchen of the family's home outside of Detroit. Liz Polemus, hunching over the Formica table, the frugal young mother and wife, working hard to stretch the dollars.

Singing to her daughter, who sat across from her, fascinated with the woman's deft hands.

> *I who love you shall be near you, all through the night.*
> *Soft the drowsy hours are creeping.*
> *Hill and vale in slumber sleeping.*

Liz felt a cramp in her right arm—the one that had never healed properly—and realized she was still gripping the receiver fiercely at the news she'd just received. That her daughter was on her way to the house.

The daughter she hadn't spoken with in more than three years.

> *I my loving vigil keeping, all through the night.*

Liz finally replaced the telephone and felt blood surge into her arm, itching, stinging. She sat down on the embroidered couch that had been in the family for years and massaged her throbbing forearm. She felt light-headed, confused, as if she wasn't sure the phone call had been real or a wispy scene from a dream.

Only the woman wasn't lost in the peace of sleep. No, Beth Anne was on her way. A half hour and she'd be at Liz's door.

Outside, the rain continued to fall steadily, tumbling into the pines that filled Liz's yard. She'd lived in this house for nearly a year, a small place miles from the nearest suburb. Most people would've thought it too small, too remote. But to Liz it was an oasis. The slim widow, mid-fifties, had a busy life and little time for housekeeping. She could clean the place quickly and get back to work. And while hardly a recluse, she preferred the buffer zone of forest that separated her from her neighbors. The minuscule size also discouraged suggestions by any male friends that, hey, got an idea, how 'bout I move in? The woman would merely look around the one-bedroom home and explain that two people would go crazy in such cramped quarters; after her husband's death she'd resolved she'd never remarry or live with another man.

Her thoughts now drifted to Jim. Their daughter had left home and cut off all contact with the family before he died. It had always stung her that the girl hadn't even called after his death, let alone attended his funeral. Anger at this instance of the girl's callousness shivered within Liz but she pushed it aside, reminding herself that whatever the young woman's purpose tonight there wouldn't be enough time to exhume even a fraction of the painful memories that lay between mother and daughter like wreckage from a plane crash.

A glance at the clock. Nearly ten minutes had sped by since the call, Liz realized with a start.

Anxious, she walked into her sewing room. This, the largest room in the house, was decorated with needlepoints of her own and her mother's and a dozen racks of spools—some dating back

to the fifties and sixties. Every shade of God's palette was represented in those threads. Boxes full of Vogue and Butterick patterns too. The centerpiece of the room was an old electric Singer.
It had none of the fancy stitch cams of the new machines, no
lights or complex gauges or knobs. The machine was a forty-
year-old, black-enameled workhorse, identical to the one that her
mother had used.

Liz had sewed since she was twelve and in difficult times the
craft sustained her. She loved every part of the process: Buying
the fabric—hearing the *thud thud thud* as the clerk would turn
the flat bolts of cloth over and over, unwinding the yardage (Liz
could tell the women with near-prefect precision when a particular amount had been unfolded). Pinning the crisp, translucent
paper onto the cloth. Cutting with the heavy pinking shears,
which left a dragon-tooth edge on the fabric. Readying the machine, winding the bobbin, threading the needle . . .

There was something so completely soothing about sewing:
taking these substances—cotton from the land, wool from animals—and blending them into something altogether new. The
worst aspect of the injury several years ago was the damage to
her right arm, which kept her off the Singer for three unbear-
able months.

Sewing was therapeutic for Liz, yes, but more than that, it
was a part of her profession and had helped her become a well-
to-do woman; nearby were racks of designer gowns, awaiting her
skillful touch.

Her eyes rose to the clock. Fifteen minutes. Another breathless slug of panic.

Picturing so clearly that day twenty-five years ago—Beth
Anne in her flannel 'jammies, sitting at the rickety kitchen table
and watching her mother's quick fingers with fascination as Liz
sang to her.

Sleep, my child, and peace attend thee . . .

This memory gave birth to dozens of others and the agitation rose in Liz's heart like the water level of the rain-swollen stream behind her house. Well, she told herself now firmly, don't just sit here . . . Do something. Keep busy. She found a navy-blue jacket in her closet, walked to her sewing table then dug through a basket until she found a matching remnant of wool. She'd use this to make a pocket for the garment. Liz went to work, smoothing the cloth, marking it with tailor's chalk, finding the scissors, cutting carefully. She focused on her task but the distraction wasn't enough to take her mind off the impending visit—and memories from years ago.

The shoplifting incident, for instance. When the girl was twelve.

Liz recalled the phone ringing, answering it. The head of security at a nearby department store was reporting—to Liz's and Jim's shock—that Beth Anne had been caught with nearly a thousand dollars' worth of jewelry hidden in a paper bag.

The parents had pleaded with the manager not to press charges. They'd said there must've been some mistake.

"Well," the security chief said skeptically, "we found her with five watches. A necklace too. Wrapped up in this grocery bag. I mean, that don't sound like any mistake to me."

Finally after much reassurance that this was a fluke and promises she'd never come into the store again, the manager agreed to keep the police out of the matter.

Outside the store, once the family was alone, Liz turned to Beth Anne furiously, "Why on earth did you do that?"

"Why not?" was the girl's singsong response, a snide smile on her face.

"It was stupid."

"Like, I care."

"Beth Anne . . . why're you acting this way?"

"What way?" the girl'd asked in mock confusion.

Her mother had tried to engage her in a dialog—the way the

talk shows and psychologists said you should do with your kids—but Beth Anne remained bored and distracted. Liz had delivered a vague, and obviously futile, warning and had given up.

Thinking now: You put a certain amount of effort into stitching a jacket or dress and you get the garment you expect. There's no mystery. But you put a thousand times *more* effort into raising your child and the result is the opposite of what you hope and dream for. This seemed so unfair.

Liz's keen gray eyes examined the wool jacket, making sure the pocket lay flat and was pinned correctly into position. She paused, looking up, out the window toward the black spikes of the pine but what she was seeing were more hard memories of Beth Anne. What a mouth on that girl! Beth Anne would look her mother or father in the eye and say, "There is no goddamn way you're going to make me go with you." Or, "Do you have *any* fucking clue at all?"

Maybe they should've been stricter in their upbringing. In Liz's family you got whipped for cursing or talking back to adults or for not doing what your parents asked you to do. She and Jim had never spanked Beth Anne; maybe they *should've* swatted her once or twice.

One time, somebody had called in sick at the family business—a warehouse Jim had inherited—and he needed Beth Anne to help out. She'd snapped at him, "I'd rather be dead than go back inside that shithole with you."

Her father had backed down sheepishly but Liz stormed up to her daughter. "Don't talk to your father that way."

"Oh?" the girl asked in a sarcastic voice. "How *should* I talk to him? Like some obedient little daughter who does everything he wants? Maybe that's what he wanted but it's not who he got." She'd grabbed her purse, heading for the door.

"Where are you going?"

"To see some friends."

"You are not. Get back here this minute!"

Her reply was a slamming door. Jim started after her but in an instant she was gone, crunching through two-month-old gray Michigan snow.

And those "friends"?

Trish and Eric and Sean . . . kids from families with totally different values from Liz's and Jim's. They tried to forbid her from seeing them. But that, of course, had no effect.

"Don't tell me who I can hang out with," Beth Anne had said furiously. The girl was eighteen then and as tall as her mother. As she walked forward with a glower, Liz retreated uneasily. The girl continued, "And what do you know about them anyway?"

"They don't like your father and me—that's all I need to know. What's wrong with Todd and Joan's kids? Or Brad's? Your father and I've known them for years."

"What's *wrong* with them?" the girl muttered sarcastically. "Try, they're losers." This time grabbing both her purse and the cigarettes she'd started smoking, she made another dramatic exit.

With her right foot Liz pressed the pedal of the Singer and the motor gave its distinctive grind, then broke into *clatta clatta clatta* as the needle sped up and down, vanishing into the cloth, leaving a neat row of stitches around the pocket.

Clatta, clatta, clatta . . .

In middle school the girl would never get home until seven or eight and in high school she'd arrive much later. Sometimes she'd stay away all night. Weekends too she just disappeared and had nothing to do with the family.

Clatta clatta clatta. The rhythmic grind of the Singer soothed Liz somewhat but couldn't keep her from panicking again when she looked at the clock. Her daughter could be here at any minute.

Her girl, her little baby . . .

Sleep, my child . . .

And the question that had plagued Liz for years returned now: What had gone wrong? For hours and hours she'd replay the girl's early years, trying to see what Liz had done to make Beth Anne reject her so completely. She'd been an attentive, involved mother, been consistent and fair, made meals for the family every day, washed and ironed the girl's clothes, bought her whatever she needed. All she could think of was that she'd been too strong-minded, too unyielding in her approach to raising the girl, too stern sometimes.

But this hardly seemed like much of a crime. Besides, Beth Anne had been equally mad at her father—the softie of the parents. Easygoing, doting to the point of spoiling the girl, Jim was the perfect father. He'd help Beth Anne and her friends with their homework, drive them to school himself when Liz was working, read her bedtime stories and tuck her in at night. He made up "special games" for him and Beth Anne to play. It was just the sort of parental bond that most children would love.

But the girl would fly into rages at him too and go out of her way to avoid spending time with him.

No, Liz could think of no dark incidents in the past, no traumas, no tragedies that could have turned Beth Anne into a renegade. She returned to the conclusion that she'd come to years ago: that—as unfair and cruel as it seemed—her daughter had simply been born fundamentally different from Liz; something had happened in the wiring to make the girl the rebel she was.

And looking at the cloth, smoothing it under her long, smooth fingers, Liz considered something else: Rebellious, yes, but was she a *threat* too?

Liz now admitted that part of the ill ease she felt tonight wasn't only from the impending confrontation with her wayward child; it was that the young woman scared her.

She looked up from her jacket and stared at the rain spattering her window. Her right arm tingling painfully, she recalled that terrible day several years ago—the day that drove her permanently from Detroit and still gave her breathless nightmares. Liz had walked into a jewelry store and stopped in shock, gasping as she saw a pistol swinging toward her. She could still see the yellow flash as the man pulled the trigger, hear the stunning explosion, feel the numbing shock as the bullet slammed into her arm, sending her sprawling on the tile floor, crying out in pain and confusion.

Her daughter, of course, had nothing to do with that tragedy. Yet Liz had realized that Beth Anne was just as willing and capable of pulling the trigger as that man had done during the robbery; she had proof her daughter was a dangerous woman. A few years ago, after Beth Anne had left home, Liz had gone to visit Jim's grave. The day was foggy as cotton and she was nearly to the tombstone when she realized that somebody was standing over it. To her shock she realized it was Beth Anne. Liz eased back into the mist, heart pounding fiercely. She debated for a long moment but finally decided that she didn't have the courage to confront the girl and decided to leave a note on her car's windshield.

But as she stepped to the Chevy, fishing in her handbag for a pen and some paper, she glanced inside and her heart shivered at the sight: A jacket, a clutter of papers and half-hidden beneath them a pistol and some plastic bags, which contained white powder—drugs, Liz assumed.

Oh, yes, she now thought, her daughter, little Beth Anne Polemus, was very capable of killing.

Liz's foot rose from the pedal and the Singer fell silent. She lifted the clamp and cut the dangling threads. She pulled it on and slipped a few things into the pocket, examined herself in the mirror and decided that she was satisfied with the work.

Then she stared at her dim reflection. Leave! a voice in her head said. She's a threat! Get out now before Beth Anne arrives.

But after a moment of debate Liz sighed. One of the reasons she'd moved here in the first place was that she'd learned her daughter had relocated to the Northwest. Liz had been meaning to try to track the girl down but had found herself oddly reluctant to do so. No, she'd stay, she'd meet with Beth Anne. But she wasn't going to be stupid, not after the robbery. Liz now hung the jacket on a hanger and walked to the closet. She pulled down a box from the top shelf and looked inside. There sat a small pistol. "A ladies' gun," Jim had called it when he gave it to her years ago. She took it out and stared at the weapon.

Sleep, my child . . . All through the night.

Then she shuddered in disgust. No, she couldn't possibly use a weapon against her daughter. Of course not.

The idea of putting the girl to sleep forever was inconceivable.

And yet . . . What if it were a choice between her life and her daughter's? What if the hatred within the girl had pushed her over the edge?

Could she kill Beth Anne to save her own life?

No mother should ever have to make a choice like this one.

She hesitated for a long moment then started to put the gun back. But a flash of light stopped her. Headlights filled the front yard and cast bright yellow cat's eyes on the sewing room wall beside Liz.

The woman glanced once more at the gun and, rather than put it away in the closet, set it on a dresser near the door and covered it with a doily. She walked into the living room and stared out the window at the car in her driveway, which sat motionless, lights still on, wipers whipping back and forth fast, her daughter hesitating to climb out; Liz suspected it wasn't the bad weather that kept the girl inside.

A long, long moment later the headlights went dark.

Well, think positive, Liz told herself. Maybe her daughter had changed. Maybe the point of the visit was reaching out to make amends for all the betrayal over the years. They could finally begin to work on having a normal relationship.

Still, she glanced back at the sewing room, where the gun sat on the dresser, and told herself: Take it. Keep it in your pocket.

Then: No, put it back in the closet.

Liz did neither. Leaving the gun on the dresser, she strode to the front door of her house and opened it, feeling cold mist coat her face.

She stood back from the approaching silhouetted form of the slim young woman as Beth Anne walked through the doorway and stopped. A pause then she swung the door shut behind her.

Liz remained in the middle of the living room, pressing her hands together nervously.

Pulling back the hood of her windbreaker, Beth Anne wiped rain off her face. The young woman's face was weathered, ruddy. She wore no makeup. She'd be twenty-eight, Liz knew, but she looked older. Her hair was now short, revealing tiny earrings. For some reason, Liz wondered if someone had given them to the girl or if she'd bought them for herself.

"Well, hello, honey."

"Mother."

A hesitation then a brief, humorless laugh from Liz. "You used to call me 'Mom.'"

"Did I?"

"Yes. Don't you remember?"

A shake of the head. But Liz thought that in fact she did remember but was reluctant to acknowledge the memory. She looked her daughter over carefully.

Beth Anne glanced around the small living room. Her eye settled on a picture of herself and her father together—they were on the boat dock near the family home in Michigan.

Liz asked, "When you called you said somebody told you I was here. Who?"

"It doesn't matter. Just somebody. You've been living here since . . ." Her voice faded.

"A couple of years. Do you want a drink?"

"No."

Liz remembered that she'd found the girl sneaking some beer when she was sixteen and wondered if she'd continued to drink and now had a problem with alcohol.

"Tea, then? Coffee?"

"No."

"You knew I moved to the Northwest?" Beth Anne asked.

"You always talked about the area, getting away from . . . well, getting out of Michigan and coming here. Then after you moved out you got some mail at the house. From somebody in Seattle."

Beth Anne nodded. Was there a slight grimace too? As if she was angry with herself for carelessly leaving a clue to her whereabouts. "And you moved to Portland to be near me?"

Liz smiled. "I guess I did. I started to look you up but I lost the nerve." Liz felt tears welling in her eyes as her daughter continued her examination of the room. The house was small, yes, but the furniture, electronics and appointments were the best—the rewards of Liz's hard work in recent years. Two feelings vied within the woman: She half-hoped the girl would be tempted to reconnect with her mother when she saw how much money Liz had but, simultaneously, she was ashamed of the opulence; her daughter's clothes and cheap costume jewelry suggested she was struggling.

The silence was like fire. It burned Liz's skin and heart.

Beth Anne unclenched her left hand and her mother noticed a minuscule engagement ring and a simple gold band. The tears now rolled from her eyes. "You—?"

The young woman followed her mother's gaze to the ring. She nodded.

Liz wondered what sort of man her son-in-law was. Would he be someone soft like Jim, someone who could temper the girl's wayward personality? Or would he be hard? Like Beth Anne herself?

"You have children?" Liz asked.

"That's not for you to know."

"Are you working?"

"Are you asking if I've changed, Mother?"

Liz didn't want to hear the answer to this question and continued quickly, pitching her case. "I was thinking," she said, desperation creeping into her voice, "that maybe I could go up to Seattle. We could see each other . . . we could even work together. We could be partners. Fifty-fifty. We'd have so much fun. I always thought we'd be great together. I always dreamed—"

"You and me working together, Mother?" She glanced into the sewing room, nodded toward the machine, the racks of dresses. "That's not my life. It never was. It never could be. After all these years, you really don't understand that, do you?" The words and their cold tone answered Liz's question firmly: No, the girl hadn't changed one bit.

Her voice went harsh. "Then why're you here? What's your point in coming?"

"I think you know, don't you?"

"No, Beth Anne, I *don't* know. Some kind of psycho revenge?"

"You could say that, I guess." She looked around the room again. "Let's go."

Liz's breath was coming fast. "Why? Everything we ever did was for you."

"I'd say you did it *to* me." A gun appeared in her daughter's hand and the black muzzle lolled in Liz's direction. "Outside," she whispered.

"My God! No!" She inhaled a gasp as the memory of the shooting in the jewelry store came back to her hard. Her arm tingled and tears streaked down her cheeks.

She pictured the gun on the dresser.

Sleep, my child . . .

"I'm not going anywhere!" Liz said, wiping her eyes.

"Yes, you are. Outside."

"What are you going to do?" she asked desperately.

"What I should've done a long time ago."

Liz leaned against a chair for support. Her daughter noticed the woman's left hand, which had eased to within inches of the telephone.

"No!" the girl barked. "Get away from it."

Liz gave a hopeless glance at the receiver and then did as she was told.

"Come with me."

"Now? In the rain."

The girl nodded.

"Let me get a coat."

"There's one by the door."

"It's not warm enough."

The girl hesitated, as if she was going to say that the warmth of her mother's coat was irrelevant, considering what was about to happen. But then she nodded. "But don't try to use the phone. I'll be watching."

Stepping into the doorway of the sewing room, Liz picked up the blue jacket she'd just been working on. She slowly put it on, her eyes riveted to the doily and the hump of the pistol beneath it. She glanced back into the living room. Her daughter was staring at a framed snapshot of herself at eleven or twelve standing next to her father and mother.

Quickly she reached down and picked up the gun. She could turn fast, point it at her daughter. Scream to her to throw away her own gun.

Mother, I can feel you near me, all through the night . . .
Father, I know you can hear me, all through the night . . .

But what if Beth Anne *didn't* give up the gun?

What if she raised it, intending to shoot?

What would Liz do then?

To save her own life could she kill her daughter?

Sleep, my child . . .

Beth Anne was still turned away, examining the picture. Liz would be able to do it—turn, one fast shot. She felt the pistol, its weight tugging at her throbbing arm.

But then she sighed.

The answer was no. A deafening no. She'd never hurt her daughter. Whatever was going to happen next, outside in the rain, she could never hurt the girl.

Replacing the gun, Liz joined Beth Anne.

"Let's go," her daughter said and, shoving her own pistol into the waistband of her jeans, she led the woman outside, gripped her mother roughly by the arm. This was, Liz realized, the first physical contact in at least four years.

They stopped on the porch and Liz spun around to face her daughter. "If you do this, you'll regret it for the rest of your life."

"No," the girl said. "I'd regret *not* doing it."

Liz felt a spatter of rain join the tears on her cheeks. She glanced at her daughter. The young woman's face was wet and red too, but this was, her mother knew, solely from the rain; her eyes were completely tearless. In a whisper she asked, "What've I ever done to make you hate me?"

This question went unanswered as the first of the squad cars pulled into the yard, red and blue and white lights igniting the fat raindrops around them like sparks at a Fourth of July celebration. A man in his thirties, wearing a dark windbreaker and a badge around his neck, climbed out of the first car and walked toward the house, two uniformed state troopers behind him. He nodded to Beth Anne. "I'm Dan Heath, Oregon State Police."

The young woman shook his hand. "Detective Beth Anne Polemus, Seattle PD."

"Welcome to Portland," he said.

She gave an ironic shrug, took the handcuffs he held and cuffed her mother's hands securely.

■

Numb from the cold rain—and from the emotional fusion of the meeting—Beth Anne listened as Heath recited to the older woman, "Elizabeth Polemus, you're under arrest for murder, attempted murder, assault, armed robbery and dealing in stolen goods." He read her her rights and explained that she'd be arraigned in Oregon on local charges but was subject to an extradition order back to Michigan on a number of outstanding warrants there, including capital murder.

Beth Anne gestured to the young OSP officer who'd met her at the airport. She hadn't had time to do the paperwork that'd allow her to bring her own service weapon into another state so the trooper had loaned her one of theirs. She returned it to him now and turned back to watch a trooper search her mother.

"Honey," her mother began, the voice miserable, pleading.

Beth Anne ignored her, and Heath nodded to the young uniformed trooper, who led the woman toward a squad car. But Beth Anne stopped him and called, "Hold on. Frisk her better."

The uniformed trooper blinked, looking over the slim, slight captive, who seemed as unthreatening as a child. But, with a nod from Heath, he motioned over a policewoman, who expertly patted her down. The officer frowned when she came to the small of Liz's back. The mother gave a piercing glance to her daughter as the officer pulled up the woman's navy-blue jacket, revealing a small pocket sewn into the inside back of the garment. Inside was a small switchblade knife and a universal handcuff key.

"Jesus," whispered the officer. He nodded to the policewoman, who searched her again. No other surprises were found.

Beth Anne said, "That was a trick I remember from the old days. She'd sew secret pockets into her clothes. For shoplifting and hiding weapons." A cold laugh from the young woman. "Sewing and robbery. Those're her talents." The smile faded. "Killing too, of course."

"How could you do this to your mother?" Liz snapped viciously. "You Judas."

Beth Anne watched, detached, as the woman was led to a squad car.

Heath and Beth Anne stepped into the living room of the house. As the policewoman again surveyed the hundreds of thousands of dollars' of stolen property filling the bungalow, Heath said, "Thanks, Detective. I know this was hard for you. But we were desperate to collar her without anybody else getting hurt."

Capturing Liz Polemus could indeed have turned into a bloodbath. It had happened before. Several years ago, when her mother and her lover, Brad Selbit, had tried to knock over a jewelry store in Ann Arbor, Liz had been surprised by the security guards. He'd shot her in the arm. But that hadn't stopped her from grabbing her pistol with her other hand and killing him and a customer and then later shooting one of the responding police officers. She'd managed to escape. She'd left Michigan for Portland, where she and Brad had started up her operation again, sticking with her forte—knocking over jewelry stores and boutiques selling designer clothes, which she'd use her skills as a seamstress to alter and then would sell to fences in other states.

An informant had told the Oregon State Police that Liz Polemus was the one behind the string of recent robberies in the Northwest and was living under a fake name in a bungalow here. The OSP detectives on the case had learned that her daughter was a detective with the Seattle police department and had helicoptered Beth Anne to Portland Airport. She'd driven here alone to get her mother to surrender peacefully.

"She was on two states' ten-most-wanted lists. And I heard she was making a name for herself in California too. Imagine that—your own mother." Heath's voice faded, thinking this might be indelicate.

But Beth Anne didn't care. She mused, "That was my childhood—armed robbery, burglary, money laundering. . . . My father owned a warehouse where they fenced the stuff. That was their front—they'd inherited it from his father. Who was in the business too, by the way."

"Your *grandfather*?"

She nodded. "That warehouse . . . I can still see it so clear. Smell it. Feel the cold. And I was only there once. When I was about eight, I guess. It was full of perped merch. My father left me in the office alone for a few minutes and I peeked out the door and saw him and one of his buddies beating the hell out of this guy. Nearly killed him."

"Doesn't sound like they tried to keep anything very secret from you."

"Secret? Hell, they did everything they could to get me *into* the business. My father had these 'special games,' he called them. Oh, I was supposed to go over to friends' houses and scope out if they had valuables and where they were. Or check out TVs and VCRs at school and let him know where they kept them and what kind of locks were on the doors."

Heath shook his head in astonishment. Then he asked, "But you never had any run-ins with the law?"

She laughed. "Actually, yeah—I got busted once for shoplifting."

Heath nodded. "I copped a pack of cigarettes when I was fourteen. I can still feel my daddy's belt on my butt for that one."

"No, no," Beth Anne said. "I got busted *returning* some crap my mother stole."

"You what?"

"She took me to the store as cover. You know, a mother and daughter wouldn't be as suspicious as a woman by herself. I saw her pocket some watches and a necklace. When we got home I put the merch in a bag and took it back to the store. The guard saw me looking guilty, I guess, and he nailed me before I could replace anything. I took the rap. I mean, I wasn't going to drop a dime on my parents, was I? . . . My mother was so mad. . . . They honestly couldn't figure out why I didn't want to follow in their footsteps."

"You need some time with Dr. Phil or somebody."

"Been there. Still am."

She nodded as memories came back to her. "From, like, twelve or thirteen on, I tried to stay as far away from home as I could. I did every after-school activity I could. Volunteered at a hospital on weekends. My friends really helped me out. They were the best . . . I probably picked them because they were one-eighty from my parents' criminal crowd. I'd hang with the National Merit scholars, the debate team, Latin club. Anybody who was decent and normal. I wasn't a great student but I spent so much time at the library or studying at friends' houses I got a full scholarship and put myself through college."

"Where'd you go?"

"Ann Arbor. Criminal justice major. I took the CS exam and landed a spot on Detroit PD. Worked there for a while. Narcotics mostly. Then moved out here and joined the force in Seattle."

"And you've got your gold shield. You made detective fast." Heath looked over the house. "She lived here by herself? Where's your father?"

"Dead," Beth Anne said matter-of-factly. "She killed him."

"*What?*"

"Wait'll you read the extradition order from Michigan. Nobody knew it at the time, of course. The original coroner's report was an accident. But a few months ago this guy in prison in Michigan confessed that he'd helped her. Mother found out my father was skimming money from their operation and sharing it with some girlfriend. She hired this guy to kill him and make it look like an accidental drowning."

"I'm sorry, Detective."

Beth Anne shrugged. "I always wondered if I could forgive them. I remember once, I was still working Narc in Detroit. I'd just run a big bust out on Six Mile. Confiscated a bunch of smack. I was on my way to log the stuff into Evidence back at the station and I saw I was driving past the cemetery where my father was buried. I'd never been there. I pulled in and walked up to the grave and tried to forgive him. But I couldn't. I realized then that I never could—not him or my mother. That's when I decided I had to leave Michigan."

"Your mother ever remarry?"

"She took up with Selbit a few years ago but she never married him. You collared him yet?"

"No. He's around here somewhere but he's gone to ground."

Beth Anne gave a nod toward the phone. "Mother tried to grab the phone when I came in tonight. She might've been trying to get a message to him. I'd check out the phone records. That might lead you to him."

"Good idea, Detective. I'll get a warrant tonight."

Beth Anne stared through the rain, toward where the squad car bearing her mother had vanished some minutes ago. "The weird part was that she believed she was doing the right thing for me, trying to get me into the business. Being a crook was her nature; she thought it was my nature too. She and Dad were born bad. They couldn't figure out why I was born good and wouldn't change."

"You have a family?" Heath asked.

"My husband's a sergeant in Juvenile." Then Beth Anne smiled. "And we're expecting. Our first."

"Hey, very cool."

"I'm on the job until June. Then I'm taking a LOA for a couple of years to be a mom." She felt an urge to add "Because children come first before anything." But, under the circumstances, she didn't think she needed to elaborate.

"Crime Scene's going to seal the place," Heath said. "But if you want to take a look around, that'd be okay. Maybe there's some pictures or something you want. Nobody'd care if you took some personal effects."

Beth Anne tapped her head. "I got more mementos up here than I need."

"Got it."

She zipped up her windbreaker, pulled the hood up. Another hollow laugh.

Heath lifted an eyebrow.

"You know my earliest memory?" she asked.

"What's that?"

"In the kitchen of my parents' first house outside of Detroit. I was sitting at the table. I must've been three. My mother was singing to me."

"Singing? Just like a real mother."

Beth Anne mused, "I don't know what song it was. I just remember her singing to keep me distracted. So I wouldn't play with what she was working on at the table."

"What was she doing, sewing?" Heath nodded toward the room containing a sewing machine and racks of stolen dresses.

"Nope," the woman answered. "She was reloading ammunition."

"You serious?"

A nod. "I figured out when I was older what she was doing. My folks didn't have much money then and they'd buy empty brass cartridges at gun shows and reload them. All I remember is the bullets were shiny and I wanted to play with them. She said if I didn't touch them she'd sing to me."

This story brought the conversation to a halt. The two officers listened to the rain falling on the roof.

Born bad . . .

"All right," Beth Anne finally said, "I'm going home."

Heath walked her outside and they said their good-byes. Beth Anne started the rental car and drove up the muddy, winding road toward the state highway.

Suddenly, from somewhere in the folds of her memory, a melody came into her head. She hummed a few bars out loud but couldn't place the tune. It left her vaguely unsettled. So Beth Anne flicked the radio on and found Jammin' 95.5, filling your night with solid-gold hits, party on, Portland. . . . She turned the volume up high and, thumping the steering wheel in time to the music, headed north toward the airport.

Interrogation

He's in the last room."

The man nodded to the sergeant and continued down the long corridor, grit underfoot. The walls were yellow cinderblock but the hallway reminded him of an old English prison, bricky and soot-washed.

As he approached the room he heard a bell somewhere nearby, a delicate ringing. He used to come here regularly but hadn't been in this portion of the building for months. The sound wasn't familiar and, despite the cheerful jingling, it was oddly unsettling.

He was halfway down the hallway when the sergeant called, "Captain?"

He turned.

"That was a good job you guys did. Getting him, I mean."

Boyle, a thick file under his arm, nodded and continued down the windowless corridor to room I-7.

What he saw through the square window: a benign-looking man of about forty, not big, not small, thick hair shot with gray. His amused eyes were on the wall, also cinderblock. His slippered feet were chained, his hands too, the silvery links looped through a waist bracelet.

Boyle unlocked and opened the door. The man grinned, looked the detective over.

"Hello, James," Boyle said.

"So you're him."

Boyle'd been tracking down and putting away murderers for nineteen years. He saw in James Kit Phelan's face what he always saw in such men and women at times like this. Insolence, anger, pride, fear.

The lean face, with a one- or two-days' growth of salt-and-pepper beard, the eyes blue as Dutch china.

But something was missing, Boyle decided. What? Yes, that was it, he concluded. Behind the eyes of most prisoners was a pool of bewilderment. In James Phelan this was absent.

The cop dropped the file on the table. Flipped through it quickly.

"You're the one," Phelan muttered.

"Oh, I don't deserve all the credit, James. We had a lotta folks out looking for you."

"But the word is they wouldn't've kept going if you hadn't been riding their tails. No sleep for your boys and girls's what I heard."

Boyle, a captain and the head of Homicide, had overseen the Granville Park murder task force of five men and women working full-time—and dozens of others working part-time (though everyone seemed to have logged at least ten, twelve hours a day). Still, Boyle had not testified in court, had never had a conversation with Phelan before today, never seen him up close. He expected to find the man looking very ordinary. Boyle was surprised to see another quality in the blue eyes. Something indescribable. There'd been no trace of this in the interrogation videos. What was it?

But James Phelan's eyes grew enigmatic once again as he studied Boyle's sports clothes. Jeans, Nikes, a purple Izod shirt. Phelan wore an orange jumpsuit.

Anyway, what it was, I killed her.

"That's a one-way mirror, ain't it?"

"Yes."

"Who's behind there?" He peered at the dim mirror, never once, Boyle noticed, glancing at his own reflection.

"We sometimes bring witnesses in to check out suspects. But there's nobody there now. Don't need 'em, do we?" Phelan sat back in the blue fiberglass chair. Boyle opened his notebook, took out a Bic pen. Boyle outweighed the prisoner by forty pounds, most of it muscle. Still, he set the pen far out of the man's reach.

Anyway, what it was . . .

"I've been asking to see you for almost a month," Boyle said amiably. "You haven't agreed to a meeting until now."

Sentencing was on Monday and after the judge pronounced one of the two sentences he was deciding upon at this very moment—life imprisonment or death by lethal injection—James Kit Phelan would be permanently giving up the county's hospitality for the state's.

"'Meeting,'" Phelan repeated. He seemed amused. "Wouldn't 'interrogation' be more like it? That's what you have in mind, right?"

"You've confessed, James. Why would I want to interrogate you?"

"Dunno. Why'd you put in, let's see, was it something like a dozen phone calls to my lawyer over the past coupla months wanting to 'meet' with me?"

"Just some loose ends on the case. Nothing important."

In fact Boyle kept his excitement under wraps. He'd despaired of ever having a chance to talk to Phelan face to face; the longer the captain's requests had gone unanswered the more he brooded that he'd never learn what he was desperate to know. It was Saturday and only an hour ago he'd been packing up turkey sandwiches for a picnic with the family when the call from Phelan's lawyer came. He'd sent Judith and the kids on ahead and sped to the county lockup at 90 m.p.h.

Nothing important . . .

"I didn't want to see you 'fore this," Phelan said slowly, "'cause I was thinking maybe you just wanted to, you know, gloat."

Boyle shook his head good-naturedly. But he also admitted to himself that he certainly had something to gloat about. When there was no arrest immediately following the murder, the case turned sour and it turned personal. Chief of Homicide Boyle versus the elusive, unknown killer.

The contest between the two adversaries had raged in the tabloids and in the police department and—more importantly—in Boyle's mind. Still taped up behind Boyle's desk was the front page of the *Post*, which showed a picture of dark-haired, swarthy Boyle glaring at the camera from the right-hand side of the paper and the police artist's composite of Anna Devereaux's killer from the left. The two pieces of art were separated by a bold, black *VS.*, and the detective's was by far the scariest shot.

Boyle remembered the press conference held six months to the day after the murder in which he promised the people of the town of Granville that though the investigation had bogged down they weren't giving up hope and that the killer would be caught. Boyle had concluded, "That man is *not* getting away. There's only one way this's going to end. Not in a draw. In a checkmate." The comment—which a few months later became an embarrassing reminder of his failure—had, at last, been validated. The headline of every story about Phelan's arrest read, of course, CHECKMATE!

There was a time when Boyle would have taken the high ground and sneered down the suggestion that he was gloating over a fallen enemy. But now he wondered. Phelan had for no apparent reason killed a defenseless woman and had eluded the police for almost a year. It had been the hardest case Boyle had ever run, and he'd despaired many times of ever finding the perp. But, by God, he'd won. So, maybe there *was* a part of him that had come to look over his trophy.

. . . I killed her. . . . And there's nothing else I have to say.

"I just have a few questions to ask you," Boyle said. "Do you mind?"

"Talking about it? Guess not. It's kinda boring. Ain't that the truth about the past? Boring."

"Sometimes."

"That's not much of an answer. The past. Is. Boring. You ever shot anybody?"

Boyle had. Twice. And killed them both. "We're here to talk about you."

"I'm here 'cause I got caught. *You're* here to talk about me."

Phelan slouched in the chair. The chains clinked softly. It reminded him of the bell he'd heard when he entered the interrogation room corridor.

He looked down at the open file.

"So what do you want to know?" Phelan asked.

"Only one thing," Boyle said, opening the battered manila folder. "Why'd you kill her?"

■

"Why?" Phelan repeated slowly. "Yeah, everybody asked me about the motive. Now 'motive' . . . that's a big word. A ten-dollar word, my father'd say. But 'Why.' That cuts right to the chase."

"And the answer is?"

"Why's it so important?"

It wasn't. Not legally. You only need to establish motive if the case is going to trial or if the confession is uncorroborated or unsupported by physical evidence. But it had been Phelan's fingerprints found at the crime scene and the DNA testing verified Phelan's skin was the tissue dug from beneath Anna Devereaux's perfect dusty-rose–polished fingernails. The judge accepted the confession without any state presentation of motive, though even he had suggested to the prisoner that he have the decency to explain why he'd committed this terrible crime. Phelan had remained silent and let the judge read him the guilty verdict.

"We just want to complete the report."

"'Complete the report.' Well, if that ain't some bureaucratic crap, I don't know what is."

In fact Boyle wanted the answer for a personal, not professional, reason. So he could get some sleep. The mystery of why this drifter and petty criminal had killed the thirty-six-year-old wife and mother had been growing in his mind like a tumor. He sometimes woke up thinking about it. In the past week alone—when it looked like Phelan was going down to Katonah maximum security without ever agreeing to meet Boyle—the captain would wake up sweating, plagued by what he called Phelan-mares. The dreams had nothing to do with Anna Devereaux's murder; they were a series of gut-wrenching scenes in which the prisoner was whispering something to Boyle, words that the detective was desperate to hear but could not.

"Makes no difference in the world to us or you at this point," Boyle said evenly. "But we just want to know."

"'We'?" the prisoner asked coyly and Boyle felt he'd been caught at something. Phelan continued, "Suppose you folks have some theories."

"Not really."

"No?"

Phelan swung the chain against the table and kept looking over the captain with that odd gaze of his. Boyle was uncomfortable. Prisoners swore at him all the time. Occasionally they spit at him and some had even attacked him. But Phelan slipped that curious expression on his face—what the hell was it?—and adjusted his smile. He kept studying Boyle.

"That's a weird sound, ain't it, Captain? The chain. Hey, you like horror films?"

"Some. Not the gory ones."

Three ringing taps. Phelan laughed. "Good sound effect for a Stephen King movie, don'tcha think? Or Clive Barker. Chains at night."

"How 'bout if we go through the facts again? What happened. Might refresh your memory."

"You mean my confession? Why not? Haven't seen it since the trial."

"I don't have the video. How 'bout if I just read the transcript?"

"I'm all ears."

■

"On September 13 you were in the town of Granville. You were riding a stolen Honda Nighthawk motorcycle."

"That's right."

Boyle lowered his head and in his best jury-pleasing baritone read from the transcript, "'I was riding around just, you know, seeing what was there. And I heard they had this fair or festival or something, and I kept hearing this music when I cut back the throttle. And I followed it to this park in the middle of town.

"'There was pony rides and all kinds of food and crafts and stuff like that. Okay, so I park the bike and go looking at what they got. Only it was boring, so I walked off along this little river and before I went too far it went into this forest and I seen a flash of white or color or something I don't remember. And I went closer and there was this woman sitting on a log, looking at the river. I remember her from town. She worked in some charity store downtown. You know, where they donate stuff and sell it and the money goes to a hospital or something. I thought her name was Anne or Annie or Anna or something.'"

Anna Devereaux. . . .

"'She was having a cigarette, like she'd snuck off to have one, like she'd promised everybody she wasn't going to but had to have one. The first thing she did when she heard me come up was drop the cigarette on the ground and crush it out. Without even looking at me first. Then she did and looked pretty freaked. I say, "Hey." She nodded and said something I couldn't hear and looked at her watch, like she had someplace she really had to be. Right. She started to walk away. And when she passed me I hit her hard in the neck and she fell down. Then I sat on her and grabbed this scarf she was wearing and pulled it real tight and I squeezed until she stopped moving, then I still kept squeezing. The cloth felt good on my wrists. I got off her, found the cigarette. It was still burning. She didn't crush it out. I finished it and walked back to the fair. I got a snow cone. It was cherry. And got on my bike and left.

"'Anyway, what it is, I killed her. I took that pretty blue scarf in my hands and killed her with it. And there's nothing else I have to say.'"

Boyle'd heard similar words hundreds of times. He now felt something he hadn't for years. An icy shiver down his spine.

"So that's about it, James?"

"Yeah. That's all true. Every word."

"I've been through the confession with a magnifying glass, I've been through your statements to the detectives, I watched that interview, you know, the one you did with that TV reporter . . ."

"She was a fox."

"But you never said a word about motive."

The ringing again. The waist chain, swinging like a pendulum against the metal table leg.

"Why'd you kill her, James?" Boyle whispered.

Phelan shook his head. "I don't exactly. . . . It's all muddy."

"You must've thought about it some."

Phelan laughed. "Hell, I thought about it tons. I spent days talking it over with that friend of mine."

"Who? Your biker buddy?"

Phelan shrugged. "Maybe."

"What was his name again?"

Phelan smiled.

It was known that while Phelan was generally a loner, he had several friends who ran with a tough crowd. In particular, witnesses reported seeing him in the company of a biker who'd hid Phelan after the Devereaux murder. The man's identity never came to light. Boyle wanted him on aiding and abetting but was too focused on collaring Phelan himself to spend time on an accessory.

Phelan continued, "Anyway, what it was, him and me, we'd pass a bottle around and spend days talking 'bout it. See, he's a tough son of a bitch. He's hurt people in his day. But it was always 'cause they crossed him. Or for money. Or something like that. He couldn't figure out why I'd just up and kill that lady."

"Well?"

"We didn't come up with no answers. I'm just telling you that it ain't like I didn't think about it."

"So you drink some, do you, James?"

"Yeah. But I wasn't drinking the day I killed her. Nothing but lemonade."

"How well did you know her? Anna Devereaux?"

"Know her? I didn't know her."

"I thought you said you did." Boyle looked down at the confession.

"I said I'd seen her. Same as I seen the pope on TV one time. And Julia Roberts in the movies and I've seen as much of Sheri Starr the porn queen as there is to see. But that don't mean I *know* 'em."

"She had a husband and a child."

"I heard."

The ringing again. It wasn't the chains. The sound came from outside. The bell he'd heard when he first entered the interrogation room corridor. Boyle frowned. When he looked back Phelan was watching him, a bemused smile on his face. "That's the coffee break cart, Captain. Comes around every morning and afternoon."

"It's new."

"Started about a month ago. When they closed the cafeteria."

Boyle nodded, looked down at his blank notebook. He said, "They'd talked about getting divorced. Anna and her husband."

"What's his name?" Phelan asked. "The husband? He that gray-haired guy sitting in the back of the courtroom?"

"He's gray-haired, yes. His name's Bob."

The victim's husband was known as Robert to everyone. Boyle hoped that Phelan would somehow stumble over the name difference and give something away.

"So you're thinking he hired me to kill her."

"Did he?"

Phelan grunted. "No, he didn't."

The cloth felt good on my wrists . . .

Robert Devereaux had seemed to the interrogating detectives to be the model of a grieving husband. He'd passed a voluntary lie detector test and it didn't seem likely that he'd had his wife murdered for a fifty-thousand-dollar insurance policy. This wasn't much of a motive but Boyle was determined to pursue any possibility.

Anna Devereaux. Thirty-six. Well liked in the town.

Wife and mother.

A woman losing the battle to quit smoking.

I took that pretty blue scarf in my hands and killed her with it. And there's nothing else I have to say.

An old scar on her neck—from a cut when she was seventeen; she often wore scarves to conceal it. The day she'd been killed, last September, the scarf she'd worn had been a silk Christian Dior and the shade of blue was described in the police report as aquamarine.

"She was a good-looking woman, wasn't she?" Boyle asked.

"I don't remember."

The most recent photos of Anna Devereaux that either of the two men had seen had been at trial. Her eyes were open, frosted with death, and her long-nailed hand was held outward in a plea for mercy. Even in those pictures you could see how beautiful she was.

"I didn't fool around with her, if that's what you're getting at. Or even want to."

The profiling came back negative for lust-driven killing. Phelan had had normal heterosexual responses to the Rorschach and free association tests.

"I'm just thinking out loud, James. You were walking through the forest?"

"That day I killed her? I got bored with the fair and just started walking. I ended up in the forest."

"And there she was, just sitting there, smoking."

"Uh-huh," Phelan responded patiently.

"What did she say to you?"

"I said, 'Hey.' And she said something I couldn't hear."

"What else happened?"

"Nothing. That was it."

"Maybe you were mad 'cause you didn't like her muttering at you."

"I didn't care. Why'd I care about that?"

"I've heard you say a couple times the thing you hate most is being bored."

Phelan looked at the cinderblock. He seemed to be counting. "Yeah. I don't like to be bored."

"How much," Boyle asked, "do you hate it?" He gave a laugh. "On a scale of one to—"

"But people don't kill 'causa hate. Oh, they *think* about killing who they hate, they *talk* about it. But they really only kill two kindsa people—folk they're scared of and folk they're mad at. What exactly do *you* hate, Detective? Ponder it for a minute. Lotta things, I'll bet. But you wouldn't kill anyone 'causa that. Would you?"

"She had some jewelry on her."

"That's a question?"

"Did you rob her? And kill her when she wouldn't give you her wedding and engagement rings?"

"If she was getting divorced why wouldn't she give me her rings?"

Phelan meant this only rhetorically. To point out the flaw in Boyle's logic.

Homicide had discounted robbery as a motive immediately. Anna Devereaux's purse, eight feet from her body, had contained eleven credit cards and $180 cash.

Boyle picked up the manila folder, read some more, dropped it on the tabletop.

Why? . . . .

It seemed appropriate that the operative word when it came to James Kit Phelan's life would be a question. Why had he killed Anna Devereaux? Why had he committed the other crimes he'd been arrested for? Many of them gratuitous. Never murder, but dozens of assaults. Drunk and disorderlies. A kidnapping that got knocked down to an aggravated assault. And who exactly *was* James Kit Phelan? He'd never talked much about his past. Even the *Current Affair* story had managed to track down only two former cellmates of Phelan for on-camera interviews. No relatives, no friends, no ex-wives, no high school teacher or bosses.

Boyle asked, "James, what I hear you saying is, you yourself don't have the faintest idea why you killed her."

Phelan pressed his wrists together and swung the chain so that it rang against the table again. "Maybe it's something in my mind," he said after some reflection.

They'd given him the standard battery of tests and found nothing particularly illuminating and the department shrinks concluded that "the prisoner presents with a fairly strong tendency to act out what are classic antisocial proclivities"—a diagnosis Boyle had responded to by saying, "Thanks, Doc, his rap sheet says the same thing. Only in English."

"You know," Phelan continued slowly, "I sometimes feel something gets outta control in me." His pale lids closed over the blue eyes and Boyle imagined for a moment that the crescents of flesh were translucent and that the eyes continued to peer out into the small room.

"How do you mean, James?" The captain felt his heart rate increase. Wondered: Are we really closing in on the key to the county's perp of the decade?

"Some of it might have to do with my family. There was a lotta crap when I was growing up."

"How bad?"

"Really bad. My father did time. Theft, domestics, drunk and disorderlies. Things like that. He'd beat me a lot. He and my mother were supposedly this great couple at first. Really in love. That's what I heard but that's not what it looked like to me. You married, Captain?" Phelan glanced at his left hand. There was no band. He never wore one; as a rule Boyle tried to keep his personal life separate from the office. "I am, yes."

"How long?"

"Twenty years."

"Man," Phelan laughed. "Long time."

"I met Judith when I was in the academy."

"You been a cop all your life. I read that profile of you." He laughed. "In that newspaper issue with the headline, after you caught me. 'Checkmate.' That was funny." Then the smile faded. "See, after my mother was gone, my father never had anybody in his life for more'n a year. Part of it was he couldn't never keep a job. We moved all the time. I mean, we lived in twenty states, easy. The article said you'd lived 'round here most of your life."

He's opening up, Boyle thought excitedly. Keep him going.

"Lived three miles from here, in Marymount, going on twenty-one years."

"I've been through there. Pretty place. I lived in plenty of small towns. It was tough. School was the worst. New kid in class. I always got the crap beat out of me. Hey, that'd be one advantage, having a cop for a dad. Nobody'd pick on you."

Boyle said, "That may be true but there's another problem. I've got my share of enemies, you can imagine. So we keep moving the kids from one school to another. Try to keep 'em out of public schools."

"You send 'em to private?"

"We're Catholic. They're in a parochial school."

"That one in Granville? That place looks like a college campus. Must set you back some. Man."

"No, they're up in Edgemont. It's smaller but it still costs a bundle. You ever have kids?"

Phelan put on a tough face. They were getting close to something, Boyle could sense.

"In a way."

Encourage him. Gentle, gentle.

"How's that?"

"My mama died when I was ten."

"I'm sorry, James."

"I had two little sisters. Twins. They were four years younger'n me. I pretty much had to take care of them. My father, he ran around a lot, like I was saying. I sorta learned what it was like to be a father by the time I was twelve."

Boyle nodded. He'd been thirty-six when Jon was born. He still wasn't sure he knew what it was like to be a father. When he told Phelan this the prisoner laughed. "How old're your kids?"

"Jonathon, he's ten. Alice is nine." Boyle resisted a ridiculous urge to flash his wallet pictures.

Phelan suddenly grew somber. The chains clinked.

"See, the twins were always wanting something from me. Toys, my time, my attention, help 'em read this, what does this mean? . . . Jesus."

Boyle noted the anger on the face. Keep going, he urged silently. He didn't write any notes, afraid that he might break the stream of thought. That could lead to the magic *why*.

"Man, it damn near drove me nuts. And I had to do it all by myself. My father was always on a date—well, *he* called 'em dates—or was passed out drunk." He looked up quickly. "Hell, you don't know what I'm talking about, do you?"

Boyle was stung by the sudden coldness in the prisoner's voice.

"I sure do," the captain said sincerely. "Judith works. A lotta times I end up with the kids. I love them and everything—just like you loved your sisters, I'm sure—but, man, it takes a lot out of you."

Phelan drifted away for a moment. Eyes as glazed as Anna Devereaux's. "Your wife works, does she? My mama wanted to work too. My father wouldn't let her."

He calls his mother "Mama," but his father by the more formal name. What do I make of that?

"They fought about it all the time. Once, he broke her jaw when he found her looking through the want ads."

And when she passed me I hit her hard in the neck and she fell down.

"What's your wife do?" Phelan asked.

"She's a nurse. At St. Mary's."

"That's a good job," Phelan said. "My mother liked people, liked to help them. She'da been a good nurse." His face grew dark again. "I think about all those times my father hit her. . . . That's what started her taking pills and stuff. And she never stopped taking 'em. Until she died." He leaned forward and whispered, "But you know the terrible thing." Avoiding Boyle's eyes.

"What, James? Tell me."

"See, sometimes I get this feeling . . . I sorta blame it all on my mother. If she hadn't whined so much about getting a job, if she'd just been happy staying home. . . . Stayed home with me and the girls, then Dad wouldn't've *had* to hit her."

Then I sat on her and grabbed this scarf she was wearing and pulled it real tight and I squeezed until she stopped moving, then I still kept squeezing.

"And she wouldn't've started drinking and taking those pills and she'd still be here." He choked. "I sometimes feel good thinking about him hitting her."

The cloth felt good on my wrists.

He blew a long stream of air from his lungs. "Ain't a pretty thing to say, is it?"

"Life ain't pretty sometimes, James."

Phelan looked up at the ceiling and seemed to be counting acoustical tiles. "Hell, I don't even know why I'm bringing all this up. It just kinda . . . was there. What was going through my mind." He began to say something else but fell silent and Boyle didn't dare interrupt his train of thought. When the prisoner spoke again he was more cheerful. "You do things with your family, Captain? That's something I think was the hardest of all. We never did a single damn thing together. Never took a vacation, never went to a ball game."

"If I wasn't talking to you here right now, I'd be with them all on a picnic."

"Yeah?"

Boyle worried for a moment that Phelan would be jealous of Boyle's family life. But the prisoner's eyes lit up. "That's nice, Captain. I always pictured us—my mama and my father, when he wasn't drinking, and the twins. We'd be out, doing just what you're talking about. Having a picnic in some town square, a park, sitting in front of the bandshell, you know."

I kept hearing this music when I cut back the throttle. And I followed it to this park in the middle of town.

"That what you and your family were going to do?"

"Well, we're the unsocial types," Boyle said, laughing. "We stay away from crowds. My parents've got a little place upstate."

"A family house?" Phelan asked slowly, maybe picturing it.

"On Taconic Lake. We go up there usually."

The prisoner fell silent for some moments then finally said, "You know, Captain, I've got this weird idea." His eyes counted cinderblocks. "We have all this knowledge in our heads. Everything people ever knew. Or'll know in the future. Like how to kill a mastodon or how to make a nuclear spaceship or how to talk in a different language. It's all there in everybody's mind. Only they have to find it."

What's he saying? Boyle wondered. That *I* know why he did it?

"And how you find all this stuff is you sit real quiet and then the thought comes into your head. Just bang, there it is. Does that ever happen to you?"

Boyle didn't know what to say. But Phelan didn't seem to expect an answer.

Outside, in the corridor, footsteps approached then receded.

Anyway, what it is, I killed her. I took that pretty blue scarf in my hands. . . .

Phelan sighed. "It's not that I was trying to keep anything from you all. I just can't really give you the kinda answer you want."

Boyle closed the notebook. "That's all right, James. You've told me plenty. I appreciate it."

I took that pretty blue scarf in my hands and killed her with it. And there's nothing else I have to say.

■

"Got it," Boyle announced into the pay phone. He stood in the dim corridor outside the cafeteria in the courthouse, where he'd just had a celebratory lunch with some of the other cops on the Phelan team.

"All right!" the district attorney's enthusiastic voice came through the phone. Most of the senior prosecutors had known that Boyle was going to conduct the final interrogation of James Phelan and were waiting anxiously to find out why he'd killed Anna Devereaux. It had become *the* question in the county prosecutor's department. Boyle had even heard rumors that some guys were running a macabre pool, laying serious money on the answer.

"It's complicated," Boyle continued. "I think what happened was we didn't do enough psychological testing. It's got to do with his mother's death."

"Phelan's mother?"

"Yeah. He's got a thing about families. He's mad because his mother abandoned him by dying when he was ten and he had to raise his sisters."

"What?"

"I know, it sounds like psychobabble. But it all fits. Call Dr. Hirschorn. Have him—"

"Boyle, Phelan's parents are still alive. Both of 'em."

Silence.

"Boyle? You there?"

After a moment: "Keep going."

"And he was an only child. He didn't have any sisters."

Boyle absently pressed his thumb on the chrome number plate of the phone, leaving a pattern of fat fingerprints on the cold metal.

"And his parents . . . they ran up big debts getting him doctors and counselors to try to help 'im. They were saints. . . . Captain? You there?"

Why would Phelan lie? Was this all just a big joke? He replayed the events in his mind. I ask a dozen times to see him. He refuses until just before he's sentenced. He finally agrees. But why?

Why? . . .

Boyle bolted upright, his solid shoulder slamming into the side of the phone kiosk.

In despair he lifted his left hand to his face and closed his eyes. He realized he'd just given Phelan the name of every member of his family. Where Judith worked, where the kids went to school.

Hell, he'd told them where they were right now! Alone, at Taconic Lake.

The captain stared at his distorted reflection in the phone's chrome number pad, realizing the enormity of what he'd done. Phelan had been planning this for months. It was why he'd held out saying anything about the motive: to draw Boyle in close, to make the captain himself desperate to talk, to get information out of *him*, and to deliver the message that his family was in danger.

Wait, calm down. He's locked up. He can't do anything to anybody. He's not getting out—

Oh, no . . .

Boyle's gut ran cold.

Phelan's friend, the biker! Assuming he lived nearby, he could be at Taconic Lake in thirty minutes.

"Hey, Boyle, what the hell's going on?"

The answer to the query about James Phelan's motive for killing Anna Devereaux meant nothing. The question *itself* was the murderer's last weapon—and he was using it on the cop who'd become obsessed with bringing him down.

Why, why, why . . .

Boyle dropped the phone and raced up the hall to the prisoner lockup. "Where's Phelan?" he screamed.

The guard blinked at the frantic detective. "He's right there. In the lockup, Captain. You can see him."

Boyle glanced through the double glass at the prisoner sitting calmly on a bench.

"What's he been doing since I left?"

"Reading. That's all. Oh, and he made a few phone calls."

Boyle lunged across the desk and grabbed the guard's phone. "Hey!"

He punched in the number of the lake house. It began to ring. Three times, four . . .

It was then that Phelan looked at Boyle and smiled. He mouthed something. The captain couldn't hear through the bulletproof glass, of course, but he knew without a doubt that the man had just uttered the word "Checkmate."

Boyle lowered his head to the receiver and, like a prayer, whispered, "Answer, please answer," as the phone rang again and again and again.

Afraid

Where are we going?" the woman asked as the black Audi sped away from Florence's Piazza della Stazione, where her train had just arrived from Milan.

Antonio shifted gears smoothly and replied, "It's a surprise."

Marissa clicked on her seat belt as the car plunged down the narrow, winding streets. She was soon hopelessly lost. A Milan resident for all of her thirty-four years, she knew only the city center of Florence. Antonio, on the other hand, was a native Florentine and sped assuredly along an unfathomable route of streets and alleys.

A surprise? she wondered. Well, he'd wanted to pick the location for their long weekend together and she'd agreed. So, she told herself, sit back and enjoy the ride. . . . Her job had been particularly stressful in the past month; it was time to let someone else make the decisions.

Slim and blonde, with features of the north, Marissa Carrefiglio had been a runway model in her early twenties but then took up fashion design, which she loved. But three years ago her brother had quit the family business and she'd been forced to take over management of the arts and antiques operation. She wasn't happy about it but her stern father wasn't a man you could say no to.

Another series of sharp turns. Marissa gave an uneasy laugh at Antonio's aggressive driving and looked away from the streets as she told him about the train ride from Milan, about news from her brother in America, about recent acquisitions at her family's store in the Brera.

He, in turn, described a new car he was thinking of buying, a problem with the tenant in one of his properties and a gastronomic coup he'd pulled off yesterday: some white truffles he'd found at a farmers' market near his home and had bought right out from under the nose of an obnoxious chef.

Another sharp turn and a fast change of gears. Only the low setting sun, in her eyes, gave her a clue of the direction they were traveling.

She hadn't known Antonio very long. They'd met in Florence a month ago at a gallery off the Via Maggio, where Marissa's company occasionally consigned art and antiques. She had just delivered several works: eighteenth-century tapestries from the famed Gobelins Manufactory in France. After they were hung, she was drawn to a dark medieval tapestry taking up a whole wall in the gallery. Woven by an anonymous artist, it depicted beautiful angels descending from heaven to fight beasts roaming the countryside, attacking the innocent.

As she stood transfixed by the gruesome scene a voice had whispered, "A nice work but there's an obvious problem with it."

She blinked in surprise and turned to the handsome man standing close. Marissa frowned. "Problem?"

His eyes remained fixed on the tapestry as he said, "Yes. The most beautiful angel has escaped from the scene." He turned and smiled. "And landed on the floor beside me."

She'd scoffed laughingly at the obvious come-on line. But he'd delivered it with such self-effacing charm that her initial reaction—to walk away—faded quickly. They struck up a conversation about art and, a half hour later, were sharing prosecco, cheese and conversation.

Antonio was muscular and trim, with thick, dark hair and brown eyes, a ready smile. He was in the computer field. She couldn't quite understand exactly what he did—something about networks—but he must've been successful. He was wealthy and seemed to have a lot of free time.

They had much in common, it turned out. They'd both gone to college in Piemonte, had traveled extensively in France and shared an interest in fashion (though while she liked to design, he preferred to wear). A year younger than she, he'd never been married (she was divorced), and, like her, he only had one living parent; her mother had passed away ten years ago, and Antonio's father, five.

Marissa found him easy to talk to. That night they'd met she'd rambled on about her life—complaining about her domineering father, her regret at leaving fashion for a boring job, and her former husband, to whom she occasionally loaned money that was never paid back. When she'd realized how moody and complaining she sounded, she'd blushed and apologized. But he hadn't minded at all; he enjoyed hearing what she had to say, he admitted. What a departure from most of the men she dated, who focused only on her looks—and on themselves.

They'd walked along the Arno, then strolled across the Ponte Vecchio, where a young boy tried to sell him roses for his "wife." Instead he bought her a tourist souvenir: a Lucretia Borgia poison ring. She'd laughed hard and she kissed him on the cheek.

The next week he came to visit her in the Navigli in Milan; she'd seen him twice after that on business here in Florence. This was to be their first weekend away. They were not yet lovers but Marissa knew that would soon change.

Now, on their way to the "surprise" destination, Antonio made another sharp turn down a dim residential street. The neighborhood was run-down. Marissa was troubled that he was taking this shortcut—and troubled all the more when he abruptly skidded to a stop at the curb.

What was this? she wondered.

He climbed out. "Just have an errand. I'll be right back." He hesitated. "You might want to leave the doors locked." He strode to a decrepit house, looked around him and entered without knocking. Marissa noticed that he'd taken the car keys with him, which made her feel trapped. She loved to drive—her car was a silver Maserati—and she didn't take well to the role of passenger. She decided to follow his advice and checked to make sure all the doors were locked. As she was looking at his side of the car she glanced out the window. She saw two twin boys, about ten years old, standing motionless, side by side, across the street. They stared at her, unsmiling. One whispered something. The other nodded gravely. She felt a shiver at the unnerving sight.

Then, turning back, Marissa gasped in shock. An old woman's skull-like face stared at her, merely a foot away on the passenger side of the Audi. The woman must have been sick and near death.

Through the half-open window Marissa stammered, "Can I help you?"

Wearing dirty, torn clothing, the scrawny woman rocked unsteadily on her feet. Her yellow eyes glanced over her shoulder quickly, as if she was concerned about being seen. She then glanced at the car, which seemed familiar to her.

"Do you know Antonio?" Marissa asked, calming.

"I'm Olga. I'm the queen of the Via Magdelena. I know everyone . . ." A frown. "I have come to offer you my sympathies."

"About what?"

"Why, the death of your sister, of course."

"My sister? I don't have a sister."

"You're not Lucia's sister?"

"I don't know a Lucia."

The woman shook her head. "But you so resemble her."

Marissa could hardly bear to look into the woman's wet, jaundiced eyes.

"I've troubled you unnecessarily," Olga said. "Forgive me."

She turned away.

"Wait," Marissa called. "Who was she, this Lucia?"

The woman paused. She leaned down and whispered, "An artist. She made dolls. I am not speaking of toys. They were works of art. She made them out of porcelain. The woman was a magician. It was as if she could capture human souls and place them in her dolls."

"And she died?"

"Last year, yes."

"How did you know her?"

Olga glanced one more time at the building Antonio had gone into. "Forgive me if I troubled you. I was mistaken, it seems." She hobbled away.

Antonio returned a moment later, carrying a small, gray paper bag. He set this in the back seat. He said nothing about his errand other than to apologize that it took longer than he planned. As he dropped into the driver's seat, Marissa looked past him to the opposite side of the street. The twins were gone.

Antonio shoved the shifter into gear and they sped away. Marissa asked him about the old woman. He blinked in surprise. He hesitated then gave a laugh. "Olga . . . she's crazy. Not right in the head."

"Do you know a Lucia?"

Antonio shook his head. "Did she say I did?"

"No. But . . . it seemed she was telling me about her because she recognized your car."

"Well, as I say, she's crazy."

Antonio fell silent and wound his way out of town, eventually catching the A7. He then turned south onto the SS222, the famous Chiantigiana highway, which winds through the wine region between Florence and Siena.

As Marissa gripped the handhold above the door in the car, they raced through Strada then past the magnificent Castello di Uzzano, then Greve and into the sparser region south of Panzano. This was beautiful country—but there was an eeriness about it. Not too many kilometers north, the Monster of Florence had butchered more than a dozen people from the late sixties to the mid-eighties and here, south, two other madmen had not long ago tortured and slaughtered several women. These recent killers had been captured and were in prison, but the deaths were particularly gruesome and had occurred not far from where they were at the moment. Now that she'd thought of them Marissa couldn't put the murders out of her mind.

She was about to ask that Antonio turn the radio on, when suddenly, about three kilometers from Quercegrossa, he turned sharply onto a one-lane dirt road. They drove for nearly a kilometer before Marissa finally asked, her voice uneasy, "Where are we, Antonio? I wish you'd tell me."

He glanced at her troubled face. Then he smiled. "I'm sorry." He abandoned the mystery and solemnity he'd been displaying. The old Antonio was back. "I didn't mean to make you uncomfortable. I was just being dramatic. I'm taking you to my family's country home. It was an old mill. My father and I renovated it ourselves. It's a special place and I wanted to share it with you."

Marissa relaxed and placed her hand on his leg. "I'm sorry. I wasn't cross-examining you. . . . There's just been so much pressure at work . . . and trying to persuade my father to let me have a few days off—oh, it was a nightmare."

"Well, you can relax now." His hand closed around hers.

She lowered her window and breathed in the fragrant air. "It's lovely out here."

"It is, yes. Pure peace and quiet. No neighbors for several kilometers."

They drove five more minutes then parked. He retrieved the gray bag he'd collected at that ramshackle place in Florence and then removed the suitcases and a bag of groceries from the trunk. They walked fifty meters along a path through an overgrown, thorny olive grove and then he nodded toward a footbridge over a fast-moving stream. "There it is."

In the low light of dusk she could just make out the house on the opposite shore. It was quite an impressive place, though far more gothic than romantic—an ancient, two-story stone mill with small windows barred with metal rods.

They crossed the bridge and he set the suitcases down at the front door. He fished for the key. Marissa turned and looked down. Black and fast moving, the stream seemed quite deep. Only a low railing separated her from a sheer, twenty-foot drop into the water.

His voice, close to her ear, made her jump. He'd come up behind her. "I know what you're thinking."

"What?" she asked, her heart beating fast.

He put his arm around her and said, "You're thinking about that urge."

"Urge?"

"To throw yourself in. It's the same thing people feel when standing on observation decks or the edge of a cliff—that strange desire to step off into space. No reason, no logic. But it's always there. As if—" He released her shoulder. "—I were to let go there'd be nothing to stop you from jumping in. Do you know what I mean?"

Marissa shivered—largely because she knew exactly what he meant. But she said nothing. To change the course of the conversation she pointed at the far shore, at a small white, wooden cross, surrounded by flowers. "What's that?"

He squinted. "Again? Ah, trespassers leave them. It happens often. It's quite irritating."

"Why?"

After a moment he said, "A boy died here. Before we owned the mill. . . . He lived up the road. Nobody knows exactly what happened but it seems he was playing with a soccer ball and it rolled into the water. He fell in trying to get it. The water's very fast—you can see. He was sucked into the sluice there and was wedged upside down."

Marissa was claustrophobic. This thought terrified her.

"It took him a half hour to die. Now his relatives come to leave the memorial. They claim they don't. They say the crosses and flowers just appear out of nowhere. But of course they're lying."

Her eyes were riveted on the dark, narrow intake, where the child had died. What a terrible way to end your life.

Antonio's loud voice startled her again. But this time he was laughing. "Now, enough morbid stories. Let's eat!"

Gratefully, Marissa followed him inside. She was relieved to see that the interior was very comfortable, actually cozy. It was nicely painted and on the wall hung expensive paintings and tapestries. Antonio lit candles and opened prosecco. They toasted their first long weekend together and began to prepare dinner. Marissa whipped up an antipasto platter of marinated vegetables and ham but Antonio did most of the cooking. He made linguine with butter and the white truffles for the first course and trout with herbs for the main. She was impressed, watching his assured hands cut and mix and whisk and assemble. Enjoying his skill, yes, but she was saddened slightly too, regretting that her long hours at the shop prevented her from spending as much time as she would have liked in her own kitchen, making meals for friends.

Marissa set the table while he went downstairs to the wine cellar and returned with a 1990 Chianti from a famous local vineyard. A lover of wine, Marissa lifted an eyebrow and remarked that it was a wonderful vintage, hard to find; even the labels were collectors' items. "You must have a wonderful wine cellar. Can I see it?"

But as she stepped toward the door he pulled it shut, wincing slightly. "Oh, it's a mess down there. I'm embarrassed. I didn't get a chance to straighten it. Perhaps later."

"Of course," she agreed.

He set the food out and, in candlelight, they ate a leisurely dinner, talking the entire time. He told her about the crazy neighbors, a bad-tempered tomcat that thought he owned the property, the difficulty he and his father had had in finding period accessories to restore the mill.

Afterwards, they carried the dishes into the kitchen and Antonio suggested they have grappa in the parlor. He pointed it out to her. She walked into the small, intimate room and sat on the couch, then heard the squeal of the wine cellar door and his footsteps descending the stairs. He returned five minutes later with two filled glasses. They sat together, sipping the liquor. It seemed more bitter than most of the grappas she'd had but she was sure that, given Antonio's good taste, it was an expensive distillation.

She was feeling warm, feeling comfortable, feeling giddy.

Leaning back against his strong shoulder, she lifted her face and kissed him. Antonio kissed back, hard. Then whispered, "There's a present for you in there." He pointed to a nearby bathroom.

"A present?"

"Go see."

She rose and, in the room, found an antique silk robe on a hanger. The garment was golden, with tiny flowers on it and lace at the edging.

"It's beautiful," she called. She debated. Should she put it on? That would be a clear message to him. . . . Did she want to send it or not?

Yes, she decided, she did.

She stripped her clothes off, slipped the thin robe on then returned to the parlor. He smiled and took her hand, stared into her eyes. "You're so beautiful. You look just like . . . an angel."

His words echoed the line he'd used when they met. But there was something slightly off about his tone, as if he'd intended to say that she looked like something else and caught himself just in time.

Then she laughed to herself. You're used to your father—parsing everything he says, looking for double meanings and subtle criticisms. Relax.

Marissa sat down beside Antonio once more. They kissed passionately. He pulled the clip out of her hair and let it tumble to her shoulders then took her face in both hands and stared into her eyes for a long moment. He kissed her again. She was very light-headed from his touch and the liquor. When he whispered, "Let's go into the bedroom," she nodded.

"It's through there." He pointed to the kitchen. "I think there're some candles beside the bed. Why don't you light them? I'll lock up."

Picking up some matches, Marissa walked into the kitchen. She noticed that he'd left the wine cellar door open. She glanced down the steep stairs and could see much of the room. It wasn't messy at all, as he'd said. In fact, the place was spotlessly clean, well organized. She heard Antonio closing a window or door in another part of the house and, out of curiosity, walked quietly halfway down the stairs. She paused, frowning, staring at something under a table nearby. It was a soccer ball, half-deflated.

She recalled that the boy who'd drowned had been playing with a ball like this. Was it his?

Continuing down the steps, Marissa stooped and picked it up. The ball was a special one, commemorating one of Milan's big wins last year; the date was printed on it. So it couldn't have been the dead boy's—Antonio had said he'd drowned when the previous owner was living here. But Antonio had been the owner for at least five years—which is when his father, who'd helped renovate the place, had died. It was just a strange coincidence.

But wait. . . . Thinking back to his account of the incident, Marissa recalled that Antonio had said that nobody knew exactly what happened to the youngster. But if that was true, then how could he possibly know it'd taken the boy a half hour to die?

Fear began to grow deep inside her. She heard the creak of his footsteps above her. She put the ball back and turned to the stairs. But then she stopped and gasped. On a stone wall to the right of the steps was a photograph. It was of Antonio and a woman who looked very much like Marissa, her hair dangling to her shoulders. They were both wearing wedding rings—even though he said he'd never been married.

And the woman was wearing the same robe that Marissa now wore.

She was, of course, Lucia.

Who'd died last year.

With stunning clarity, Marissa understood: Antonio had murdered his wife. The boy with the football had perhaps heard her screams for help or had witnessed the killing. Antonio had chased him and flung him into the stream where he'd been pulled into the sluice and drowned while the mad husband watched him die.

Her heart pounding, she walked closer to the sideboard underneath the photograph. There was the gray bag that Antonio had picked up in Florence. It was sitting beside the bottle of grappa he'd just opened. Marissa opened the bag. Inside was a bottle of barbiturates, half empty. A glance at the top of the sideboard showed a dusting of powder, the same color as the pills— as yellow as the jaundiced eyes of the old woman who'd come up to Antonio's car.

It was as if he'd crushed some of the drugs.

To mix into her grappa, Marissa realized.

A searing wave of panic raced through her and pooled in her belly. Marissa had never been so afraid in her life. His plan was to drug her and—and then what?

She couldn't waste time speculating. She had to escape. Now!

Starting up the stairs, Marissa froze.

Antonio was standing above her. In his hand was a carving knife. "I told you I didn't want you in the wine cellar, Lucia."

"What?" Marissa whispered, weak with terror.

"Why did you come back?" he whispered. Then gave a chilling laugh. "Ah, Lucia, Lucia . . . you came back from the dead. Why? You deserved to die. You made me fall in love with you, you took my heart and my soul and you were going to just walk away and leave me alone."

"Antonio," Marissa said, her voice cracking. "I'm not—"

"You thought I was just one of your dolls, didn't you? Something you could create and then sell and abandon?"

He started down the stairs, closing the door behind him.

"No, Antonio. Listen to me—"

"How could you come back?"

"I'm not Lucia!" she screamed.

She thought back to their initial meeting. It wasn't an angel he thought she resembled when they first met; it was the wife he'd murdered.

"Lucia," he moaned.

He reached up to the wall and clicked out the lights. The room was utterly dark.

"God, no. Please!" She backed away, her bare feet stinging on the cold floor.

She could hear his footsteps descending toward her—the creaking wood gave him away. But then he stepped onto the stone floor and she lost track of where he was.

No. . . . Tears dotted her eyes.

He called, "Did you come back to turn me into another one of your dolls?"

Marissa backed away. Where was he? She couldn't hear him. *Where?*

Was he—?

A stream of hot breath kissed her left cheek. He was no more than a foot away.

"Lucia!"

She screamed and dropped to her knees. She couldn't move forward, toward where she believed the stairs were—he was in her way—but she remembered seeing a small door against the far wall. Maybe it led to the backyard. Feeling her way along the wall, she finally located it, ripped the door open and tumbled inside, slamming it behind her.

Sobbing, she struck a match.

No!

She found herself in a tiny cell, four feet high and six square. No windows, no other doorways.

Through her tears of panic, she saw an object on the floor in front of her. Easing forward, hands shaking, heart stuttering, she saw that it was a porcelain doll, its black eyes staring at the ceiling.

And on the wall were dark brown streaks—blood, Marissa understood—left by the prior occupant of this chamber, Lucia, who spent the last days of her life in terror, trying vainly to scratch through the stone with her bare fingers.

The match went out, and darkness surrounded her.

Marissa collapsed on the floor in panic, sobbing. What a fool I've been, she thought.

I'll die here, I'll die here, I'll die—

But then, from outside the cell, she heard Antonio's voice, sounding suddenly quite normal.

He called, "It's all right, Marissa. Don't worry. There's a light switch behind a loose stone to the left of the door. Turn it on. Read the note hidden inside the doll."

What was happening? Marissa wondered. She wiped the tears from her eyes and found the switch, clicked it on. Blinking against the bright light, she bent down and pulled a folded piece of paper from the hollowed-out doll. She read.

Marissa—
The wall to your left is false. It's plastic. Pull it down and you'll see a door and a window. The door is unlocked. When you're ready to leave, push it open outward. But first look out the window.

She ripped the plastic away. There was indeed a window. She looked out and saw the footbridge. Unlike before, the property was now well lit with spotlights from the mill. She saw Antonio, with his suitcase, heading over the bridge. He paused, must have seen the light through the window of the cell and knew she was watching. He waved. Then he disappeared toward the parking lot. A moment later she heard his car start and the sound of him driving away.

What the hell's going on?

She pushed the door open and stepped outside.

There was her suitcase and purse. She tore off the robe, dressed quickly with trembling hands and pulled her cell phone from her purse, gripping it the way a scared child clings to a stuffed animal. She continued with the note.

You are safe. You have always been safe.

I am on my way back to Florence now, nowhere near the mill. But believe that I'm no psychotic killer. There is no Lucia. The old woman who told you about her was paid 100 euros for her performance. There was no little boy who drowned; I put the flowers and cross by the stream myself before I came to pick you up at the station today. The football was merely a prop. The blood on the wall of the cell is paint. The drugs were candy (though the grappa was real— and quite rare, I may add). The photograph of me and my "wife" was created by computer.

As for what is true: My name is Antonio, I have never been married, I made a fortune in computers, and this is my vacation house.

What, you are wondering, is this all about?

I must explain:

As a child I spent much time in loneliness and boredom. I immersed myself in the books of the great writers of horror. They were terrifying, yes, but they also exhilarated me. I would see an audience watching a horror film and think: They are scared but they are alive.

Those experiences moved me to become an artist. Like any truly great musician or painter, my goal is not simply to create beauty but to open people's eyes and rearrange their views and perceptions, the only difference being that instead of musical notes or paint, my medium is fear. When I see people like you who, as Dante writes, have lost the true path in life, I consider it my mission to help them find it. The night in Florence, the night we met, I singled you out because I saw that your eyes were dead. And I soon learned why—your unhappiness at your job, your oppressive father, your needy ex-husband. But I knew I could help you.

Oh, at this moment you hate me, of course; you are furious. Who wouldn't be?

But, Marissa, ask yourself this question, ask it in your heart: Don't you think that being so afraid has made you feel exquisitely alive?

Below are three phone numbers.

One is for a car service that will take you back to the train station in Florence.

The second is for the local police precinct.

The third is my mobile.

The choice of whom you call is yours. I sincerely hope you call the last of these numbers, but if you wish not to— tonight or in the future—I, of course, will understand. After all, it's the nature of art that the artist must sometimes send his creation into the world, never to see it again.

Yours, Antonio

Furious, tearful, quivering, Marissa walked to a stone bench at the edge of the water. She sat and breathed deeply, clutching the note in one hand, the phone in the other. Her eyes rose, gazing at the stars. Suddenly she blinked, startled. A large bat, a dark shape in the darker sky, zigzagged overheard in a complex yet elegant pattern. Marissa stared at it intently until the creature vanished over the trees.

She looked back to the stream, hearing the urgent murmur of the black water's passage. Holding the note into the beam of a light from the side of the mill, she read one of the numbers he'd given her. She punched it into her phone.

But then she paused, listening again to the water, breathing in the cool air with its scent of loam and hay and lavender. Marissa cleared the screen of her mobile. And she dialed another number.

Double Jeopardy

There *is* no one better than me."

"Uh-huh, uh-huh. What're my options?'

Paul Lescroix leaned back in the old oak chair and glanced down at the arm, picking at a piece of varnish the shape of Illinois. "You ever pray?" his baritone voice asked in response.

The shackles rattled as Jerry Pilsett lifted his hands and flicked his earlobe. Lescroix had known the young man all of four hours and Pilsett must've tapped that right earlobe a dozen times. "Nup," said the skinny young man with the crooked teeth. "Don't pray."

"Well, you ought to take it up. And thank the good Lord that I'm here, Jerry. You're at the end of the road."

"There's Mr. Goodwin."

Hmm. Goodwin, a twenty-nine-year-old public defender. Unwitting co-conspirator—with the local judges—in getting his clients sentenced to terms two or three times longer than they deserved. A rube among rubes.

"Keep Goodwin, if you want." Lescroix planted his chestnut-brown Italian shoes on the concrete floor and scooted the chair back. "I could care."

"Wait. Just that he's been my lawyer since I was arrested." He added significantly, "Five months."

"I've read the documents, Jerry," Lescroix said dryly. "I know how long you two've been in bed together."

Pilsett blinked. When he couldn't process that expression, he asked, "You're saying you're better'n him? That it?" He stopped looking shifty-eyed and took in Lescroix's perfect silver hair, trim waist and wise, jowly face.

"You really don't know who I am, do you?" Lescroix, who would otherwise have been outraged by this lapse, wasn't surprised. Here he was, after all, in Hamilton, a hick-filled county whose entire population was less than Lescroix's home neighborhood, the Upper East Side of Manhattan.

"All's I know is Harry, he's the head jailor today, comes in and tells me to shut off *Regis 'n' Kathie Lee* an' get the hell down to the conference rooms. There's this lawyer wants to see me, and now here you are telling me you want to take my case and I'm supposed to fire Mr. Goodwin. Mr. Goodwin, who's been decent to me all along."

"Well, see, Jerry, from what I've heard, Goodwin's decent to everybody. He's decent to the judge, he's decent to the prosecution, he's decent to the prosecution's witnesses. That's why he's one bad lawyer and why you're in real deep trouble."

Pilsett was feeling pushed into a corner, which was what sitting with Lescroix for more than five minutes made you feel. So he decided to hit back. (Probably, Lescroix reflected, just what had happened on that night in June.) "Who 'xactly says you're any good? Answer me that."

Should I eviscerate him with my résumé? Lescroix wondered. Rattle off my role in the Menendez brothers' first trial? Last year's acquittal of the Sacramento wife for the premeditated arson murder of her husband with a novel abuse defense (embarrassment in front of friends being abuse too)? The luscious not-guilty awarded to Fred Johnson, the pretty thief from Cabrini-Green in Chicago, who was *brainwashed*, yes, brainwashed, ladies and gentlemen, into helping a militant *cell*, no not a gang, a revolutionary cell, murder three customers in a Southside check-cashing store. The infamous *Time* magazine profile? The *Hard Copy* piece?

But Lescroix merely repeated, "There is no one better than me, Jerry." And let the sizzling lasers of his eyes seal the argument.

"The trial's *tomorrow*. Whatta you know 'bout the case? Can we get it, you know, continued?" The three syllables sounded smooth in his mouth, too smooth: he'd taken a long time to learn what the word meant and how it was pronounced.

"Don't need to. I've read the entire file. Spent the last three days on it."

"Three days." Another blink. An earlobe tweak. This was their first meeting: Why would Lescroix have been reviewing the file for the past three days?

But Lescroix didn't explain. He never explained anything to anyone unless he absolutely had to. Especially clients.

"But didn't you say you was from New York or something? Can you just do a trial here?"

"Goodwin'll let me 'do' the trial. No problem."

Because he's a decent fellow.

And a spineless wimp.

"But he don't charge me nothing. You gonna handle the case for free?"

He really *doesn't* know anything about me. Amazing. "No, Jerry. I never work for free. People don't respect you when you work for free."

"Mr. Goodwin—"

"People don't respect Goodwin."

"I do."

"Your respect doesn't count, Jerry. Your uncle's picking up the tab."

"Uncle James?"

Lescroix nodded.

"He's a good man. Hope he didn't hock his farm."

He's not a good man, Jerry, Lescroix thought. He's a fool.

Because he thinks there's still some hope for you. And I don't give a rat's ass whether he mortgaged the farm or not. "So, what do you say, Jerry?"

"Well, I guess. Only there's something you have to know." Scooting closer, shackles rattling. The young, stubbly face leaned forward and the thin lips leveraged into a lopsided smile.

But Lescroix held up an index finger that ended in a snappy, manicured nail. "Now, you're going to tell me a big secret, right? That you didn't kill Patricia Cabot. That you're completely innocent. That you've been framed. That this's all a terrible mistake. That you just happened to be at the crime scene."

"I—"

"Well, Jerry, no, it's not a mistake."

Pilsett looked uneasily at Lescroix, which was just the way the lawyer loved to be looked at. He was a force, he was a phenomenon. No prosecutor ever beat him, no client ever upstaged him.

"Two months ago—on June second—you were hired by Charles Arnold Cabot to mow his lawn and cart off a stack of rotten firewood near his house in Bentana, the ritziest burgh in Hamilton. He'd hired you before a few times and you didn't really like him—Cabot's a country club sort of guy—but of course you did the work and you took the fifty dollars he agreed to pay you. He didn't give you a tip. You got drunk that night and the more you drank, the madder you got 'cause you remembered that he never paid you enough—even though you never bargained with him and you kept coming back when he called you."

"Wait—"

"Shhhh. The next day, when Cabot and his wife were both out, you were still drunk and still mad. You broke into the house and while you were cutting the wires that connected their two-thousand-dollar stereo receiver to the speakers, Patricia Cabot came back home unexpectedly. She scared the hell out of you and you hit her with the hammer you'd used to break open the door from the garage to the kitchen. You knocked her out. But didn't kill her. You tied her up. Thinking maybe you'd rape her later. Ah, ah, ah—let me finish. Thinking maybe you'd rape her later. Don't gimme that *look*, Jerry. She was thirty-four, beautiful and unconscious. And look at you. You even have a girlfriend? I don't think so.

"Then you got spooked. The woman came to and started to scream. You finished things up with the hammer and started to run out the door. The husband saw you in the doorway with the bloody hammer and the stereo and their CD collection under your arm. He called the cops and they nailed you. A fair representation of events?"

"Wasn't all their CDs. I didn't take the Michael Bolton."

"Don't ever try to be funny with me."

Pilsett flicked his earlobe again. "Was pretty much what happened."

"All right, Jerry. Listen. This's a small town and people here're plenty stupid. I consider myself the best defense lawyer in the country but this case is open and shut. You did it, everyone knows you did it, and the evidence is completely against you. They don't have the death penalty in this state but they're damn generous when it comes to handing out life terms with no chance for parole. So. That's the future you're facing."

"Yup. And know what it tells me? Tells me *you're* the one can't lose on this here situation." Pilsett grinned.

Maybe they weren't as dumb in Hamilton as he thought.

The young man continued, "You come all the way here from New York. You do the trial and you leave. If you get me off, you're a celebrity and you get paid and on *Geraldo* or *Oprah* or some such for winning a hopeless case. And if you lose, you get paid and nobody gives a damn because I got put away like I oughta."

Lescroix had to grin. "Jerry, Jerry, Jerry. That's one thing I just love about this line of work. No charades between us."

"What's charades?"

"Doesn't matter."

"Gotta question." He frowned.

Take your time . . .

"Say you was to get me off. Could they come after me again?"

"Nope. That'd be double jeopardy. That's what's so great about this country. Once a jury's said you're innocent, you're free, and the prosecutor can't do diddly. . . . Come on, you gonna hire me and boot that Goodwin back to the law library, where he belongs?"

He flicked his earlobe again. The chains clinked. "Guess I will."

"Then let's get to work."

■

Paul Lescroix's résumé had been amply massaged over the years. He'd gone to a city law school at night. Which wouldn't of course play in the many new stories he fantasized would feature him, so after he graduated he signed up fast for continuing ed courses in Cambridge, which were open to any lawyer willing to pay five hundred bucks. Accordingly the claim that he was "Harvard educated" was true.

He got a job at minimum wage transcribing and filing judicial opinions for traffic court magistrates. So he could say that he'd served his apprenticeship clerking and writing opinions for criminal court judges.

He opened a solo practice above Great Eastern Cantonese carry-out in a sooty building off Maiden Lane in downtown Manhattan. Hence, he became "a partner in a Wall Street firm, specializing in white-collar crime."

But these little hiccups in the history of Paul Lescroix (all right, originally Paul Vito Lacosta), these little glitches didn't detract from his one gift—the uncanny ability to decimate his opponents in court. Which is one talent no lawyer can fake. He'd unearth every fact he could about the case, the parties, the judge, the prosecutor, then he'd squeeze them hard, pinch them, mold them like Play-Doh. They were facts still, but facts mutated; in his hands they became weapons, shields, viruses, disguises.

The night before the Pilsett trial, he spent one hour emptying poor Al Goodwin of whatever insights he might have about the case, two hours meeting with reporters and ten hours reviewing two things; the police report, and a lengthy document prepared by his own private investigator, hired three days ago when James Pilsett, Jerry's uncle, came to him with the retainer fee.

Lescroix immediately noticed that while the circumstantial evidence against Pilsett was substantial, the biggest threat came from Charles Cabot himself. They were lucky of course that he was the only witness but unfortunate that he happened to be the husband of the woman who was killed. It's a dangerous risk to attack the credibility of a witness who's also suffered because of the crime.

But Paul Victor Lescroix, Esq., was paid four hundred dollars an hour against five-figure retainers for the very reason that he was willing—no, *eager*—to take risks like that.

Smiling to himself, he called room service for a large pot of coffee and, while murderer Jerry Pilsett and decent Al Goodwin and all the simple folk of Hamilton County dreamt their simple dreams, Lescroix planned for battle.

He arrived at the courtroom early, as he always did, and sat primly at the defense table as the witnesses and spectators and (yes, thank you, Lord, the press) showed up. He mugged subtly for the cameras and scoped out the prosecutor (state U grad, Lescroix had learned, top 40 percent, fifteen years under his belt and numb from being mired in a dead-end career he should have left thirteen years ago).

Lescroix then turned his eyes to a man sitting in the back of the courtroom. Charles Cabot. He sat beside a woman in her six-ties—mother or mother-in-law, Lescroix reckoned, gauging by the tears. The lawyer was slightly troubled. He'd expected Cabot to be a stiff, upper-middle-class suburbanite, someone who'd elicit little sympathy from the jury. But the man—though he was about forty—seemed boyish. He had mussed hair, dark blond, and wore a rumpled sports coat and slacks, striped tie. A friendly insurance salesman. He comforted the woman and dropped a few tears himself. He was the sort of widower a jury could easily fall in love with.

Well, Lescroix had been in worse straits. He'd had cases where he'd had to attack grieving mothers and widowed wives and even bewildered children. He'd just have to feel his way along, like a musician sensing the audience's reaction and adjusting his playing carefully. He could—

Lescroix realized suddenly that Cabot was staring at him. The man's eyes were like cold ball bearings. Lescroix actually shivered—*that* had never before happened in court—and he struggled to maintain eye contact. It was a moment. Yet Lescroix was glad for the challenge. Something in that look of Cabot's made this whole thing personal, made it far easier to do what he was about to do. Their eyes locked, the electricity sparking between them. Then a door clicked open and everyone stood as the clerk entered.

"Oyez, oyez, oyez, criminal court for the county of Hamilton, First District, is now in session. The right honorable Jennings P. Martell presiding, all ye with business before this court come forward and be heard."

Pilsett, wearing a goofy brown suit, was led cautiously out of the lockup. He sat down next to his lawyer. The defendant grinned stupidly until Lescroix told him to stop. He flicked his earlobe several times with an unshackled finger.

When Lescroix looked back to Cabot the metallic eyes had shifted from the lawyer and were drilling into the back of the man who'd killed his wife with a $4.99 Sears Craftsman claw hammer.

The prosecutor presented the forensic evidence first and Lescroix spent a half hour chipping away at the testimony of the lab technicians and the cops—though the crime-scene work had been surprisingly well handled for such a small police department. A minor victory for the prosecution, Lescroix conceded to himself.

Then the state called Charles Cabot.

The widower straightened his tie, hugged the woman beside him and walked to the stand.

Guided by the prosecutor's pedestrian questions, the man gave an unemotional account of what he'd seen on June third. Monosyllables of grief. A few tears, Lescroix rated the performance uncompelling, though the man's broken words certainly held the jury's attention. But he'd expected this; we love tragedies as much as romance and nearly as much as sex.

"No further questions, Your Honor," the prosecutor said and glanced dismissively at Lescroix.

The lawyer rose slowly, unbuttoned his jacket, ran his hand through his hair, mussing it ever so slightly. He paced slowly in front of the witness. When he spoke he spoke to the jury. "I'm so very sorry for your misfortune, Mr. Cabot."

The witness nodded, though his eyes were wary.

Lescroix continued, "The death of a young woman is a terrible thing. Just terrible. *Inexcusable*."

"Yes, well. Thank you."

The jury's collective eyes scanned Lescroix's troubled face. He glanced at the witness stand. Cabot didn't know what to say. He'd been expecting an attack. He was uneasy. The eyes were no longer steely hard. They were cautious. Good. People detest wary truth-tellers far more than self-assured liars.

Lescroix turned back to the twelve men and women in his audience.

He smiled. No one smiled back.

That was all right. This was just the overture.

He walked to the table and picked up a folder. Strode back to the jury box. "Mr. Cabot, what do you do for a living?"

The question caught him off guard. He looked around the courtroom. "Well, I own a company. It manufactures housings for computers and related equipment."

"Do you make a lot of money at it?"

"Objection."

"Overruled. But you'll bring this back to earth sometime soon, Mr. Lescroix?"

"You bet I will, Your Honor. Now, Mr. Cabot, please answer."

"We had sales of eight million last year."

"Your salary was what?"

"I took home about two hundred thousand."

"And your wife, was she employed by the company too?"

"Part-time. As a director on the board. And she did some consulting work."

"I see. And how much did she make?"

"I don't know exactly."

"Toss an estimate our way, Mr. Cabot."

"Well, in the neighborhood of a hundred thousand."

"Really? Interesting."

Flipping slowly through the folder, while the jury wondered what could be interesting about this piece of news.

Lescroix looked up. "How was your company originally financed?"

"Objection, Your Honor," the gray-faced prosecutor said. His young assistant nodded vigorously, as if every bob of his head was a legal citation supporting his boss.

The judge asked, "Going anywhere real, Mr. Lescroix, or're we being treated to one of your famous fishing trips?"

Perfect. Lescroix turned to the jury, eyes upraised slightly; the judge didn't notice. See what I've got to deal with? he asked tacitly. He was rewarded with a single conspiratorial smile from a juror.

And then, God bless me, another.

"I'm going someplace very real, Your Honor. Even if there are people present who won't be very happy where that might be."

This raised a few murmurs.

The judge grunted. "We'll see. Overruled. Go ahead, Mr. Cabot."

"If I recall, the financing was very complicated."

"Then let's make it easy. Your wife's father is a wealthy businessman, right?"

"I don't know what you mean by wealthy." Cabot swallowed.

"Net worth of twelve million'd fall *somewhere* in that definition, wouldn't it?"

"I suppose, somewhere."

Several jurors joined Lescroix in chuckling.

"Didn't your father-in-law stake you to your company?"

"I paid back every penny—"

"Mr. Cabot," Lescroix asked patiently, "did your father-in-law stake you to your company or did he not?"

A pause. Then a sullen "Yes."

"How much of the company did your wife own?"

"If I remember, there were some complicated formulas—"

"More complexity?" Lescroix sighed. "Let's make it simple, why don't we. Just tell us what *percentage* of the company your wife owned."

Another hesitation. "Forty-nine."

"And you?"

"Forty-nine."

"And who owns the other two percent?"

"That would be her father."

"And on her death, who gets her shares?"

A moment's hesitation. "If we'd had any children—"

"*Do* you have children?"

"No."

"I see. Then let's hear what will in *fact* happen to your wife's shares."

"I guess I'll receive them. I hadn't thought about it."

Play 'em right. Just like an orchestra conductor. Light hand on the baton. Don't add, "So you're the one who's profited from your wife's death." Or: "So then you'd be in control of the company." They're dim, but even the dimmest are beginning to see where we're headed.

Cabot took a sip of water, spilled some on his jacket and brushed the drops away.

"Mr. Cabot, let's think back to June, all right? You hired Jerry Pilsett to do some work for you on the second, the day before your wife died, correct?"

Not *before she was murdered.* Always keep it neutral.

"Yes."

"And you'd hired him several times before, right?"

"Yes."

"Starting when?"

"I don't know, maybe six months ago."

"How long have you known that Jerry lived in Hamilton?"

"I guess five, six years."

"So even though you've known him for six years, you never hired him before last spring?"

"Well, no, but—"

"Even though you had plenty of opportunities to."

"No. But I was going to say—"

"Now June second was what day of the week, Mr. Cabot?"

After a glance at the judge, Cabot said, "I don't remember."

"It was a Friday."

"If you say so," the witness replied churlishly.

"*I* don't say so, Mr. Cabot. My Hallmark calendar does." And he held up a pocket calendar emblazoned with a photo of fuzzy puppies.

A wheeze of laughter from several members of the jury.

"And what time of day was he supposed to do the work?"

"I don't know."

"Early?"

"Not real early."

"'Not real early,'" Lescroix repeated slowly. Then snapped, "Wasn't it in fact late afternoon and evening?"

"Maybe it was."

Frowning, pacing. "Isn't it odd that you hired somebody to do yard work on a Friday night?"

"It wasn't night. It was dusk and—"

"Please answer the question."

"It didn't occur to me there was anything odd about it."

"I see. Could you tell us exactly what you hired him to do?"

A surly glance from Cabot. Then: "He mowed the lawn and took away some rotten firewood."

"Rotten?"

"Well, termite infested."

"Was it *all* termite infested?"

Cabot looked at the prosecutor, whose milky face shone with concern, and then at the D.A.'s young assistant, who would probably have been concerned too if he hadn't been so confused at the moment. Jerry Pilsett merely flicked his earlobe and stared morosely at the floor.

"Go ahead," the judge prompted. "Answer the question."

"I don't know. I saw termite holes. I have a wood-framed house and I didn't want to take the chance they'd get into the house."

"So you saw some *evidence* of termites but the pile of wood wasn't completely rotten, was it?"

"I don't know. Maybe not." Cabot gave an uneasy laugh.

"So there was some—maybe a lot—of good wood there."

"Maybe. What difference—?"

"But for some reason you wanted Jerry Pilsett to haul the entire pile away. And to do so on this particular Friday night."

"Why are you asking me all these questions?"

"To get to the truth," Lescroix spat out. "That's what we're here for, isn't it? Now, tell us, sir, was the pile of wood covered with anything?"

A slight frown. He'd only be wondering why Lescroix was focusing on this fact but the result was a wonderfully suspicious expression.

"Yes. By an old tarp."

"And was the tarp stacked to the ground?"

"Yes, it was."

"And you'd put the tarp over the wood yourself?"

"Yes."

"When?" Lescroix demanded.

"I don't remember."

"No? Could it have been just a few days before you hired Jerry?"

"No. . . . Well, maybe."

"Did Jerry say anything about the tarp?"

"I don't recall."

Lescroix said patiently, "Didn't Jerry say to you that the stakes were pounded into the ground too hard to pull out and that he'd have to loosen them somehow to uncover the wood?"

Cabot looked up at the judge, uneasy. He swallowed again, seemed to think about taking a sip of water but didn't. Maybe his hands were shaking too badly. "Do I have to answer these questions?"

"Yes, you do," the judge said solemnly.

"Maybe."

"And did you tell him there were some tools in the garage he could use if he needed them?"

Another weighty pause. Cabot sought the answer in the murky plaster heaven above them. "I might have."

"Ah." Lescroix's face lit up. Easily half the jury was with him now, floating along with the music, wondering where the tune was going. "Could you tell our friends on the jury how many tools you have in your garage, sir?"

"For Christ's sake, I don't know."

A sacrilege in front of the jury. Deliciously bad form.

"Let me be more specific," Lescroix said helpfully. "How many *hammers* do you own?"

"Hammers?" He glanced at the murder weapon, a claw hammer, sitting, brown with his wife's stale blood, on the prosecution's table. The jury looked at it too.

"Just one. That one."

"So," Lescroix's voice rose, "when you told Jerry to get a tool from the garage to loosen the stakes you'd pounded into the ground, you knew there was only one tool he could pick. That hammer right there?"

"No. . . . I mean, I don't know what he used—"

"You didn't know he used that hammer to loosen the stakes?"

"Well, I knew that. Yes. But. . . " The eyes grew dark. "Why're you ac—?"

"Why am I what, sir?"

Cabot sat back.

Lescroix leaned toward the witness. "Accusing you? Is that what you were going to say? Why would I accuse you of anything?"

"Nothing. I'm sorry."

The judge muttered, "Okay, Mr. Lescroix. Let's move along."

"Of course, Your Honor. And therefore, as a result of directing him to use that hammer, his fingerprints are now on the murder weapon. Isn't that the case?"

Cabot stared at the prosecutor's disgusted face. "I don't know."

"You don't know?"

Sonata for witness and jury.

"Maybe it's true. But—"

"Sir, let's go on. On that day, the second of June, after Jerry Pilsett had mowed the lawn and loaded the wood into his pickup truck to be carted off, you asked him inside to pay him, right?"

"Yes, I think so."

"And you asked him into your living room. Right?"

"I don't remember."

Lescroix flipped through a number of sheets in the folder, as if they were chock full of crime scene data and witnesses transcripts. He stared at one page for a moment, as blank as the others. Then closed the folder.

"You don't?"

Cabot too stared at the folder. "Well, I guess I did, yes."

"You gave him a glass of water."

"Maybe."

"Did you or didn't you?"

"Yes! I did."

"And you showed him your latest possession, your new stereo. The one you later *claimed* he stole."

"We were talking about music and I thought he might be interested in it."

"I see." Lescroix was frowning. "I'm sorry, Mr. Cabot, but help me out here. This seems odd. Here's a man who's been working for hours in the summer heat. He's full of dirt, sweat, grass stains . . . and you ask him inside. Not into the entry hall, not into the kitchen, but into the living room."

"I was just being civil."

"Good of you. Only the result of this . . . this *civility* was to put his shoeprints on the carpet and his fingerprints on the stereo, a water glass, doorknobs and who knows what else?"

"What are you *saying*?" Cabot asked. His expression was even better than Lescroix could have hoped for. It was supposed to be shocked but it looked mean and sneaky. A Nixon look.

"Please answer, sir."

"I suppose some footprints were there, and his fingerprints might be on some things. But that doesn't—"

"Thank you. Now, Mr. Cabot, would you tell the jury whether or not you asked Jerry Pilsett to come back the following day."

"What?"

"Did you ask Jerry to come back to your house the next day? That would be Saturday, June third."

"No, I didn't."

Lescroix frowned dramatically. He opened the folder again, found another important blank sheet, and pretended to read. "You didn't say to Jerry Pilsett, and I quote, 'You did a good job, Jerry. Come back about five tomorrow and I'll have some more work for you'?"

"I didn't say that. No."

A breathless scoff. "You're denying you said that?"

He hesitated, glanced at the prosecutor and offered a weak "Yes."

"Mr. Cabot, His Honor will remind you that lying under oath is perjury and that's a serious crime. Now answer the question. Did you or did you not ask Jerry Pilsett to come back to your house at five p.m. on Saturday, June third?"

"No, I didn't. Really, I swear." His voice was high from stress. Lescroix loved it when that happened since even the saintliest witness sounded like a liar. And qualifiers like "really" and "I swear" added to the cadence of deception.

You poor bastard.

Lescroix turning toward the jury, puffing air through cheeks. A few more sympathetic smiles. Some shaking heads too, revealing shared exasperation at a lying witness. The second movement of Lescroix's performance seemed to have gone over well.

"All right," the lawyer muttered skeptically. "Let's go back to the events of June third, sir."

Cabot put his hands in his lap. Purely a defensive gesture, again in response to the stress that he'd be feeling. Yet juries sometimes read another message in the pose: guilt. "You told the court that you came home about five p.m. Correct?"

"Yes."

"Where had you been?"

"The office."

"On Saturday?"

Cabot managed a smile. "When you have your own business you frequently work on Saturdays. I do, at any rate."

"You came back at five and found Jerry Pilsett standing in the doorway."

"Yes, holding the hammer."

"The bloody hammer."

"Yes."

"It *was* bloody, right?"

"Yes."

Another examination of the infamous file, this time looking over a document with actual writing on it. "Hmm. Now the police found your car on the parking strip fifty feet from the door where you allegedly saw Jerry. Is that what you claimed?"

"It's where the car *was*. It's the truth."

Lescroix forged on. "Why was the car that far away from the house?"

"I . . . well, when I was driving up to the house I panicked and drove over the curb. I was worried about my wife."

"But you couldn't see your wife, could you?"

A pause. "Well, no. But I could see the hammer, the blood."

"Fifty feet away's a pretty good distance. You could actually see the hammer in Jerry's hand?"

Calling him "Jerry," never "the defendant" or "Pilsett." Make him human. Make him a buddy of every member of the jury. Make *him* the victim here.

"Sure, I could."

"And the blood on it?"

"I'm sure I could. I—"

Lescroix pounced. "You're *sure* you could." Just the faintest glissando of sarcasm. He scanned another page, shaking his head. "Your vision's not very good, is it?" The lawyer looked up. "In fact, isn't it illegal for you to drive without your glasses or contacts?"

"I . . . " Taken aback by the amount of research Lescroix had done. Then he smiled. "That's right. And I had my glasses on when I drove up to the house. So I could see the bloody hammer in his hand."

"Well, sir, if that's the case, then why did an officer bring them to you in the house later that evening? When he needed you to look over some items in the house. He found them in your car."

It was in the police report.

"I don't . . . Wait, I must've . . . I probably took them off to dial the cell phone in the car—to call the police. They're distance glasses. I must've forgotten to put them back on."

"I see. So you claim you saw a man in your doorway with a bloody hammer, you took off your driving glasses and you called nine-one-one."

"Yes, I guess that's about right."

He didn't notice the "you claim" part of the comment; the jury always does.

"So that means you called nine-one-one from inside the car?"

"I called right away, of course."

"But from inside the car? You claim you see a man in your doorway with a bloody hammer and yet you park fifty feet away from the house, you stay in the safety of the car to call for help? Why didn't you jump out of the car and go see what was going on? See about your wife?"

"Well, I did."

"But after you called nine-one-one."

"I don't know. I . . . Maybe I called later."

"But then your glasses wouldn't have been in the car."

Cabot was now as disoriented as a hooked pike. "I don't know. I panicked. I don't remember what happened."

Which was, of course, the complete truth.

And, accordingly, of no interest to Lescroix.

He walked ten feet away from the witness stand, stopped and

turned toward Cabot. The jury seemed to be leaning forward, awaiting the next movement.

"At what time did you leave the office on Saturday, June third?"

"I don't know."

"Well, you arrived home at about five, you claimed. It's a ten-minute drive from your office. So you must have left about four-thirty. Did you go straight home?"

"I . . . I think I had some errands to run."

"What errands? Where?"

"I don't recall. How do you expect me to recall?"

"But you'd think it'd be easy to remember at least one or two places you stopped during the course of two hours."

"Two hours?" Cabot frowned.

"You left the office at three p.m."

The witness stared at his inquisitor.

"According to the video security tape in your building's lobby."

"Okay, maybe I did leave then. It was a while ago. And this's all so hard for me. It's not easy to remember . . ."

His voice faded as Lescroix opened the private eye's report and found photocopies of Cabot's banking statements and canceled checks.

"Who," the lawyer asked pointedly, "is Mary Henstroth?"

Cabot's eyes slipped away from the lawyer's. "How did you know about . . . ?"

I do my goddamn homework, Lescroix might have explained. "Who is she?"

"A friend. She—"

"A friend. I see. How long have you known her?"

"I don't know. A few years."

"Where does she live?"

"In Gilroy."

"Gilroy's a fifteen-minute drive from Hamilton, is that right?"

"It depends."

"Depends? On how eager you are to get to Gilroy?"

"Objection."

"Sustained. Please, Mr. Lescroix."

"Sorry, Your Honor. Now, Mr. Cabot, on June third of this year, did you write a check to Ms. Henstroth in the amount of five hundred dollars?"

Cabot closed his eyes. His jaw clenched. He nodded.

"Answer for the court reporter, please."

"Yes."

"And did you deliver this check in person?"

"I don't remember," he said weakly.

"After you left work, you didn't drive to Gilroy and, during the course of your . . . *visit,* give Ms. Henstroth a check for five hundred dollars?"

"I might have."

"Have you written her other checks over the past several years?"

"Yes." Whispered.

"Louder, please, sir?"

"Yes."

"And did you give these other checks to Ms. Henstroth in person?"

"Some of them. Most of them."

"So it's reasonable to assume that the check you wrote on June third was delivered in person too."

"I said I might have," he muttered.

"These checks that you wrote to your 'friend' over the past few years were on your company account, not your joint home account, correct?"

"Yes."

"So is it safe to assume that your wife would not be receiving the statement from the bank showing that you'd written these checks? Is that correct too?"

"Yes." The witness's shoulders dipped. A slight gesture, but Lescroix was sure a number of the jurors saw it.

They all saw the prosecutor toss his pencil onto the table in disgust. He whispered something to his sheepish assistant, who nodded even more sheepishly.

"What was this money for?"

"I . . . don't remember."

Perfect. Better to let the evasive answer stand than to push it and have Cabot come up with a credible lie.

"I see. Did you tell your wife you were going to see Ms. Henstroth that afternoon?"

"I . . . no, I didn't."

"I don't suppose you would," Lescroix muttered, eyes on the rapt jury; they loved this new movement of his symphony.

"Your Honor," the prosecutor snapped.

"Withdrawn," Lescroix said. He lifted a wrinkled piece of paper from the file; it contained several handwritten paragraphs and looked like a letter, though it was in fact an early draft of a speech Lescroix had given to the American Association of Trial Lawyers last year. He read the first paragraph slowly, shaking his head. Even the prosecutors seemed to be straining forward, waiting. Then he replaced the letter and looked up. "Isn't your relationship with Ms. Henstroth romantic in nature, sir?" he asked bluntly.

Cabot tried to look indignant. He sputtered, "I resent—"

"Oh, please, Mr. Cabot. You have the gall to accuse an innocent man of murder and you *resent* that I ask you a few questions about your mistress?"

"Objection!"

"Withdrawn, Your Honor."

Lescroix shook his head and glanced at the jury, asking, What kind of monster are we dealing with here? Lescroix paced as he flipped to the last page of the file. He read for a moment, shook his head, then threw the papers onto the defense table with a huge slap. He whirled to Cabot and shouted, "Isn't it true you've been having an affair with Mary Henstroth for the past several years?"

"No!"

"Isn't it true that you were afraid if you divorced your wife you'd lose control of the company she and her father owned fifty-one percent of?"

"That's a lie!" Cabot shouted.

"Isn't it true that on June third of this year you left work early, stopped by Mary Henstroth's house in Gilroy, had sex with her, then proceeded to your house where you lay in wait for your wife with a hammer in your hand? That hammer there, People's Exhibit A?"

"No, no, no!"

"And then you beat her to death. You returned to your car and waited until Jerry Pilsett showed up, just like you'd asked him to do. And when he arrived you took off your glasses to look at your cell phone and called the police to report him—an innocent man—as the murderer?"

"No, that's not true! It's ridiculous!"

"Objection!"

"Isn't it true?" Lescroix cried, "that you killed Patricia, your loving wife, in cold blood?"

"No!"

"Sustained! Mr. Lescroix, enough of this. I won't have these theatrics in my courtroom."

But the lawyer would not be deflected by a mule-county judge. His energy was unstoppable, fueled by the murmurs and gasps from the spectators, and his outraged voice soared to the far reaches of the courtroom, reciting, "Isn't it true, isn't it true, isn't it true?"

His audience in the jury box sat forward as if they wanted to leap from their chairs and give the conductor a standing ovation, and Charles Cabot's horrified eyes, dots of steely anger no more, scanned the courtroom in panic. He was speechless, his voice choked off. As if his dead wife had materialized behind him and closed her arms around his throat to squeeze out what little life remained in his guilty heart.

■

Three hours to acquit on all charges.

Not a record but good enough, Lescroix reflected as he sat in his hotel room that evening. He was angry he'd missed the last of the two daily flights out of Hamilton but he had some whiskey in a glass at his side, music on his portable CD player and his feet were resting on the windowsill, revealing Italian socks as sheer as a woman's black stockings. He was passing the time replaying his victory and trying to decide if he should spend some of his fee on getting those jowl tucks done.

There was a knock on the door.

Lescroix rose and let Jerry Pilsett's uncle into the room. The lawyer hadn't paid much attention to him the first time they'd met and he realized now that with his quick eyes and tailored clothes this was no dirt jockey. He must've been connected with one of the big corporate farming companies. Probably hadn't had to hock the family spread at all and Lescroix regretted charging him only seventy-five K for the case; should've gone for an even hundred. Oh well.

The elder Pilsett accepted a glass of whiskey and drank a large swallow. "Yessir. Need that after all of today's excitement. Yessir."

He pulled an envelope out of his pocket and set it on the table. "Rest of your fee. Have to say, I didn't think you could do it. Didn't even get him on the burglary charges," the man added with some surprise.

"Well, they couldn't very well do that, could they? Either he was guilty of everything or guilty of nothing."

"Reckon."

Lescroix nodded toward the fee. "A lot of people wouldn't've done this. Even for family."

"I'm a firm believer in kin sticking together. Doing whatever has to be done."

"That's a good sentiment," the lawyer offered.

"You say that like you don't believe in sentiments. Or don't believe in kin."

"Haven't had occasion to believe or disbelieve in either of them," Lescroix answered. "My life's my job."

"Getting people out of jail."

"Protecting justice's what I like to call it."

"Justice?" the old man snorted. "Y'know, I watched that O.J. trial. And I heard a commentator after the verdict. He said it just goes to show if you have money—whatever your race—you can buy justice. I laughed at that. What'd he mean, *justice*? If you have money you can buy *freedom*. That's not necessarily justice at all."

Lescroix tapped the envelope. "So what're *you* buying?"

Pilsett laughed. "Peace of mind. That's what. Better'n justice and freedom put together. So, how'd my nephew stand his ordeal?"

"He survived."

"He's not at home. He staying here?"

Lescroix shook his head. "He didn't think he'd be too welcome in Hamilton for a while. He's at a place on Route 32 West. Skyview Motel. I think he wants to see you. Thank you in person."

"We'll give him a call, the wife and I, take him out to dinner." The man finished the whiskey and set the glass down. "Well, mister, it's a hard job you have. I don't envy you it." He appraised the lawyer with those sharp eyes. "Mostly I don't envy you staying up at night. With that conscience of yours."

A faint frown crossed Lescroix's face, hearing this. But then it blossomed into a smile. "I sleep like a baby, sir. Always have."

They shook hands and walked to the door. Jerry's uncle

stepped into the corridor but then stopped and turned. "Oh, 'nother thing. I'd listen to the news, I was you." He added cryptically, "You'll be hearing some things you might want to think on."

Lescroix closed the door and returned to the uncomfortable chair and his sumptuous whiskey.

Things I want to think on?

At six he picked up the remote control and clicked the TV set on, found the local news. He was watching a pretty young newscaster holding a microphone in front of her mouth.

"It was this afternoon, while prosecutors were asking freed suspect Gerald Pilsett about the role of Charles Cabot in his wife's death, that Pilsett gave the shocking admission. A claim he later repeated for reporters."

Oh, my Lord. No. He didn't!

Lescroix sat forward, mouth agape.

Jerry came on-screen, grinning that crooked smile and tapping a finger against his earlobe. "Sure I killed her. I told my lawyer that right up front. But there's nothing nobody can do about it. He said they can't try me again. It's called double jeopardy. Hey, their case wasn't good enough to get me the first time, that ain't my fault."

Lescroix's skin crawled.

Back to the blonde newscaster. "That very lawyer, Paul Lescroix, of New York City, created a stir in court earlier today when he suggested that Hamilton businessman Charles Cabot himself killed his wife because he was in love with another woman. Police, however, have discovered that the woman Lescroix accused Cabot of having an affair with is Sister Mary Helen Henstroth, a seventy-five-year-old nun who runs a youth center in Gilroy. Cabot and his wife frequently served as volunteers at the center and donated thousands of dollars to it.

"Police also dispelled Lescroix's other theory that Cabot might have killed his wife to take control of the company of which he is president. Even though he owned a minority of the shares, a review of the corporate documents revealed that Patricia Cabot and her father had voluntarily handed over one hundred percent voting control to Cabot after he paid back fifty thousand dollars her father had loaned him to start the business five years ago.

"State prosecutors are looking into whether charges can be brought against Lescroix for defamation and misuse of the legal process."

Furious, Lescroix flung the remote control across the room. It shattered in a dozen pieces.

The phone rang.

"Mr. Lescroix, I'm with WPIJ news. Could you comment on the claim that you knowingly accused an innocent man—"

"No." *Click*.

It rang again.

"'Lo?"

"I'm a reporter with the *New York Times*—"

Click .

"Yeah?"

"This that gawdamn shyster? I find you I'm gonna—"

Click .

Lescroix unplugged the phone, stood and paced. Don't panic. It's no big deal. Everybody'd forget about it in a few days. This wasn't *his* fault. His duty was to represent a client to the best of his ability. Though even as he tried to reassure himself, he was picturing the ethics investigation, explaining the matter to his clients, his golfing buddies, his girlfriends. . . .

Pilsett. What an utter fool. He—

Lescroix froze. On the TV screen was a man in his fifties. Unshaven. Rumpled white shirt. An unseen newscaster was asking him his reaction to the Pilsett verdict. But what had snagged Lescroix's attention was the super at the bottom of the screen: *James Pilsett, Uncle of Acquitted Suspect.*

It wasn't the man who'd hired him, who'd been here in the room an hour ago to deliver his fee.

"Wayl," the uncle drawled. "Jurry wus alwus a problem. Weren't never doing what he ought. Deserved ever' lick he got. Him gitting off today . . . I don' unnerstand that one bit. Don' seem right to me."

Lescroix leapt to the desk and opened the envelope. The full amount of the rest of the fee was enclosed. But it wasn't a check. It was cash, like the retainer. There was no note, nothing with a name on it.

Who the hell was he?

He plugged the phone in and dialed the Skyview Motel.

The phone rang, rang, rang.

Finally it was answered. "Hello?"

"Jerry, it's Lescroix. Listen to me—"

"I'm sorry," the man's voice said. "Jerry's tied up right now."

"Who's this?"

A pause.

"Hello, counselor."

"Who are you?" Lescroix demanded.

There was a soft chuckle on the other end. "Don't you recognize me? And after our long talk in court this morning. I'm disappointed."

Cabot! It was Charles Cabot.

How had he gotten to Jerry's motel room? Lescroix was the only one who knew where the man was hiding out.

"Confused, counselor?"

But, no, Lescroix recalled, he *wasn't* the only one who knew. He'd told the man impersonating Jerry's uncle about the Skyview. "Who was he?" Lescroix whispered. "Who was the man who paid me?"

"Can't you guess?"

"No."

But even as he said that, he understood. Lescroix closed his eyes. Sat on the bed. "Your father-in-law."

The rich businessman. Patricia's father.

I'm a firm believer in kin sticking together. . . .

"He hired me?"

"We both did," Cabot said.

"To defend your wife's killer? Why?"

Cabot sighed. "Why do you think, counselor?"

Slowly, Lescroix's thoughts were forming—like ice on a November pond. He said, "Because there's no death penalty in this state."

"That's right, counselor. Maybe Jerry'd go to prison for life but that wasn't good enough for us."

And the only way Cabot and his father-in-law could get to Jerry was to make sure he was acquitted. So they hired the best criminal attorney in the country.

Lescroix laughed in disgust. Why, Cabot was the one playing *him* in the trial. Acting guilty, never explaining what he might've explained, cringing at Lescroix's far-fetched innuendos.

Suddenly the lawyer remembered Cabot's words: *Jerry's tied up right now* . . .

"Oh my God, are you going to kill him?"

"Jerry? Oh, we're just visiting right now," Cabot said. "Jerry and I and Patsy's dad. But I should tell you, I'm afraid he's pretty depressed, Jerry is. I'm worried that he might do himself some harm. He's even threatened to hang himself. That'd be a shame. But of course it's a man's own decision. Who'm I to interfere?"

"I'll tell the police," Lescroix warned.

"Will you now, counselor? I guess you could do that. But it'll be my word against yours, and I have to say that after the trial today your stock's none too high 'round here at the moment. And neither's Jerry's."

"So what're you buying?"

"Peace of mind. That's what."

"Sorry to cut this short," Cabot continued. "I think I hear some funny noises from the other room. Where Jerry is. I better run, check on him. Seem to recall seeing a rope in there."

A low, desperate moaning sounded through the line, distant.

"What was that?" Lescroix cried.

"Oh-oh, looks like I better go. So long, counselor. Hope you enjoyed your stay in Hamilton."

"Wait!"

Click.

Tunnel Girl

Sorry to bother you so early, sir."

An alarmed Ron Badgett, in a 6:00 a.m. morning daze, blinked at the suited man on his doorstep, holding a police department shield.

"I'm Detective Larry Perillo."

"What's wrong, officer?"

"You own the building at Seventy-seven Humbolt Way?"

"That's right. My company's there." Ron Badgett felt another jolt of concern course through him. He'd been fuzzy-headed and exhausted three minutes ago. Now he was thoroughly awake. "There been a fire or something?" The paunchy, middle-aged man, with thinning hair, pulled his beige terry-cloth bathrobe belt tight.

It was a cool September Saturday morning, and the two men were standing in the doorway of Ron's well-worn suburban colonial house, which hadn't quite recovered from the previous owners' three children, who'd apparently run and jumped and pounded on every accessible surface. Ron and his wife spent most of their free time fixing it up.

"No, sir, your office's fine. But we're hoping you can help us. You know the old building behind yours, across the parking lot?"

"The condemned one?"

"That's it."

Sandra, Ron's wife of eighteen years, appeared in the doorway, frowning. She wore a blue quilted robe and slippers. Her hair was mussed, and she had a sleepy, morning look that Ron still found appealing, even after eighteen years of marriage. "What's the matter, honey?"

"There's some problem with an old building behind the office." He introduced her to the policeman.

"Oh, that one they're going to tear down?" Sandra, at the moment working only occasional freelance jobs, had spent a week helping Ron move into the building. One day, at the back loading dock, she'd commented that the old building looked dangerous.

"That's right, ma'am." Perillo then added, "It seems that yesterday evening a coed from City College was taking a shortcut through the courtyard back there. Part of the building collapsed. She's trapped in one of those old delivery tunnels that used to connect the factories and warehouses in the neighborhood."

"My God," Sandra whispered.

"But she's alive?" Ron asked.

"So far. We can hear her calling for help but she doesn't sound very strong."

His wife shook her head. Ron and Sandra had a seventeen-year-old daughter, currently in school in Washington, DC, and the woman was undoubtedly thinking about their own child hurt or trapped. Nobody's as sympathetic as fellow parents.

The policeman glanced down at the morning newspaper, sitting nearby in a plastic bag on the lawn. He picked it up and extracted the paper, showed them the headline: CAN THEY SAVE TUNNEL GIRL?

A photo revealed dozens of rescue workers standing around a pile of rubble. A police dog was in the foreground, sniffing at a gaping hole in the ground. A grim-faced couple stood nearby; they were identified as the parents of the trapped girl, Tonya Gilbert. Another photo was the girl's high school yearbook picture. Ron scanned the article and learned some things about Tonya. She'd just started her senior year at City College, after spending the summer as a hiking guide at a state park on the Appalachian Trail. She was a public health major. Her father was a businessman, her mother a volunteer for a number of local charities. Tonya was an only child.

Ron tapped a sidebar article. "Hey, look at that." PARENTS OFFER $500K REWARD FOR GIRL'S RESCUE read this headline.

A half million? he thought. Then he recalled the girl's last name sounded familiar. Her father was probably the same Gilbert who owned a big financial analysis and investment bank in the city and was always appearing in the press at charity auctions and cultural benefits.

Sandra asked the detective, "How can we help?"

Perillo said, "Our rescue teams tried to get to her from the surface but it's too dangerous. The rest of the building could collapse at any minute. The city engineers'd like to try to get to her through the basement of your office."

Sandra shook her head. "But how will that help? It's nowhere near the old building."

"Our people looked over old maps of buildings that used to be in the area. There're some basements under the parking lot between your building and the collapsed one that we think haven't been filled in. We're hoping somebody can work their way to the girl from underground."

"Oh, sure, of course," Ron said. "Whatever we can do."

"Thanks much, sir."

"I'll come down right away and let you in. Just give us a few minutes to throw on some clothes."

"You can follow me." The detective gestured toward his dark blue unmarked police car.

Ron and Sandra hurried back into the house, his wife whispering, "That poor girl. . . . Let's hurry."

In the bedroom, Ron tossed his robe and pajamas onto the floor, while Sandra stepped into her dressing room to change. As he pulled on jeans and a sweatshirt, Ron clicked on the local TV station. A news crew was at the scene, and a reporter was telling the anchorman that another portion of the wall had just collapsed, but the debris had missed Tonya. She was still alive.

Thank God for that, Ron thought. He slipped on his jacket, staring at the TV screen. The camera panned to two young women standing at the police line. One wiped tears while the other held up a sign. It read: We ♥ You, Tunnel Girl.

■

RB Graphic Design was in an old coffee warehouse, a small one, near the river and across the street from City College.

Two years ago a dozen developers had decided to turn around this former industrial district of the city and convert it to lofts, chic restaurants, theaters and artsy professional quarters—the way a lot of towns seemed to be doing lately, in more or less desperate attempts to reverse the trend of flight to the homogenous mall-land of the 'burbs.

The real estate companies sunk big bucks into renovation and new construction in the eight-square-block area, while the city itself agreed to some tax breaks to get people and companies to move in and paid for some cheap street sculpture, signage and a public relations firm, which came up with a name for the district: "NeDo," for "New Downtown." This term had already been printed up on street signs and in promotional materials when it was discovered that people weren't pronouncing it "Nue-Dow," as planned, but "Nee-Due," which sounded pretty lame, like a hair spray or soft drink. But by then the name had stuck. Despite the awkward name and some other bad planning (such as forgetting that those going to chic restaurants, theaters and jobs in artsy offices might want to park their cars someplace), the development caught on. Ron Badgett, for one, knew immediately that he wanted to move his company into the area and was particularly taken by the former coffee warehouse. He couldn't explain it, he told Sandra, but he knew instinctively that it suited his personality perfectly.

Ron was also ready to move from his original office. He felt he'd exhausted the benefits of the old place, which was in the traditional city center, a boring neighborhood of 1950s office buildings, the bus station and a recently defunct secretarial school. It was a ghost town at night. Violent crime had increased in the past couple of years and Sandra hated driving to the area alone in the evenings to meet Ron after work.

But even though NeDo was starting to catch on, the move didn't work out financially for his company the way Ron had hoped. It seemed that a number of his clients preferred the old neighborhood (which offered uncongested streets, ample parking and restaurants that weren't noisy and pretentious). He'd lost a half-dozen clients, and though he'd picked up a few new ones he was still hurting from the dip in business and the cost of the move, which had been more than he'd figured on.

The money was a problem, especially to Sandra. She was more ambitious—and had more expensive tastes—than her husband, and their income had taken a hit when she'd been laid off from her job as an engineer with an energy company six months ago. He knew she would've liked him to get a steady job with a big ad agency, but he couldn't bring himself to. Ron Badgett had always been open with his wife about the fact that he had other goals than amassing money. "I have to work for myself. You know, I need to follow my creative spirit." He'd grinned ruefully. "I know that sounds stupid. But I can't help it. I have to be true to myself."

Ultimately, he believed, Sandra understood this and supported him. Besides, he loved being in NeDo and had no desire to move.

As the Badgetts now followed the speeding police car, these thoughts about the neighborhood and their fiscal situation, and personalities, however, were far from his mind; all he could think of was Tonya Gilbert, Tunnel Girl, lying beneath the collapsed building.

Ahead of them they saw the bustle of the drama: scores of emergency workers, fire trucks, police cars, onlookers kept back by yellow police tape. The press too, of course, a half-dozen vans with their station logos on the sides and crowned with satellite dishes pointed skyward.

Ron skidded to a stop in front of his building—under a prominent No Parking sign—and, with Sandra, jumped out. They followed the detective to the front door of RB Graphic Design, where several somber police and fire officials stood. They were big men, and solid women, some wearing jumpsuits and belts encrusted with rescue equipment, some in business suits or uniforms.

One of them, a white-haired man in a navy-blue uniform that had ribbons and badges on the chest, shook the Badgetts' hands as Perillo introduced them. "I'm Fire Chief Knoblock. Sure appreciate you coming down to help us out. We've got ourselves some situation here."

"My Lord, she's underneath all of that?" Sandra asked, staring through the alley beside Ron's building at a huge pile of rubble. The remaining walls of the building hovered precariously above gaping holes in the ground. They seemed ready to tumble down at any minute. A cloud of dust from the recent collapse hung in the air like gray fog.

"'Fraid so." The chief continued, "She's down about twenty-five, thirty feet in a section of an old tunnel they used to make deliveries in when these were working factories and warehouses. Miracle she's alive." The tall man, with perfect posture, shook his head. "All to save a couple blocks' walk."

"They should've had warning signs up, or something," Ron said.

"Probably did," the chief responded. "I'd guess she just ignored 'em. You know kids," Knoblock added with the air of a man who'd seen a lot of tragedy caused by teenage foolishness.

"Why did it collapse?" Ron asked.

"Nobody quite knows. The inspectors said a lot of the support beams were rotting but they didn't think it was in danger of coming down anytime soon, otherwise they would've fenced it off."

"Well, come on inside," Ron said. He opened the door and led Knoblock and the others into the building, then down into the basement. The developer hadn't spent much time renovating this part of the building and it was musty and dimly lit, but clean, thanks to Sandra's hard work during the move.

Detective Perillo asked, "One thing I was thinking, Chief. Did she have a cell phone? Maybe you could call her. She could tell you how bad she's hurt or maybe something about how we could get to her."

"Oh, she's got a phone," the chief said. "We checked the records. She made a couple of calls last night as she was leaving school—just before she fell in, we're figuring. But the cell company said it's shut off. She probably can't find it in the dark. Or maybe she can't reach it."

"Might be broken," Sandra offered.

"No," the chief explained. "The company can tell that. Phones still have some signal, even when they're off. Has to be she just can't get to it."

A fireman in a jumpsuit walked down the stairs, looked around, then cleared graphic arts supplies off an old drafting table. He spread out a map of the area around Ron's building. Two others rigged spotlights—one on the map, the other on a portion of the basement wall in the back of the building.

Knoblock took a call on his own phone. "Yes, sir . . . yes. We'll let you know."

The chief hung up. He shook his head and said in a low voice to Ron and his wife, "That was her father. Poor guy. He's pretty upset. I was talking to his wife and it seems that he and Tonya've been having some problems lately. She banged up her car over the summer and he wouldn't give her the money to fix it up. That's why she had to walk to the bus stop."

"So," Sandra said, "he thinks it's his fault she had the accident."

"And, you ask me, it's why he's offering a reward like that. I mean, five hundred thousand dollars . . . I never heard of that before. Not 'round here."

A voice called down from the top of the stairs. "Langley just showed up. He'll be down in a minute."

"Our rescue specialist," the chief explained.

"Who is he?" Ron asked.

"The number-one search-and-rescue specialist in the country. Runs a company out of Texas. Greg Langley. You ever hear of him?"

Sandra shook her head. But Ron lifted an eyebrow. "I think so. Yeah. He was on the Discovery Channel, or something."

"A and E," the chief said. "He's pretty good, from what I hear. His outfit rescues climbers and hikers who get stuck on mountains or in caves, workers trapped on oil rigs, avalanches, you name it. He's got this sort of a sixth sense, or something, for finding and saving people."

"He and his crew were in Ohio," Detective Perillo said. "Drove all night to get here."

"You were lucky you could catch him when he was free," Ron said.

Chief Knoblock said, "Actually, *he* called *us* just after the story broke about midnight. I couldn't figure out how he heard about it. But he said he's got people listening to news stories all over the country and they let him know if it sounds like a job he could take on." The chief added in a whisper, "Man seems a bit too interested in the reward for my taste. But as long as he saves that girl, that's all I care about."

The firemen finished rigging the power lines and clicked the lights on, filling the space with brilliant white illumination, just as footsteps sounded on the stairs. A group of three men and two women arrived in the basement, carting ropes and hard hats, lights, radios, metal clamps and hooks and tools that looked to Ron like mountain climbing gear. They all wore yellow jumpsuits with the words stitched on the back *Langley Services. Houston, TX.*

One of these men introduced himself as Greg Langley. He was in his forties, about five foot ten, slim but clearly strong. He had a round, freckled face, curly red hair and eyes brimming with self-assuredness.

Introductions were made. Langley glanced at Ron and Sandra, but didn't even acknowledge them. Ron felt a bit offended but gave no outward reaction to the snub.

"What's the situation?" Langley asked the officials.

Knoblock described the accident and the girl's location in the tunnel, touching places on the map, and explained about the basements connecting Ron's building with the collapsed factory.

Langley asked, "She in immediate danger?"

"We can probably get food and water to her somehow," Knoblock said. "And in this weather she's not going to die of exposure. But her voice is real weak. Makes us think she was pretty badly hurt in the fall. She could be bleeding, could have broken limbs. We just don't know."

Another fireman added, "The big danger is another cave-in. The entire site's real unstable."

"Where do we go in?" Langley asked, glancing at the cellar wall.

A city engineer examined the map and then tapped a spot on the brick. "On the other side of this wall was an old building that was torn down years ago and paved over. But most of the sub-basement rooms're intact. We think you can pick your way through them to a wooden doorway . . . about here." He touched the map. "That'll get you into this delivery tunnel." He traced along the map to an adjoining tunnel. "The girl's in the one next to it."

It was then that a faint rumbling filled the basement.

"My God," Sandra said, grabbing Ron's arm.

Knoblock lifted his radio. "What was that?" he called into the microphone.

Some static, an indiscernible word or two. Then a voice, "Another cave-in, chief."

"Oh, damn . . . is she okay?"

"Hold on. . . . We can't hear anything. Hold on."

No one in the basement spoke for a moment.

"Please," Ron whispered.

Then the chief's radio clattered again and they heard: "Okay, okay—we can hear her. Can't make out much, but it sounds like she's saying, 'Please help me.'"

"Okay," Langley snapped. "Let's get moving. I want that wall down in five minutes."

"Yessir," Knoblock said and lifted his radio again.

"No," the rescue specialist barked. "My people'll do it. It's got to be done just right. Can't leave it to . . . " His voice faded, and Ron wondered what sort of unwitting insult he'd been about to deliver. He turned to another assistant, a young woman. "Oh, here, call her father. Tell him this's the account I want the money wired to as soon as she's safe."

The woman took the slip of paper and scurried upstairs to make a call. There was silence for a moment, as the fire department and police officials looked at one another uneasily. Langley caught their eye. His glance said simply, I'm a professional. I expect to get paid for producing results. You got a problem with that, go hire somebody else.

Knoblock, Perillo and the others seemed to get the message and they turned back to the chart. The chief asked, "You want one of our people to go with you?"

"No, I'll go in alone," Langley said and began to assemble his gear.

"Got a question," Ron said. Langley ignored him. Knoblock raised an eyebrow. The graphic designer pointed down at the map. "What's this?" He traced his finger along what seemed to be a shaft leading from a street nearby to the tunnel adjacent to the one the girl was in.

One of the firemen said, "It's an old sluice. Before they put the levee in, there was a lot of flooding in those tunnels when the river overflowed. They needed serious drainage."

"How big is it?"

"I don't know . . . I'd guess three feet across."

"Could somebody get through it?"

Langley glanced up and finally spoke to him, "Who're you again?"

"I own this building."

The rescue specialist turned back to the map. "Only an idiot'd go that way. Can't you see? It goes right underneath the unstable portion of the building. It's probably already sealed off after the first collapse. Even if it wasn't, you bump one support, you *breathe* wrong, and it all comes down on top of you. Then I'd have *two* people to rescue." He gave a grim laugh. "Tunnel Girl and Tunnel Asshole."

"Sounds like you've checked it out already," Ron said pointedly, irritated at the man's haughtiness. "You work fast."

"I've been in this business a long time. I have a sense of what's a reasonable risk and what isn't. That drain isn't."

"Really?"

"Yeah, *really,*" Langley muttered."You know, this is a pretty tricky operation. You two might want to leave. We're going to bring in some heavy equipment here. People have a way of getting hurt in situations like this." He looked at Ron, then glanced at Sandra.

When Ron didn't move, Langley added, "Chief? We on the same page here?" Langley strapped on a yellow hard hat and clipped an impressive-looking cell phone to his belt.

"Uhm, Mr. Badgett," Knoblock said uneasily to Ron and Sandra. "I appreciate you helping us out. But it might be better if—"

"That's okay," the graphic designer said. "We were just leaving."

■

Outside, Ron got into the car and nodded for Sandra to join him. He drove slowly up the street, away from the site of the collapsed building and the rescue efforts, the cacophony of the lights and crowds.

"Aren't we going to stay?" she asked. "See what happens?"

"No."

"What's wrong?" she asked uneasily, watching her husband troll slowly down the deserted street, looking into the alleys and the vacant lots overrun with grass and filled with trash—locales scheduled to become part of NeDo in the future but at the moment nothing more than evidence of what the neighborhood had once been.

Finally he stopped, staring down at the ground. He climbed out of the car. Sandra joined him.

"What are you . . . ?" Her voice faded. "No."

Ron was looking at an entrance to a large drain—the one he'd pointed out on the map.

"You're not . . . No, Ron, you're not going in there."

"Five hundred thousand dollars," he whispered. "Where else are we going to get a chance for money like that?"

"No, honey. You heard what Greg said. It's dangerous."

"A half million dollars. Think about it. . . . You know business's been slow. The move set me back a lot more than I thought."

"It'll get better. You'll get more clients." Her face was a grim mask. "I don't want you to go. Really."

Ron was staring at the grate of the drainage ditch, the blackness on the other side. "I don't think it's dangerous at all. . . . Didn't it seem there was something weird about what Langley said?"

"Weird?"

"He didn't even check the sluice out. But he goes on and on about how risky it is. You're an engineer; what do you think? Isn't this the best way to get to her?"

She shrugged. "I don't do geologic work, you know that."

"Well, even to *me* it seems like the best way. . . . It was like Langley was telling everybody that there was only one way to get to the girl, his route. So nobody'd even try the drain." He nodded toward the grating. "That way he's sure he gets the reward."

Sandra fell silent for a moment. Then she shook her head. "I didn't really get that sense. He's pretty arrogant and insulting. But even if what you're saying is true, going in there still has to be risky." She pointed toward the collapsed building. "You still have to go underneath it."

"Five hundred thousand dollars, baby," he whispered.

"It's not worth getting killed."

"I'm going to do it."

"Please, Ron, no."

"I have to."

She sighed, grimacing. "I've always sensed there're sides to you that I don't know, Ron. Things that you don't share with me. But playing knight in shining armor to save some girl? I never thought of you that way. Or is it that you're just pissed off he insulted us and threw us out of our own building?" Ron didn't answer. Sandra then added, "And to be honest, honey, you aren't really in the best shape, you know."

"I'm going to be crawling, not running a marathon." He laughed, shook his head. "Something's not right about this whole thing. Langley's working some angle. And I'm not going to let him get away with it. I'm going to get that money."

"You've made up your mind," she asked in a soft voice, "haven't you?"

"That's one thing you *do* know about me: Once I've decided what I want to do, nothing's going to stop me."

Ron reached into the glove compartment and took out the flashlight. Then he walked to the trunk and found the tire iron. "My coal mining gear," he said with a weak laugh as he held up the bent metal rod. He looked at the blackness of the drain opening.

Sandra took her cell phone from the car, gripping it firmly in her hand. "Call if anything happens. I'll get somebody there as soon as I can."

He kissed her hard. And the knight—in faded jeans and an old sweatshirt, not shining armor—started into the murky opening.

■

The route through the drain was, in fact, much less risky than the doomsaying egomaniac Langley had predicted—at least in the beginning. Ron had about three hundred feet of steady crawling, impeded only by a few roots, clumps of dirt and sewage-related detritus, which was hardly pleasant but not dangerous.

He encountered a few rats but they were frightened and scurried away from him quickly. (Ron wondered if they were charging into the spot where the rescue specialist was now working his way toward Tonya. He had to admit he liked the idea of sharp-toothed rodents scaring the hell out of his rival—yeah, Sandra was partly right; Langley *had* pissed him off.)

Closer to the building, the drain became increasingly clogged. Roots had broken through the concrete walls and clustered together like pythons frozen in rigor mortis, and the way was partly blocked by piles of dried mud nearly as hard as concrete. His back in agony, his legs cramping, Ron now made slower progress. Still, he could see that—not surprisingly—Langley had been wrong. The drain walls were solid and in no danger of collapse.

Tunnel Asshole . . .

Ron kept going, checking his progress by looking through the access holes that opened into basements and the old delivery tunnels. Finally he arrived at the narrow one that, he recalled from the map, led to a wooden door opening into the tunnel where Tonya Gilbert was. He put his ear to the opening and listened.

"Help me," the girl's muted voice rasped. "Please help me . . ." She was probably no more than thirty feet from him.

The opening into this side tunnel was small, but by working a few old bricks out of the wall with the tire iron he was able to create enough space to crawl through. He climbed onto the dry earth of the tunnel and, standing, shone his light around. Yes, it was the one right next to the girl's.

He'd done it! He gotten to Tunnel Girl first.

Then he heard a noise:

Thud . . . thud . . .

What was it? Was the girl signaling?

No, the sound was coming from a different place.

Thud . . .

Ron suddenly realized what it was. Greg Langley had arrived. He was at the far wall of the tunnel, breaking his way through another old door, which connected this shaft to the deserted basement next door. The sound of breaking wood told Ron that Langley would be inside in three or four minutes. Then the pounding stopped, and Ron heard the man's muffled voice. Ron shut the light out, alarmed. What if Langley wasn't alone? He walked quietly to the door the rescue specialist had been breaking through and listened. He heard the man say, "I'll call you back."

So, he was only on his phone. But who was he talking to? And what had he been saying? Had someone found out Ron was coming and was a threat to getting the reward?

Thud . . .

Langley had resumed breaking through the wooden door. Ron flattened himself against the wall beside the wooden door. Suddenly there was a loud crack and several boards fell inward, creating about a two-by-two-foot opening. Light from Langley's lantern shone into the dim tunnel. Ron pressed hard against the wall, breathing shallowly, not moving.

Finally something emerged from the opening, a wicked-looking pickax. It seemed more like a weapon than a tool. Then a beam from another flashlight—a powerful one—shot throughout the tunnel and swung from side to side. It narrowly missed catching Ron in its circle of light. He squinted and leaned back against the wall as hard as he could, rubbing his eyes to get them used to the brilliance.

There was a pause and then finally he could make out Langley's head emerging through the opening. He got halfway through, then once again started to play the flashlight around the tunnel.

Just before the illumination hit Ron's legs, the graphic designer lifted the tire iron and swung it hard into the back of Langley's head, just below the hard hat. It struck him solidly and the man grunted and collapsed onto his belly.

Once I've decided what I want to do, nothing's going to stop me. . . .

As quietly as he could, Ron gathered rocks and bricks from the floor and began piling them onto the unconscious Greg Langley, creating what he felt was a very realistic scene of a man caught by a surprise cave-in.

■

Two days later Ron Badgett and his wife were standing near the podium in front of City College, awaiting the start of the press conference. A hundred people milled about. Behind the lectern was a blow-up from a local newspaper, mounted to a curtain that rippled in the wind. The headline read: TUNNEL GIRL SAVED!

Sandra had her arm hooked through her husband's. He enjoyed her proximity and the flowery smell of her perfume. She had a smile on her face. The atmosphere among the crowd was festive, giddy even. There's nothing like rescuing trapped children to supercharge community spirit.

Waving and smiling, Chief Knoblock, Tonya Gilbert and her parents walked through the crowd and up to the podium. After a lengthy round of cheers and applause, the chief quieted the onlookers like a conductor in front of an orchestra and said, "Ladies and gentlemen, could I have your attention please? . . . Thank you. I'm delighted to present to you Tonya Gilbert. She was just released from Memorial Hospital this morning. I know she wants to say a word to you."

More wild clapping and shouts.

The pretty girl, with a small bandage over her forehead and a blue cast on her ankle and another on her wrist, stepped shyly to the microphone. Blushing fiercely, she started to say something, but her throat caught. She started over. "Like, I just want to say, you know, thanks to everybody. I was pretty freaked. So, you know . . . uhm, thanks."

Her lack of articulation didn't stop the crowd from exploding in applause and cheers once again.

Then the chief introduced the girl's parents. The businessman, in a blue blazer and gray slacks, stepped forward to the microphone, while his wife, beaming a smile, put her arm around her daughter's shoulders. The businessman thanked the fire department and police for their heroic efforts, and the citizens of the town for their support.

"But my deepest appreciation goes to the man who risked his life to save my little girl. And as a token of that appreciation I want to give him this." The businessman held up a framed, three-foot-long mock-up of a check for $500,000. "Which represents the sum I've ordered deposited into his account."

More raucous applause; large sums of money, just like rescued youngsters, are guaranteed crowd-pleasers.

Gilbert added, "Please join me in thanking . . . Mr. Greg Langley."

A brace on his neck, a bandage on his hand, the rescue specialist walked slowly to the podium, limping. He seemed agitated, though Ron guessed it had less to do with the pain from the injuries than his impatience with hokeyness like this. He took the big check and passed it quickly to his assistant.

Tonya's father continued, "What he did took great personal courage and sacrifice. Even after being buried in a cave-in and nearly killed, Mr. Langley continued to crawl to the tunnel where our Tonya was trapped and got her to safety. You'll have the gratitude of our family forever."

The crowd seemed to want a speech but all Langley said was an impatient "Thanks a lot." He waved and left fast—on to more rescues and more rewards, Ron assumed. He felt a burst of regret he'd only brained the guy when he'd simulated the cave-in and hadn't caused more serious damage; he definitely deserved a broken wrist or jawbone.

As they drove home, Sandra was clearly pleased the girl had been rescued but she said with some genuine sympathy in her voice, "Sorry you missed out on the reward, honey."

What he'd told his wife was that the drain was so clogged with roots and mud that he'd only gotten halfway to the tunnel.

She added, "I know you're disappointed you didn't get what you'd wanted. But at least the girl's safe . . . and so are you. That's the important thing."

He kissed her hair.

Thinking: Ah, but you're wrong, dear. I got *exactly* what I wanted.

Though he could hardly share this thought with her. Just like there was a *lot* about him he couldn't share: Such as why he'd picked the old coffee warehouse in the first place: because it had windows facing the main door of City College—providing a perfect view for watching the girls leave, making it easy to pick who'd be his victims. This is what he'd meant when he'd told her the place suited his personality; it had nothing to do with having an artsy office in a vibrant redevelopment. He needed a new hunting ground after the secretarial school across from his old office had closed—the school from which he'd kidnaped two coeds within the past year and videotaped their leisurely murders. (Ironically Ron Badgett himself was one of the reasons that violent crime had increased lately in the old city center.)

A few weeks ago, just after he'd moved to the new building, Ron had spotted gorgeous Tonya Gilbert leaving class. He couldn't stop thinking about the clinging pink tank top she wore, her long hair flying in the breeze, her slim legs—couldn't stop picturing her tied down in a cellar, Ron slipping the garrote around her beautiful neck.

Deciding that Tonya'd be his first victim in NeDo, he'd followed her for several days and learned she always took a shortcut from the school down the alley beside his office and continued through the courtyard of the deserted building behind it. Ron had planned the abduction carefully. He'd found that an old tunnel went right underneath her route and had laid a trap—removing a grate and covering it with thin Sheetrock, painted to look like concrete. When she'd walked over it last night, she'd fallen through and dropped twenty feet to the floor of the tunnel. He'd climbed down to her, made sure she was unconscious, shut off her cell phone and threw it down a drainpipe (he'd been troubled to learn from helpful Chief Knoblock that cell phones still have a signal when they're off; he'd have to remember that in the future).

Leaving her in the tunnel, he'd returned to the surface to seal up the open grate with plywood. But as he was hammering the grate back into place he must've hit a weakened beam. It collapsed and, as he'd scrabbled to safety, half the building came down. There was no way to get back inside from there. Worse, one of the sub-basement walls had collapsed too, exposing the tunnel where the girl lay.

Tonya was still unconscious and wouldn't know what Ron had done, nor could she identify him. But rescue workers would undoubtedly find the workroom off the adjacent tunnel where he had his knives and ropes and video camera, all of which bore his fingerprints. There was also a videotape in the camera that he sure as hell didn't want the police to see. He'd tried to climb back down to get his things but the building was far too unstable. He was looking for another route down when the first fire trucks arrived—somebody must have heard the collapse and called 9-1-1—and Ron had fled.

He'd returned back home, desperately trying to figure out how to return for the damning evidence. While Sandra slept, he'd stayed transfixed to the TV all night, watching the coverage about Tunnel Girl, praying that they wouldn't get into the tunnel before he had a chance, somehow, to beat them to it. Praying too that she wouldn't die—his only hope to get to the workroom was to pretend he was trying to rescue her himself.

Then, after a tortured, sleepless night, the police arrived at his doorstep (his alarm at seeing Detective Perillo had nothing to do with the possibility of a fire-damaged office, of course).

Despite this scare, though, it worked out for the best that they'd asked for his help; it was through Knoblock and the city engineers that he learned that there might be another way to get back into the tunnel and collect what he'd left behind last night. After working his way through the drain and knocking Langley out, he'd managed to get all his gear, obliterate his foot- and fingerprints and slip out of the tunnel without Tonya's hearing him. On the way back down the sluice he'd disposed of the weapons, ropes and camera by pitching them down fissures in the drain and filling in the spaces with dirt and mud. (He did, of course, keep the videotape of the student he'd last killed; it was one of his better ones.)

Oh, he was a bit sorry he couldn't be the one to rescue the girl and collect the reward. But, if he had, the press might've looked into his life and learned a few interesting things—for instance, the fact that he'd always chosen to live or work near colleges from which coeds had disappeared over the years.

Besides, he'd been honest with Sandra regarding one other thing: That he had values other than making money. The reward meant little. There was indeed, as she'd observed, another side to him, a more important side.

I need to follow my creative spirit. I have to be true to myself. . . .

Of course, that creative spirit didn't involve graphic design; it centered around ropes and knives and beautiful college girls.

"I've got to say," Sandra said, "I'm still not convinced that everything was the way it seemed to be."

Ron eyed his wife cautiously. "No?" He hoped she wasn't on to him; he loved her, and he'd prefer not to kill her.

"It was just odd, Langley calling right after the accident. You know, I actually wondered if maybe he was behind the whole thing."

"No kidding?"

"Yeah, maybe he travels around and booby-traps buildings and oil rigs, then after somebody's trapped he calls and gets a reward or a fee to rescue the victims." She gave a soft giggle. "And you know what else I thought?"

"What's that?"

"That maybe Tonya and Langley were in on it together."

"Together?" Seeing that his wife's suspicions were headed in a harmless direction, he could laugh.

"I mean, she and her father were having problems—he wouldn't pay to fix her car, remember? She might've wanted to get even with him. Oh, and did you see that she was a hiking guide on the Appalachian Trail? Maybe she met Langley when he was rescuing somebody at the park. I mean, she wasn't very badly hurt. Maybe they staged the whole thing together, Tonya and Langley, to split the reward."

Ron supposed this might make sense to an outside observer. Of course, now that he thought about it, that same observer might also speculate that Sandra *herself* could've been in collusion with Langley, whom she might've met through her work for an oil company and, as an engineer, rigged a trap for the girl after she'd noticed the building during Ron's move.

Interesting takes on the incident, thought an amused Ron Badgett, who was, of course, the only one in the world who knew exactly what had happened to the girl.

"Could be," he said. "But I guess that's between Gilbert and Langley now."

Ron steered the car into the driveway and, leaving the engine running, climbed out and opened the door for his wife. "I'm going to head back to the office, see how they're coming with the basement wall." The city was paying to have the hole in his cellar repaired.

Sandra kissed him good-bye and said she'd have dinner ready when he got back home.

Ron climbed back into the driver's seat and drove eagerly to NeDo. In truth, he couldn't care less about the basement wall. The last daytime classes at City College were over in twenty minutes and he wanted to be at his desk by then, in front of his window, so he could watch the coeds leaving the school on their way home.

Tunnel Girl had been saved; Ron Badgett needed someone new.

Locard's Principle

I t's politically sensitive."

"Politics." Lincoln Rhyme offered a distracted grunt to the heavyset, disheveled man who was leaning against a dresser in the bedroom of the criminalist's Upper West Side town house.

"No, it's important."

"And *sensitive*," Rhyme echoed. He wasn't pleased with visitors in general; was much less pleased with visitors at eight-thirty in the morning.

Detective Lon Sellitto pushed away from the dresser and took the coffee Rhyme's aide, Thom, offered. He sipped.

"That's not bad."

"Thanks," Thom said.

"No," Sellitto corrected. "I mean his hand. Look."

A quadriplegic, injured while running a crime scene some years ago, Rhyme had been undergoing therapy and had regained some slight movement in his right hand. He was immensely proud of the accomplishment but it was against his nature to gloat—about personal achievements, at least; he ignored Sellitto and continued squeezing a soft rubber ball. Yes, some movement in his hand had indeed returned but the feelings were haywire. He felt textures and temperatures that didn't match the properties of the sponge rubber.

Another grunt. He flicked the ball away with his index finger. "I'm not really crazy about drop-ins, Lon."

"We got a crunch, Linc."

A politically sensitive one. Rhyme continued, "Amelia and I've got a few other cases going on at the moment, you know." He sipped the strong coffee through a straw. The tumbler was mounted on the headboard to his right. To his left was a microphone, connected to a voice recognition system that in turn was hooked into an environmental control unit, the central nervous system of his bedroom.

"Like I said, a crunch."

"Hmm." More coffee.

Rhyme carefully examined Sellitto—the Major Cases detective with whom he used to work frequently when Rhyme had run NYPD's crime scene unit. He seemed tired. Rhyme reflected that however early Rhyme had wakened, Sellitto had probably been up several hours before, responding to the 10–29 homicide call.

Sellitto explained that the entrepreneur and philanthropist Ronald Larkin, fifty-five, had just been shot to death in the bedroom of his Upper East Side town house. The first responders found a dead body, a wounded and sobbing wife, very little evidence and no witnesses whatsoever.

Both the feds and the NYPD upper echelons wanted Rhyme and his partner, Amelia Sachs, to work the scene, with Sellitto as lead detective. Rhyme was often the choice for big cases because, despite his reclusive nature, he was well known to the public and his presence suggested the mayor and brass were serious about a collar.

"You know Larkin?"

"Refresh my memory." Unless facts had to do with his job—consulting forensic scientist, or "criminalist"—Rhyme didn't pay much attention to trivia.

"Ronald Larkin, come on, Linc. Everybody knows him."

"Lon, the sooner you tell me, the sooner I'll be able to say no."

"He's been in that kind of mood," Thom told Sellitto.

"Yeah, for the last twenty years."

"Onward and upward," Rhyme said with cheerful impatience, sipping more coffee through the straw.

"Ronald Larkin hit it big in energy. Pipelines, electricity, water, geothermal."

"He was a good guy," Thom interjected, feeding Rhyme a breakfast of eggs and a bagel. "Environmentally conscious."

"Happy day," Rhyme said sourly.

Sellitto helped himself to a second bagel and continued, "He'd retired last year, turns the company over to somebody else and starts a foundation with his brother. Doing good things in Africa, Asia and Latin America. He lives in LA but he and his wife have a place here. They flew into town last night. Early this morning they're in bed and somebody fires through the window, takes him out."

"Robbery?"

"Nope."

Really? Rhyme grew more intrigued. He turned quickly away from the incoming bagel, like a baby avoiding a spoon of mashed carrots.

"Lincoln," Thom said.

"I'll eat later. The wife?"

"She got hit but rolled onto the floor, grabbed the phone, called nine-one-one. The shooter didn't wait around to finish the job."

"What'd she see?"

"Not much, I don't think. She's in the hospital. Haven't had a chance to talk to her more than a few words. She's hysterical. They only got married a month ago."

"Ah, a recent wife. . . . Even if she was wounded, that doesn't mean she didn't *hire* somebody to kill hubby and hurt her a little in the process."

"You know, Linc, I've done this before. . . . I checked already. There's no motive. She's got money of her own from Daddy. And she signed a prenup. In the event of his death all she gets is a hundred thousand and can keep the engagement ring. Not worth the needle, you know."

"That's the deal he cut with his wife? No wonder he's rich. You mentioned politically sensitive?"

"Here's one of the richest men in the country, way involved in the Third World, and he gets offed in our backyard. The mayor's not happy. The brass isn't happy."

"Which means you must be one sad puppy."

"They want you and Amelia, Linc. Come on, it's an interesting case. You like challenges."

After the accident at the subway crime scene that left him disabled, Rhyme's life became very different from his life before. Back then he would prowl through the playground that is New York City, observing people and where they lived and what they did, collecting samples of soil, building materials, plants, insects, trash, rocks . . . anything that might help him run a case. His inability to do this now was terribly frustrating. And, always independent, he detested relying on anyone else.

But Lincoln Rhyme had always lived a cerebral life. Before the accident, boredom had been his worst enemy. Now, it was the same. And Sellitto—intentionally, of course—had just teased him with two words that often got his attention.

Interesting . . . challenge . . .

"So, what do you say, Linc?"

Another pause. He glanced at the half-eaten bagel. He'd lost his appetite altogether. "Let's get downstairs. See if we can find out a little more about Mr. Larkin's demise."

"Good," said Thom, sounding relieved. He was the one who often took the brunt of Rhyme's bad moods when he was involved in *uninteresting, unchallenging* cases, as had been the situation lately.

The handsome blond aide, far stronger than his slim physique suggested, dressed Rhyme in sweats and executed a sitting transfer to move him from the elaborate motorized bed into an elaborate motorized wheelchair, a sporty red Storm Arrow. Using the one working finger of his left hand, the ring finger, Rhyme maneuvered the chair into the tiny elevator that took him down to the first floor of the Central Park West town house.

Once there, he steered into the parlor, which bore no resemblance to the Victorian sitting room it had once been. The place was now a forensic lab that would rival those in a medium-size town anywhere in America. Computers, microscopes, chemicals, petri dishes, beakers, pipettes, shelves containing books and supplies. Not a square inch was unoccupied, except for the examination tables. Wires like sleeping snakes lay everywhere.

Sellitto clomped down the stairs, finishing the bagel—either his or Rhyme's.

"I better track down Amelia," Rhyme said. "Let her know we've got a scene to run."

"Oh, kinda forgot to mention," Sellitto said as he chewed. "I called her already. She's probably at the scene by now."

■

Amelia Sachs never got over the somber curtain that surrounded the site of a homicide.

She believed this was good, though. To feel the sorrow and the outrage at intentional death pushed her to do the job that much better.

Standing in front of the three-story town house on Manhattan's Upper East Side, the tall, redheaded detective was aware of this pall now, and perhaps felt it a bit more than she normally would have, knowing that Ron Larkin's death could affect many, many needy people around the world. What would happen to the foundation now that he was gone?

"Sachs? Where are we?" Rhyme's impatient voice cut through her headset. She turned the volume down.

"Just got here," she replied, worrying her fingernail. She tended to hurt herself in small, compulsive ways—particularly when she was about to search a scene where a tragedy like this had occurred. She felt the pressure of getting it right. To make sure the killer was identified and collared.

She was in working clothes: not the dark suits she favored as a detective, but the white hooded overalls worn by crime scene searchers, to make certain that they didn't contaminate the scene with their own hair, sloughed-off epidermal cells and any of the thousands of bits of trace evidence we constantly carry around with us.

"I don't see anything, Sachs. What's the problem?"

"There. How's that?" She clicked a switch on her headset.

"Ah, perfect. Hmm. Did that used to be a geranium?"

Sachs was looking at a planter containing a shriveled plant beside the front door. "You're talking to the wrong girl, Rhyme. I buy 'em, I plant 'em, I kill 'em."

"I'm told they need water occasionally."

Rhyme was in his town house about a mile and a half away, across Central Park, at the moment but was seeing exactly what Sachs saw, thanks to a high-definition video feed, running from a tiny camera mounted on her headset to the CSU's rapid response vehicle. From there it continued its wireless journey onward, ending up on a flat-screen monitor two feet in front of the criminalist. They'd worked together for years, with Rhyme generally in his lab or bedroom and Sachs working the crime scenes herself, reporting to him via radio. They'd tried video in the past but the resulting image wasn't clear enough to be helpful; Rhyme had bullied the NYPD into paying some big bucks for an HD system.

They'd tested it before but this was the first time it would be used on a case.

Carrying the basic crime scene equipment, Sachs started forward. She glanced down at the doormat, which contained a lightning bolt above the letters LES, for Larkin Energy Services.

"His logo?"

"I'd guess," she replied. "You read the article about him, Rhyme?"

"Missed it."

"He was one of the most popular bosses in the country."

Rhyme grunted. "All it takes is one disgruntled employee. I always wondered about that word. Is a happy employee 'gruntled'? Where's the scene?"

She continued into the town house.

A uniformed officer stood downstairs. He looked up and nodded.

"Where's his wife?" Sachs asked. She wanted to get the chronology of events.

But the woman, the officer explained, was still at the hospital being treated for a wound. She was expected to be released soon. Two detectives from Major Cases were with her.

"I'll want to talk to her, Rhyme."

"We'll have Lon get her over here after she's released. Where's the bedroom. I can't see it." His tone suggested he was struggling not to be impatient.

Sachs sometimes thought that his gruffness was a means to shelter himself from the emotional dangers of police work. Sometimes she believed that it was simply his nature to be gruff.

"Bedroom?"

"Upstairs, Detective." The patrolman nodded.

She went up two flights of steep, narrow steps.

The site of the murder was a large bedroom decorated in French provincial style. The furniture and art were undoubtedly expensive but Sachs found that there were so many flourishes and scrolls and draped cloth—in gaudy yellows and greens and golds—that the room set her on edge. A designer's room, not a homeowner's room.

Near the far window was the bed, ironically underneath an old painting of shot birds on a kitchen table. The bedclothes were on the floor, flung there by the medical crews attending to Ronald Larkin, she supposed. The sheet and pillows revealed a large brown bloodstain.

Sachs stepped closer and wondered if there'd been—

"Any slug penetration?" Rhyme asked.

She smiled. Those words were going to be the next in her thoughts. She'd forgotten he was seeing exactly what she was.

"Doesn't seem to be." She could find no bullet holes on Larkin's side of the bed. "We'll have to check with the medical examiner."

"Tells me he might've used fragmenting bullets."

Professional killers sometimes bought or made rounds that broke apart when they hit flesh—to cause more damage and be more likely to inflict fatal wounds. Fired from this close—about six feet away—you would have expected a normal slug to continue through the skull and exit.

"What's that?" Rhyme asked. "To your left."

"There we go." She was looking at a bullet hole in the side of a gilded bedside table, bits of fiber protruded. Sachs picked up the pillow. The slugs had pierced it and continued on. She found another hole in the wall. And on the floor a smaller bloodstain, from the wife's wound, she supposed. There were bits of dull lead on the floor. "Yep. Frags."

She shook her head.

"What're you doing, Sachs? You're making me dizzy."

"Oh. Forgot we're attached, Rhyme. I was just thinking about the slugs. The pain."

Fragmenting bullets tend to be less numbing than regular rounds and cause more agony as the pieces fan out in the body.

"Yes, well." Rhyme added nothing more.

Sachs would take samples and photos later. Now she wanted to get a sense of how the crime had occurred. She stepped outside onto the small balcony—the home of three more drought-stricken plants. It was clear where the killer had stood, aiming through the window. He might've intended to break in and shoot from closer but had been deterred by the locked windows and French door. Rather than waking his victims by trying to jimmy the lock he'd smashed the glass and fired through the hole.

"How'd he get there? From the roof?" Rhyme asked. "Ah, no, I see. What the hell's on the hook?"

Sachs was wondering the same. She was gazing at a grappling hook, from which a rope dangled into the backyard garden below. She examined the hook.

"Cloth, Rhyme. Flannel. Looks like he cut a shirt up."

"So nobody'd hear it make contact when he threw it. Clever boy. I assume it's a knotted rope?"

"Yeah, how'd you know?" She looked over the balcony at the thirty-foot black rope. The cord had knots tied in it about every two feet.

"Even the best athletes can't climb a rope thinner than about an inch. You can climb *down* one but not up. Gravity—one of the four universal forces in physics, by the way. It's the weakest one, but it still works pretty damn well. Hard to beat it. Okay, Sachs, walk the grid and collect the collectibles. Then come on home."

■

"Been having a *dis*-cussion with one of my buddies. Here we are, all cozy in BK. Hey, hey, smile when I'm talking 'bout you."

Fred Dellray was on the other end of the phone, in Brooklyn apparently. Rhyme could picture him with one of his CIs. The tall, lanky FBI agent, with piercing eyes as dark as his skin, ran a network of confidential informants—the chic term for snitches. Much of Dellray's work nowadays was counterterrorism and he'd developed a number of international connections.

One of whom was apparently discussing rumors with Dellray about the Ronald Larkin killing. (Though CIs never really *discussed* anything with the agent. Either they told him what he wanted to know or they didn't, and in the case of the latter, good luck.)

"Word is goin' 'round, Lincoln, that this shooter is a serious *pro*-fessional, know what I mean? Just in case you couldn'ta figured that one out on your own. I mean, money, money, money. No dollar *a*-mount but think way outside the Wal-Mart price tag for a kill."

"Any details on the shooter? Description?"

"Only deets are: U.S. citizen but may have other passports. Spent a lot of time overseas, trained in Europe, word is. Africa, and Middle East connections lately. But then all the bad boys do."

"Mercenary?"

"Most likely."

Rhyme had assisted in several cases involving mercenary soldiers, one not too long ago, in fact, an arms importing scheme in Brooklyn. Rhyme had dealt with many types of criminals in his career but he'd found the mercenaries to be, on the whole, far more dangerous than your average street thug, even those in the mob. They often felt a moral justification in killing, were extremely smart and often had a worldwide network of contacts. Unlike a punk in Tony Soprano's crew, they knew how to slip across borders and disappear into jurisdictions where you'd never find them.

"Any thoughts on who hired him?"

"Nup, not a skinny li'l fact on *that* one."

"Working with backup?"

"Dunno. But lots of 'em do."

"Why was Larkin hit?" Rhyme asked into the speakerphone.

"Ah, that'd be the other *un*-known. . . ." He apparently turned aside to say something to his snitch, who replied in a fast, eager-to-please voice, though Rhyme couldn't make out his words. Dellray came back on. "Sorry, Lincoln. No reasons my good friend here heard about. And I *know* he'd share with me. 'Cause that's the kinda friend he aspires to be. Wish I had more for you, Lincoln. I'll keep lookin."

"Appreciate it, Fred." They hung up.

He turned to the man sitting on a stool next to him and nodded a greeting.

Mel Cooper had arrived when Rhyme was on the phone with Dellray. He was a slightly built, balding man somewhere in his thirties, precise of movement (he was a champion ballroom dancer). Cooper was a forensic lab technician, based in the Crime Scene headquarters in Queens. Rhyme, who'd hired the tech at the NYPD years ago, occasionally still shanghaied him to work on cases here in the town house. He now shoved his thick glasses up on his nose. They discussed the mercenary angle, though Rhyme could see that the news didn't mean much to him. Cooper preferred dealing with the information provided by microscopes, density gradient units and computers to that offered by human beings.

A prejudice that Rhyme largely shared.

A few minutes later the criminalist heard the front door open and Amelia Sachs's confident stride on the marble. Then silence as she hit the carpet and finally a different sound on the wood floor.

She stepped inside, bearing two cartons of evidence.

A smiling greeting to Mel Cooper, then she kissed Rhyme and set the cartons down on an examining table.

Cooper and Sachs both pulled on powder-free latex gloves.

And they got to work.

"Weapon first," Rhyme said.

They pieced together the bullets and learned that they were .32 caliber, probably fired from an automatic—Sachs found bits of fireproof fiber that would have come from a sound suppressor, and silencers are not effective with revolvers, only autoloaders or single-shot weapons. Rhyme noted again the killer's professional quality that Dellray had alluded to, since he'd taken the time to pick up the spent shell casings from the balcony; automatics eject the used brass.

Unfortunately the bullets were too shattered to reveal anything about the lands and grooves—the rifling in the barrel—

which could in turn help identify the type of pistol the killer had used. The medical examiner might find some intact slugs during the autopsy, but Rhyme doubted it; bone will easily shatter fragile bullets like these.

"Friction ridges?" The technical term for fingerprints.

"Zip. Some latex glove marks on the window. Looks like he wiped some dirt away to get a better shot."

Rhyme grunted in frustration. "Shoe tread marks?"

"None on the balcony. And in the garden at the foot of the rope? He obliterated his prints before he left."

The grappling hook was a CMI brand with epoxy-coated tines. They'd been wrapped in strips of gray and blue flannel, cut, as Sachs speculated, from an old shirt—no identifying label, of course.

Pro-fessional . . .

The knotted rope was Mil-Spec 550 chute cord, black, with a nylon braided shroud over seven inner lines.

Cooper, who'd gone online to get a profile of the rope, looked up from the computer and reported, "Sold all over the country. And it's cheap. He'd've paid cash for it."

It was far better to have expensive evidence, bought with traceable credit cards.

Sachs handed a small plastic envelope to Mel Cooper. "I found this near the grappling hook."

"What is it?" he asked, looking at the small fleck inside.

"Lint, I think. Might be from his pockets. I figured he pulled out his weapon as soon as he climbed over the railing."

"I'll burn a sample," Cooper said and turned to a large machine sitting in the corner of the lab, switching it on.

"How about trace?" Rhyme asked.

"Nothing in the garden or the wall he scaled to get into the backyard. On the balcony, we've got a few things. Dirt from the garden. Then sand and some other dirt that doesn't match what's in the garden or the planters. A bit of rubber—maybe from the sole of a boot or shoe. Two hairs—black and curly. No bulb attached."

This meant that there could be no DNA analysis; you need the root of the hair for that. Still, the strands had most likely come from the killer. Ron Larkin had pure gray hair and his wife was a redhead.

Mel Cooper looked up from the computer screen of the gas chromatograph mass spectrometer, which had run an analysis of the lint. "He's a bodybuilder, I'd guess. Dianabol. Steroid used by athletes."

"What kind of sports?" Rhyme asked.

"You're asking the wrong person, Lincoln. I don't do a performance-enhanced foxtrot or waltz. But if he's got traces in his pocket lint I think it's safe to say he's serious about it."

"And then this . . ." Sachs held up another plastic bag. At first glance, it appeared empty. But with his magnifying glasses on, Cooper found and extracted a small brown fiber. He held it up for Rhyme to see.

"Good catch, Sachs," Rhyme said, straining his head closer. "Nothing gets by you. What is it?"

Cooper put the fiber under an optical stereo microscope and bent over the twin eyepieces. He then turned to a computer and typed with lightning-fast fingers. "I think . . ." He looked back to the microscope. "It's coir fiber."

"Which is?"

"I'm finding out." Cooper read for a moment then reported: "Used for ropes mostly. Also rugs, runners, coasters, decorative nicknacks."

"But not the rope he rode in on?" Rhyme asked.

"No. That's pure nylon. This is something else. Coir comes from coconut. The biggest producers are in Malaysia, Indonesia and Africa."

"Doesn't exactly point directly to his front door now, does it? What else do we have?"

"That's it."

"Check the sand and dirt. GC 'em."

A gas chromatograph test revealed that the trace contained significant levels of diesel fuel and saltwater.

"But a special kind of fuel," he said, reading the screen of the nearby computer. "It's got microbiocides in it. With the saltwater that means its probably marine fuel. Diesel fuel in ships often gets contaminated with microorganisms. The manufacturers put in an additive to prevent that."

Sachs said, "So, he's got a boat. Or lives near a dock."

"Or came ashore by boat," Rhyme said. Vessels were still the most untraceable way to get into the country on the Eastern Seaboard—and also one of the best ways to avoid roadblocks and surveillance if you wanted to travel around the New York area.

"Let's add it all to a chart. Thom! If you'd be . . . Thom?"

"Yes?" The aide walked into the parlor. Like Sachs and Cooper he was wearing gloves but his were yellow and had the name *Playtex* on them.

"Could you jot down our findings to date?" Rhyme nodded toward the whiteboard and Thom stripped off the gloves and wrote what his boss dictated.

RONALD LARKIN HOMICIDE

- Coir fiber.
- Dirt from garden below the balcony.
- Dark hairs, curly. No bulb attached.
- Bit of rubber, black, possibly from sole of shoe.
- Dirt and sand with traces of marine diesel fuel, saltwater.
- No friction ridges, tread marks, tool marks.
- Lint containing traces of Dianabol steroid. Athlete?
- .32 caliber automatic, sound suppressor, fragmentation bullets.

- CMI grappling hook, wrapped in strips of old flannel shirt.
- Mil-Spec 550 rope, knotted. Black.

Suspect:
- U.S. citizen, other passports?
- trained in Europe.
- mercenary with African, Middle East connections.
- no motive.
- high fee.
- employer unknown.

Rhyme scanned the list. His eyes fixed on one item.

"The rope," Rhyme said.

"Well . . . " Sachs looked at Cooper. "I thought—"

"I *know* it's nylon. And it's untraceable. But what about it's so *interesting*?"

Sachs shook her head. "I give."

"The knots. They've been compressed ever since he tied them."

Cooper said, "Still don't get it, Lincoln."

He smiled. "Look at them like little surprise packages of evidence. I wonder what's inside, don't you? Let's open them up."

"You mean me, right?" Cooper said.

"I'd love to help, Mel. But . . ." Rhyme gave a smile.

The tech picked up the rope in his gloved hands. He started to untie a knot. "Like iron."

"So much the better for us. Whatever's inside has been trapped nice and tight since he tied them."

"*If* there's anything there at all," Cooper said. "This could be a total waste of time."

"I like that, Mel. It sums up the whole business of crime scene work, wouldn't you say?"

■

When Rhyme had lived alone, the front parlor of his town house— across the hall from the lab—had been used as a storeroom. But now that Sachs was living here part of the time she and Thom had redecorated, turned it into a comfortable living room.

There were contemporary Asian paintings and silk screens, from NoHo and East Village galleries, a large portrait of Houdini (a present from a woman they'd worked with on a case some years ago), a Blue Dog print, two large flower arrangements and comfortable furniture imported all the way from New Jersey.

On the mantel rested pictures of Sachs's father and mother and of her as a teenage girl, peeking out from under the hood of a '68 Dodge Charger she and her father worked on for months before finally admitting to themselves that the patient was terminal.

And her history wasn't the only one represented in the parlor.

She'd sent Thom on a mission into the basement of the town house where he'd rummaged through boxes and returned with framed decorations and citations from Rhyme's days with the NYPD. Personal photographs, as well. Several of them showed Rhyme during his Illinois childhood, with his parents and other relatives. One was of the boy and his folks in front of their house, beside a large blue sedan. The parents smiled at the camera. Lincoln was smiling as well, but his was a different expression—one of curiosity—and the eyes were looking to the side at something off camera.

One snapshot depicted a slim, intense, teenage Lincoln. He was wearing a school track uniform.

Thom now opened the front door and ushered three people into the room: Lon Sellitto, as well as a portly sixtyish man in a gray suit and minister's collar and, gripping his arm, a woman with pale skin and eyes as red as her hair. She had no reaction to the wheelchair.

"Mrs. Larkin," the criminalist said. "I'm Lincoln Rhyme. This is Amelia Sachs."

"Call me Kitty, please." She nodded a greeting.

"John Markel," the reverend said and shook Sachs's hand, gave a sallow smile to Rhyme.

He explained that his diocese, on Manhattan's Upper East Side, operated several charities in the Sudan and Liberia and ran a school in the Congo. "Ron and I have worked together for years. We were going to have lunch today, about our work over there." He sighed and shook his head. "Then I heard the news."

He'd hurried to the hospital to be with Kitty and then said he'd accompany her here.

"You don't have to stay, John," the widow said. "But thank you for coming."

"Edith and I want you to spend the night with us. We don't want you alone," the man said.

"Oh, thank you, John, but I should be with Ron's brother and his family. And his son too."

"I understand. But if you need anything, please call."

She nodded and embraced him.

Before he left, Sachs asked the minister if he had any ideas about who the killer might be. The question caught him off guard. "Killing someone like Ron Larkin? It's inexplicable. I'd have no idea who'd want him dead."

Thom saw the minister out, and Kitty sat on a couch. The aide returned a moment later with a tray of coffee. Kitty took a cup but didn't sip any. She let it sit between her clasped hands.

Sachs nodded at the large bandage on her forearm. "Are you all right?"

"Yes," she said, as if the only pain came from speaking. She stared at her arm. "The doctor said it was part of one of the bullets. It broke apart." She looked up. "It might have been from the one that killed Ron. I don't know what to think about that."

Rhyme deferred to Sachs, who had more people skills than he, and the detective asked her about the shooting.

Kitty and her husband had been traveling around the country to meet with the heads of companies and other not-for-profits. Last night they'd flown in from Atlanta, where they'd been meeting with one of the suppliers the charity was purchasing baby formula from. The limo had picked them up at LaGuardia and then taken them to the town house, around midnight.

"The car dropped us off. We went inside and went to bed right away—it was late, we were exhausted. Then early this morning I heard something. It woke me up. A shuffle, I don't know. Or a scraping sound. I remember I was so tired I didn't move. I just lay there with my eyes open."

That probably saved her life, Rhyme reflected. If she'd rolled over or gotten out of bed, the killer would have shot her first.

Then she saw something on the balcony, the form of a man.

"At first I thought it was a window washer. I mean, I knew it couldn't be but I was groggy and he looked like he was holding a squeegee. But it wasn't that at all."

The .32.

She heard glass breaking and pops, then her husband grunting.

"I screamed and rolled out of bed. I called nine-one-one. I didn't even realize I'd been shot until later and I saw I was bleeding."

Sachs drew her out and got some more information. The killer was a white man with dark curly hair, wearing some kind of dark clothes. He had broad shoulders.

Steroids . . .

The light, Kitty said, was too dim to see his face.

Recalling the HD images of the town house, Rhyme asked, "Did you happen to go out on the balcony when you got home? Was there anything unusual there? Any furniture moved?"

"No, we just went right to bed."

Sachs asked, "How could the killer have found out you'd be there last night?"

"It was in the papers. We were here for several fund-raisers and to meet with the heads of other philanthropic foundations. The *Times* had an article on it, I think."

Sellitto asked, "You have any thoughts about why he might've been killed?"

Her hands were knotted together. Rhyme wondered if she was going to break down. She took a breath and said, "I know he had enemies. When he was in Africa or the Far East he had a security detail. But here . . . I don't know. It was all so new to me. . . . You might want to talk to his brother. I spoke to him this morning. He's flying back from Kenya with his wife now. They'll be here tonight. Or if you want to talk to somebody now, you could call

Bob Kelsey. He was Ron's right-hand man in the foundation. He's pretty upset but he'd want to help."

And with that her voice stopped working. She choked and began to sob.

Sachs looked at Rhyme, who nodded.

She said, "That's all, Kitty. We don't want to keep you any longer."

Finally she controlled herself.

Thom walked into the room and gave her a Kleenex. She thanked him and wiped her face.

"Now," Lon Sellitto said, "we're going to have someone keep an eye on you."

Kitty shook her head and gave a faint laugh. "I know I'm a little shaky. But I'll be okay. I just . . . It's all so overwhelming. I'll stay with Ron's brother when they get back. And I have family in the area too. Oh, and Ron's son and his wife are flying back from China." A deep breath. "That was the hardest call. His son."

"Well, Mrs. Larkin, I'm talking about a bodyguard."

"A . . . guard? Why?"

Sachs said, "You're a material witness. He tried to kill you too. There's a chance he might try again."

"But I didn't see anything, really."

Rhyme pointed out, "He doesn't know that."

The policewoman said, "And there's more to being a material witness than identifying the perp. You could testify as to the time the incident occurred, the sound of the shots, where he was standing, how he stood, how he held the gun. All those things can help convict him."

"Well, we have security people in the company."

Sellitto said, "Probably better to stick with a police officer, you know."

"I guess . . . Sure. I just can't imagine anybody'd go to the trouble to hurt me. "

Rhyme noticed Lon Sellitto trying to put a good front on. "Hey," the rumpled detective said, "the odds're a thousand to one against it. But, you know, why not be on the safe side?"

■

A burly man stood at the window of the little-used kitchen in his house in New Jersey. His back was to the view—not a bad one: skyline of Manhattan—and he was watching a small, flat-screen TV in the living room.

"I'm watching it right now, Captain."

It had been some years since Carter had been a soldier—he was now a "security consultant," which was as good a job description as any—but after all the military training he felt most comfortable addressing people by rank. He himself was simply Carter. To the people who hired him, to the people he worked with. Carter.

On the TV a commentator was mentioning that Ronald Larkin's wife had survived the attack. She was described as a material witness.

"Hmm." Carter grunted.

When Carter was overseas on his "security" assignments, he often relied on journalists for information. He was amazed at how much sensitive material they gave away, in exchange for what he told them—which was usually just a bunch of crap.

A second newscaster came on and the story turned into one about all the good done by the Larkin Foundation, how much money it gave away.

Carter had been involved with a lot of really rich people. Only a couple of sheiks in the Mideast had as much money as Ronald Larkin, he believed.

Oh, there was that French businessman . . .

But, like Larkin, he wasn't rich anymore. He was dead.

"Larkin had come to town to meet with executives from other nonprofits about merging their organizations into a super-charity to consolidate their efforts in Africa, where famine and illness are rampant. And now let's go to our correspondent in the Darfur region of Western Sudan, where . . ."

Yadda, yadda, yadda. Carter shut the set off, the remote a tiny thing in his massive hand.

Carter was then listening carefully to the captain, who was pretty troubled.

After a moment of silence, Carter said, "I'll take care of it, Captain. I'll make sure it gets done right."

After he hung up, Carter walked into his bedroom and looked through the closet, where he found a business suit. He started to pull on the navy-blue trousers but then stopped. He replaced the suit in the closet and picked one that was a size 48. It was much easier to carry a gun inconspicuously when you wore a suit that was one size too large.

Ten minutes later he was in his forest-green Jeep Cherokee, heading toward Manhattan.

■

Robert Kelsey, a balding, fit businessman, was the operations director for the Larkin Foundation, which meant his job was to give away about three billion dollars a year.

"It's not as easy as it sounds."

Rhyme agreed, after the man explained: government regulations, tax laws, Washington politics, Third World politics and, perhaps the most daunting of all, fielding requests from the thousands of people and organizations who came to you, needing money for their heartbreaking causes—people you had to send away empty-handed.

The man was on the same couch as Kitty Larkin an hour before. He too had that distracted, disheveled air of someone wakened early with tragic news and was as yet unable to fully absorb it.

"We've got some evidence, a few leads," Lon Sellitto said, "but we don't have a clear motive yet. You have any ideas who'd want him dead? Mrs. Larkin didn't have any thoughts on that."

Lincoln Rhyme was rarely interested in a suspect's motives—he considered them to be the weakest leg of a case. (Evidence was, of course, to him strongest.) Still, obvious motives can point you in the direction of good evidence that *will* get a conviction.

"Who'd want him dead?" Kelsey repeated with a grim smile. "For a man who gave away billions to kids who were starving or sick, you'd be amazed at how many enemies he had. But I'll try to give you an idea. Our big drives for the past couple of years have been getting food and HIV drugs to Africa and funding for education in Asia and Latin America. The hardest place to work has been Africa. Darfur, Rwanda, the Congo, Somalia. . . . Ron refused to give money directly to the government. It'd just disappear into the pockets of the local officials. So what we do is buy the food here or in Europe and ship it to where it's needed. Same with the medicine. Not that that cuts out corruption. The minute a ship docks, there'll be somebody with a gun helping himself to your rice or wheat. The baby formula's stolen and either sold or used to cut drugs. And the HIV medicine's transferred into new bottles and sold across the borders to people with money to pay the going rate. The sick ones it was intended for get watered-down versions. Or sometimes just water."

"That bad?" Sellitto asked. "Jesus."

"Oh, yeah. We lose fifteen, twenty percent a year of our African donations to theft and hijacking. Tens of millions. And we're luckier than most charities over there. . . . That's why Ron was so unpopular. He insists that we control the *distribution* of the food and medicine over there. We cut deals with the best local organizations who'd get the job done. Sometimes those groups, like Liberian Relief, are allied with the opposition politi-cal parties. So, right there, that means he's a threat to the govern-ment in power.

"Then there're other regions where the government's legit and he distributes through them. Which makes him a threat to the *opposition* party. Then there're the warlords. And the fundamen-talist Islamic groups who don't want any Western aid at all. And the armies and militias who *want* people famished because they use hunger as a tool . . . Oh, it's a nightmare."

Kelsey gave a bitter laugh. "Then anti-U.S. countries around the world: the Arab bloc, Iran and Pakistan, Indonesia and Malaysia in the Far East. . . . The foundation's private, of course, but over there they see us as an arm of Washington. And, in a way, we are. Oh, and that's just overseas. Now, let's talk about America."

"Here?" Sachs asked. "He had enemies here?"

"Oh, yeah. You think the business of charity is filled with saints? Guess again. My background was corporate accounting, and I'll tell you that the most ruthless corporate raiders are noth-ing compared to the CEO's of a charity. Ron bought the food from a half-dozen suppliers here and in Europe. I can't tell you how many tons of rotten rice and corn they tried to sell us. Ron reported a half-dozen of them to the FDA.

"Then some executives seem to think charity begins at home. One organization wanted to work with us and Ron found out that the head was getting a salary of five hundred thousand a year and flew around the country in a private jet that was paid for by the endowment.

"Ron dropped them cold, called up the *Times* and gave them the story. The CEO was fired the next day."

Kelsey realized he was getting worked up. "Sorry. It's hard to do good nowadays. And, now, with him gone? It's going to be that much harder."

"What about Larkin's personal life?"

"His first wife died ten years ago," Kelsey said. "He has a grown son who's involved in energy joint ventures in China. They had a very good relationship. He'll be devastated by this."

"What about his new wife?"

"Oh, Kitty? She was good for him, and she loved him too. See, she's got money of her own—her father had a textile business or something. Ron'd meet a lot of women who were just after one thing, you can imagine. It was hard for him. But she was genuine."

"His brother?" Sellitto asked.

"Peter? What about . . . ? Oh, you mean, could *he* have been involved in his death?" A laugh. "No, no, impossible. They were very close. He's successful too. Has his own company. Not as rich as Ron, but I'm talking thirty billion instead of a hundred. He didn't need any money. Besides, they had the same values, worked hard for the foundation. It was Ron's full-time job, but Peter still put in twenty, thirty hours a week, on top of his full schedule as CEO of his own company."

Sellitto then asked for a specific list of people who might have a grudge against Ron Larkin—from all of the categories Kelsey had mentioned. He wrote for some time.

Kelsey handed Sellitto the sheet and said he'd try to think of anyone else. The man, looking dazed, said good-bye and left.

Mel Cooper came out of the lab flexing his hands.

"How's the mission?" Rhyme asked.

"Do you know how many knots there were?"

"Twenty-four," Rhyme said. "And I noted the tense of the verb. You're finished."

"I think I have carpal tunnel. But we were successful."

"You find his business card?"

"Maybe something just as good. A husk. A very small husk."

"Of what?"

"Rice."

Rhyme nodded, pursing his lips. And Sachs said exactly what he was thinking: "Shipments of food that the foundation sent to Africa? So the shooter might've been recruited there."

"Or by somebody who owns a farm. Or sells rice. The one who sold the rotten shipments maybe."

"And the marine diesel oil," Mel Cooper said, nodding at the chart. "Cargo ships."

Sachs added the entry to their chart.

"Let's look over the list that Kelsey made for us."

Sachs taped the page on a whiteboard.

"The *usual* suspects?" Rhyme snorted a cold laugh. "Typical homicides have, what? Four or five tops? And what pond are we fishing in here?" A nod at the list. "Most of the Third World, half of the Middle East and Europe and a good chunk of the Fortune Five Hundred corporations."

"And all he was doing," Sachs said, "was giving away money to people who needed it."

"Don't you know that expression?" Sellitto muttered. "No good deed goes unpunished."

RONALD LARKIN HOMICIDE

- Coir fiber.
- Dirt from garden below the balcony.
- Dark hairs, curly. No bulb attached.
- Bit of rubber, black, possibly from sole of shoe.
- Dirt and sand with traces of marine diesel fuel, saltwater.
- No friction ridges, tread marks, tool marks.
- Lint containing traces of Dianabol steroid. Athlete?
- .32 caliber automatic, sound suppressor, fragmentation bullets.

- CMI grappling hook, wrapped in strips of old flannel shirt.
- Mil-Spec 550 rope, knotted. Black.
- Rice husk, trapped in knot.

- Suspect:
  - U.S. citizen, other passports?
  - trained in Europe.
  - mercenary with African, Middle East connections.
  - no motive.
  - high fee.
  - employer unknown.

The young officer wasn't comfortable.

He was a newly appointed detective, still awaiting rank, and had been given the thankless job of escorting the poor widow back to her town house to collect some clothes, then hand her over to a bodyguard.

Not that she was beating up on him or anything. No, it was just the opposite. She seemed so distant and upset and weepy that he didn't know what to say to her, how to act. He wished his wife were here; she'd calm the woman down pretty fast. But the detective himself? Nope, wasn't his strength. He was sympathetic, sure, but he didn't know how to express it. He'd been on the force only five years, mostly in Patrol, and he'd had very few opportunities to meet grieving relatives. Once, a garbage truck plowed into the side of a parked SUV, killing the woman driver. He'd had to tell the husband what had happened, and it had taken him weeks to get over the look of horror and sorrow in the man's face.

Now, he was working as a detective in Narcotics. Occasional bodies, occasional widows. None of them grieving like this. A lot didn't seem to care their husbands were dead.

He watched Kitty Larkin standing in the front doorway of her town house, paralyzed, it seemed.

"Is something wrong?" he asked, then mentally kicked himself.

Duh . . .

He meant, of course, was there something out of the ordinary about the house, something he should be looking into, calling Lieutenant Sellitto about. His hand strayed to his Glock, which he'd drawn a half dozen times in his career, but never fired.

Kitty shook her head. "No," she whispered, and seemed to realize that she'd stopped walking. "Sorry." She continued into the house. "I'll just be a few minutes. I'll pack a bag."

The detective was making a circuit from the front to the back of the house when he saw a black sedan pull up in the street.

An African American woman in a dark suit climbed out and walked up to him. She flashed a badge.

U.S. Department of State.

"I'm taking over security for Mrs. Larkin," she said with a faint accent the man couldn't place.

"You're—"

"Taking over security for Mrs. Larkin," the woman repeated slowly.

Good, the officer thought, relieved that he wouldn't have to sit around and watch the woman cry. But then he thought: Hold on.

"Just a second."

"What do you mean?"

The cop pulled out his phone and called Lieutenant Sellitto.

"Yeah?" the gruff Major Cases cop asked.

"Detective, just wanted to let you know that the bodyguard got here, for the Larkin woman. She's from the State Department, though, not us."

"The what?"

"State Department."

"Yeah? What's her name?"

The detective asked to see her ID again and she showed it to him. "Norma Sedgwick."

"Hold on a minute."

He said to Norma. "Just have to check."

She didn't seem mad but her face registered a bit of "whatever." It seemed like a rookie putdown. Okay, you feddie bitch, *you* ever get shot at by a crank-crazed eighteen-year-old armed with a SIG-Sauer and a knife? Which is how he'd spent last Monday evening.

He just smiled at her.

On the other end of the line Sellitto's hand was over the receiver and he was talking with someone else. The detective wondered if it was the legendary Lincoln Rhyme. He knew Sellitto worked with him from time to time. He'd never met Rhyme. There were rumors that he didn't really exist.

A few minutes later—it seemed like forever—Sellitto came back on the line.

"Yeah, it's okay."

Thank you, the detective thought. He could leave Mrs. Larkin and her grief and flee back to the place where he was a lot more comfortable: the drug world of East New York and the South Bronx.

■

"Norma, where're we going?" Kitty, in the backseat, asked the stocky, attractive State Department agent, driving the Lincoln Town Car.

"A hotel near our office in Midtown. We basically own one of the upper floors, so the staff doesn't put any guests there without our okay. Right now it's empty. You'll be the only one there. I'll be staying in the room across the hall, and another agent'll be there through the night. It's not the best hotel in the world, probably not what you're used to, but not bad. In any case, it's safer than you staying in your town house."

"Maybe," the widow said softly. "But I'm going back there as soon as I can." She looked up and, in the rearview mirror, saw the agent's dark face studying her. "Let's hope everything's resolved soon."

They drove in silence for a few minutes. Then Norma asked, "How's your arm?"

"It's nothing, really." The widow touched the bandage. Her wound still stung badly but she'd stopped taking the painkillers the doctor had prescribed for her.

"Why is the State Department interested in me? I don't quite understand."

"Well, your husband's work overseas."

"What do you mean?"

"Sensitive issues. You know." She didn't add anything more.

And Kitty thought: This is ridiculous. The last thing in the world she wanted was a bodyguard. She'd try to have the woman sent back to her office as soon as Peter Larkin and his wife arrived.

Kitty was thinking of Peter and his family when she became aware that Norma Sedgwick had stiffened. Her shoulders hunched and she kept glancing into the rearview mirror. "Mrs. Larkin, I think there's a vehicle following us."

"What?" Kitty turned around. "Impossible."

"No, I'm pretty sure. I've been practicing evasive turns but he's stayed with me the whole time."

"That green Jeep?"

"That's it, yes."

"Who's driving?"

"A man, I think. White. Seems to be alone."

Kitty looked. Couldn't see inside. The windows were tinted. Norma picked up her cell phone and started to make a call.

This was crazy, Kitty thought. It made no sense for—

"Look out!" Norma cried.

In a burst of speed the Cherokee accelerated right toward them and then drove them off the street over the curb into the park.

"What's he doing?" Norma barked.

"I can't tell!"

Into her phone the agent said, "This is Sedgwick. We've got an assailant! Madison and Twenty-third. The park. He's—"

The Jeep then backed up and accelerated directly toward them.

Kitty screamed, lowered her head and waited for the impact.

But Norma accelerated and drove the car farther onto the grass of the park, stopping just before slamming into a temporary chain-link fence around a construction site. The Jeep bounded over the curb and came to a stop nearby.

"Get out, get the hell out!" Norma shouted. "Move!" She

jumped from the front seat and, gun in her hand, ripped the back door open.

Clutching her purse, Kitty scrabbled out of the car. Norma took her by the arm and virtually dragged her into a stand of bushes, while pedestrians and park sitters fled. The Jeep stopped. The door flew open and Kitty believed the driver slid out.

"Are you all right?" Holding her weapon, Norma looked her over carefully.

"Yes, yes!" Kitty shouted. "I'm fine. Watch him! He's out of the car."

The attacker, a solid white man in a dark suit and white shirt, moved quickly through the bushes toward them, then vanished behind a pile of construction material.

"Where is he? *Where*?"

Kitty glanced down at the gun in the woman's hand. She held it steady and seemed to know what she was doing. But she'd driven them into a cul de sac. There was nowhere to run. Kitty looked back toward the car. Nothing.

Motion above them.

Norma barked a scream, and Kitty looked up to see a figure hanging over the fence, a gun in his hand.

But it wasn't the attacker. They were looking at a uniformed NYPD officer. He saw the ID around Norma's neck but he wasn't taking chances. His gun was aimed directly toward the agent.

"Lower the weapon and identify yourself!"

"I'm State Department. Security."

"Lower the weapon and show me."

"Jesus Christ," Kitty snapped. "She's guarding me. There's a man after us."

Norma pointed her gun toward the ground and with her other hand held out her ID. He read it and nodded. "You should've called it in."

"It just happened. Look, over there. Your two o'clock. White male, big guy. Drove us off the street. Probably armed."

"What's he after?"

"She's a homicide witness."

Then the officer frowned. "Is that him?" He was gazing at Norma's car. Kitty saw a man crouching behind it.

"Yeah," Norma said. Then to Kitty, "Get down!" And shoved her onto the asphalt walkway they were crouching on. Kitty was furious. She should've insisted they stay at the town house.

"You, wait!" the officer called, starting forward. "Police. Don't move!"

But by then the attacker had realized that he was outnumbered. He raced back to his Jeep. He backed the vehicle over the curb and sped up Madison, leaving a trail of blue smoke in his wake.

■

Via the high-def video system, Lincoln Rhyme, in his lab, was watching Kitty Larkin talk to Sellitto and Sachs inside the black Town Car. The widow was giving them an account of the incident in a shaky voice.

Rhyme was thinking: This system is quite an invention. It was as if the people were right there in front of him.

"I couldn't really say what happened," Kitty said. "It was all so fast. I didn't even see him clearly."

Norma Sedgwick gave a similar account of the incident. They differed in the color of the Jeep's shade of green, in the height of the assailant, in the color of his shirt.

Witnesses . . . Rhyme didn't have much faith in them. Even honest ones get confused. They miss things. They misinterpret what they do see.

He was impatient. "Sachs?"

He saw the screen jump a little as she heard his voice.

"Excuse me," she said to Kitty and Sellitto. The scene swiveled as she climbed out of the car and walked away.

"What, Rhyme?"

"We don't need to worry about what they saw or didn't see. I want the scene searched. Every inch."

"Okay, Rhyme. I'll get to work."

Sachs walked the grid—Rhyme's term for the most comprehensive, some would say compulsive, way of searching a crime scene—with her usual diligence. A lab tech from Queens processed the evidence in the back of the Crime Scene's rapid response vehicle. But the only things relating to the Larkin killing were two more of the coir fibers like the one on the balcony. One of the fibers was pressed into a small black fleck, which might've come from an old leather-bound book; Rhyme remembered similar evidence from a case some years ago.

"Nothing else?" he asked, irritated.

"Nope."

Rhyme sighed.

There is a well-known rule in forensics called Locard's Principle. The Frenchman Edmond Locard, one of the fathers of forensic science, came up with a rule that posited an inevitable exchange of trace evidence (he spoke of "dust") between the perpetrator and either the crime scene or the victim.

Rhyme believed in Locard's Principle; in fact, it was the underlying force that drove him to relentlessly push those who worked for him—and to push himself too. If that connection, however fragile, can be established, then the perp might be found, crimes solved and future tragedies prevented.

But making that link assumes the investigator can locate, identify and grasp the implications of that trace evidence. In the case of the Larkin homicide Rhyme wasn't sure that he could. Circumstance might play a role in this—the environment, third parties, fate. Then too the killer might simply be too smart and diligent. Too *pro*-fessional, as Fred Dellray had observed.

Sachs took every defeat personally. "Sorry, Rhyme. I know it's important."

He said something dismissive. Not to worry, we'll keep looking over things in the lab here, maybe the autopsy will reveal something helpful. . . .

But he supposed his reassurance rang false to her.

It certainly did to him.

■

"Are you all right?" Norma asked.

"Knees hurt. When I went down on the ground."

"Sorry about that," the agent said, looking over Kitty from the rearview mirror. Norma had high cheekbones and exotic Egyptian eyes.

"Don't be silly. You saved my life." Kitty, though, was still angry. She lapsed into silence.

They drove for another twenty minutes. Kitty realized they were going in circles a lot and doubling back. She looked behind her once and saw that they *were* being followed—only this time it was an unmarked police car driven by that tall officer with hair as red as her own, Amelia Sachs.

Norma's phone rang. She picked it up, had a conversation and then disconnected.

"That was her, the policewoman behind us. No sign of the Jeep."

Kitty nodded. "And nobody saw the license plate?"

"No. But they're probably stolen tags."

They continued on, driving in a random pattern. Sachs would disappear occasionally, driving up one street and down another, apparently looking for the man's Jeep.

The agent began, "I guess—"

Her phone rang. "Agent Sedgwick . . . What?"

Kitty looked in the mirror, alarmed. What now? She was getting sick of the intrigue.

"It's Amelia," Norma said to her. "She said she spotted the Jeep! He's nearby."

"Where?"

"A block! He was driving parallel to us. How? There's no way he could've followed us!"

She listened into the phone again. Then reported to Kitty, "She's in pursuit. She's called in some other units. He's headed toward the FDR." Into the phone she asked, "How did he find us? . . . You think? Hold on."

Norma asked Kitty, "He was hiding behind our car in Madison Square Park, right?"

"Yes."

She relayed this to the policewoman. There was a pause. "Okay, maybe. We'll check."

Norma disconnected. "She thinks he might not've been trying to hurt you back in the park. He wanted to get us out of the car to plant a tracker after we jumped out."

"A tracker?"

"Like a GPS, a homing device. I'm going to look." She parked and climbed out, saying, "You check the backseat. And your suitcases. He might've slipped it in there. It would be a small plastic or metal box."

Lord, what a nightmare this was, Kitty thought, even angrier now. Who the hell was this guy? Who'd hired him?

Kitty tore open her two suitcases and dumped the contents on the seat, looking through everything carefully.

Nothing.

But then she heard: "Hey, check it out."

Kitty looked out the window and saw the State Department agent holding a small white cylinder about three inches across, resting on a tissue so she wouldn't disturb fingerprints, Kitty guessed. "Magnetized, stuck up in the wheel well. It's a big one. Probably has a range of five miles. He could've found us anywhere in the area. Damn, that was a good call." She set it on the street near the curb, hunched down and, using the tissue, tinkered, apparently disabling it.

A moment later Norma's phone rang again. The agent listened and then reported in a grim voice, "He got away. Disappeared on the Lower East Side."

Kitty rubbed her face, disgusted.

Norma told the detective about the tracking device and added that they were going on to the hotel.

"Wait," said Kitty as she repacked the suitcases. "Why do you think he only left *one* tracker?"

The agent blinked. Then nodded. She said into the phone, "Detective Sachs, you think you could give us a ride?"

■

Fifteen minutes later Amelia Sachs arrived. Norma handed her the tracker and she put it in a plastic bag.

Then the agent hustled Kitty Larkin into the detective's car and together the three women drove to the hotel. On the way the agent arranged for another State Department security person to pick up the Town Car and get it back to the pool for a complete inspection. There was even some speculation that the killer might've planted an explosive device at the same time he stuck the tracker in the wheel well, so the NYPD bomb squad would have a look as well.

Sachs dropped the women off, explaining that she'd take the tracker back to the town house of that officer in the wheelchair, or consultant, whatever he was, Lincoln Rhyme. She sped off.

Norma escorted Kitty inside the hotel. It was a pretty seedy place, the woman thought. She would have expected material witnesses and security-conscious diplomats to be housed in better digs.

The agent spoke to someone at the front desk, handed him an envelope and returned to Kitty.

"Do I need to check in?"

"No, everything's taken care of."

They got out on the fourteenth floor. Norma showed her to a room, checked it out herself and handed her the key. "You can call room service for anything you want."

"I just want to call my family and Peter and then get some rest."

"Sure, dear, you go right ahead. I'll be across the hall if you need anything."

Kitty hung the Do Not Disturb sign on the knob and stepped into the room. It was just as tacky as the lobby suggested and smelled of mildew. She sat heavily on the bed, sighing. She noticed the window shades were up, which seemed a stupid idea for a hotel where they stashed witnesses. She rose and pulled the drapes shut, then turned the lights on in the room.

She called the number of Peter Larkin's office and identified herself. She accepted the gush of sympathy the man's secretary offered and then asked when Peter and his wife would be arriving. It would be around nine that night. She left a message for him to call her as soon as they got in.

Then she kicked her shoes off, lay back on the bed, closed her eyes and fell into a troubled sleep.

■

Rhyme pressed his head back into the headrest of his wheelchair. He felt Sachs's hand curl around his neck and massage. He could feel her hand at one moment and then, though he knew she continued the massage, the sensation vanished as her fingers moved down, below the fourth cervical vertebra, the site of his disabling injury.

At another time, this might give rise to reflections—either on his condition, or on his relationship with Amelia Sachs. But now he was aware of nothing but the urgency to nail the killer of Ron Larkin, the man who gave away billions.

"How're we doing, Mel?"

"Give me a minute."

"You've had plenty of them. What's going on?"

The massaging sensation stopped, but this was due not to the migration of her hand but because she'd stepped away and was helping Cooper prepare a slide for examination under the microscope.

Rhyme looked over the updated evidence chart for the hundredth time.

The answer was there. It *had* to be. There were no other options. No witnesses, no clear motives, no succinct list of suspects.

The evidence, the minuscule bits of trace, held the key.

Locard's Principle . . .

Rhyme glanced at the clock.

"Mel?"

Without looking up from the Bausch and Lomb, the tech repeated patiently, "It should only be a minute."

But every minute that passed meant that the killer was sixty seconds closer to escaping.

Or, Rhyme feared, sixty seconds closer to murdering once again.

■

Carter was sitting in his green Jeep, looking over Brooklyn from a spot near the South Street Seaport.

He was sipping coffee and enjoying the view. The tall-masted clipper ship, the bridges, the boat traffic.

Carter had no boss except the people who hired him, and he kept his own hours. Sometimes he'd get up early—four a.m.— and, when the Fulton Fish Market was still operating, drive here. He'd wander past stalls, staring at the tuna, the squid, the flounder, the crabs. It reminded him of seaports overseas.

He was sorry the fish market had closed. Financial problems, he guessed. Or unions maybe.

Carter had solved a lot of union problems in his day.

His cell phone rang. He glanced down at caller ID.

"Captain," he said in a respectful voice.

He listened carefully, then said, "Sure. I can do that." He disconnected and placed a call overseas.

Carter was glad he didn't have to go anywhere for a few minutes. A small cargo ship was steaming up the East River and he enjoyed watching its progress.

"*Oui?*" a voice answered from the other side of the world.

Carter began a conversation, not even aware that he'd lapsed into French.

■

Kitty awoke to a phone call.

She picked it up. "Hello?"

Peter Larkin's voice said, "Kitty. How are you?"

She'd seen plenty of pictures of him, but only met the man once, at the wedding. She remembered him clearly: tall, lean, with thinning hair. He resembled his brother only in facial structure.

"Oh, Peter, this is so terrible."

"Are you doing okay?"

"I suppose." She cleared her throat. "I was just asleep, and I was dreaming about him. I woke up and for a minute I was fine. Then I remembered what had happened. It's so terrible. How are *you*?"

"I can't even think. We didn't sleep on the plane. . . ."

They commiserated for a few minutes more, then Peter explained they were at the airport and their luggage had just arrived. He and his wife would be in the town house in an hour or two. His daughter, a college student at Yale, was already there.

Kitty glanced at her watch, the one Ron had given her. It was simple and elegant and probably worth ten thousand dollars.

"Why don't you get some rest tonight and I'll come by in the morning."

"Of course. You have the address?"

"It's somewhere. I . . . I don't know where. I'm just not thinking straight."

He gave it to her again.

"It'll be good to see you, Kitty."

"Family has to be together at times like this."

■

Kitty went into the bathroom and washed her face in icy water, rinsing away the last dullness of sleep.

She returned to the room and gazed at herself in the wall mirror, thinking how different she looked from the woman she really was. Not Kitty Larkin at all, but someone named Priscilla Endicott, a name lost behind a lengthy string of aliases.

When you were a professional killer, you couldn't afford to be yourself of course.

A left-wing radical in the United States, an advocate—and occasional practitioner—of political violence, Priscilla had moved overseas after college, where she'd floated among several underground movements and ended up helping out political terrorists in Ireland and Italy. But by the age of thirty she realized that politics don't pay the bill, at least not simple-minded communist and socialist politics, and she decided to offer her talents to those who'd pay: security consultants in Eastern Europe, the Middle East and Africa. When even that didn't pay enough, she changed her line of work again, keeping the title but taking on a whole new job description, which she described as "problem solver."

Four months ago, while sunbathing at a pool in the United Arab Emirates, she'd gotten a phone call from a trusted contact. After some negotiation, she'd been hired, for $5 million U.S., to kill Ron Larkin and his brother and wife, the three people instrumental in overseeing the Larkin Foundation.

Priscilla had changed her appearance: weight gain, dyed hair, colored contact lenses, strategic collagen injections. She became Catherine "Kitty" Biddle Simpson, created a credible biography and managed to get close to Larkin through some charities in Los Angeles. She'd spent plenty of time in Africa and could discuss the region intelligently. She even knew a great deal about the plight of the children, having turned a number of them into orphans.

Kitty laid on the charm (and a few other skills, of course), they began dating and she looked for a chance to complete her contract. But it wasn't easy. Oh, she could've killed him at any time, but murdering a very public and popular man like Ronald Larkin, not to mention his brother and sister-in-law too, and getting away, of course, was much harder than she'd thought.

But then Ron Larkin himself provided a solution. Amusing her no end, he proposed to her.

As his wife she'd have complete access to his life, without the security people around, and his brother and sister-in-law would automatically trust her.

The first thing she said was, "Yes, dear, but I don't want a penny of your money."

"Well . . ."

"No, I've got my father's trust fund," she'd explained. "Besides, honey, what I like about you isn't the dollar signs. It's what you do for people. And, okay, you got a decent body for an old guy," she'd joked.

Under those circumstances, who could possibly suspect her?

Then after a bout of marital bliss (occasional sex, many rich dinners, countless boring businesspeople), it was time to act.

On Tuesday night they'd arrived at LaGuardia (flying on a private jet, she could bring her guns and the other accoutrements of her trade with her), driven to the town house and gone to bed. At 4:30 a.m., she'd dressed and pulled on latex gloves, screwed the suppressor onto the barrel of her favorite .32 automatic and stepped outside onto the balcony, feeling the cool, electric smell of New York City air in the morning. She'd distributed the planted evidence—the trace she scattered around to lead the police off—then rested the grappling hook on the railing, tossed the rope over the side. She'd returned to the window, cracked the pane and fired—hitting Ron three times and sending the fourth and fifth rounds into her own pillow.

Then she called 9-1-1, hysterical, to report the attack. After hanging up she'd unscrewed the back of the television, put the gun, silencer, ammunition and gloves inside, and with her cuticle scissors, slit her arm and jammed a fragment of shattered bullet into the wound. Then she staggered downstairs to await the police. Ron's brother and sister-in-law would arrive as soon as possible, of course, and she'd kill them too, making it look like the same man was behind their deaths.

Planned perfectly . . .

But, of course, while plans can be perfect, the execution—so to speak—never is.

My God, a *real* hit man—the guy in the Jeep—had showed up, trying to take her out.

The best she could figure was that one of her enemies—she'd made plenty over the years—had recognized her from the news about Ron, despite her effort not to be photographed in public and her changed appearance.

Or maybe it had nothing to do with Priscilla Endicott; maybe the man's goal was to kill Mrs. Kitty Larkin. Hired by a former mistress of Larkin's? she wondered. Or a jilted girlfriend?

She gave a bitter laugh at the irony. Here, the police and State Department were protecting her from a killer—just not the particular killer they believed him to be.

Priscilla now dialed a number on her mobile (she wouldn't trust a hotel phone).

"Hello?" a man answered.

"It's me."

"My God, what the hell is going on? I see the stories—somebody's after *you*?"

"Relax."

"Who the hell is he?"

"I don't know for sure. I did a job in the Congo last year and one of the targets got away. Maybe him."

"So he has nothing to do with us?"

"No."

"But what're we going to do about it?"

"You sound panicked," Priscilla said.

"Of course I'm panicking. What—"

"Take a deep breath."

"What're we going to do?" he repeated, sounding even *more* panicked.

"I say we have a goddamn good laugh about it."

Silence. Maybe he thought she was hysterical. Then he asked, "What do you mean?"

"Our biggest problem has always been giving the police another suspect, somebody other than you and me."

"Right."

"Well, now we've *got* one. Peter and his wife'll be at their town house in about an hour. I'll sneak out of where I am now, kill them and get back before I'm missed. They'll think the guy in the Jeep did it. He's not stupid. When he hears that they're looking for *him* for the homicide, he'll probably take off. I'll be safe, you'll be safe."

The man was quiet for a moment. Then gave a brief chuckle. "It could work," he said.

"It *will* work. What's the status of the second installment?"

"In your account."

"Good. I won't call again. Just watch the news. Oh, one thing. I don't know if it's going to bother you. . . . It seems that Peter's daughter just got into town from college. She'll be with them when I get there."

The man didn't hesitate before asking, "What's the problem with that?"

"I guess that means," Priscilla said, "that there isn't one."

■

Two hours later the woman slipped out the side door of the hotel, unseen by the desk clerk. She'd taken a cab to a street corner two blocks from the town house of Peter and Sandra Larkin, then walked the rest of the way.

The wealthy lifestyle of these particular targets, with their private homes in Manhattan, was very helpful. Getting into a doorman building unseen could be a bitch.

She paused outside the town house and looked into her purse, checking the weapon, which she'd retrieved from the TV in the bedroom of Ron Larkin's town house when she'd gone there to pack her suitcases earlier.

She now climbed the stairs, looked up and down the street. No one. She pulled on latex gloves and pressed the buzzer.

A moment later.

"Hello?"

"Peter, it's Kitty. I have to see you."

"Oh, Kitty," the brother said. "We weren't expecting you till tomorrow. But we're glad you're here. Come on up. We're all in the living room. Second floor. The door's open. Come on in."

The buzz of the door lock echoed through the misty night.

Priscilla pushed inside.

She was thinking of the sequence. If they were all together, hit the most dangerous target first and fast: That would be any bodyguards. And the daughter's boyfriend, if there was one. Then Peter Larkin. He was a large man and could be a threat. A head shot for him. Then the daughter, who'd be younger and possibly more athletic. Finally the wife.

Then she'd leave more of the planted evidence to link this killing to Ron's: the steroids, the dark curly hairs (stolen from a barbershop trash bin), another fleck of rubber peeled off a running shoe she later discarded, more of the sand and dirt she'd scraped up from a marina in L.A.

Priscilla recited: Find the target, look for guards, check the backdrop, possible security systems, especially cameras. Aim, squeeze, count your rounds.

Climbing the stairs, she was aware of the musty smell of an apartment not much used, but the place was very elegant nonetheless. Both Peter's and Ron's fortunes were obscene. Billions. Thinking that this much money was controlled by just two individuals reignited some of her latent political views about inequality in the distribution of wealth, despite their charitable efforts. Still, Priscilla Endicott couldn't very well take the high moral ground any longer; she herself was a wealthy woman now—and it was her craft of killing that had made her one.

Reaching into her purse, Priscilla lifted her gun, clicked the safety off.

She walked inside the living room quickly, the gun behind her back.

"Hello?"

She stopped fast, staring at the empty room.

Had she gotten the wrong room? she wondered.

The TV was on. The stereo too. But not a single human being was here.

Oh, no . . .

She turned to flee.

Which is when the tactical team—five officers—pushed from the two side doorways, shoving their weapons toward her, shouting, screaming, grabbing. In less than a second the .32 was out of her hands and she was on the floor, with her wrists cuffed behind her.

■

Lincoln Rhyme surveyed the town house from the sidewalk.

"Pretty nice place," Amelia Sachs said.

"Seems okay." Architecture, like décor, didn't mean a lot to him.

Lon Sellitto glanced up at the tall building too. "Jesus. I knew they were rich, but really." He was standing with the lieutenant from Emergency Services, the man who'd directed the takedown.

A moment later the door opened and the woman who'd been hired to kill Ron Larkin, his brother and sister-in-law was escorted out, cuffed. Given her ruthlessness and ingenuity, Rhyme and Sellitto had ordered her feet shackled too.

The officers accompanying her paused, and the criminalist looked her over.

"*Miranda?*" Rhyme asked one of the tactical cops.

He nodded.

But the killer didn't seem to care about having her lawyer present when she spoke. She leaned toward Rhyme and whispered harshly, "How? How the hell did you do it?"

Locard's Principle, the criminalist thought. But his answer to her was: "The fiber. The coir fiber made me suspicious right away."

She shook her head.

Rhyme explained, "Amelia found it on the balcony. I remembered seeing the Larkin Energy logo on the doormat in front of the town house when Amelia got there to search the scene. And I remembered that coir fibers are used in making rugs and mats. She checked later and found out the fiber *did* come from the same mat.

"Now, how did the fiber get from the doormat to the balcony?

It couldn't've been when you and Ron arrived at the house to-gether last night. You said you hadn't been on the balcony. And obviously you hadn't been there for a long time—otherwise you would've watered the houseplants. Same for any caretakers. The mysterious killer? Would he have wiped his feet on the doormat on a busy street then walked around to the back of the building, climbed the rope to the balcony? Didn't make sense. So," he re-peated dramatically, "how did the fiber get there?

"I'll tell you, Kitty: *You* picked it up from the mat on your shoe when you got in from the airport. And *you* left it on the balcony early this morning when you stepped outside to kill Ron."

She blinked, shaking her head no, but Rhyme could see from the dismay in her face that the words struck close to home. She'd thought of almost everything. But as Locard might've said, Almost isn't good enough when it comes to evidence.

"Then the other clues on the balcony? The steroid, the rubber, the lint, sand and dirt with the diesel traces, the hairs. I suspected they were planted by you to support your story of the bodybuild-ing hit man. But proving it was something else. So I—"

It was then that Kitty, or whatever her name was, stiffened. "God, no. It's him! He's going to—"

Rhyme swiveled around in the chair to see a green Jeep Cherokee pull up and double-park next to them. Climbing out was a solidly built man with a crew cut, wearing a conservative suit. He snapped closed a cell phone and walked toward them.

"No!" Kitty cried.

"Captain," the man said, nodding at Rhyme. The criminalist was amused that Jed Carter insisted on using Rhyme's rank when he was with the NYPD.

Carter was a freelance security consultant for companies doing business in Africa and the Middle East. Rhyme had met him on that Brooklyn illegal arms case a few months ago, when the former mercenary soldier had helped the FBI and the NYPD take down the principal gunrunner. Carter was humorless and stiff—and surely had a past Rhyme didn't want to know too much about—but he'd proved invaluable in nailing the perp. (He also seemed eager to make amends for some of his own past missions in Third World countries.)

Carter shook Sellitto's hand, then the tactical officer's. He nodded respectfully to Amelia Sachs.

"What is this?" Kitty gasped.

Sachs said, "Like Lincoln was saying, we suspected you but we ran your prints and you weren't on file anywhere."

"Will be soon, though," Sellitto pointed out cheerfully.

"So we didn't have enough proof to get a search warrant."

"Not on the basis of one fiber. So I enlisted the help of Mr. Carter here—and Agent Sedgwick."

Norma, from State Department security, worked regularly with Fred Dellray. He'd contacted her and explained that they'd needed someone to play bodyguard and to help them fake an assault. She'd agreed. They'd arranged the undercover set for Madison Square Park, along with an officer from Patrol, in hopes that they'd find some more of the trace that Rhyme suspected was planted. If so, it had to come from Kitty and would place her on the balcony, justifying a search warrant.

But his idea didn't work. Sachs searched Madison Square Park around where Kitty had lain, as well as the Lincoln, inside and out, but she could find none of the planted evidence or any trace linking her to the weapon.

So they'd tried once more. Rhyme decided that they needed to search her suitcases. Sachs called Norma about a tracking device that the supposed killer had planted. While Norma pretended to find one under the car—it was her Olay skin cream jar—Kitty had dumped the contents of her suitcases out into the backseat to look for the device.

After Sachs dropped them off at the hotel, she returned immediately to the sedan and searched the hell out of it. She found traces of the steroid, a bit more of the diesel-laden sand and dirt and another grain of rice. Ironically, it turned out the rice husk in the rope and the grain of rice in the State Department sedan weren't from any shipments of food to Africa. Their source was a spoonful of dried rice in a lace ball tied with a silver ribbon, a souvenir from Kitty's and Ron's wedding. The woman had neglected to take it out of her suitcase.

Rhyme added, "Detective Sellitto went to the courthouse, got a warrant and a wiretap."

"A tap?" Kitty whispered.

"Yep. On your cell."

"Shit." Kitty closed her eyes, a bitter grimace on her face.

"Oh, yeah," Sellitto muttered. "We got the asshole who hired you."

It wasn't a warlord, vengeful employee, Third World dictator or corrupt CEO who wanted Ron and his brother dead. And it wasn't the Reverend John Markel—briefly a suspect because of the fleck of leather at the Madison Square scene, possibly shed by a Bible.

No, Robert Kelsey, the operations director of the foundation, was whom she'd called an hour ago. When he'd learned that Ron Larkin was thinking of merging with several other foundations, Kelsey knew there'd be a complete audit of the operation and it would be discovered that he'd been taking money from warlords and corrupt government officials in Africa in exchange for information about where the ship containing food and drugs would be docking.

Oh, yeah. We lose fifteen, twenty percent a year of our African donations to theft and hijacking. Tens of millions. . . .

He had to kill them, he reasoned, to stop any mergers.

Kelsey had confessed, in exchange for an agreement not to seek the death penalty. But he swore he didn't know Kitty's real identity. Sachs and Sellitto believed him; Kitty wasn't a stupid woman, and she'd have to operate through a number of anony-mous identities.

That's why Rhyme had called Carter not long ago, to see if the former mercenary could learn more about her. The man now said, "I've been speaking to some of my associates in Marseilles, Bahrain and Cape Town, Captain. They're asking about her now. They think it won't take too long to get an ID. I mean, she's not exactly your typical merc."

Amen, thought Lincoln Rhyme.

"This is a mistake," Kitty growled at Rhyme. Which could be interpreted to mean either he was erroneous or that stopping her was foolhardy and dangerous.

Whatever the message, her opinion meant nothing to him.

Lon Sellitto escorted her to a squad car and got in his own Crown Victoria. The entourage headed downtown to Central Booking.

Soon all the tactical officers were gone. Jed Carter promised he'd call as soon as he heard about anyone who fit Kitty's de-scription. "Good-bye, Captain. Ma'am." He ambled off to his green Jeep.

Rhyme and Sachs were alone on the street. "Okay," he said, meaning, Let's get home. He wanted the Glenmorangie whisky Thom had denied him in anticipation of the operation here. ("It's not like I'm going to be fighting anybody hand-to-hand." Still, as often, the aide won.)

He asked Sachs to call Thom now; he was parked up the street in Rhyme's custom-made van.

But Sachs frowned. "Oh, we can't leave yet."

"Why?"

"There're some people who want to meet you. Ron Larkin's brother and family." They had been ushered into an upstairs bed-room with armed guards as soon as Kitty had arrived. She glanced at the third-floor window and waved at the faces of a middle-aged couple looking down at Rhyme and Sachs at the moment.

"Do we have to?"

"You saved their lives, Rhyme."

"Isn't that enough? I have to make small talk too?"

She laughed. "Five minutes. It'll mean a lot to them."

"Well, I'd love to," he said, offering a rather insincere smile. "But it's not exactly accessible." Nodding at the stairs and then his wheelchair.

"Oh, don't worry, Rhyme," Sachs said, resting her hand on his shoulder. "I'll bet they'll come to us."

A Dish Served Cold

We have reason to believe there's a man who wants to cause you some harm, sir."

Standing on the hot sidewalk in front of his office building, compact, muscular Stephen York rocked back and forth on his Bally shoes.

Cause you some harm.

The hell's that supposed to mean?

York set down his gym bag. The fifty-one-year-old investment banker looked from the Scottsdale Police Department senior detective who'd delivered this news to the man's younger partner. The cops were easy to tell apart. Older, blond Bill Lampert was pale as milk, as if he'd come to Scottsdale via Minnesota—a migration that happened pretty frequently, York had learned. The other cop, Juan Alvarado, undoubtedly had roots in the vicinity.

"Who?" York asked.

"His name's Raymond Trotter."

York thought about it, then shook his head. "Never heard of him." He peered at the picture the cop held out. From DMV, it seemed. "Doesn't look familiar. Who is he?"

"Lives here in town. Runs a landscaping company."

"Wait, I know the place. Out off the interstate?" York thought Carole had shopped there.

"Yeah, the big one." Lampert wiped his forehead.

"He's got a problem with me? What sort?" York pulled his Armani shades on. The three p.m. sun in Arizona was like a blowtorch.

"We don't know."

"Well, what *do* you know?"

Alvarado explained. "We arrested a day laborer for drugs. An illegal. Hector Diaz. He wanted to cut a deal on the charge and he told us he had some information about a possible crime. Seems he's worked for this Trotter off and on. A few days ago Trotter comes to him and offers him a thousand dollars to stop by your house and see if you needed yard work done. While he was there he was supposed to check out your alarm system."

"You're kidding."

"Nope."

What was all *this* about? Despite the temperature hovering at 105 degrees York felt a chill run through him. "Alarms? Why?"

"All Trotter told Diaz was he was interested in payback for something you did."

"Payback?" York shook his head in frustration. "Jesus, you come and tell me this crap, somebody's going to—quote—cause me some harm—and you don't have any idea what it's about?"

"No, sir. We were hoping you could tell us."

"Well, I can't."

"Okay, we'll check this Trotter out. But we'd recommend you keep an eye out for anything odd."

"Why don't you arrest him?"

"He hasn't committed a crime," Lampert said. "I'm afraid that without evidence of an overt act, there's nothing we can do."

Cause some harm . . .

Evidence of an overt act . . .

Maybe if they stopped talking like sociology professors they'd do some real goddamn police work. York came close to telling them this but he guessed the disgusted look on his face was message enough.

■

Trying to put the encounter with the cops out of his thoughts, York drove to the gym. Man, he needed some muscle time. He'd just come through a grind of a negotiation with two men who owned a small manufacturing company he was trying to buy. The old guys'd been a lot wilier than he'd expected. They'd made some savvy demands that were going to cost York big money. He'd looked them over, real condescending, and stormed out of their lawyer's office. Let 'em stew for a day or two before. He'd probably concede but he wasn't going to let them think they'd bullied him.

He parked in the health club lot. Climbed out of the car and walked through the fierce sun to the front door.

"Hi, Mr. York. You're early today."

A nod to the daytime desk manager, Gavin.

"Yeah, snuck out when nobody was looking."

He changed clothes and headed for the aerobics room, empty at the moment. He flopped down on the mats to stretch. After ten minutes of limbering up, he headed off to the machines, pushing hard, doing his regular circuit of twenty reps on each before moving on, ending up with crunches; his job as one of the three partners in a major Scottsdale venture capital firm had him doing a lot of entertaining and spending serious time at his desk; his belly had been testing the waistband of his slacks lately.

He didn't like flabby. Neither did women, whatever they told you. A platinum Amex card lets you get away with a lot but when it's bedtime the dolls love solid abs.

After the crunches he hopped on the treadmill for his run.

Mile one, mile two, three . . .

Trying to push the difficult business deal out of his head— goddamn it, what was with those decrepit farts? How could they be so sharp? They oughta be in an old folks' home.

Running, running . . .

Mile five . . .

And who was this Raymond Trotter?

Payback . . .

He scanned his memory again but could come up with no hits on the name.

He fell into the rhythm of his pounding feet. At seven miles he slowed to a walk, cooled off and shut the treadmill down. York pulled a towel over his neck and, ignoring a flirtatious glance from a woman who was pretty but a few years past being worth the risk, returned to the locker room. There he stripped and grabbed a clean towel then headed for the sauna.

York liked this part of the club because it was out of the way and very few members came here at this time of day. Now it was completely deserted. York wandered down the tile corridor. He heard a noise from around the corner. A click, then what sounded like footsteps, though he couldn't tell for sure. Was somebody here? He got to the junction and looked. No, the hallway was empty. But he paused. Something was different. What? He realized the place was unusually dark. He glanced up at the light fixtures. Several bulbs were missing. Four thousand bucks a year for membership and they couldn't replace the bulbs? Man, he'd give Gavin some crap for that. The murkiness, along with a faint, snaky hiss from the ventilation, made the place eerie.

He continued to the door of the redwood sauna, hanging his towel on a hook and turning the temperature selector to high. He'd just started inside when a sharp pain shot through into his foot.

"Hell!' he shouted and danced back, lifting his sole to see what had stabbed him. A wooden splinter was sticking out of the ball of his foot. He pulled it out and pressed his hand against the tiny, bleeding wound. He squinted at the floor where he'd stepped and noted several other splinters.

Oh, Gavin was going to get an earful today. But York's anger faded as he glanced down and found what he supposed was the source of the splinters: two slim wooden shims, hand carved, it looked like, lying on the floor near the doorway. They were like door stops, except that the only door here—to the sauna—was at the top of a two-step stairway. The door couldn't be wedged open.

But the shims could be used to wedge the door *closed* if somebody pounded them into the jamb when the door was shut. They'd fit perfectly. But it'd be crazy to do that. Somebody trapped inside would have no way of turning down the temperature or calling for help; there were no controls inside the unit. And heat in a sauna could kill; York and his wife had just seen a local TV story about a Phoenix woman who'd died in a sauna after she'd fainted in hers.

Holding the shims, staring down at them, a sudden click from nearby made him jump. York turned and saw a shadow against the wall, like that of a person pausing. Then it vanished.

"Hello?" York called.

Silence.

York walked into the hallway. He could see nobody. Then he glanced at the emergency exit door, which didn't seem to be closed all the way. He looked out. The alley was empty. Turning back, he noticed something on the edge of the door. Somebody had taped the latch down so he could get inside without being seen from anyone in the lobby.

Cause you some harm . . .

Five minutes later, showerless, York was hurrying out of the club, not bothering to give Gavin the lecture he deserved. The businessman was carrying the shims and bit of duct tape, wrapped in paper towels. He was careful. Like everybody who watched TV nowadays he knew all about the art of preserving fingerprints.

■

"They're in here."

Stephen York handed the paper towel to pale-skinned detective Bill Lampert. "I didn't touch them—I used tissues."

"At your health club, you said?" asked the detective, looking over the shims and the tape.

"That's right." York couldn't resist adding the name of the exclusive place.

Lampert didn't seem impressed. He stepped to the doorway and handed the evidence to Alvarado. "Prints, tool marks, stat." The young officer vanished.

Turning back to York. "But nobody actually tried to detain you in the sauna?"

Detain? York asked himself wryly. You mean: *Lock me inside to roast me to death*. "No." He pulled out a cigar. "You mind?"

"There's no smoking in the building," Lampert replied.

"Maybe not technically, but . . ."

"There's no smoking in the building."

York put the stogie away. "The way I read it, Trotter found out my routine. He got into the club and taped the back door open so he could get in without anybody seeing him from the lobby."

"How'd he do that? He a member?"

"I don't know."

Lampert held up a finger. He called the club and had a brief conversation. "No record of him as a member or a guest in the last month."

"Then he had a fake ID or something to try a guest membership."

"Fake ID? That's a little . . . complicated, isn't it?"

"Well, somehow, the asshole got inside. He was going to seal me inside but I think I surprised him and he ditched the shims and took off."

Alvarado walked into his boss's office. "No prints. Tool marks aren't distinctive but if we find a plane or chisel we might make a match."

York laughed. "No prints? That's proof of something right there, isn't it?"

Lampert ignored him. He lifted a sheet of paper from his desk and looked it over. "Well, we've looked into this Trotter fellow. Seems like any normal guy. No police record except for a few traffic tickets. But there is something. I talked to the Veterans Administration in Phoenix. Turns out they have a file on him. He was in Kuwait, the first Gulf War. His unit got hit hard. Half his men were killed and he was badly wounded. After he got discharged he moved here, spent a year in counseling. The file has his shrink's notes in it. That's all privileged—doctor-patient—and we're not supposed to see it but I've got a buddy in the VA and he gave me the gist. Apparently after Trotter got out of the service he ended up hanging with a bad crowd here and in Albuquerque. Did some strong-arm stuff. For hire. That was a while ago, and he was never arrested but still . . . "

"Christ. . . . So maybe somebody hired him?"

"Who've you pissed off bad enough they'd go to this kind of trouble to get even?"

"I don't know. I'd have to think about it."

Alvarado said, "You know that expression 'Revenge is a dish best served cold'?"

"Yeah, I think I heard of that."

"Might be somebody from your distant past. Think way back."

A dish served cold . . .

"Okay. But what're we going to do in the meantime?" York asked, wiping his sweating palms on his pants.

"Let's go have a talk with him. See what he has to say." The detective picked up the phone and placed a call.

"Mr. Trotter please. . . . I see. Could you tell me when? . . . Thanks. No message." He hung up. "He just left for Tucson. He'll be back tomorrow morning."

"Aren't you going to stop him?"

"Why?"

"Maybe he's trying to escape, go to Mexico. "

Lampert shrugged and opened a file from another case. "Then I guess you're off the hook."

■

Pulling up to their five-million-dollar mini-mansion on the edge of the desert, York climbed out of his Mercedes, locked the doors and looked around to make sure he hadn't been followed. No sign of anyone. Still, when he walked inside he double-locked the door behind him.

"Hey, honey." Carole joined him in the entryway, wearing her workout Spandex. His third wife was frosted blonde and beautiful. ("You guys give good visuals," an associate once said.) They'd been together three years. A former secretary turned personal trainer, Carole had just the right mix of what York called being-on-the-ball and not-getting-it. Meaning she could carry on a conversation and not be embarrassing but she kept quiet when she knew she was supposed to—and didn't ask too many questions about where he'd been when he came home late or went on last-minute business trips.

She glanced at the door. "What's with that?" They never used the deadbolt.

He had to be careful. Carole needed things explained to her in simple terms and if she didn't understand what he told her, she'd freak. And her brand of hysteria could get ugly. He'd found that out about stupid people, how they lost it when confronted with something they didn't understand.

So he lied. "Somebody up the street got broken into yesterday."

"I didn't hear about it."

"Well, they did."

"Who?"

"I don't remember."

A faint giggle—a habit of hers he found either irritating or sexy, depending on his mood. "You don't know who? That's weird."

Today's was an irritating giggle.

"Somebody told me. I forgot. I got a lot on my mind."

"Can we go to the club for dinner?"

"I'm wasted, baby. I'll barbecue tonight. How's that?"

"Okay, sure."

He could tell she was disappointed but York knew how to bail out sinking ships; he mixed cocktails fast—doubles—and steered her to the pool, where he put on a Yanni CD. In twenty minutes the liquor and music had dulled her disappointment and she was babbling on about wanting to go visit her family in Los Angeles in a couple of weeks, would he mind baching it?

"Whatever." He gave it a minute and then, sounding casual, said, "I'm thinking of getting some plants for the office."

"You want me to help?"

"No, Marge is handling it. You ever buy anything from that landscaper out by the highway? Trotter's?"

"I don't know. I think so. A while ago."

"They ever deliver anything here?"

"No, I just bought some houseplants and brought 'em home. Why?"

"Wondering if they have good service."

"Now you're into decorating. That's wild." Another giggle.

He grunted and headed into the kitchen, pulled open the fridge.

Smoking a Macanudo and drinking his vodka and tonic, York grilled some steaks and made a salad and they ate in silence. After she'd cleared the dishes, they moved into the den and watched some TV. Carole got cuddly. Normally this meant it was time for the hot tub, or bed—or sometimes the floor—but tonight he said, "You head on upstairs, doll. I've got a few numbers to look over."

"Aw." Another pout.

"I'll be up soon."

"Oh, okay." She sighed, picked up a book and climbed the stairs.

When he heard the door click shut he walked into his study, shut the lights out and peered out at the dark sweep of moonlit desert behind the house. Shadows, rocks, cacti, stars . . . This was a vista he loved. It changed constantly. He remained here for five minutes, then, pouring a tall scotch, he kicked his shoes off and stretched out on the couch.

A sip of smoky liquor. Another.

Payback . . .

And Stephen York began a trip through his past, looking for some reason that Trotter, or anyone, wanted him dead.

Because he had ditsy Carole on his mind, he thought first of the women who'd been in his life. He considered his ex-wives. York had been the one who'd ended each of the marriages. The first wife, Vicky, had gone off the deep end when he'd told her he was leaving. The little mouse had cried and begged him to stay even though she knew about the affair he'd been having with his secretary. But he was adamant about the divorce and soon he cut off all contact with her, except for financial matters involving their son, Randy.

But would she actually hire a killer to get even with him?

No way, he decided: Vicky's reaction to the breakup was to play victim, not vengeful ex. Besides, York had done right by her. He'd paid alimony and child support promptly and, a few years later, hadn't contested the custody order that took away his rights to see their son.

York and his second wife were together only two years. She'd proved too brittle for him, too liberal, too NPR. *That* breakup was Holyfield-Tyson, pure combat. Susan, a high-powered commercial real estate lawyer, walked away with a lot of money, more than enough to salve her injured pride (York left her for a woman sixteen years younger and twenty pounds slimmer). She also took her career too seriously to risk it by doing anything illegal to him. She had remarried—a military consultant and former army colonel she'd met negotiating a contract with the government for her client—and York was sure he'd fallen off her radar screen.

Ex-girlfriends? The usual suspects. . . . But, brother, where to start? Almost too many to count. He'd broken up badly with some of them, used some, lied. Of course, York himself had been used and lied to by women. On the whole it evened out, he figured. That was how the game worked; nobody sane would hire a hit man to kill a lover just because he'd dumped you.

Who else could it be?

Most likely, he decided, it was somebody he'd had business dealings with.

But there were a lot of fish in that sea too. Dozens came to mind. When he'd been a salesman for a pharmaceutical company, he'd reported one of his fellow detail men for cheating on his expense account (York turned him in not out of company loyalty but to pillage the guy's territory). The man was fired and vowed to get even.

He'd also been involved in the acquisition of dozens of companies over the last ten years; hundreds of employees had been fired as a result. He recalled one of these in particular—a salesman who'd come to him in tears, after he'd been let go, begging for a second chance. York, though, stuck to his decision—mostly because he didn't like the man's whining. A week later the salesman killed himself; his note said he'd failed as a man because he could no longer take care of his wife and children. York could hardly be responsible for crazy behavior like that. But his survivors might not feel that way. Maybe Trotter was this man's brother or best friend, or been hired by them.

He recalled another incident: the time he'd had a private eye check out a rival venture capitalist and found he was gay. The client that they were both wooing was a homophobe. During dinner one night York subtly dropped the skinny on the rival, and the next day York's outfit got the assignment. Had *he* found out and hired Trotter?

Any other sins?

Oh, you bet, York thought in disgust, reaching into the dim past.

A dish served cold . . .

Recalling an incident in college, a prank gone wrong—a frat hazing that resulted in a pledge getting drunk and stabbing a cop. The kid was expelled, then disappeared not long after. York couldn't remember his name. It could've been Trotter.

A dozen other incidents flooded into his thoughts, two dozen, three—people ignored and insulted, lies told, associates cheated. . . . His memory spit out not only the serious offenses, but the petty ones too: rudeness to clerks, gouging an elderly woman who'd sold him her car, laughing when a man's toupee flew off in a heavy wind . . .

Reliving them all. It was exhausting.

Another hit of scotch . . . then another.

And the next thing he knew the sun was streaming through the window. He squinted in pain from the hangover and groggily focused on his watch. Oh, damn, it was nine. . . . Why hadn't Carole wakened him? She knew he had two deals this morning. Sometimes that woman just didn't have a goddamn clue.

York staggered into the kitchen, and Carole looked up from the phone. She smiled. "Breakfast's ready."

"You let me sleep."

She told her friend she'd call back and hung up. "I figured you were tired. And you looked just too cute, all cuddled up."

Cute. Jesus Lord . . . York winced in pain. His neck was frozen from sleeping in an awkward position.

"I don't have time for breakfast," he grumbled.

"My mother always said breakfast is—"

"—the most important meal of the day. So you've told me. Like, a hundred times."

She went silent. Then rose and walked into the living room with her coffee and phone.

"Baby, I didn't mean . . . "

York sighed. Like walking on eggshells sometimes. . . . He retreated to the bedroom. He was fishing for aspirin in the medicine cabinet when the phone rang.

"For you" was his wife's cool announcement.

It was Detective Bill Lampert. "Trotter's back in town. Let's go say hi. We'll pick you up in twenty minutes."

■

"Yes, can I help you?"

"Raymond Trotter?"

"That's right."

Standing in front of Trotter Landscaping and Nursery, a rambling complex of low buildings, greenhouses and potting sheds, Bill Lampert and Juan Alvarado looked over the middle-aged man. Lampert noted that he was in very good shape: slim, with broad shoulders. His brown hair, flecked with gray, was cut short. His square-jawed face shaved perfectly, blue jogging outfit immaculate. Confident eyes. The detective wondered if they revealed surprise as he glanced at their shields and maybe a bit more surprise at the sight of Stephen York, standing behind them. Trotter set down the large cactus he was holding.

"Sir, we understand you were seeking some personal information about Mr. York here."

"Who?"

Good delivery, Lampert reflected. He nodded behind him. "The gentleman there."

Trotter frowned. "You're mistaken, I'm afraid. I don't know him."

"You're sure?"

"Yes."

"Do you know a man named Hector Diaz? Mexican, thirty-five, stocky. He used to work day labor for you."

"I've hired hundreds of day people. I don't know half their names. Is this an immigration issue? My people are supposed to check documentation."

"No, sir, it's not. This Diaz claimed you asked him about Mr. York's security."

"What?" Then Trotter squinted knowingly. "How'd this all come up. By any chance, was Diaz arrested for something?"

"That's right."

"So he made up something about a former employer to get a shorter sentence. Doesn't that happen?"

Lampert and his partner shared a look. Whatever else, this Trotter wasn't stupid. "Sometimes, sure."

"Well, I didn't do what Diaz said I did." The piercing eyes turned to York.

Alvarado took over. "Were you in the Scottsdale Health and Racquet Club yesterday?"

"The . . . oh, the fancy one? No, that's not how I spend my money. Besides, I was in Tucson."

"Before you left for Tucson."

"No. I have no idea what you're getting at but I don't know this York. I don't have any interest in his alarm systems."

Lampert felt Alvarado touch his shoulder. The young detective was pointing at a pile of wooden boards, about the same width and thickness of the shims.

"You mind if we take a couple of those with us?"

"You go right ahead . . . soon as you show me a search warrant."

"We'd appreciate your cooperation."

"I'd appreciate a warrant."

"Are you worried about what we might find?" Alvarado chimed in.

"I'm not at all worried. It's just that we've got this thing in America called the Constitution." He grinned. "What makes our country great. I play by the rules. I guess you should too."

York sighed loudly. Trotter looked him over coolly.

Alvarado said, "If you have nothing to hide then there'll be no problem."

"If *you* have probable cause there'll be no problem getting a search warrant."

"So you're telling us you have no intent to endanger Mr. York in any way."

Trotter laughed. "That's ridiculous." Then his face grew icy. "This is pretty serious, what you're suggesting. You start spreading rumors like this, it could get embarrassing. For me . . . and for you. I hope you realize that."

"Assault and breaking and entering are very serious crimes," Alvarado said.

Trotter picked up the plant. It was impressive, its wild spikes dangerous. "If there's nothing else . . ."

"No, there's nothing else. Thanks for your time." Lampert nodded to his partner and he and York started back to the cars.

When they were in the parking lot Lampert said, "He's up to something."

York nodded. "I know what you mean—that look he gave me. It was like he was saying, I'm going to get you. I swear."

"Look? That's not what I'm talking about. Didn't you hear him? He said he wasn't interested in your 'alarms.' I never told him that's what Diaz said. I only mentioned 'security.' That could mean anything. Makes me believe Diaz was telling the truth."

York was impressed. "I never noticed it. Good catch. So what do we do now?"

"You have that list I wanted? Of anybody might have a grudge against you?"

He handed over a sheet of paper. "Anything else I should do?"

Looking at the list, Lampert said, "One thing. You might want to think about a bodyguard."

■

Stan Eberhart looked a bit like Lampert—solid, sculpted hair, humorless, focused as a terrier—only with a tan. The big man stood in the doorway of York's home. The businessman ushered him in.

"Morning, sir." He spoke with a faint drawl and was the epitome of calm. Eberhart was the head of security for York's company—York-McMillan-Winston Investments. After his meeting with the cops and Trotter, York had called the man into his office and told him the situation. Eberhart agreed to "put together a comprehensive SP that'll take in all contingencies for the situation." Sounding just like the Scottsdale cops (not too surprising; Eberhart had been a detective in Phoenix).

An SP, it turned out, was a security plan, and York figured it would be a good one. Eberhart was a heavy hitter in corporate security. In addition to working homicide in Phoenix he'd been a federal drug agent and a private eye. He was a black- or red- or some kick-ass-belt karate expert and flew helicopters and owned a hundred guns. Security people, York learned, did all that Outdoor Life Network crap. Tough guys. York didn't get it. If making money, golf, martinis and women weren't involved, what was the point?

Alone now in the house—Carole was at her tennis lesson— the men walked into the large sunroom, which the security man studied with a face that suggested he wasn't happy.

Why? Did he think it was too exposed because of the glass? He's worried about goddamn snipers? York laughed to himself.

Eberhart suggested they go into the kitchen, away from the glass windows.

York shrugged and played along. They sat at the kitchen island. The man unbuttoned his jacket—he always wore a suit and tie, whatever the temperature. "First off, let me tell you what I've found out about Trotter. He was born in New Hampshire, majored in engineering in Boston. He got married and went into the army. After he was discharged he came back here. Whatever happened after that—the stuff in the VA file—he *seemed* to turn his life around. Started the landscaping company. Then his wife died."

"Died? Maybe that's the thing—he blames me for it. What happened?"

Eberhart was shaking his head. "She had cancer. And you, your company and your clients don't have any connection with the doctors that treated her or the hospital."

"You checked that?"

"An SP is only as good as the intelligence behind it," the man recited. "Now about his family: He's got three kids. Philip, Celeste and Cindy, ages fourteen, seventeen and eighteen. All in local public schools. Good kids, no trouble with the law." He showed candid pictures that looked like they were from school yearbooks: a skinny, good-looking boy and two daughters: one round and pretty, the other lean and athletic.

"You ever hit on the girls?"

"God no." York was offended. He had *some* standards.

Eberhart didn't ask if his boss had ever made a move on the son. If he had, York would've fired him on the spot.

"Trotter was single for a while then last year he remarried, Nancy Stockard—real estate broker, thirty-nine. She got divorced about five years ago, has a ten-year-old son." Another picture emerged. "You recognize her?"

York looked at the picture. Now, *she* was somebody he could definitely go for. Pretty in a girl-next-door way. Great for a one-night stand. Or two.

But, he reflected, no such luck. He would've remembered.

Eberhart continued, "Now, Trotter seems like a good guy, loves his kids, drives 'em to soccer and swimming and their after-school jobs. Model parent, model husband and good businessman. Made a ton of money last year. Pays his taxes, even goes to church sometimes. Now, let me show you what we've come up with for the SP."

The plan provided for two teams of security specialists, one to conduct surveillance on Trotter and the other to serve as bodyguards. It would be expensive; rent-a-cops don't come cheap.

"But frankly I don't think this'll go on for too long, sir," Eberhart said. He explained that all seven people he had in mind for the security detail were former cops and knew how to run crime scenes and interview witnesses. "With all of us on it, we'll build a solid case, enough to put him away for a long time. We'll have more people and resources on this than Scottsdale Homicide."

And, Christ, the fee'll probably be the same as their annual budget.

York gave the man his and Carole's general daily routine, the stores they shopped at, restaurants and bars they went to regularly. He added that he wanted the guards to keep their distance; he still hadn't shared the story with Carole.

"She doesn't know?"

"Nope. Probably wouldn't take it too well. You know women."

Eberhart didn't seem to know what his boss meant exactly. But he said, "We'll do the best we can, sir."

York saw the security man to the door, thanked him. The man pointed out the first team, in a tan Ford, parked two doors down. York hadn't even noticed them when he'd answered the door. Which meant they knew what they were doing.

As the security specialist drove off, York's eyes again looked into the backyard, at the desert horizon. Recalling that he'd laughed about snipers earlier.

Now, the thought wasn't funny. York returned inside and pulled closed the drapes on every window that opened onto the beautiful desert vista.

∎

As the days went by there were no further incidents and York began to relax. The guard details watching York and Carole remained largely invisible, and his wife had no clue that she was being guarded when she went on her vital daily missions—to the nail salon, the hairdresser, the club and the mall.

The surveillance team kept a close watch on Trotter, who seemed oblivious to the tail. He went about his life. A few times the man fell off the surveillance radar but only for short periods and it didn't seem that he'd been trying to lose the security people. When he disappeared the teams on York and Carole stepped up protection and there were no incidents.

Meanwhile, Lampert and Alvarado continued to look into the list of people with grudges from York's past. Some seemed likely, some improbable, but in any event none of the leads panned out.

York decided to get away for a long weekend in Santa Fe for golf and shopping. York chose to leave the bodyguards behind, because they'd be too hard to hide from Carole. Eberhart thought this was okay; they'd keep a close eye on Trotter and if he left Scottsdale a team would fly to Santa Fe to cover York immediately.

The couple hit the road early. The security man told York to take a complicated route out of town, then pause at a particular vista east of the city, where he could make certain they weren't being followed, which he did. No one was following.

Once away from the city York pointed the car into the dawn sun and eased back in the Mercedes's leather seat, as the slipstream poured into the convertible and tousled their hair.

"Put on some music, doll," he called to Carole.

"Sure thing. What?"

"Something loud," he shouted.

A moment later Led Zeppelin chugged from the speakers. York punched off the cruise control and pushed the accelerator to the floor.

■

Sitting in his white surveillance van, near Ray Trotter's pink adobe house, Stan Eberhart heard his phone chirp. "Yeah?"

Julio, one of the rent-a-cops, said, "Stan, got a problem."

"Go on."

"Has he left yet?"

"York? Yeah, an hour ago."

"Hmm."

"What's the matter?"

"I'm at a NAPA dealer near the landscaping company."

Eberhart had sent people to stores near Trotter's house and business. Armed with pictures, they were querying clerks about purchases the man might've made recently. The security people were no longer in the law enforcement profession, of course, but Eberhart had learned that twenty-dollar bills open as many doors as police shields do. Probably more.

"And?"

"Two days ago this guy who looked like Trotter ordered a copy of a technical manual for Mercedes sports cars. It came in yesterday and he picked it up. The same time, he bought a set of metric wrenches and battery acid. Stan, the book was about brakes. And that was just around the time we lost Trotter for a couple of hours."

"He could've gotten to York's Mercedes, you think?"

"Not likely but possible. I think we have to assume he did."

"I'll get back to you." Eberhart hung up and immediately called York.

A distracted voice answered. "Hi."

"Mr. York, it's—"

"I'm not available at the moment. Please leave a message and I'll get back to you as soon as possible."

Eberhart hit disconnect and tried again. Each of the five times he called, the only response was the preoccupied voice on the voicemail.

■

York was nudging the Mercedes up to a hundred.

"Doesn't this rock?" he called, laughing. "Whoa!"

"Like, what?" Carole shouted back. The roar of the slipstream and Robert Plant's soaring voice had drowned out his voice.

"It's great!"

But she didn't answer. She was frowning, looking ahead. "There's, like, a turn up there." She added something else he couldn't hear.

"What?"

"Uhm, maybe you better slow down."

"This baby curves on a dime. I'm fine."

"Honey, please! Slow down!"

"I know how to drive."

They were on a straightaway, which was about to drop down a steep hill. At the bottom the road curved sharply and fed onto a bridge above a deep arroyo.

"Slow down! Honey, please! Look at the turn!"

Christ, sometimes it just wasn't worth the battle. "Okay."

He lifted his foot off the gas.

And then it happened.

He had no clue exactly what was going on. A huge swirl of sand, spinning around and around, as if the car were caught in the middle of a tornado. They lost sight of the sky. Carole, screaming, grabbed the dash. York, gripping the wheel with cramping hands, tried desperately to find the road. All he could see was sand, whipping into his face, stinging.

"We're going to die, we're going to die," Carole was wailing.

Then from somewhere above them, a tinny voice crackled, "York, stop your car immediately. Stop your car!"

He looked up to see the police helicopter thirty feet over his head, its rotors' downdraft the source of the sandstorm.

"Who's that?" Carole screamed. "Who's that?"

The voice continued, "Your brakes are going to fail! Don't start down that hill!"

"Son of a bitch," he cried. "He tampered with the brakes."

"Who, Stephen? What's going on?"

The helicopter sped forward toward the bridge and landed—presumably so the rescue workers could try to save them if the car crashed or plummeted over the cliff.

Save them, or collect the bodies.

He was doing ninety as they started over the crest of the hill. The nose of the Mercedes dropped and they began to accelerate.

He pressed the brake pedal. The calipers seemed to grip.

But if he got any farther and the brakes failed he'd have nowhere to go but into rock or over the cliff; there was no way they could make the turn doing more than thirty-five. At least here there was sand just past the shoulder.

Stephen York gripped the wheel firmly and took a deep breath. "Hold on!"

"Whatta you mean—?"

He swerved off the road.

Suitcases and soda and beer flew from the backseat, Carole screamed and York fought with all his strength to keep the car on course, but it was useless. The tires skewed, out of control, through the sand. He just missed a large boulder and plowed into the desert.

Rocks and gravel spattered the body, spidering the windshield and peppering the fender and hood like gunshots. Tumbleweeds and sagebrush pelted their faces. The car bounced and shook and pitched. Twice it nearly flipped over.

They were slowing but they were still speeding at forty miles an hour straight for a large boulder. . . . Now, though, the sand was so deep that he couldn't steer at all.

"Jesus, Jesus, Jesus. . . . " Carole was sobbing, lowering her head to her hands.

York jammed his foot onto the brake pedal with his left foot, shoved the shifter into reverse and then floored the accelerator with his right. The engine screamed, sand cascaded into the air above them.

The car came to a stop five feet from the face of the rock.

York sat forward, head against the wheel, his heart pounding, drenched in sweat. He was furious. Why hadn't they called him? What was with the *Black Hawk Down* routine?

Then he noticed his phone. The screen read, 7 *missed calls 5 messages marked urgent.*

He hadn't heard the ring. The wind and the engine . . . and the goddamn music.

Sobbing and pawing at the sand that covered her white pant suit, Carole snapped at him, "What is going on? I want to know. Now."

And, as Eberhart and Lampert walked toward them from the chopper, he told her the whole story.

■

No weekend vacation, Carole announced.

"You, like, might've mentioned it up front."

Showing some backbone for a change.

"I didn't want to worry you."

"You mean you didn't want me to ask what you did to somebody to make them want to get even with you."

"I—.

"Take me home. Now."

They'd returned to Scottsdale in silence, driving in a rental car; the Mercedes had been towed away by the police to look for evidence of tampering and repairs. An hour after walking through their front door Carole left again, suitcase in hand, headed to Los Angeles early for the family visit.

York was secretly relieved she was going. He couldn't deal both with Trotter and his wife's crazy moods. He returned inside, checked the lock on every door and window and spent the night with a bottle of Johnnie Walker and HBO.

■

Two days later, around five p.m., York was working out in the gym he'd set up in a bedroom—he was avoiding the health club and its deadly sauna. He heard the doorbell. Picking up the pistol he now kept in the entryway, he peered out. It was Eberhart. Three locks and a deadbolt later, he gestured the security man in.

"Got something you should know about. I had two teams on Trotter yesterday. He went to a multiplex for a matinee at noon."

"So?"

"There's a rule: anybody under surveillance goes to a movie by himself . . . that's suspicious. So the teams compared notes. Seems that fifteen minutes after he goes in, this guy in overalls comes out with a couple of trash bags. Then about an hour later, little over, a delivery man in a uniform shows up at the theater, carrying a big box. But my man talked to the manager. The workers there don't usually take the first trash out to the Dumpster until five or six at night. And there weren't any deliveries scheduled that day."

York grimaced. "So, he dodged you for an hour. He could get anywhere in that time."

"He didn't take his car. We had it covered. And we checked cab companies. Nobody called for one in that area."

"So he walked someplace?"

"Yep. And we're pretty sure where. Southern States Chemical is ten minutes by foot from the multiplex. And you know what's interesting?" He looked at his notes. "They make acrylonitrile, methyl methacrylate and adiponitrile."

"What the hell're those?"

"Industrial chemicals. By themselves they're not any big deal. But what *is* important is that they're used to make hydrogen cyanide."

"Jesus. Like the poison?"

"Like the poison. And one of my guys looked over Southern States. There's no security. Cans of the chemicals were sitting right out in the open by the loading dock. Trotter could've walked up, taken enough to make a batch of poison that'd kill a dozen people and nobody would've seen him. And guess who did the company's landscaping?"

"Trotter."

"So he'd know about the chemicals and where they were kept."

"Could anybody make it? The cyanide?"

"Apparently it's not that hard. And with Trotter in the landscaping business, you'd have to figure he knows chemicals and fertilizers. And remember: He was in the army too, first Gulf War. A lot of those boys got experience with chemical weapons."

The businessman slammed his hand down on the counter. "Goddamnit. So he's got this poison and I'll never know if he's slipped it into what I'm eating. Jesus."

"Well, that's not exactly true," Eberhart said reasonably. "Your house is secure. If you buy packaged food and keep an eye on things at restaurants you can control the risk."

Control the risk . . .

Disgusted, York returned to the hallway, snagged the FedEx envelope containing a delivery of his cigars, which had arrived that morning, and ripped it open. He stalked into the kitchen, unwrapping the cigars. "I can't even go outside to buy my own smokes. I'm a prisoner. That's what I am." York rummaged in a drawer for a cigar cutter, found one and nipped the end off the Macanudo. He chomped down angrily on the cigar, clicked the flame of a lighter and lifted it to his mouth.

Just at that moment a voice yelled, "No!"

Startled, York reached for his gun. But before he could reach it, he was tackled from behind and tumbled hard to the floor, the breath knocked from his lungs.

Gasping, in agony, he scrabbled back in panic. He stared around him—and saw no threat. He then shouted at the security man, "What're you doing?"

Breathing heavily, Eberhart rose and pulled his boss to his feet. "Sorry . . . I had to stop you. . . . The cigar."

"The—?"

"Cigar. Don't touch it."

The security man grabbed several Baggies. In one he put the cigars. In the other the FedEx envelope. "When I was asking you about stores you go to—for the security plan—you told me you get your cigars in Phoenix, right?"

"Right. So what?"

Eberhart held up the FedEx label. "These were sent from a Postal Plus store in the Sonora Hills strip mall."

York thought. "That's near—"

"Three minutes from Trotter's company. He could've called the store and found out when you ordered some. Then bought some himself and doctored 'em. I'll get a field test kit and see."

"Don't I need . . . I mean, don't I need to eat cyanide for it to kill me?"

"Uh-uh." The security expert sniffed the bag carefully. "Cyanide smells like almonds." He shook his head. "Can't tell. Maybe the tobacco's covering up the scent."

"Almonds," York whispered. "Almonds. . . " He smelled his fingers and began washing his hands frantically.

There was a long silence.

Rubbing his skin with paper towels, York glanced at Eberhart, who was lost in thought.

"What?" the businessman snapped.

"I think it's time for a change of plans."

■

The next day Stephen York parked his leased Mercedes in the hot, dusty lot of the Scottsdale Police Department. He looked around uneasily for Trotter's car—a dark blue Lexus sedan, they'd learned. He didn't see it.

York climbed out, carrying plastic bags containing the FedEx envelope, cigars and food from his kitchen. He carried them into the PD's building, chilly from an overeager air conditioner.

In a ground-floor conference room he found four men: the buddy team of Lampert and Alvarado, as well as Stan Eberhart and a man who was dressed in exactly the same clothes that York wore and who was his same build. The man introduced himself as Peter Billings, an undercover cop.

"Long as I'm playing the part of you for a little while, Mr. York, was wonderin', s'okay to use your pool and hot tub?"

"My—"

"Joking there," Billings said.

"Ah," York muttered humorlessly and turned to Lampert. "Here they are."

The detective took the bags and tossed them absently on an empty chair. None of the cigars or food contained poison, according to a test Eberhart conducted at York's. But bringing them here—presumably under the eye of vengeful Mr. Trotter—was an important part of their plan. They needed to make Trotter believe for the next hour or so that they were convinced he was going to poison York.

After the tests turned out negative Eberhart had concluded that Trotter was faking the whole cyanide thing; he only wanted the police to *think* he intended to poison York. Why? A diversion, of course. If the police were confident they knew the intended method of attack, they'd prepare for that and not the real one.

But what *was* the real one? How was Trotter actually going to come at York?

Eberhart had taken an extreme step to find out: breaking into Trotter's house. While the landscaper, his wife and their children were out Eberhart had disabled the alarm and surveillance cameras then examined the man's office carefully. Hidden in the desk were books on sabotage and surveillance. Two pages were marked with Post-its, marking chapters on turning propane tanks into bombs and on making remote detonators. He found another clue, as well: a note that said "Rodriguez Garden Supplies."

Which was where Stephen York went every Saturday afternoon to exchange his barbecue grill's propane tanks. Eberhart believed that Trotter's plan was to keep the police focused on a poison attack, when he was in fact going to arrange an "accidental" explosion after York picked up his new propane tank. The security man, though, couldn't go to the police with this information—he'd be admitting he'd committed trespass—so he told Bill Lampert only that he'd heard from some sources that Trotter was asking about propane tanks and where York shopped. There was no evidence for a search warrant but the detective reluctantly agreed to Eberhart's plan to catch Trotter in the act. First, they'd make it seem that they believed the cyanide threat. Since Trotter probably knew York went to the propane store every Saturday around lunchtime, the businessman would take the cigars and food to the police, apparently for testing, which would occupy them for several hours. Trotter would be following. York would then leave and run some errands, among them picking up a new propane canister. Only it wouldn't be Stephen York in the car, but Detective Peter Billings, the look-alike. Billings would collect a new propane tank from Rodriguez's—though it would be empty, for safety's sake—and then stash it in his car. He'd then return to the store to browse and Lampert and his teams would wait for Trotter to make his move.

"So where's our boy?" Lampert asked his partner.

Alvarado explained that Trotter had left his house about the same time as York and headed in the same direction. They'd lost him in traffic for a time but then picked him up at a Whole Foods grocery store lot within walking distance of Rodriguez's. One officer saw him inside.

Lampert called the other players in the setup. "It's going down," he announced.

Doing his impersonation of York, Billings walked outside, got into the car and headed into traffic. Eberhart and York climbed into one of the chase cars and eased after him, though well behind so they wouldn't get spotted by Trotter if he was, in fact, trailing Billings.

Twenty minutes later the undercover cop pulled up in front of Rodriguez's Garden Supplies, and Eberhart, York beside him, parked in a mini-mall lot a block away. Lampert and the teams moved into position nearby. "Okay," Billings radioed through his hidden mike, "I'm getting the tank, going inside."

York and Eberhart leaned forward to watch what was happening. York could just make out his Mercedes up the street.

Lampert called over the radio, "Any sign of Trotter?"

"Hasn't come out of Whole Foods yet," sounded through the speaker of the walkie-talkie dashboard.

Billings came on a moment later. "All units. I've loaded the fake tank in the car. The backseat. I'm going back inside."

Fifteen minutes later York heard a cop's voice urgently saying, "Have something. . . . Guy in a hat and sunglasses, could be Trotter approaching the Mercedes from the east. He's got a shopping bag in one hand and something in the other. Looks like a small computer. Might be a detonator. Or the device itself."

The security specialist nodded at Stephen York, sitting beside him, and said, "Here we go."

"Got him on visual," another cop said.

The surveillance officer continued. "He's looking around. . . . Hold on. . . . Okay, the suspect just walked by York's car. Couldn't see for sure, but he paused. Think he might've dropped something underneath it. Now he's crossing the street. . . . He's going into Miguel's."

Lampert radioed, "That'll be where he'll detonate the device from. . . . All right, people, let's seal off the street and get an undercover inside Miguel's to monitor him."

Eberhart lifted an eyebrow to York and smiled. "This is it."

"Hope so" was the uneasy response.

Now officers were moving in slowly, sticking close to the buildings on either side of Miguel's Bar and Grill, where Trotter'd be waiting for "York" to return to the car, detonate the device and burn him to death.

A new voice came on the radio. "I'm inside Miguel's," came a whisper from the second undercover cop. "I see the subject by the window on a stool, looking out. No weapons in sight. He's opened up what he was carrying before—a small computer or something, antenna on it. He just typed something. Assume that the device is armed."

Lampert radioed, "Roger. We're in position, three behind Miguel's, two in front. The street's been barricaded and Rodriguez's is clear; we got everybody out the back door. We're ready for the takedown."

In Eberhart's car, the security man kept up an irritating drumming with his fingertips on the steering wheel.

York tried to tune it out, wondering, Would Trotter resist? Maybe he'd panic and—

He jumped as Eberhart's hand gripped his arm hard. The security man was looking in the rearview mirror. He was frowning. "What's that?"

York turned. On the trunk was a small shopping bag. While they'd been staring at York's Mercedes, somebody had put it there.

"This is Eberhart. All units, stand by."

Lampert asked, "What's up, Stan?"

Eberhart said breathlessly, "He made us! He didn't plant anything under the Mercedes. Or if he did there's another device on our car. It's in a Whole Foods bag, a little one. We're getting out!"

"Negative, negative," another voice called over the radio. "This is Grimes with the bomb unit. It could have a pressure or rocker switch. Any movement could set it off. Stay put, we'll get an officer there."

Eberhart muttered, "It's a *double* feint. He leads us off with the poison and then a fake bomb at the Mercedes. He's been watching us all along and he's planning to get us here. . . . Jesus."

Lampert called, "All units, we're going into Miguel's. Don't let him hit the detonator."

Eberhart covered his face with his jacket.

Stephen York had his doubts that that would provide much protection from an exploding gas tank. But he did exactly the same.

■

"Ready?" Lampert whispered to Alvarado and the others on the takedown team, huddled at the back door of Miguel's.

Nods all around.

"Let's do it."

They crashed through the door fast, pistols and machine guns up, while other officers charged through the front. As soon as he stepped into the bar, Lampert sighted on Trotter's head, ready to nail him if he made any move toward the detonator.

But the suspect merely turned, alarmed and frowning in curiosity like the other patrons, at the sound of the officers.

"Hands up! You, Trotter, freeze, freeze!"

The landscaper stumbled back off the stool, eyes wide in shock. He lifted his hands.

An officer from the bomb squad stepped between Trotter and the detonator and looked it over carefully, as the tac cops threw the man to the floor and cuffed him.

"I didn't do anything! What's this all about?"

The detective called into his microphone, "We've got him. Bomb Units One and Two, proceed with the render safe operation."

■

In the car, complete silence. Eberhart and York struggled to remain motionless but York felt as if his pounding heart was going to jiggle the bomb enough so that it would detonate.

They'd learned that Trotter was in custody and couldn't push the detonator button. But that didn't mean that the device wasn't set with a hair trigger. Eberhart had spent the last five minutes lecturing York on how sensitive some bomb detonators could be—until York had told him to shut the hell up.

Wrapped in his jacket, the businessman peeked out and, in the side-view mirror, watched the policeman in a green bomb suit approach the car slowly. Through the radio's tinny speaker they heard, "Eberhart, York, stay completely still."

"Sure," Eberhart said in a throaty whisper, his lips barely moving.

York could see the policeman step closer and peer into the shopping bag. He took out a flashlight and pointed it downward, examining the contents. With a wooden probe, like a chopstick, he carefully searched the bag.

Through the speaker they heard what sounded like a gasp.

York cringed.

But it wasn't.

The sound was a laugh. Followed by: "Trash."

"It's what?"

The officer pulled his hood off and walked to the front of the car. With a shaking hand, York rolled the window down.

"Trash," the man repeated. "Somebody's lunch. They had sushi, Pringles and a Yoo-hoo. That chocolate stuff. Not a meal I myself would've picked."

"Trash?" Lampert's voice snapped through the speaker.

"That is affirmative."

The first bomb unit called in; a search of the area beneath York's Mercedes revealed nothing but a crumpled soda cup, which Trotter might or might not've thrown there.

York wiped his face and climbed out of the car, leaned against it to steady himself. "Goddamn it, he's been yanking our chain. Let's go talk to that son of a bitch."

■

Lampert looked up to see Eberhart and York angrily walking into Miguel's. The patrons had resumed eating and drinking and were clearly enjoying this real-life *Law and Order* show.

He turned back to the uniformed officer who'd just searched Trotter. "Wallet, keys, money. Nothing else."

Another detective from the bomb squad had carefully examined the "detonator" and reported that they'd been wrong; it was only a small laptop computer. As York was mulling this over, a plain-clothed cop appeared at the door and said, "We searched Trotter's car. No explosives."

"Explosives?" Trotter asked, frowning deeply.

"Don't get cute," Lampert snapped.

"But there was an empty propane tank," the cop added. "From Rodriguez's."

Trotter added, "I needed a refill. That's where I always go. I was going there after lunch." He nodded at the bar menu. "You ever try the tamales here? The best in town."

York muttered, "You played us like a fish, goddamn it. Making us think your trash was a bomb."

Another cold smile crossed the landscaper's face. "Why exactly did you think I'd have a bomb?"

Silence for a moment. Then Lampert turned toward Eberhart, who avoided everyone's eyes.

Trotter nodded at the computer. "Hit the play button."

"What?" Lampert asked.

"The play button."

Lampert paused as he looked over the computer.

"It's not a bomb. And even if it was, would I blow myself up too?" The detective hit the button.

"Oh, Christ," muttered Eberhart as a video came on the small screen.

It showed the security man prowling through an office.

"Stan? Is that you?" Lampert asked.

"I—"

"Yep, it's him," Trotter said. "He's in my office at home."

"You told us one of your sources said Trotter was asking about where York shopped and about propane tanks."

The security man said nothing.

Trotter offered, "I was going to stop by the police station after lunch and drop off the CD. But since you're here . . . it's all yours."

The officers watched Eberhart ransacking Trotter's desk.

"So what'd that be?" the landscaper asked. "Breaking and entering, trespass too. And—if you were going to ask—yeah, I want to press charges. What do you guys say? To the fullest extent of the law."

"But I . . . " the security man stammered.

"You what?" Trotter filled in. "You shut the power off? *And* the backup too? But I've been a little paranoid lately, thanks to Mr. York. So I have *two* battery backups."

"You broke into his house?" Stephen York asked Eberhart, looking shocked. "You never told me that."

"You goddamn Judas!" Eberhart exploded. "You knew exactly what I was doing. You agreed to it! You *wanted* me to!"

"I swear," York said, "this is the first I've heard about it."

Lampert shook his head. "Stan, why'd you do it? I could've overlooked some things, but a B and E? Stupid."

"I know, I know," he said, looking down. "But we were so desperate to get this guy. He's *dangerous*. He's got books on sabotage and surveillance. . . . Please, Bill, can you cut me some slack?"

"Sorry, Stan." A nod to a uniformed officer, who cuffed him. "Take him to booking."

Trotter called after him, "If you're interested, those books about bombs and things? I got them for research. I'm trying my hand at a murder mystery. Everybody seems to be doing it nowadays. I've got a couple of chapters on that computer. Why don't you check it out, if you don't believe me."

"You're lying!" Then York turned to Lampert. "You know why he did this, don't you? It's all part of his plan."

"Mr. York, just—"

"No, no, think about it. He sets up a sting to get rid of my security man and leave me unprotected. And then he does all this, with the fake bomb, to find out about your procedures—the bomb squad, how many officers you have, who your undercover cops are."

"Did you leave a Whole Foods bag on the trunk of Mr. Eberhart's car?" Alvarado asked.

Trotter replied, "No. If you think I did, why don't you check for fingerprints."

York pointed at Trotter's pocket. "Gloves, look! There won't *be* any prints. Why's he wearing gloves in this heat?"

"I'm a landscaper. I usually wear gloves when I work. Most of us do. . . . Have to say, I'm getting pretty tired of this whole thing. Because of what some day laborer said, you got it into your head that I'm a killer or something. Well, I'm sick of my house being broken into, sick of being watched all the time. I think it's time to call my lawyer. "

York stepped forward angrily. "You're lying! Tell me why you're doing this! Tell me, goddamn it! I've looked at everything I've ever done bad in my whole life. I mean *everything*. The homeless guy I told to get a job when he asked me for a quarter, the clerk I called a stupid pig—'cause she gave me the wrong order, the valet I didn't tip because he couldn't speak English. . . . Every little goddamn thing! I've been going over my life with a microscope. I don't know what I did to you. Tell me! Tell me!" His face was red and his veins jutted out. His fists were clenched at his sides.

"I don't know what you're talking about." Trotter lifted his hands, the cuffs jingling.

The detective made a decision. "Take 'em off." A patrol officer unhooked the bracelets.

Sweating, York said to Lampert, "No! This's all part of his plot!"

"I'm inclined to believe him. I think Diaz was making the whole thing up."

"But the sauna—" York began.

"Think about it, though. Nothing happened. And there was nothing wrong with the brakes on your Mercedes. We just got the report."

York snapped, "But the repair guide. He bought one!"

"Brakes?" Trotter asked.

York said, "You bought a book on Mercedes brakes. Don't deny it."

"Why would I deny it? Call DMV. I bought an old Mercedes sedan a week ago. It needs new brakes and I'm going to do the work myself. Sorry, York, but I think you need professional help."

"No, he just bought the car as a cover," York raged. "Look at him! Look at his eyes! He's just waiting for a chance to kill me."

"Bought a car as cover?" Alvarado asked, eyeing his boss.

Lampert sighed. "Mr. York, if you're so sure you're in danger, then I'd suggest you hire another babysitter. I frankly don't have time for any more of these games." He turned to the team. "Come on, people, let's pack up. We've got some real cases to get back to."

The detective noticed the bartender hovering nearby, holding Trotter's tamales. He nodded and the man walked forward and served the landscaper, who sat back down, unfolded a napkin and smoothed it on his lap.

"Good, huh?" he asked Trotter.

"The best."

Lampert nodded. "Sorry about this."

Trotter shrugged. Suddenly his mood seemed to change. Smiling, he turned to York, who was heading out the front door, and called, "Hey."

The businessman stopped and stared back.

"Good luck to you," Trotter said. And started on his lunch.

■

At ten that night Ray Trotter made the rounds of his house, saying good night to his children and stepson, as he always did. ("A serial good nighter" was how his younger daughter laughingly described him.)

Then he showered and climbed into bed, waiting for Nancy, who was finishing the dishes. A moment later the lights in the kitchen went out and she passed the doorway. His wife smiled at him and continued into the bathroom.

A moment later he heard the shower. He enjoyed the hiss of falling water. A desert dweller now, yes, but Ray still had a fondness for the sounds of the damp Northeast.

Lying back against a half dozen thick pillows, he reflected on the day's events, particularly the incident at Miguel's.

Stephen York, face red, eyes frightened. He was out of control. He was as crazed as a lunatic.

Of course, he also happened to be 100 percent right. Ray Trotter had in fact done everything that York accused him of—from approaching Diaz about the alarms to planting the trash on the trunk of Eberhart's car.

Sure, he'd done it all.

But he'd never had any intention of hurting one hair on York's coiffed, Rogained head.

He'd asked Diaz about York's security system but the next day had anonymously turned the worker in for drugs (Ray had seen him selling pot to other employees at the landscaping company), in the hopes that he'd spill the information about Ray to the cops. He'd bought the books on sabotage, as well as the one about Mercedes brakes, but would never think about making a bomb or tampering with the businessman's car. The shims at the sauna room he was never going to use. And the chemicals from Southern States he'd never planned to use to make cyanide. He'd sent an order of cigars—nice ones, by the way, and completely poison free. Even the psychologist's reports in the Veterans Administration file were Ray's creation. He'd gone to the VA's office, requested his own file and, pretending to review it, had slipped in several sheets of notes, apparently taken by a counselor during therapy sessions from years ago, documenting his "troubled years" after the service. The report was all a fiction.

Oh, yes, his heart ached for revenge against Stephen A. York. But the payback wasn't exacting physical revenge; it was simply in making the man *believe* that Trotter was going to kill him— and guaranteeing that York spent a long, long time wallowing in paranoia and misery, waiting for the other shoe to drop: for York's car to explode, his gas line to start leaking, a gunshot to shatter his bedroom window.

Was that just a stomach cramp—or the first symptom of arsenic poisoning?

And the offense that had turned Ray into an angel of vengeance?

I don't know what I did to you. Tell me, tell me, tell me. . . .

To Ray's astonishment and amusement, York himself had actually mentioned the very transgression that afternoon at Miguel's.

Ray thought back to it now, an autumn day two years ago. His daughter Celeste had returned home from her after-school job, a troubled look on her face.

"What's the matter?" he'd asked.

The sixteen-year-old hadn't answered but had walked immediately to her room, closed the door. These were the days not
long after her mother had passed away; occasional moodiness
wasn't unusual. But he'd persisted in drawing her out and that
night he'd learned the reason she was upset: an incident during
her shift at McDonald's.

Celeste confessed that she'd accidentally mixed up two orders
and given a man a chicken sandwich when he'd asked for a Big
Mac. He'd left, not realizing the mistake, then returned five minutes later, and walked up to the counter. He looked over the
heavyset girl and snapped, "So you're not only a fat pig, you're
stupid too. I want to see the manager. Now!"

Celeste had tried to be stoic about the incident but as she related it to her father a single tear ran down her cheek. Ray was
heartbroken at the sight. The next day he'd learned the identity
of the customer from the manager and filed away the name
Stephen York.

A single tear . . .

For some people, perhaps, not even worth a second thought.
But because it was his daughter's tear, Ray Trotter decided it was
payback time.

He now heard the water stop running, then detected a fragrant smell of perfume wafting from the bathroom. Nancy came
to bed, laying her head on his chest.

"You seem happy tonight," she said.

"Do I?"

"When I walked past before and saw you staring at the ceiling
you looked . . . what's the word? Content."

He thought about the word. "That describes it." Ray shut the
light out, and putting his arm around his wife, pulled her closer
to him.

"I'm glad you're in my life," she whispered.

"Me too," he replied.

Stretching out, Ray considered his next steps. He'd probably give York a month or two of peace. Then, just when the business-man was feeling comfortable, he'd start up again.

What would he do? Maybe an empty medicine vial next to York's car, along with a bit of harmless Botox on the door handle. That had some appeal to it. He'd have to check if a trace of the cosmetic gave a positive reading for botulism bacteria.

Now that he'd convinced the police that he was innocent and York was paranoid, the businessman could cry wolf as often as he liked and the cops would tune him out completely.

The playing field was wide open . . .

Maybe he could enlist York's wife. She'd be a willing ally, he believed. In his surveillance Ray had seen how badly the man treated her. He'd overheard York lose his temper at her once when she kept pressuring him to let her apply to a local college to finish her degree. He'd yelled as if she were a teenager. Carole was currently out of town—probably with that English profes-sor she'd met at Arizona State when she was sneaking classes in-stead of taking tennis lessons. The man had transferred to UCLA but she was still seeing him; they'd meet in LA or Palm Springs. Ray had also followed her to a lawyer's office several times in Scottsdale and assumed she was getting ready to divorce York.

Maybe after it was final she'd be willing to give him some in-side information that he could use.

Another idea occurred to him. He could send York an anony-mous letter, possibly with a cryptic message on it. The words wouldn't be important. The point would be the smell; he'd sprin-kle the paper with almond extract—which gave off the telltale aroma of cyanide. After all, nobody knew that he *hadn't* made a batch of poison.

Oh, the possibilities were endless . . .

He rolled onto his side, whispered to his wife that he loved her and in sixty seconds was sound asleep.

Copycat

Detective Quentin Altman rocked back, his chair squealing with the telltale caw of aging government furniture, and eyed the narrow, jittery man sitting across from him. "Go on," the cop said.

"So I check out this book from the library. Just for the fun of it. I never do that, just read a book for the fun of it. I mean, *never.* I don't get much time off, you know."

Altman hadn't known this but he could certainly have deduced it. Wallace Gordon was the Greenville *Tribune*'s sole crime reporter and must've spent sixty, seventy hours a week banging out copy, to judge by the number of stories appearing under his byline every day.

"And I'm reading along and—"

"What is it you're reading?"

"A novel—a murder mystery. I'll get to that. . . . I'm reading along and I'm irritated," the reporter continued, "because somebody'd circled some passages. In a *library* book."

Altman grunted distractedly. He was head of Homicide in a burgh with a small-town name but big-city crime statistics. The fifty-something detective was busy and he didn't have much time for reporters with crackpot theories. There were twenty-two folders of current cases on his desk and here Wallace was delivering some elliptical message about defaced books.

"I don't pay much attention at first but I go back and reread one of the circled paragraphs. It jogs my memory. Anyway, I checked the morgue—"

"Morgue?" Altman frowned, rubbing his wiry red hair, which showed not a strand of gray.

"*Our* morgue, not yours. In the newspaper office. All the old stories."

"Got it. How 'bout getting to the point?"

"I found the articles about the Kimberly Banning murder."

Quentin Altman grew more attentive. Twenty-eight-year-old Kimberly had been strangled to death eight months ago. The murder occurred two weeks after a similar killing—of a young female grad student. The two deaths appeared to be the work of the same person but there were few forensic leads and no motive that anyone could determine. The cases prompted a task force investigation but eventually the suspects were cleared and the case grew cold.

Tall and gaunt, with tendons and veins rising from his pale skin, reporter Wallace tried—usually unsuccessfully—to tone down his intimidating physique and face with brown tweed jackets, corduroy slacks and pastel shirts. He asked the cop, "You remember how the whole town was paranoid after the first girl was killed? And how everybody was double locking their doors and never letting strangers into their houses?"

Altman nodded.

"Well, look at this." The reporter pulled latex gloves out of his pocket and put them on.

"Why the gloves, Wallace?"

The man ignored the question and dug a book out of his battered briefcase. Altman got a look at the title. *Two Deaths in a Small Town*. He'd never heard of it.

"This was published six months *before* the first killing." He opened the book to a yellow Post-it tab and pushed it forward.

"Read those paragraphs." The detective pulled on his CVS drug-store glasses and leaned forward.

The Hunter knew that now that he'd killed once, the town would be more alert than ever. Its soul would be edgier, its collective nerves would be as tense as an animal trap's blue-steel spring. Women would not stroll the streets alone and those who did would be looking around constantly, alert for any risk. Only a fool would let a stranger into her house and the Hunter did not enjoy killing fools.

So on Tuesday night he waited until bedtime—11:00 p.m.—and then slipped onto Maple Street. There, he doused a parked convertible's roof with gasoline and ignited the pungent, amber liquid. A huge whoosh . . . He hid in the bushes and, hypnotized by the tornado of flames and ebony smoke swirling into the night sky above the dying car, he waited. In ten minutes behemoths of fire trucks roared up the street, their wailing sirens drawing people from their homes to find out what the excitement might be.

Among those on the sidewalk was a young, demure blonde with a heart-shaped face, Clara Steading. This was the woman the Hunter knew he had to possess—possess completely. She was love incarnate, Amore herself, she was Beauty, she was Passion. . . . And she was also completely ignorant of her role as the object of his demented desire. Clara shivered in her bathrobe, standing on the sidewalk, along with a clutch of chattery neighbors, as they watched the firemen extinguish the blaze and offered words of sympathy to the dismayed owner of the car, who lived a few doors away.

Finally the onlookers grew bored, or repulsed by the bitter smell of the burnt rubber and plastic, and they re-

turned to their beds or their late-night snacks or their mind-numbing TV. But their vigilance didn't flag; the moment they stepped inside, every one of them locked their doors and windows carefully—to make certain that the strangler would not wreak his carnage in their homes.

Though in Clara Steading's case, her diligence in securing the deadbolt and chains had a somewhat different effect: locking the Hunter inside with her.

"Jesus," Altman muttered. "That's just what happened in the Kimberly Banning case, how the perp got inside. He set fire to a car."

"A convertible," Wallace added. "And then I went back and found some passages that'd been marked. One of them was about how the killer had stalked his victim by pretending to work for the city and trimming the plants in a park across from her apartment."

This was just how the first victim of the Greenville Strangler, the pretty grad student, had been stalked.

Wallace pointed out several other passages, marked with asterisks. There were margin notes too. One said, "Check this one out. Important." Another jotting was "Used distraction." And: "Disposing of body. Note this."

"So the killer's a copycat," Altman murmured. "He used the novel for research."

Which meant that there could be evidence in the book that might lead to the perp: fingerprints, ink, handwriting. Hence, the reporter's *CSI* gloves.

Altman stared at the melodramatic dust jacket on the novel— a drawing of a man's silhouette peering into the window of a house. The detective pulled on his own latex gloves and slipped the book into an evidence envelope. He nodded at the reporter and said a heartfelt "Thanks. We haven't had a lead on this one in over eight months."

Walking into the office next to his—that of his assistant, a young crew-cut detective named Josh Randall—he instructed the man to take the book to the county lab for analysis. When he returned, Wallace was still sitting expectantly in the hard chair across from Altman's desk.

Altman wasn't surprised he hadn't left. "And the quid pro quo?" the detective asked. "For your good deed?"

"I want an exclusive. What else?"

"I figured."

Altman didn't mind this in theory; cold cases were bad for the department's image and solving cold cases was good for a cop's career. Not to mention that there was still a killer out there. He'd never liked Wallace, though, who always seemed a little out of control in a spooky way and was as irritating as most crusaders usually are.

"Okay, you've got an exclusive," Altman said. "I'll keep you posted." He rose then paused. Waited for Wallace to leave.

"Oh, I'm not going anywhere, my friend."

"This's an official investigation—"

"And it wouldn't've been one without me. I want to write this one from the inside out. Tell my readers how a homicide investigation works from your point of view."

Quentin Altman argued some more but in the end he gave in, feeling he had no choice. "All right. But just don't get in my way. You do that, you're out of here."

"Wouldn't think of it." Wallace frowned an eerie look into his long, toothy face. "I might even be helpful." Maybe it was a joke but there was nothing humorous about the delivery. He then looked up at the detective. "So whatta we do next?"

"Well, *you're* going to cool your heels. *I'm* going to review the case file."

"But—"

"Relax, Wallace. Investigations take time. Sit back, take your jacket off. Enjoy our wonderful coffee."

Wallace glanced at the closet that served as the police station's canteen. He rolled his eyes and the ominous tone of earlier was replaced with a laugh. "Funny. I didn't know they still made instant."

The detective winked and ambled down the hall on his aching bones.

■

Quentin Altman hadn't run the Greenville Strangler case.

He'd worked on it some—the whole department'd had a piece of the case—but the officer in charge had been Bob Fletcher, a sergeant who'd been on the force forever. Fletcher, who'd never remarried after his wife left him some years before, and was childless, had devoted his life to his job after the divorce and seemed to take his inability to solve the Strangler case hard; the soft-spoken man had actually given up a senior spot in Homicide and transferred to Robbery. Altman was now glad for the sergeant's sake that there was a chance to nail the killer who'd eluded him.

Altman wandered down to Robbery with the news about the novel and to see if Fletcher knew anything about it. The sergeant, though, was out in the field at the moment and so Altman left a message and then dove into the cluttered and oppressively hot records room. He found the Strangler files easily; the folders sported red stripes on the side, a harsh reminder that, while this might've been a cold case, it was still very much open.

Returning to his office, he sat back, sipping the, yeah, disgusting instant coffee, and read the file, trying to ignore Wallace's incessant scribbling on his steno pad, the scratchy noise irritatingly audible throughout the office. The events of the murders were well documented. The perp had broken into two women's apartments and strangled them. There'd been no rape, sexual molestation or postmortem mutilation. Neither woman had ever been stalked or threatened by former boyfriends and, though Kimberly had recently purchased some condoms, none of her friends knew that she'd been dating. The other victim, Becky Winthrop, her family said, hadn't dated for over a year.

Sergeant Fletcher had carried out a by-the-book investigation but most killings of this sort, without witnesses, motive or significant trace found at the scene, are generally not solved without the help of an informant—often a friend or acquaintance of the perp. But, despite extensive press coverage of the investigation and pleas on TV by the mayor and Fletcher, no one had come forward with any information about possible suspects.

An hour later, just as he closed the useless file, Altman's phone rang. The documents department had blown up images of the handwriting and was prepared to compare these to any samples found elsewhere, though until such specimens were found the officers could do nothing.

The techs had also checked for any impression evidence—to see if the killer had written something on, say, a Post-it note on top of one of the pages—but found nothing.

A ninhydrin analysis revealed a total of nearly two hundred latent fingerprints on the three pages on which the marked paragraphs appeared and another eighty on the jacket. Unfortunately many of them were old and only fragments. Technicians had located a few that were clear enough to be identified and had run them through the FBI's integrated automated fingerprint identification system in West Virginia. But all the results had come back negative.

The cover of the book, wrapped in print-friendly cellophane, yielded close to four hundred prints but they too were mostly smudges and fragments. IAFIS had provided no positive IDs for these either.

Frustrated, he thanked the technician and hung up.

"So what was that about?" Wallace asked, looking eagerly at the sheet of paper in front of Altman, which contained both notes on the conversation he'd just had—and a series of compulsive doodles.

He explained to the reporter about the forensic results.

"So no leads," Wallace summarized and jotted a note, leaving the irritated detective to wonder why the reporter'd actually found it necessary to write this observation down.

As he gazed at the reporter an idea occurred to Altman and he stood up abruptly. "Let's go."

"Where?"

"Your crime scene."

"Mine?" Wallace asked, scrambling to follow the detective as he strode out the door.

■

The library near Gordon Wallace's apartment, where he'd checked out the novel *Two Deaths in a Small Town,* was a branch in the Three Pines neighborhood of Greenville, so named because legend had it that three trees in a park here had miraculously survived the fire of 1829, which had otherwise destroyed the rest of the town. It was a nice area, populated mostly by businessmen, professionals and educators; the college was nearby (the same school where the first Strangler victim had been a student).

Altman followed Wallace inside and the reporter found the head of the branch, introduced her to the detective. Mrs. McGiver was a trim woman dressed in stylish gray; she looked more like a senior executive with a high-tech company than a librarian.

The detective explained how they suspected the book had been used by a copycat as a model for the killings. Shock registered on the woman's face as she realized that the Strangler was somebody who'd been to her library. Perhaps he was even someone she knew.

"I'd like a list of everybody who checked out that book." Altman had considered the possibility that the killer might not have checked it out but had merely looked through it here, in the library itself. But that meant he'd have to underline the passages in public and risk drawing the attention of librarians or patrons. He concluded that the only safe way for the Strangler to do his homework was at home.

"I'll see what I can find," she said.

Altman had thought that it might take days to pull together this information but Mrs. McGiver was back in minutes. Altman felt his gut churning with excitement as he gazed at the sheets of paper in her hand, relishing the sensations of the thrill of the hunt and pleasure at finding a fruitful lead.

But as he flipped through the sheets, he frowned. Every one of the thirty or so people checking out *Two Deaths* had done so recently—within the last six months. They needed the names of those who'd checked it out *before* the killings eight months ago. He explained this to her.

"Oh, but we don't have records that far back. Normally we would, but about six months ago our computer was vandalized."

"Vandalized?"

She nodded, frowning. "Somebody poured battery acid or something into the hard drives. Ruined them and destroyed all our records. The backup too. Somebody from your department handled the case. I don't remember who."

Wallace said, "I didn't hear about it."

"They never found who did it. It was very troubling but more of an inconvenience than anything. Imagine if he'd decided to destroy the books themselves."

Altman caught Wallace's eye. "Dead end," the cop said angrily. Then he asked the librarian, "How 'bout the names of everybody who had a library card then? Were their names in the computer too?"

She nodded. "Prior to six months ago, they're gone too. I'm sorry."

Forcing a smile onto his face, he thanked the librarian and walked to the doorway. But he stopped so suddenly that Wallace nearly slammed into his back.

"What?" the reporter asked.

Altman ignored him and hurried back to the main desk, calling out, "Mrs. McGiver! Hold up there! I need you to find out something for me."

Drawing glares and a couple of harsh *shhhh*'s from readers.

■

The author of *Two Deaths in a Small Town*, Andrew M. Carter, lived in Hampton Station, near Albany, about two hours away from Greenville.

Mrs. McGiver's copy of *Who's Who in Contemporary Mystery Writing* didn't include street addresses or phone numbers but Altman called the DMV and they tracked down the specifics.

The idea that occurred to Altman as he was leaving the library was that Carter might've gotten a fan letter from the Strangler. Maybe he'd written to express some admiration, maybe he'd asked for more information or how the author had done his research. If there was such a letter the county forensic handwriting expert could easily link the notation with the fan, who—if they were lucky—might have signed his real name to the letter and included his address.

Mentally crossing his fingers he placed a call to the author. A woman answered. "Hello?"

"I'm Detective Altman with the Greenville Police Department," he said. "I'd like to speak to Andrew Carter."

"I'm his wife," she said. "He's not available." The matter-of-fact tone in her voice suggested that this was her knee-jerk response to all such calls.

"When will he be available?"

"This is about the murders, isn't it?"

"That's right, ma'am."

A hesitation. "The thing is . . ." Her voice lowered and Altman suspected that her unavailable husband was in a nearby room. "He hasn't been well."

"I'm sorry," Altman said. "Is it serious?"

"You bet it's serious," she said angrily. "When the news got out that Andy's book, you know, inspired somebody to kill those girls he got real depressed. He cut himself off from everybody. He stopped writing." She hesitated. "He stopped *everything*. He just gave up."

"Must've been difficult, Mrs. Carter," Altman said sympathetically, reflecting that reporter Wallace wasn't the first person to wonder if the novel had inspired a copycat.

"You have no idea. I told him it was just a coincidence—those women getting killed like he wrote in the book. Just a weird coincidence. But these reporters and, well, *everybody*, friends, neighbors . . . They kept yammering on and on about how Andy was to blame."

Altman supposed she wasn't going to like the fact he'd found proof that her husband's book had probably been the model for the killings.

She continued, "He's been getting better lately. Anything about the case could set him back."

"I do understand that, ma'am, but you have to see my situation. We've got a possibility of catching the killer and your husband could be real helpful . . ."

The sound on the other end of the line grew muffled and Altman could hear her talking to someone else.

Quentin Altman wasn't surprised when she said, "My husband just got back. I'll put him on."

"Hello?" came a soft, uneasy voice. "This's Andy Carter."

Altman identified himself.

"Were you the policeman I talked to a while back?"

"Me? No. That might've been the case detective. Sergeant Bob Fletcher."

"Right. That was the name."

So Fletcher *had* talked to the author. There was no reference in the case file that he recalled. He must've missed it. He reiterated to Carter what he'd told the author's wife and the man said immediately, "I can't help you. And frankly, I don't *want* to. . . . This's been the worst time of my life."

"I appreciate that, sir. But that killer's still free. And—"

"But I don't *know* anything. I mean, what could I possibly tell you that—"

"We may have a sample of the killer's handwriting—we found some notes in a copy of your book that make us think he might've written them. And we'd like to compare it to any letters from fans you might've received."

There was a long pause. Finally the author whispered, "So he *did* use my book as a model."

In a kind voice Altman said, "It's looking that way, Mr. Carter. The underlined passages are the ones that fit the M.O. of the two murders. I'm afraid they're identical."

Altman heard nothing for a moment then he asked, "Sir, are you all right?"

The author cleared his throat. "I'm sorry. I can't help you. I just . . . it'd be too much for me."

Quentin Altman often told young officers who worked for him that a detective's most important trait is persistence. He said in an even voice, "You're the only one who can help us trace the book back to the killer. He destroyed the library computer so we don't have the names of who checked out your book. There's no match on the fingerprints either. . . . I want to catch this man real bad. And I suspect you do too, Mr. Carter. Don't you, now?"

There was no response. Finally the faint voice continued, "Do you know that *strangers* sent me clippings about the killings?

Perfect strangers. Hundreds of them. They blamed *me*. They called my book a 'blueprint for murder.' I had to go into the hospital for a month afterwards, I was so depressed. . . . I *caused* those murders! Don't you understand that?"

Altman looked up at Wallace and shook his head.

The reporter gestured for the phone. Altman figured, Why not?

"Mr. Carter, there's a person here I'm going to put on the line. I'd like him to have a word with you."

"Who?"

The cop handed the receiver over and sat back, listening to the one-sided conversation.

"Hello, Mr. Carter." The reporter's gaunt frame hunched over the phone and he gripped the receiver in astonishingly long, strong fingers. "You don't know me. My name is Wallace Gordon. I'm a fan of your book—I loved it. I'm a reporter for the *Tribune* here in Greenville. . . . I got that. I understand how you feel—my colleagues step over a lot of lines. But I don't operate that way. And I know you're reluctant to get involved here. I'm sure you've been through a tough time but let me just say one thing: I'm no talented novelist like you—I'm just a hack journalist—but I *am* a writer and if I have any important belief in my life it's in the freedom to write whatever moves us. Now . . . No, please, Mr. Carter, let me finish. I heard that you stopped writing after the murders. . . . . Well, you and your talent were as much a victim of those crimes as those women were. You exercised your God-given right to express yourself and a terrible accident happened. That's how I'd look at this madman: an act of God. You can't do anything about those women. But you can help yourself and your family to move on. . . . And there's something else to consider: You're in a position to make sure nobody else ever gets hurt by this guy again."

Altman lifted an impressed eyebrow at the reporter's sales pitch. Wallace held the receiver to his ear for a moment, listening. Finally he nodded and glanced at Altman. "He wants to talk to you."

Altman took the phone. "Yessir?"

"What exactly would you want me to do?" came the tentative voice through the phone.

"All I need is to go through the fan mail you got about the book."

A bitter laugh. "Hate mail, you mean. That's mostly what I got."

"Whatever you received. We're mostly interested in handwritten letters, so we can match physical evidence. But any emails you got, we'd like to see too."

A pause. Was he going to balk? Then the detective heard the man say, "It'll take me a day or two. I kind of stopped . . . well, let me just say things haven't been too organized around my office lately."

"That's fine." Altman gave the author the directions to the police station and told him to wear kitchen gloves and handle the handwritten letters by the edges to make sure he didn't mess up the fingerprints.

"All right," Carter said sullenly.

Altman wondered if he'd really come. He started to tell the author how much he appreciated the help but after a moment he realized that the man had hung up and he was listening to dead air.

■

Andy Clark did indeed make the journey to Greenville.

He turned out not to resemble either a sinister artist or a glitzy celebrity but rather any one of the hundreds of white, middle-aged men who populated this region of the Northeast. Thick, graying hair, neatly trimmed. A slight paunch (much slighter than Altman's own, thanks to the cop's fondness for his wife's casseroles). His outfit wasn't an arm-patch sports jacket or any other authorial garb, but an L.L.Bean windbreaker, Polo shirt and corduroy slacks.

It had been two days since Altman had spoken to Carter. The man now stood uneasily in the cop's office, taking the coffee that the young detective Josh Randall offered and nodding greetings to the cops and to Gordon Wallace. Carter slipped off his windbreaker, tossing it on an unoccupied chair. The author's only moment of ill ease in this meeting was when he glanced on Altman's desk and blinked as he saw the case file that was headed, *Banning, Kimberly—Homicide #13–04*. A brief look of dismay filled his face. Quentin Altman was grateful that he'd had the foresight to slip the crime scene photos of the victim's body to the bottom of the folder.

They made small talk for a minute or two and then Altman nodded at a large white envelope in the author's hand. "You find some letters you think might be helpful?"

"Helpful?" Carter asked, rubbing his red eyes. "I don't know. You'll have to decide that." He handed the envelope to the detective.

Altman opened the envelope and, donning latex gloves, pulled out what must've been about two hundred or so sheets.

The detective led the men into the department conference room and spread the letters out on the table. Randall joined them.

Some of them were typed or printed out from a computer— but these were signed, offering a small sample of the correspondent's handwriting. Some were written in cursive, some in block letters. They were on many different types and sizes of paper and colors of ink or pencil. Crayons too.

For an hour the men, each wearing rubber gloves, pored over the letters. Altman could understand the author's dismay. Many of them were truly vicious. Finally he divided them into several piles. First, the emails, none of which seemed to have been written by potential killers. Second were the handwritten letters that seemed like the typical innocent opinions of readers. None of these asked for details about how he'd researched the novel or seemed in any way incriminating, though some were angry and some were disturbingly personal ("Come and see us in Sioux City if your in town and the wife and me will treat you to our special full body massege out side on the deck behind our trailer").

"Ick," said young officer Randall.

The final pile, Altman explained, "included letters that were reasonable and calm and cautious . . . Just like the Strangler. See, he's an organized offender. He's not going to give anything away by ranting. If he has any questions he's going to ask them politely and carefully—he'll want some detail but not too much; that'd arouse suspicion." Altman gathered up this stack—about ten letters—placed them in an evidence envelope and handed them to the young detective. "Over to the county lab, stat."

A man stuck his head in the door—Detective Bob Fletcher. The even-keeled sergeant introduced himself to Carter. "We never met but I spoke to you on the phone about the case," the cop said.

"I remember." They shook hands.

Fletcher nodded at Altman, smiling ruefully. "He's a better cop than me. I never thought that the killer might've tried to write you."

The sergeant, it turned out, had contacted Carter not about fan mail but to ask if the author'd based the story on any previous true crimes, thinking there might be a connection between them and the Strangler murders. It had been a good idea but Carter had explained that the plot for *Two Deaths* was a product of his imagination.

The sergeant's eyes took in the stacks of letters. "Any luck?" he asked.

"We'll have to see what the lab finds." Altman then nodded toward the author. "But I have to say that Mr. Carter here's been a huge help. We'd be stymied for sure, if it wasn't for him."

Appraising Carter carefully, Fletcher said, "I have to admit I never got a chance to read your book but I always wanted to meet you. An honest-to-God famous author. Don't think I've ever shook one's hand before."

Carter gave an embarrassed laugh. "Not very famous to look at my sales figures."

"Well, all I know is my girlfriend read your book and she said it was the best thriller she'd read in years."

Carter said, "I appreciate that. Is she around town? I could autograph her copy."

"Oh," Fletcher said hesitantly, "well, we're not going out anymore. She left the area. But thanks for the offer." He headed back to Robbery.

There was now nothing to do but wait for the lab results to come back, so Wallace suggested coffee at Starbucks. The men wandered down the street, ordered and sat sipping the drinks, as Wallace pumped Carter for information about breaking into fiction writing, and Altman simply enjoyed the feel of the hot sun on his face.

The men's recess ended abruptly, though, fifteen minutes later when Altman's cell phone rang.

"Detective," came the enthusiastic voice of his youthful assistant, Josh Randall, "we've got a match! The handwriting in one of Mr. Carter's fan letters matches the notes in the margins of the book. The ink's the same too."

The detective said, "Please tell me there's a name and address on the letter."

"You bet there is. Howard Desmond's his name. And his place is over in Warwick." A small town twenty minutes from the sites of both of the Greenville Strangler's attacks.

The detective told his assistant to pull together as much information on Desmond as he could. He snapped the phone shut and, grinning, announced, "We've found him. We've got our copycat."

But, as it turned out, they didn't have him at all.

At least not the flesh-and-blood suspect.

Single, forty-two-year-old Howard Desmond, a veterinary technician, had skipped town six months before, leaving in a huge hurry. One day he'd called his landlord and announced that he was moving. He'd left virtually overnight, abandoning everything in the apartment but his valuables. There was no forwarding address. Altman had hoped to go through whatever he'd left behind but the landlord explained that he'd sold everything to make up for the lost rent. What didn't sell he'd thrown out. The detective called the state public records departments to see if they had any information about him.

Altman spoke to the vet in whose clinic Desmond had worked and the doctor's report was similar to the landlord's. In April Desmond had called and quit his job, effective immediately, saying only that he was moving to Oregon to take care of his elderly grandmother. He'd never called back with a forwarding address for his last check, as he said he would.

The vet described Desmond as quiet and affectionate to the animals in his care but with little patience for people.

Altman contacted the authorities in Oregon and found no record of any Howard Desmonds in the DMV files or on the property or income tax rolls. A bit more digging revealed that all of Desmond's grandparents—his parents too—had died years before; the story about the move to Oregon was apparently a complete lie.

The few relatives the detective could track down confirmed that he'd just disappeared and they didn't know where he might be. They echoed his boss's assessment, describing the man as intelligent but a recluse, one who—significantly—loved to read and often lost himself in novels, appropriate for a killer who took his homicidal inspiration from a book.

"What'd his letter to Andy say?" Wallace asked.

With an okaying nod from Altman, Randall handed it to the reporter, who then summarized out loud. "He asks how Mr. Carter did the research for his book. What were the sources he used? How did he learn about the most efficient way a murderer would kill someone? And he's curious about the mental makeup of a killer. Why did some people find it easy to kill while others couldn't possibly hurt anyone?"

Altman shook his head. "No clue as to where he might've gone. We'll get his name into NCIC and VICAP but, hell, he could be anywhere. South America, Europe, Singapore . . ."

Since Bob Fletcher's Robbery Division would've handled the vandalism at the Greenville Library's Three Pines branch, which they now knew Desmond was responsible for, Altman sent Randall to ask the sergeant if he'd found any leads as part of the investigation that would be helpful.

The other men found themselves staring at Desmond's fan letter as if it were a corpse at a wake, silence surrounding them.

Altman's phone rang and he took the call. It was the county clerk, who explained that Desmond owned a small vacation home about sixty miles from Greenville, on the shores of Lake Muskegon, tucked into the backwater, piney wilderness.

"You think he's hiding out there?" Wallace asked.

"I say we go find out. Even if he's hightailed it out of the state, though, there could be some leads there as to where he did go. Maybe airline receipts or something, notes, phone message on an answering machine."

Wallace grabbed his jacket and his reporter's notebook. "Let's go."

"No, no, no," Quentin Altman said firmly. "You get an exclusive. You don't get to go into the line of fire."

"Nice of you to think of me," Wallace said sourly.

"Basically I just don't want to get sued by your newspaper if Desmond decides to use you for target practice."

The reporter gave a scowl and dropped down into an officer chair.

Josh Randall returned to report that Sergeant Bob Fletcher had no helpful information in the library vandalism case.

But Altman said, "Doesn't matter. We've got a better lead. Suit up, Josh."

"Where're we going?"

"For a ride in the country. What else on a nice fall day like this?"

■

Lake Muskegon is a large but shallow body of water bordered by willow, tall grass and ugly pine. Altman didn't know the place well. He'd brought his family here for a couple of picnics over the years and he and Bob Fletcher had come to the lake once on a halfhearted fishing expedition, of which Altman had only vague memories: gray, drizzly weather and a nearly empty creel at the end of the day.

As he and Randall drove north through the increasingly deserted landscape he briefed the young man. "Now, I'm ninety-nine percent sure Desmond's not here. But what we're going to do first is clear the house—I mean closet by closet—and then I want you stationed in the front to keep an eye out while I look for evidence. Okay?"

"Sure, boss."

They passed Desmond's overgrown driveway and pulled off the road then eased into a stand of thick forsythia.

Together, the men cautiously made their way down the weedy drive toward the "vacation house," a dignified term for the tiny, shabby cottage sitting in a three-foot-high sea of grass and brush. A path had been beaten through the foliage—somebody had been here recently—but it might not have been Desmond; Altman had been a teenager once himself and knew that nothing attracts adolescent attention like a deserted house.

They drew their weapons and Altman pounded on the door, calling, "Police. Open up."

Silence.

He hesitated a moment, adjusted the grip on his gun and kicked the door in.

Filled with cheap, dust-covered furniture, buzzing with stuporous fall flies, the place appeared deserted. They checked the four small rooms carefully and found no sign of Desmond. Outside, they glanced in the window of the garage and saw that it was empty. Then Altman sent Randall to the front of the driveway to hide in the bushes and report anybody's approach.

He then returned to the house and began to search, wondering just how hot the cold case was about to become.

■

Two hundred yards from the driveway that led to Howard Desmond's cottage a battered, ten-year-old Toyota pulled onto the shoulder of Route 207 and then eased into the woods, out of sight of any drivers along the road.

A man got out and, satisfied that his car was well hidden, squinted into the forest, getting his bearings. He noticed the line of the brown lake to his left and figured the vacation house was in the ten-o'clock position ahead of him. Through dense underbrush like this it would take him about fifteen minutes to get to the place, he estimated.

That'd make the time pretty tight. He'd have to move as quickly as he could and still keep the noise to a minimum.

The man started forward but then stopped suddenly and patted his pocket. He'd been in such a hurry to get to the house he couldn't remember if he'd taken what he wanted from the glove compartment. But, yes, he had it with him.

Hunched over and picking his way carefully to avoid stepping on noisy branches, Gordon Wallace continued on toward the cabin where, he hoped, Detective Altman was lost in police work and would be utterly oblivious to his furtive approach.

■

The search of the house revealed virtually nothing that would indicate that Desmond had been here recently—or where the man might now be. Quentin Altman found some bills and cancelled checks. But the address on them was Desmond's apartment in Warwick.

He decided to check the garage, thinking he might come across something helpful the killer had tossed out of the car and forgotten about—maybe a sheet containing directions or a map or receipt.

Altman discovered something far more interesting than evidence, though; he found Howard Desmond himself.

That is to say, his corpse.

The moment Altman opened the old-fashioned double doors of the garage he detected the smell of decaying flesh. He knew where it had to be coming from: a large coal bin in the back. Steeling himself, he flipped up the lid.

The mostly skeletal remains of a man about six feet tall were inside, lying on his back, fully clothed. He'd been dead about six months—just around the time Desmond disappeared, Altman recalled.

DNA would tell for certain if this was the vet tech but Altman discovered the man's wallet in his hip pocket and, sure enough, the driver's license inside was Desmond's. DNA or dental records would tell for certain.

The man's skull was shattered; the cause of death was probably trauma to the head by a blunt object. There was no weapon in the bin itself but after a careful examination of the garage he found a heavy mallet wrapped in a rag and hidden in the bottom of a trash-filled oil drum. There were some hairs adhering to the mallet that resembled Desmond's. Altman set the tool on a workbench, wondering what the hell was going on.

Somebody had murdered the Strangler. Who? And why? Revenge?

But then Altman did one of the things he did best—let his mind run free. Too many detectives get an idea into their heads and can't see past their initial conclusions. Altman, though, always fought against this tendency and he now asked himself: But what if Desmond *wasn't* the Strangler?

They knew for certain that he was the one who'd underlined the passages in the library's copy of *Two Deaths in a Small Town*. But what if he'd done so *after* the killings? The letter Desmond had written to Carter was undated. Maybe—just like the reporter Gordon Wallace himself had done—he'd read the book after the murders and been struck by the similarity. He'd started to investigate the crime himself and the Strangler had found out and murdered him.

But then who was the killer?

Just like Gordon Wallace had done . . .

Altman felt another little tap in his far-ranging mind, as fragments of facts lined up for him to consider—facts that all had to do with the reporter. For instance, Wallace was physically imposing, abrasive, temperamental. At times he could be threatening, scary. He was obsessed with crime and he knew police and forensic procedures better than most cops, which also meant that he knew how to anticipate investigators' moves. (He'd sure blustered his way right into the middle of the reopened case just the other day, Altman reflected.) Wallace owned a Motorola police scanner and would've been able to listen in on calls about the victims. His apartment was a few blocks from the college where the first victim was killed.

The detective considered: Let's say that Desmond had read

the passages, become suspicious and circled them, then made a few phone calls to find out more about the case. He might've called Wallace, who, as the *Tribune*'s crime reporter, would be a logical source for more information.

Desmond had met with the reporter, who'd then killed him and hid the body here.

Impossible . . . Why, for instance, would Gordon have brought the book to the police's attention?

Maybe to preempt suspicion?

Altman returned to the disgusting, impromptu crypt once again to search it more carefully, trying to unearth some answers.

■

Gordon Wallace caught a glimpse of Altman in the garage.

The reporter had crept up to a spot only thirty feet away and was hiding behind a bush. The detective wasn't paying any attention to who might be outside, apparently relying on Josh Randall to alert him to intruders. The young detective was at the head of the driveway, a good two hundred feet away, his back to the garage.

Breathing heavily in the autumn heat, the reporter started through the grass in a crouch. He stopped beside the building and glanced into the side window fast, noting that Altman was standing over a coal bin in the rear of the garage, squinting at something in his hand.

Perfect, Wallace thought and, reaching into his pocket, eased to the open doorway, where his aim would be completely unobstructed.

■

The detective had found something in Desmond's wallet and was staring at it—a business card—when he heard the snap of a twig behind him and, alarmed, turned.

A silhouette of a figure was standing in the doorway. He seemed to be holding his hands at chest level.

Blinded by the glare, Altman gasped, "Who're—?"

A huge flash filled the room.

The detective stumbled backward, groping for his pistol.

"Damn," came a voice he recognized.

Altman squinted against the back lighting. "Wallace! You goddamn son of a bitch! What the hell're you doing here?"

The reporter scowled and held up the camera in his hand, looking just as unhappy as Altman. "I was trying to get a candid of you on the job. But you turned around. You ruined it."

"*I* ruined it? I told you not to come. You can't—"

"I've got a First Amendment right to be here," the man snapped. "Freedom of the press."

"And I've got a right to throw your ass in jail. This's a crime scene."

"Well, that's why I want the pictures," he said petulantly. Then he frowned. "What's that smell?" The camera sagged and the reporter started to breathe in shallow gasps. He looked queasy.

"It's Desmond. Somebody murdered him. He's in the coal bin."

"Murdered *him*? So he's not the killer?"

Altman lifted his radio and barked to Randall, "We've got visitors back here."

"What?"

"We're in the garage."

The young officer showed up a moment later, trotting fast. A disdainful look at Wallace. "Where the hell did you come from?"

"How'd you let him get past?" Altman snapped.

"Not his fault," the reporter said, shivering at the smell. "I parked up the road. How 'bout we get some fresh air?"

Angry, Altman took perverse pleasure in the reporter's discomfort. "I oughta throw you in jail."

Wallace held his breath and started for the coal bin, raising the camera.

"Don't even think about it," Altman growled and pulled the reporter away.

"Who did it?" Randall asked, nodding at the body.

Altman didn't share that for a moment he'd actually suspected Wallace Gordon himself. Just before the photo op incident he'd found a stunning clue as to who Desmond's—and the two women's—killer probably was. He held up a business card. "I found this on the body."

On the card was written, "Detective Sergeant Robert Fletcher, Greenville Police Department."

"Bob?" Randall whispered in shock.

"I don't want to believe it," Altman muttered slowly, "but back at the office he didn't let on he even knew about Desmond, let alone that they'd met at some point."

"True."

"And," he continued, nodding at the mallet, "Bob does all that metalwork—his hobby, remember? That could be one of his."

Randall looked uneasily at the murder weapon.

Altman's heart pounded furiously at the betrayal. He now speculated about what had happened. Fletcher bobbled the case intentionally—because *he* was the killer, probably destroying any evidence that led to him. A loner, a history of short, difficult relationships, obsessed with violence and military history and artifacts and hunting. . . . He'd lied to them about not reading *Two Deaths* and *had* used it as a model to kill those women. Then— *after* the killings—Desmond happened to read the book too, underlined the passages and, being a good citizen, contacted case officer Fletcher, who was none other than the killer himself. The sergeant murdered him, dumped the body here and then destroyed the library's computer. Of course, he never made any effort to pursue the vandalism investigation.

Alarmed, Quentin Altman had another thought. He turned to the reporter. "Where was Fletcher when you left the office? Did you see him at the station?" The detective's hand strayed to his pistol as he looked around the tall grass, wondering if the sergeant had followed him here and intended to kill them as well. Fletcher was a crack rifle shot.

But Randall replied, "He was in the conference room with Andy Carter."

No! Altman realized that they weren't the only ones at risk; the author was a witness too—and therefore a potential victim of Fletcher's. Altman grabbed his cell phone and called the central dispatcher. He asked for Carter.

"He's not here, sir," the woman said.

"What?"

"It was getting late so he decided to get a hotel room for the night."

"Which one's he staying at?"

"I think it's the Sutton Inn."

"You have the number?"

"I do, sure. But he's not there right now."

"Where is he?"

"He went out to dinner. I don't know where but if you need to get in touch with him you can call Bob Fletcher's phone. They were going together."

■

Twenty minutes from town, driving at twice the posted limit.

Altman tried again to call Fletcher but the sergeant wasn't answering. There wasn't much Altman could do except try to reason with the sergeant, have him give himself up, plead with him not to kill Carter too. He prayed that the cop hadn't already done so.

Another try. Still no answer.

He skidded the squad car through the intersection at Route 202, nearly sideswiping one of the ubiquitous dairy tankers in these parts.

"Okay, that was exciting," Randall whispered, removing his sweaty palm from the dashboard as the truck's horn brayed in angry protest behind them.

Altman was about to call Fletcher's phone again when a voice clattered over the car's radio, "All units. Reports of shots fired on Route One-twenty-eight just west of Ralphs grocery. Repeat, shots fired. All units respond."

"You think that's them?"

"We're three minutes away. We're about to find out." Altman called in their position and then pushed the accelerator to the floor; they broke into three-digit speed.

After a brief, harrowing ride, the squad car crested a hill. Randall called breathlessly, "Look!"

Altman could see Bob Fletcher's Police Interceptor half on, half off the road. He skidded to a stop nearby and the two officers jumped out. Wallace's car—which'd been hitching an illegal ride on their light bar and siren—braked to a stop fifty feet behind them. The reporter too jumped out, ignoring the detective's shout to stay back.

Altman felt Randall grip his arm. The young officer was pointing at the shoulder about fifty feet away. In the dim light they could just make out the form of Andrew Carter lying face down in a patch of bloody dirt.

Oh, goddamn it! They weren't in time; the sergeant had added the author to the list of his victims.

Crouching beside the car, Altman whispered to Randall, "Head up the road that way. Look out for Fletcher. He's someplace close."

Scanning the bushes, in a crouch, Altman ran toward the author's body. As he did he happened to glance to his left and gasped. There was Bob Fletcher on the ground, holding a sheriff's department shotgun.

He shouted to Randall, "Look out!" And dropped flat. But as he swung the gun toward Fletcher he noted that the sergeant wasn't moving. The detective hit the man with his flashlight beam. Fletcher's eyes were glazed over and there was blood on his chest.

Wallace was crouching over Carter. The reporter called, "He's alive!"

The detective rose, pulled the scattergun out of Fletcher's lifeless hands and trotted over to the author. Fletcher had shot him and he was unconscious.

"Andy, stay with us!" Altman called, pressing his hand onto the bloody wound in the author's belly. Over the crest of the road the detective could see the flashing lights and hear the sirens, growing steadily louder. He leaned down and whispered into the man's ear, "Hang in there! You'll be all right, you'll be all right, you'll be all right . . ."

■

His book had saved his life, the author was explaining with a laugh that turned into a wince.

It was the next morning, and Quentin Altman and Carter's wife—a handsome, middle-aged blonde—were standing at his bedside in Greenville Hospital. Fletcher's bullet had missed vital organs but had snapped a rib and the author was in major pain despite the happy pills he'd been given.

Carter told them what had happened last evening: "Fletcher says let's go to dinner—he knew some good barbecue place in the country. We were driving along this deserted road and I was talking about *Two Deaths* and said that this was just the sort of road I had in mind when I wrote that scene where the Hunter was stalking the first victim after he sees her at McDonald's. Then, Fletcher said that *he* pictured that road being in cornfields, not forests."

"But he said he hadn't read the book," Altman said.

"Exactly. . . . He realized he'd screwed up. He got real quiet for a minute, and I was thinking something's wrong. I was even going to jump out of the car. But then he pulls his gun out and I grab it but he still shoots me. I reach over with my foot and slam on the brake. We go off the road and he slams his head into the window or something. I grab the gun and roll out of the car. I'm heading for the bushes to hide in but I see him getting the shotgun from the trunk. He starts toward me and I shoot him." He shook his head. "Man, if it hadn't been for the book, what he said about it, I never would've known what he was going to do."

Since Altman was involved in the incident, the investigation of the shooting went to another detective, who reported that the forensics bore out Carter's story. There was GSR—gunshot residue—on Fletcher's hand, which meant he'd fired the pistol, and a bullet with Carter's blood on it embedded in the cruiser passenger door. Evidence also proved that Fletcher was indeed the Greenville Strangler. The sergeant's fingerprints were all over the mallet and a search of the sergeant's house revealed several items—stockings and lingerie—that had been taken from the homes of the victims. Murdering Howard Desmond and trying to murder Andy Carter—well, those had been to cover up his original crimes. But what had been the sergeant's motive for killing the two women in Greenville? Maybe the anger at being left by his wife had boiled over. Maybe he'd had a secret affair with one of the victims, which had turned sour, and he'd decided to stage her death as a random act of violence. Maybe someday an answer would come to light.

Or maybe, Altman reflected, unlike in a mystery novel, they'd never know what had driven the man to step over the edge into the dark world of the killers he'd once hunted.

It was then that Wallace Gordon loped into the hospital room, saying, "Hot off the presses." He handed a copy of the *Tribune* to Carter. On the front page was Wallace's story about the solving of the Greenville Strangler case.

"Keep that," Wallace said. "A souvenir."

Thanking him, Carter's wife folded the paper up and set it aside with the stiff gesture of someone who has no interest in memorabilia about a difficult episode in one's life.

Quentin Altman walked to the door and, just as he was about to leave, paused. He turned back. "Oh, one thing, Andy—how's that book of yours end? Do the police ever find the Hunter?"

Carter caught himself as he was about to answer. The author gave a grin. "You know, Detective—you want to find that out, I'm afraid you're just going to have to buy yourself a copy."

■

Several days later Andrew Carter slipped out of his bed, where he'd lain, wide-awake, for the past three hours. It was two a.m.

He glanced at the quiescent form of his sleeping wife and— with the help of his cane—limped to his closet, where he found and pulled on an old pair of faded jeans, sneakers and a Boston University sweatshirt—his good-luck writing clothes, which he hadn't donned in well over a year.

Still in pain from the gunshot, he walked slowly down the hall to his office and went inside, turning on the light. Sitting at his desk, he clicked on his computer and stared at the screen for a long moment.

Then suddenly he began to write. His keyboarding was clumsy at first, his fingers jabbing two keys at once or missing the intended one altogether. Still, as the hours passed, his skill as a typist returned and soon the words were pouring from his mind onto the screen flawlessly and fast.

By the time the sky began to glow with pink-gray light and a morning bird's cell-phone trill sounded from the crisp holly bush outside his window, he'd finished the story completely—thirty-nine double-spaced pages.

He moved the cursor to the top of the document, thought about an appropriate title and typed: *Copycat*.

Then Andy Carter sat back in his comfortable chair and carefully read his work from start to finish.

The story opened with a reporter finding a suspense novel that contained several circled passages, which were strikingly similar to two real-life murders that had occurred earlier. The reporter takes the book to a detective, who concludes that the man who circled the paragraphs is the perpetrator, a copycat inspired by the novel to kill.

Reviving the case, the detective enlists the aid of the novel's author, who reluctantly agrees to help and brings the police some fan letters, one of which leads to the suspected killer.

But when the police track the suspect to his summer home they find that *he's* been murdered too. He wasn't the killer at all but had presumably circled the passages only because he, like the reporter, was struck by the similarity between the novel and the real-life crimes.

Then the detective gets a big shock: On the fan's body he finds clues that prove that a local police sergeant is the real killer. The author, who happens to be with this very officer at that moment, is nearly killed but manages to wrestle the gun away and shoot the cop in self-defense.

Case closed.

Or so it seems . . .

But Andy Carter hadn't ended the story there. He added yet another twist. Readers learn at the very end that the sergeant was innocent. He'd been set up as a fall guy by the real Strangler.

Who happened to be the author himself.

Racked by writer's block after his first novel was published, unable to follow it up with another, the author had descended into madness. Desperate and demented, he came to believe that he might jump-start his writing by actually reenacting scenes from his novel so he stalked and strangled two women, exactly as his fictional villain had done.

The murders hadn't revived his ability to write, however, and he slumped further into depression. And then, even more troubling, he heard from the fan who'd grown suspicious about the similarities between certain passages in the novel and the real crimes. The author had no choice: He met with the fan at his lakeside cottage and beat him to death, hiding the body in the garage and covering up the disappearance by pretending to be the fan and telling his boss and landlord that he was leaving town unexpectedly.

The author believed he was safe. But his contentment didn't last. Enter the reporter who'd found the underlined passages, and the investigation started anew; the police called, asking him for fan letters. The author knew the only way to be safe was to give the police a scapegoat. So he agreed to meet with the police—but in fact he'd arrived in town a day before his planned meeting with the detective. He broke into the police sergeant's house, planted some incriminating clothing he'd taken from the dead women's houses and stole one of the cop's mallets and a business card. He then went out to the dead fan's lake house, where he'd hidden the body, and used the tool to crush the skull of the decomposed body and hid the mallet, along with some of the dead man's hairs, in an oil drum. The card he slipped into the wallet. The next day he showed up at the police station with the fan letter that led to the cottage— and ultimately to the sergeant.

The author, who'd asked the unsuspecting sergeant to drive to dinner, grabbed his gun, made him stop the car and get out. Then he shot him, rested the pistol near the dead cop's hands and fired it into the woods to get gunshot residue on the man's finger (writers know as much about forensics as most cops). The author had gotten the shotgun from the trunk, left it with the sergeant and then climbed back into the squad car, where he'd taken a deep breath and shot himself in the belly—as superficially as he could.

He'd then crawled onto the road to wait for a passing car to come to their aid.

The police bought the entire story.

In the final scene the author returned home to try to resume his writing, having literally gotten away with murder.

Carter now finished rereading the story, his heart thumping hard with pride and excitement. True, it needed polishing but, considering that he hadn't written a word for more than a year, it was a glorious accomplishment.

He was a writer once again.

The only problem was that he couldn't publish the story. He couldn't even *show* it to a soul.

For the simple reason, of course, that it wasn't fiction; every word was true. Andy Carter himself was the homicidal author.

Still, he thought, as he erased the entire story from his computer, publishing it didn't matter one bit. The important thing was that by writing it he'd managed to kill his writer's block as ruthlessly and efficiently as he'd murdered Bob Fletcher and Howard Desmond and the two women in Greenville. And, even better, he knew too how to make sure that he'd never be blocked again: From now on he'd give up fiction and pursue what he'd realized he was destined to write: true crime.

What a perfect solution this was! He'd never want for ideas again; TV news, magazines and the papers would provide dozens of story leads he could choose from.

And, he reflected, limping downstairs to make a pot of coffee, if it turned out that there were no crimes that particularly interested him . . . well, Andy Carter knew that he was fully capable of taking matters into his own hands and whipping up a bit of inspiration all by himself.

The Voyeur

He had no serious chance for her, of course.

She was way out of his league.

Still, Rodney Pullman, forty-four both in age and in waist-band, couldn't help being seduced by the sight of the Resident in 10B when she'd moved into his Santa Monica apartment complex six months ago. After all, a man can dream, can't he?

With focused hopes but diffuse energy, Pullman had moved to LA from Des Moines two years ago to become a movie producer and spent months papering Tinseltown with his résumés. The results were unremarkable and he finally concluded that success at selling Saturns and industrial air conditioners in the Midwest would never open doors at companies whose products included TomKat, George Clooney and J-Lo.

But, despite the rejection, Pullman got into the Southern California groove, as he'd write to his parents. Sure, maybe folks out here were a little more superficial than in Iowa and occasionally he felt like he was coasting. But what a place to be adrift! This was a promised land—wide highways, silky fog on the beach, sand between your toes, gigaplex movie theaters, all-night noodle restaurants and a January low that matched the temperature of a typical May Day in Des Moines.

Pullman shrugged off his failure to become a mogul, took a job as a manager at a chain bookstore in Westwood and settled into a pleasant life.

He was content.

Well, almost. There *was* the love life situation . . .

Oh, that.

Pullman was divorced, ten years, from a woman he'd married just after they'd graduated from State. After the breakup he'd dated some but had found that it was hard to connect on a serious level. None of the women he went out with, mostly blind dates, knew much at all about movies, his true passion in life. (Oh, that is *so* weird, Rod, *I* love the classics too. Like, I've seen *Titanic* a hundred times. I mean, I *own* it. . . . Now, tell me about this Orbison Welles guy you mentioned.) Generally conversation settled into boring bragging about their kids and rants about how bad their ex-husbands had treated them. His dates also tended to dress themselves at the unglamorous places like Gap or L.L.Bean and were generally of—how could he put it?—solid Midwestern builds.

Oh, he met a few attractive women—like Sally Vaughn, the runner-up for Miss Iowa 2002, no less—but that relationship never went anywhere and after her he found himself longing for greener pastures in the girl department.

Which perfectly described LA. Here was a massive inventory of the most gorgeous creatures on earth. But they weren't just pretty. No, these lasses also had substance. He'd overhear them in the coffee bar of the bookstore, sitting over skim lattés and talking art and politics, brilliant, animated, funny. Just yesterday he'd listened to a couple of twenty-somethings in tight-fitting workout clothes arguing about the odd-sounding instrument on the soundtrack of *The Third Man*. A dulcimer, no, it was an accordion, no, it was—

A zither! Pullman had wanted to shout, but sensed an intrusion wouldn't be welcome (and sensed too that the one who'd been wrong would be royally pissed, putting the kibosh on any chance to hang out with either of them).

Your typical LA girl's DVD collection surely wouldn't include any sappy tearjerkers. They'd have *The Bicycle Thief, The Man Who Knew Too Much, Battleship Potemkin, Wings of Desire, The Manchurian Candidate.*

Ah, but how to meet one . . . That was the problem. How he hated the cold leap, the Hi-My-Name's-Rod-What's-Yours stage. Pudgy, clumsy, shy, he always clutched.

He'd hoped his job at the bookstore would connect him with glamorous Hollywoodians. Put him in a situation where he had a purpose—like being a salesman—or where somebody came up to *him*, then he could charm a woman with the best of them. But at the store, the instant he answered a customer's question, she had no more use for him. As for his fellow workers, they were either middle-aged losers or youngsters obsessed with their own careers (trying to, guess what, write, act in or direct movies, of course).

Out of sheer exhaustion, Pullman had given up on romance.

But then the Resident in 10B moved in.

Tammy Hudson—he'd asked the super her name the next morning—was a bit older than the stunning young things you'd see at Ivy or the back bar at the Beverly Wilshire. Pullman put her at thirty-three or thirty-four, which was good, a manageable age gap. She was gorgeous. Long hair, black as a raven's wings, often tied up in a jaunty ponytail or pinned into a flirtatious bun. She was tall and, as her yellow-and-black spandex jogging outfit proved, slim and muscular. She ran every day, and sometimes on his way to open the bookstore in the morning he'd see her in the backyard of the complex, standing in the cool, foggy air, practicing some kind of martial art.

One other thing he liked: Tammy had a great joy of life. She traveled often and—based on what he'd overheard—had a place down in Baja, or knew someone who did; she often spent weekends there. She rode a bright-red Vespa motor scooter, reminding him of Audrey Hepburn in *Roman Holiday*. Her auto was an old MG and she drove it lightning fast.

He hadn't been surprised to find that nearly every day she'd leave her apartment with her portfolio; of course she'd be involved in films. With her expressive face, she'd make a great character actor. Had he seen her in anything? he wondered. There were not many films Rodney Pullman *hadn't* seen.

He debated, and decided it wasn't completely out of the question that they could go out and that something serious might develop between them. He wasn't really bad looking. Too much gut, sure, but that was true of a lot of successful businessmen; women didn't mind, if you had the charm to offset it. He had a full head of brown hair, not a trace of gray, and a solid jaw that largely covered his double chin. He didn't smoke and drank only wine, and that in moderation. He always picked up the check at dinner.

But instantly, as always, the doubts swarmed like bees. How could the shy man meet her some way other than simply walking up and introducing himself? And once you've blown your initial chance, he knew all too well, you can't go back and start over again, not with a beautiful woman like Tammy.

So for months Pullman worshiped her from afar, struggling to come up with some way to break the ice and not make a fool of himself.

Then, this cool April evening, he got a break.

Around seven, Pullman was standing by his window, looking down into the courtyard, when he noticed motion from the bushes across the sidewalk from Tammy's bedroom. It was repeated a moment later and this time he saw a faint flash of light, like a reflection off glass.

Pullman shut his lights out and pulled the blinds down. Dropping to his knees, he peered outside and saw that a man was crouching in the bushes. He seemed to be staring into Tammy's window. He wore one of the gray uniforms of the apartment complex's groundskeepers. Pullman rose and slipped into his bedroom, where he'd have a better view of the courtyard. Yes, there was no doubt. The skinny young guy was peeping. He had a small pair of binoculars. Goddamn pervert!

Pullman's initial reaction was to call 9–1–1 and he grabbed the phone.

But he hit only the first digit, then thought, hold on . . . maybe he could *use* this somehow. He set the phone down.

Tammy's curtains closed. He focused on the voyeur and he felt a chill as the maintenance guy's shoulders slumped in disappointment—like he'd been hoping to get a look at her stripping for the shower. Still, the man stayed in position, waiting for a chance to resume his spying. But then Tammy's door opened and she stepped outside. She was wearing her pink top and tight floral pants. Her blue leather Coach purse was over her shoulder and sunglasses rode high on her head, stuck into her hair, which was loose tonight.

The voyeur crouched down into the bushes, out of sight.

Tammy locked her door and walked down the sidewalk toward the parking lot. Where was the maintenance man? Pullman wondered in alarm. Was he crawling closer to her? But just as Pullman snatched up the phone and started to push 9, he saw the stalker rise. He hadn't been about to pounce; he'd only been gathering up his tools. Carrying them, he turned away from Tammy and walked in the opposite direction, toward the back of the building.

Tammy disappeared into the lot and a moment later the rattle of her MG engine and the whine of the gears filled the night as she sped away in the little green car.

That evening Pullman stayed close to home, ordering in a pizza and keeping a close eye on the courtyard. Hours passed without any sign of Tammy or her stalker. He nearly fell asleep, but he made some coffee, drank it down black and hot, and forced himself to stay awake so he could scope out the courtyard. Reflecting, with a shiver of excitement, that this was just like the Hitchcock thriller, *Rear Window,* where Jimmy Stewart, housebound in a wheelchair, spends his time peering through his neighbors' windows. It was Pullman's favorite movie; he wondered if Tammy had ever seen it. He had a feeling she had.

At nine p.m., still seeing no sign of Tammy or the skinny voyeur, Pullman went downstairs and around the back of his building, where he found the superintendent. He asked the man, "Who's that young maintenance guy? The blond?"

"Blond?" the heavyset janitor asked, pulling a strand of greasy hair off his forehead. He smelled of beer.

"Yeah, the short guy."

"You said 'blond.'"

"Right, the one with blond hair," Pullman said, frowning in frustration. "You understand who I mean?" The janitor was Anglo; there was no language barrier. Maybe he was just stupid.

"I thought, you called somebody 'the blonde,' that meant a girl. Like 'Look at the blonde.' Nobody says that about a man. You don't call a man *'the* blond.'"

"Yeah? Well, I don't know about that. But he's blond. And short. He was trimming the hedges and raking today. You know who I mean?"

"Yeah, yeah. Him."

"What's his name?"

"I dunno. I didn't hire him. I don't do the grounds work. The board hired him."

"What's his story?"

"Story? He sweeps up, he rakes, he cuts the grass. That's the story. Why?"

"He works for a service?"

"Yeah, a service. I guess."

"Is the company bonded?" Pullman asked.

"He works for?"

"Yeah, that company."

"I guess. I told you it was the board—"

"Hired him. I know. So you don't know *anything* about him."

"Why?"

"Just curious."

The super waddled back to his apartment, frowning as if he'd been wrongly accused of something, and Pullman hurried back upstairs.

At one a.m. Tammy returned. Looking as vibrant and sexy as when she'd left, she walked to her door and unlocked it. With a look over her shoulder, she stepped inside and slammed the door shut.

She'd seemed a bit uneasy at the doorstep, Pullman decided, as if she'd seen or heard an intruder, and so he grabbed some binoculars and scanned the bushes. It didn't seem that the peeper was back but he wasn't going to take any chances. He stepped into the hallway and padded downstairs. He stood in the shadows near the stand of bushes where the voyeur had perched earlier to play his sick game.

Flies buzzed, lights flickered through the bushes and Pullman could hear the distant howl of coyotes in the hills on the way to Malibu. But the scene was otherwise quiet and still.

No sign of the maintenance man.

After Tammy's lights went out, Pullman waited a half hour and, seeing nothing but the resident tomcat prowl past, returned to his apartment, vaguely aware that this situation could be a gold mine for his love life, but wondering how best to exploit it.

Well, the first thing to consider: was the guy a serious threat? Pullman'd heard that voyeurs were like people with foot fetishes and exhibitionists. They weren't generally dangerous. They substitute the emotionally distant—and to them safer—act of watching men or women and fantasizing about them for normal sexual relationships, even though they *think* they want the latter.

It was true, of course, that rapists would sometimes spy on their victims to learn their habits and patterns before assaulting them but the vast majority of voyeurs would never even think of speaking to their victims, much less assaulting them. The odds were that the groundskeeper was harmless. Besides, he was a slim, meek-looking little punk. With her karate training, Tammy could deck him with a single jab. No, Pullman decided, there was little risk to the woman if he didn't blow the whistle on the stalker just yet.

He fell into bed and closed his eyes but was unable to fall asleep; his overheated brain continued to wrestle with the problem of how to parlay the stalking into a chance to ask Tammy out. Tossing uncomfortably, he beat the alarm to sleep by half an hour. When it blared on at seven he stumbled out of bed and looked outside. The lights were on in Tammy's apartment. He pictured her doing her morning workout or enjoying a breakfast of yogurt and berries and herbal tea, content in her ignorance of the stalker.

And of him, Pullman saw nothing.

This was troubling. Had this apartment complex been just a one-day assignment for the guy? What if he never returned? That would ruin all of the plans.

He remained at the window for as long as he could, hoping for the maintenance man's return. But at eight, he could wait no longer; he had to be at work in fifteen minutes.

Pullman showered fast and staggered outside to the parking lot, head aching from the lack of sleep, eyes stinging in the fierce sunlight. He was just about to get into his battered Saturn when a Pacific Landscaping Services pickup truck pulled into the lot.

He held his breath.

Yes, it was the stalker! He climbed out, collected his tools and a drink cooler and headed toward the courtyard. Pullman stepped behind his car and crouched down. The voyeur slipped into the same bushes where he'd kept his vigil yesterday and started to clip a hedge that was already perfectly trimmed. His hungry eyes didn't even glance at the clippers; they were focused on Tammy's bedroom window.

Thank you, Pullman offered to the god his Midwest upbringing suggested might exist and hurried back to his apartment, taking the back path to stay out of the stalker's view. He was supposed to open the bookstore but he wasn't going to pass up this chance. He pulled out his cell phone and called the Human Resources director of the store. He faked a raspy voice and told her that he was sick; he wouldn't be coming in.

"Oh," she said uncertainly. Pullman remembered that the other assistant manager was scheduled to start vacation today, which meant the HR woman'd have a hell of time finding somebody who could open the store. Pullman coughed hard but the woman offered no sympathy. She said coolly, "Let me know if you'll be in tomorrow. Give me a little more warning next time."

"I—"

Click.

Pullman shrugged. He had more important things to worry about. As he walked to his apartment he was running through some of the plans he'd been thinking of as he lay in bed last night.

"Hi, you don't know me but I live across the way. I just thought you should know . . . "

Or maybe: *"Hi, I'm your neighbor. Don't think we've met. Don't want to alarm you but there's a man in those bushes who's been staring at you for two days."*

No, don't say *two* days. She'd wondered why he didn't say anything earlier.

"Listen, miss, you don't know me, but don't look around. There's a man in those bushes across the walk. He's been staring at your apartment with some binoculars. I think he's a stalker or something."

But after some debate he decided he didn't like any of those approaches. She might just respond by saying, "Oh, thanks." Then closing the door on him and calling the cops.

End of Rodney Pullman.

No, he needed to do something dramatic—something that would impress a woman as sleek and cool and, well, unimpressible as Tammy Hudson surely was.

Squinting into the courtyard, Pullman saw that the voyeur had moved closer to her apartment, eyes still focused obsessively on her window. The sunlight glinted off the blades of the clippers, which gave an ominous *swick, swick*. The tool was long and seemed well-honed. He wondered if his earlier assessment had been wrong. Maybe this guy *was* dangerous.

Which finally gave him the idea—how to best orchestrate an introduction to the beautiful Resident in 10B.

Pullman rose and walked to his closet, rummaged through it and finally found his old baseball bat. He'd never been much for sports but he'd bought a bat and glove when he'd been hired at the bookstore and learned that they had a team. He'd thought it would be a good way to meet some of the girl clerks. As it turned out, though, the only players were guys and he soon dropped off the team.

A glance outside—no sign of Tammy, though the voyeur was still there, clipping away fervently with the shears.

Swick, swick . . .

Gripping the bat, Pullman left his apartment and slipped downstairs to the first-floor walkway then edged quietly to the shadows behind the stalker.

His plan was to wait until Tammy left for her regular morning auditions. As soon as she passed the voyeur, Pullman would jog up to the man, brandish the bat and shout to her to call the police, this man was stalking her.

He'd make the guy lie on his belly until the cops arrived; he and Tammy would have a good ten minutes to talk.

No, no, it was nothing. . . My name's Rod Pullman, by the way. And you're? . . . Nice to meet you, Tammy. . . . No, really, just being a good citizen. . . . Well, okay then, tell you what, if you really want to repay me, you can let me take you out to dinner.

Wiping his sweating hand on his slacks, he got a firmer grip on the taped bat handle.

Sure, Saturday'd work for me. Maybe—

The opening front door of Tammy's apartment interrupted the fantasy.

She stepped outside and pulled her expensive shades down over her eyes. Today, her black hair sported a bright-red headband, which matched her finger- and toenail polish. She had her blue purse over her shoulder and was carrying her portfolio. She started down the walk.

The voyeur tensed. The clipping ceased.

Pullman gripped the bat harder yet. He took a deep breath, rehearsed his lines once more.

Ready, set . . .

But then the voyeur stepped back. He set down the clippers and began fumbling with the front of his overalls.

What—?

Oh, Jesus, he was unzipping himself and reaching inside.

He *is* going to rape her!

"No!" Pullman shouted and ran forward, waving the bat over his head.

"Hey!" The rapist blinked in panic and stumbled back, tripping over a small wicket fence around a mulch bed. He landed hard and cried out in pain, his breath knocked out of his lungs, gasping.

Tammy stopped, turning toward the commotion, frowning.

Pullman yelled to her, "Call the police! This guy's been watching you. He's a rapist!" He turned back to the blond man, waving the bat. "Don't move! I'll—"

His words were cut off by the stunning explosion of gunshots from directly behind him.

Pullman howled in panic and dropped to his knees as the bullets slammed into the stalker's head and neck, leaving a bloody mist around him. The man shivered once and slumped to the ground, dead.

"Christ!" Pullman whispered in shock and slowly rose to his feet. He turned toward Tammy and frowned in astonishment to see her holding a large black pistol, which she'd pulled out of her Coach purse. She was crouching and looking around like a soldier in an ambush.

So she didn't just study karate for self-protection; she had a license to carry a gun too. Well, a lot of women in LA did, he'd heard. On the other hand, Pullman wasn't sure you could just shoot a man who was lying harmlessly on the ground, when he hadn't actually attacked you.

"Hey, you," Tammy called, stepping closer.

Pullman turned. He got a good look at the woman's beautiful blue eyes and her diamond earrings sparkling in the sun, and he smelled a flowery perfume mixed with the acrid firecracker smell of smoke from the gun.

"Me?" he asked.

"Yeah, here." She handed the portfolio to him.

"This's for me?"

But she didn't answer. She turned away and sprinted into the alley behind the apartment complex, a flash of vivacious color that vanished an instant later.

As Pullman was staring in confusion at the portfolio, he heard a rustle of feet behind him and an instant later was grabbed by a half-dozen massive hands. The next thing he knew he was being slammed face-first into a patch of extremely well-raked lawn.

■

Tammy Hudson, Rodney Pullman learned from his lawyer, was one of Southern California's most successful, and most elusive, drug dealers.

It seemed that she'd been responsible for importing thousands of pounds of high-quality cocaine from Mexico over the past year. (Hence, her frequent trips south of the border.) Driving a beat-up old sports car and living in a pathetic place like the Pacific Arms Apartments kept her off the radar screen of DEA and police officials, who found it easier to find and track the high-living kingpins in Beverly Hills and Palm Springs.

Sitting in the LA detention center across from Pullman, the lawyer now delivered the bad news that the D.A. had no intention of dropping any of the charges against him.

"But I didn't do anything," Pullman whined.

The lawyer, a tanned forty-year-old with a fringe of curly hair, gave a chuckle, as if he'd heard that line ten thousand times. He continued, explaining that the prosecutor was out for blood. For one thing, a cop had been killed; the blond man, the apparent voyeur, had actually been an undercover LAPD officer pretending to work for the landscape maintenance company. His job was to report whenever Tammy left the apartment. Other officers or DEA agents would then take over surveillance and follow her in unmarked cars or vans. (When Pullman thought that he was reaching into his pants in preparation for a rape, the officer was in fact merely fishing his radio out of an inside pocket to tell the other surveillance team that she was leaving.)

"But—"

"Let me finish." The lawyer added that the cops were also outraged that, because of Pullman, Tammy had successfully escaped. She'd disappeared completely and the FBI and DEA believed she was probably out of the country by now.

"But they can't think I was working with her! Is that what they think?"

"In a word, yeah." He went on to say that Pullman's explanation for the past several days' events raised eyebrows. "To put it mildly." For instance, the police were curious why, if he'd noticed the supposed voyeur the day before, he hadn't told her then. If his concern, as he claimed, was for an innocent woman's safety, why didn't he tell her she was in danger when he'd first found out about it?

His red-faced explanation that he wanted to use the voyeur as an excuse to introduce himself to Tammy was greeted with an expression in the lawyer's eyes that could be read as either skepticism or embarrassment for a pathetic client. The man recorded this explanation in a few anemic notes.

And why would he lie to his employer about being sick today? To the police, that made sense only if he was serving as Tammy's lookout. Today's was to be a big drug transfer and they reasoned that Pullman had stayed home to make sure Tammy got away safely to deliver the goods. Their theory was that he had figured the maintenance worker for law and attacked him to give Tammy the chance to flee.

Physical evidence too: both his fingerprints and hers were on the portfolio, which happened to contain no headshot photos or audition tapes but rather a kilo of very pure cocaine. "She gave it to me," he'd said weakly. "To create a diversion, I'll bet. So she could escape."

The lawyer didn't even bother to write that one down.

But the most damning of all was the problem with his claim that he didn't know her. "See," his lawyer said, "if you really didn't know her or have any connection with her, we might get a jury to believe everything else you're claiming."

"But I *don't* know her. I swear."

The attorney gave a faint wince. "See, Rodney, there's a problem with that."

"I prefer 'Rod.' Like I've said."

"A problem."

"What?" Pullman scratched his head; the cuffs jingled like dull bells.

"They searched your apartment."

"Oh. They did? They can do that?"

A laugh. "You were arrested on felony murder, assault, aiding and abetting and drug charges. Yes, Rod, they can do that."

"Oh."

"And you know what they found?"

He knew perfectly well what they found. He sat back, stared at the floor and played absently with the handcuffs as the lawyer read from a sheet of paper.

"Some old Yoplait containers with Tammy's fingerprints on them, ditto, two wine bottles, a box of herbal tea and empty strawberry cartons. Magazines with her name on the address label. A charge card receipt of hers from a store in the Beverly Center. A Starbucks cup with her lipstick and DNA on the rim."

"DNA? They checked that, did they?"

"That's what cops do."

"I swear, she was never in my apartment. All that stuff . . . I just . . . I kind of . . . picked it up in her trash."

"Her trash?"

"I just saw some things out behind her apartment. I didn't think it was a big deal."

"You had two dozen snapshots of her on your dresser."

"I just took a few candids is all. She wasn't looking at the camera—you can tell the cops that. If I knew her, she'd be looking at the camera, wouldn't she?"

"Rod."

"No, listen! If we *had been* together somewhere she'd be looking at me, looking *into* the lens." Pullman's voice broke in desperation. "Like, 'Say, cheese,' you know? But she wasn't. That means we weren't together. It's just logic. Doesn't that make sense?" He fell silent. After a moment he added, "I just wanted to meet her. I didn't know how."

"They found some binoculars too. They figured you used those to keep an eye on her door to warn her if anybody was going to raid her place."

"That was just so I could . . . so I could look at her. She's really pretty." Pullman shrugged. His eyes returned to the floor.

"I think the only thing we can do is talk to the DA about a plea bargain. We *don't* want to go to trial on this one, believe me. I may be able to get you a deal for fifteen, twenty years . . ."

"Twenty years?"

"I'll talk to them. See what they say."

The lawyer stepped to the door of the interview room and rapped on it to summon the guard. A moment later it opened.

"One thing," Pullman said.

His attorney turned and lifted an eyebrow.

"Sally Vaughn."

"Who?"

"A runner-up for Miss Iowa. Few years ago."

"What about her?"

"I sold her a car and we went out once but she wasn't interested in seeing me anymore. The same thing sort of happened with her."

"Same thing?"

"Like with Tammy. I was kind of watching her more than I should have."

"Peeping?"

He started to object to the word but then nodded. "I got arrested. That's why I moved here. I wanted to start over. Meet somebody for real."

"What was your sentence in Iowa?"

"Six months suspended, counseling for a year."

"It didn't take, the counseling."

"Didn't take, no."

"I'll get the records. The DA might buy it. But he lost a prime perp because of you, so he's going to want something. Probably stalking and privacy charges. You'd have to do a year, eighteen months, I'd guess."

"Better than twenty."

"I'll see what I can do." The lawyer stepped through the door.

"One other question?" Pullman asked, looking up.

"What?"

The prisoner said, "Will the police use all of those things they found? For evidence?"

"From your apartment?"

"Right."

"Probably not. They usually pick the best ones."

"Then you think I could have a couple of the pictures of Tammy to put up on my wall here? There's no window. There's nothing to look at."

The lawyer hesitated, as if Pullman were joking. When he concluded that apparently the prisoner wasn't, he said, "You know, Rodney, that's probably not the best idea in the world."

"Just a thought."

The attorney left and a large guard stepped inside. He took Rodney Pullman by the arm and led him to the corridor that would take him back to his cell.

The Poker Lesson

Poker is a game in which each man plays his own hand as he elects. No consideration should be expected by one player from another.

—JOHN SCARNE

I want into one of your games," the boy said.

Sitting hunched over a hamburger in Angela's Diner, Keller looked up at the blond kid, who stood with his hip cocked and arms crossed, trying to be cool but looking like an animal awkwardly trying to stand on its hind legs. Handsome enough even though he wore black-rimmed nerd glasses and was pale and skinny.

Keller decided not to ask the kid to sit down. "What games?" He ate more of his burger and glanced at his watch.

The kid noticed the move and said, "Well, the one that's starting at eight tonight, for instance."

Keller grunted a laugh.

He heard the rumble of one of the freight trains that bisected this neighborhood on the north side of town. He had a fond memory of a diesel rattling bar glasses six months ago just as he lay down a flush to take a $56,320 pot away from three businessmen who were from the south of France. He'd won that pot twenty minutes after the first ante. The men had scowled French scowls but continued to lose another seventy thousand over the course of the rainy night.

"What's your name?"

"Tony Stigler."

"How old're you?"

"Eighteen."

"Even if there *was* a game, which there isn't, you couldn't play. You're a kid. You couldn't get into a bar."

"It's in Sal's back room. It's not in the bar."

"How do you *know* that?" Keller muttered. In his late forties, the dark-complected man was as strong and solid as he'd been twenty years ago. When he asked questions in this tone you stopped being cute and answered straight.

"My buddy works at Marconi Pizza. He hears things."

"Well, your buddy oughta watch out what he hears. And he *really* oughta watch who he *tells* what he hears." He returned to his lunch.

"Look." The kid dug into his pocket and pulled out a wad of bills. Hundreds mostly. Keller'd been gambling since he was younger than this boy and he knew how to size up a roll. The kid was holding close to five thousand. Tony said, "I'm serious, man. I want to play with you."

"Where'd you get that?"

A shrug. "I got it."

"Don't give any *Sopranos* crap. You gonna play poker, you play by the rules. And one of the rules is you play with your own money. If that's stolen you can hike your ass outta here right now."

"It's not stolen," the kid said, lowering his voice. "I won it."

"At cards," Keller asked wryly, "or the lottery?"

"Draw and stud."

Keller enjoyed a particularly good bite of hamburger and studied the boy again. "Why my game? You got dozens you could pick."

The fading city of Ellridge, population 200,000 or so, squatted in steel-mill territory on the flat, gray Indiana River. What it lacked in class, though, the city more than made up for in sin. Hookers and lap dance bars, of course. But the town's big business was underground gambling—for a very practical reason: Atlantic City and Nevada weren't within a day's drive and the few

Indian casinos with licensed poker tables were filled with low-stakes amateurs.

"Why you?" Tony answered, "'Cause you're the best player in town and I want to play against the best."

"What's this, some John Wayne gunfighter bullshit?"

"Who's John Wayne?"

"Christ . . . you're way outta our league, kid."

"There's more where this came from." Hefting the wad. "A lot more."

Keller gestured at the cash and looked around. "Put that away."

The kid did.

Keller ate more burger, thinking of the times when, not much older than this boy, he'd blustered and lied his way into plenty of poker games. The only way to learn the game poker is to play—for money—against the best players you can find, day after day after day. Losing and winning.

"How long you played?"

"Since I was twelve."

"Whatta your parents think about what you're doing?"

"They're dead," he said unemotionally. "I live with my uncle. When he's around. Which he isn't much."

"Sorry."

Tony shrugged.

"Well, I don't let anybody into the game without somebody vouches for them. So—"

"I played in a couple games with Jimmy Logan. You know him, don't you?"

Logan lived up in Michigan and was a respected player. The stakes tended to be small but Keller'd played some damn good poker against the man.

Keller said, "Go get a soda or something. Come back in twenty minutes."

"Come on, man, I don't want—"

"Go get a soda," he snapped. "And you call me 'man' again I'll break your fingers."

"But—"

"Go," he muttered harshly.

So this's what'd be like to have kids, thought Keller, whose life as a professional gambler over the past thirty years had left no room for a wife and children.

"I'll be over there." Tony nodded across the street at the green awning of a Starbucks.

Keller pulled out his cell phone and called Logan. He had to be cautious about who he let into games. A few months ago some crusading reporters'd gotten tired of writing about all of Ellridge's local government corruption and CEO scandals so they'd done a series on gambling (THE CITY'S SHAME was the yawner of a head-line). The police were under pressure from the mayor to close up the bigger games and Keller had to be careful. But Jimmy Logan confirmed that he'd checked the boy out carefully a month or so ago. He'd come into the game with serious money and had lost bad one day but'd had the balls to come back the next. He covered his loss and kept going; he walked away the big winner. Logan had also found out that Tony's parents'd left him close to $300,000 in cash when they'd died. The money had been in a trust fund but had been released on his eighteenth birthday, last month.

With this news Keller's interest perked up.

After the call he finished his lunch. Tony delayed a defiant half hour before returning. He and his attitude ambled back into the diner slowly.

Keller told him, "Okay. I'll let you sit in tonight for a couple hours. But you leave before the high-stakes game starts."

A scoff. "But—"

"That's the deal. Take it or leave it."

"I guess."

"Bring at least ten thousand. . . . And try not to lose it all in the first five minutes, okay?"

■

The moments before a game begins are magic.

Sure, everyone's looking forward to lighting up the sour-smooth Cuban cigars, arguing about the Steelers or the Pistons or the Knicks, telling the jokes that men can tell only among themselves.

But the anticipation of those small pleasures was nothing compared with the one overriding thought: Am I going to win?

Forget the talk about the loving of the game, the thrill of the chase . . . those were all true, yes. But the thing that set real gamblers apart from dilettantes was their consuming drive to walk away from the table with more money than they sat down with. Any gambler who says otherwise is a liar.

Keller felt this rush now, sitting in the pungent, dark back room of Sal's Tavern, amid cartons of napkins, straws and coffee, an ancient Pabst Blue Ribbon beer sign, a ton of empties growing mold, broken bar stools. Tonight's game would start small (Keller considered it penny ante, despite the ten-large admission price) but would move to high stakes later in the night, when two serious players from Chicago arrived. A lot more money would change hands then. But the electric anticipation he felt with big stakes wasn't a bit different from what he felt now or if they'd only been playing for pocket change. Looking over the bare wood table, seeing the unopened decks of the red and blue Bicycle cards stacked up, one question sizzled in his mind: Am I going to win?

The other players arrived. Keller nodded a greeting to Frank Wendall, head of bookkeeping at Great Lakes Metal Works. Round and nervous and perpetually sweating, Wendall acted as if they were about to be raided at any minute. Wendall was the smart boy in Keller's poker circle. He'd drop lines into the conversation like, "You know, there're a total of 5,108 possible flushes in a fifty-two-card deck but only seventy-eight possible pairs. Odd but it makes sense when you look at the numbers." And he'd then happily launch into a lecture on those numbers, which'd keep going until somebody told him to shut up.

Squat, loud, chain-smoking Quentin Lasky, the owner of a string of body shops, was the least educated but the richest man in the room. People in Ellridge must've been particularly bad drivers because his shops were always packed. Lasky played ruthlessly—and recklessly—and would win and lose big.

The last of the group was the opposite of Lasky. Somewhere in his late sixties, lean, gray Larry Stanton had grown up here, worked for another local manufacturer all his life and then retired. He was only in Ellridge part of the year; winters he spent in Florida. A widower, he was on a fixed income and was a conservative, cautious player, who never won or lost large sums. Keller looked at the old guy as a sort of mascot of the game.

Finally the youngster arrived. Trying to be cool but obviously excited to be in a serious game, Tony stepped into the room. He wore baggy slacks, a T-shirt and a stocking cap and he toted a Starbucks coffee. Such a goddamn teenager, Keller laughed to himself.

Introductions were made. Keller noticed that Stanton seemed troubled. "It's okay. I checked him out."

"Well, it's just that, he's a little young, don't you think?"

"Maybe you're a *little* old," the kid came back. But he smiled good-naturedly and the frown that crossed Stanton's face slowly vanished.

Stanton was the banker and took cash from everybody and began handing out chips. Whites were one dollar, reds were five, blues ten and yellows twenty-five.

"Okay, Tony, listen up. I'll be telling you the rules as we go along. Now—"

"I know the rules," Tony interrupted. "Everything according to Hoyle."

"No, everything according to *me,*" Keller said, laughing. "Forget Hoyle. He never even heard of poker."

"Whatta you mean? He wrote the rules for all the games," Lasky countered.

"No, he didn't," Keller said. "That's what people think. But Hoyle was just some Brit lawyer in the seventeen hundreds. He wrote this little book about three bullshit games: whist, quadrille and piquet. Nothing else, no Kankakee, pass the garbage, put-and-take stud or high-low roll 'em over. And try going into the MGM Grand and asking for a game of whist. . . . They'll laugh you out on your ass."

"But you see Hoyle books everywhere," Wendall said.

"Some publishers kept the idea going and they added poker and all the modern games."

"I didn't know that," Tony said distractedly. He shoved his geek glasses higher on his nose and tried to look interested.

Keller said sternly, "Sorry if we're boring you, kid, but I got news: It's knowing everything about the game—even the little shit—that separates the men from the boys in poker." He looked him over carefully. "You keep your ears open, you might just learn something."

"How the hell can he hear anything even *if* he keeps his ears open?" Lasky muttered and glanced at the boy's stocking cap. "What're you, some kind of fucking rapper? Lose the hat. Show some respect."

Tony took his time removing the hat and tossing it on the counter. He pulled the lid off his Starbucks cup and sipped the coffee.

Keller examined the messy pile of chips in front of the boy and said, "Now, whatever Jimmy Logan told you about playing poker, whatever you think you know from Hoyle, forget about it. We use the big boys' rules here, and rule number one: We play fair. Always keep your chips organized in front of you so everybody at the table knows how much you've got. Okay?"

"Sure." The kid began stacking the chips into neat stacks.

"And," Wendall said, "let's say a miracle happens and you start to win big and somebody can't see exactly how many chips you have. If they ask you, you tell them. Down to the last dollar. Got that?"

"Tell 'em, sure." The boy nodded.

They cut for the deal and Wendall won. He began shuffling with his fat fingers.

Keller gazed at the riffling cards in pleasure, thinking: There's nothing like poker, nothing like it in the world.

The game went back nearly two hundred years. It started as a Mississippi river boat cheaters' game to replace three-card monte, which even the most gullible slickers quickly learned was just a scam to take their money. Poker, played back then with only the ten through the ace, seemed to give them more of a fighting chance. But it didn't, of course, not in the hands of expert sharks (the innocents might've been more reluctant to play if they'd known that the game's name probably came from the nineteenth-century slang for wallet, "poke," the emptying of which was the true object of play).

"Ante up," Wendall called. "The game is five-card draw."

There are dozens of variations of poker games. But in Keller's games, five-card draw—"closed poker" or "jackpot" were the official names—was what they played, high hand the winner. Over the years he'd played every kind of poker known to man—from California lowball draw (the most popular poker game west of the Rockies) to standard stud to Texas Hold 'Em. They were all interesting and exciting in their own ways but Keller liked basic jackpot best because there were no gimmicks, no arcane rules; it was you against the cards and the other players, like bare-knuckle boxing. Man to man.

In jackpot, players are dealt five cards and then have the option of exchanging up to three in hopes of bettering their hands. Good players, like Keller, had long ago memorized the odds of drawing certain combinations. Say he was dealt a pair of threes, a jack, a seven and a two. If he decided to keep the pair and the jack and draw substitutes for the other two, he'd have a one-in-five chance of getting another jack to make a two-pair hand. To draw the remaining threes in the deck—to make four of a kind—his chances dropped to one in 1,060. But if he chose to keep only the pair and draw three new cards, the odds of getting that four of a kind improved to 1 in 359. Knowing these numbers, and dozens more, were what separated amateur players from pros, and Keller made a very good living as a pro.

They tossed in the ante and Wendall began dealing.

Keller focused on Tony's strategy. He'd expected the kid to play recklessly but on the whole he was cautious and seemed to be getting a feel for the table and the players. A lot of teenagers would've been loud and obnoxious, Keller supposed, but the boy sat back quietly and just played cards.

Which wasn't to say he didn't need advice.

"Tony, don't play with your chips. Makes you look nervous."

"I wasn't playing with them. I—"

"And here's another rule—don't argue with the guys giving you rules. You're good. You got it in you to be a great player— but you gotta shut up and listen to the experts."

Lasky grumbled, "Listen to him, kid. He's the best. I figure I bought his friggin' Mercedes for him, all the money I lost here. And does he bring it into my shop to get the dings out? Hell, no. . . . Call you." He shoved chips forward.

"I don't get dings, Lasky. I'm a good driver. Just like I'm a good poker player. . . . Say hi to the ladies." Keller laid down three queens and took the $900 pot.

"Fuck me," Lasky snapped angrily.

"Now there's *another* rule," Keller said, nodding at the body-shop man then turning to Tony. "Never show emotion—losing *or* winning. It gives your opponent some information they can use against you."

"Excuse me for breaking the rules," Lasky muttered to Keller. "I meant to say fuck *you*."

Twenty minutes later Tony'd had a string of losses. On the next hand he looked at the five cards he'd been dealt and, when Stanton bet ten dollars, shook his head. He folded without drawing any cards and glumly toyed with the lid of his Starbucks cup.

Keller frowned. "Why'd you fold?"

"Losing streak."

Keller scoffed. "There's no such thing as a losing streak."

Wendall nodded, pushing the cards toward Tony to deal. The resident Mr. Wizard of poker said, "Remember that. Every hand of poker starts with a fresh shuffle so it's not like blackjack—there's no connection between hands. The laws of probability rule."

The boy nodded and, sure enough, played his way through Stanton's bluff to take a $850 pot.

"Hey, there you go," Keller said. "Good for you."

"So what? You in school, kid?" Lasky asked after a few lack-luster hands.

"Two cards," the boy said to Keller, then dealing. He replied to Lasky, "Been in computer science at the community college for a year. But it's boring. I'm going to drop out."

"Computers?" Wendall asked, laughing derisively. "High-tech stocks? I'll take craps or roulette wheel any day. At least you know what the odds are."

"And what do you want to do for a living?" Keller asked.

"Play cards professionally."

"Three cards," Lasky muttered to Keller. Then to Tony he gave a gruff laugh. "Pro card playing? Nobody does that. Well, Keller does. But nobody else I know of." A glance at Stanton. "How 'bout you, Grandpa, you ever play pro?"

"Actually, the name's Larry. Two cards."

"No offense, *Larry*."

"And two cards for the dealer," Keller said.

The old man arranged his cards. "No, I never even thought

about it." A nod at the pile of chips in front of him—he was just about even for the night. "I play all right but the odds're still against you. Anything serious I do with money? I make sure the odds're on my side."

Lasky sneered. "That's what makes you a man, for Christ's sake. Having the balls to play even *if* the odds're against you." A glance at Tony. "You look like you got balls. Do you?"

"You tell *me*," the boy asked and lay down two pair to win a $1,100 pot.

Lasky looked at him and snapped, "And fuck you *too*."

Keller said, "Think that means yes." Everyone at the table—except Lasky—laughed.

The play continued with a series of big pots, Lasky and Tony being the big winners. Finally Wendall was tapped out.

"Okay, that's it. I'm out of here. Gentlemen . . . been a pleasure playing with you." As always, he pulled a baseball cap on and ducked out the back door, looking hugely relieved he'd escaped without being arrested.

Keller's cell phone rang and he took the call. "Yeah? . . . Okay. You know where, right? . . . See you then." When he disconnected he lit a cigar and sat back, scanned the boy's chips. He said to Tony. "You played good tonight. But time for you to cash in."

"What? I'm just getting warmed up. It's only ten."

He nodded at his cell phone. "The big guns'll be here in twenty minutes. You're through for the night."

"Whatta you mean? I want to keep playing."

"This's the big time. Guys I know from Chicago."

"I'm playing fine. You said so yourself."

"You don't understand, Tony," Larry Stanton said, nodding at the chips. "The whites go up to ten bucks each. The yellows'll be two-fifty. You can't play with stakes like that."

"I've got. . . " He looked over his chips. ". . . almost forty thousand."

"And you could lose that in three, four hands."

"I'm not going to lose it."

"Oh, brother," Lasky said, rolling his eyes. "The voice of youth."

Keller said, "In my high-stakes game, everybody comes in with a hundred large."

"I can get it."

"This time of night?"

"I inherited some money a few years ago. I keep a lot of it in cash for playing. I've got it at home—just a couple miles from here."

"No," Stanton said. "It's not for you. It's a whole different game with that much money involved."

"Goddamn it, everybody's treating me like a child. You've seen me play. I'm good, right?"

Keller fell silent. He looked at the boy's defiant gaze and finally said, "You're back here in a half hour with a hundred G's, okay."

After the boy left, Keller announced a break until the Chicago contingent arrived. Lasky went to get a sandwich and Stanton and Keller wandered into the bar proper for a couple of beers.

Stanton sipped his Newcastle and said, "Kid's quite a player."

"Has potential," Keller said.

"So how bad you going to hook him? For his whole stake, the whole hundred thousand plus?"

"What's that?"

"'Rule number one is we play fair'?" Stanton whispered sarcastically. "What the hell was *that* all about? You're setting him up. You've been spending most of the game—and half your money—catching his draws."

Keller smiled and blew a stream of cigar smoke toward the ceiling of the bar. The old guy was right. Keller'd been going all the way with losing hands just to see how Tony drew cards. And the reconnaissance had been very illuminating. The boy had his strengths but the one thing he lacked was knowledge of the odds of poker. He was drawing blind. Keller was no rocket scientist but he'd worked hard over the years to learn the mathematics of the game; Tony, on the other hand, might've been a computer guru, but he didn't have a clue what his chances were of drawing a flush or a full house or even a second pair. Combined with the boy's atrocious skills at bluffing, which Keller'd spotted immediately, his ignorance of the odds made him a sitting duck.

"You've also been sandbagging," Stanton said in disgust.

Score another one for Grandpa. He'd spotted that Keller had been passing on the bet and folding good hands on purpose—to build up Tony's confidence and to make him believe that Keller was a lousy bluffer.

"You're setting him up for a big hit."

Keller shrugged. "I tried to talk him into walking away."

"Bullshit," Stanton countered. "You take a kid like that and tell 'em to leave, what's their first reaction? To stay. . . . Come on, Keller, he hasn't got that kind of money to lose."

"He inherited a shitload of cash."

"So you invited him into the game as soon as you found that out?"

"No, as a matter of fact, he came to *me*. . . . You're just pissed 'cause he treats you like a has-been."

"You're taking advantage of him."

Keller shot back with: "Here's my real rule number one in poker: As long as you don't cheat you can do whatever you want to trick your opponents."

"You going to share that rule with Tony?" Stanton asked.

"I'm going to do better than that—I'm going to give him a firsthand demonstration. He wants to learn poker? Well, this'll be the best lesson he ever gets."

"You think breaking him and taking his tuition money's going to make him a better player?" Stanton asked.

"Yeah, I do. He doesn't want to be in school anyway."

"That's not the point. The point is you're an expert and he's a boy."

"He claims he's a man. And one of the things about being a man is getting knocked on your ass and learning from it."

"In penny ante, sure. But not a game like this."

"You have a problem with this, Grandpa?" Angry, Keller turned ominously toward him.

Stanton looked away and held up his hands. "Do what you want. It's your game. I'm just trying to be the voice of conscience."

"If you play by the rules you'll always have a clear conscience."

A voice called from the doorway, Lasky's. He said, "They're here."

Keller slapped Stanton on his bony shoulders. "Let's go win some money."

■

More cigar smoke was filling the back room. The source: Elliott Rothstein and Harry Piemonte, businessmen from the Windy City. Keller'd played with them several times previously but he didn't know much about them; the two men revealed as little about their personal lives as their faces shared what cards they held. They might've been organized crime capos or they might have been directors of a charity for orphans. All Keller knew was they were solid players, paid their losses without griping and won without lording it over the losers.

Both men wore dark suits and expensive, tailored white shirts. Rothstein had a diamond pinkie ring and Piemonte a heavy gold bracelet. Wedding bands encircled both of their left ring fingers. They now stripped off their suit jackets, sat down at the table and were making small talk with Stanton and Lasky when Tony returned. He sat down at his place and pulled the lid off his new Starbucks, nodding at Rothstein and Piemonte.

They frowned and looked at Keller. "Who's this?" Rothstein muttered.

"He's okay."

Piemonte frowned. "We got a rule, we don't play with kids."

Tony laughed and shoved his nerd glasses high on his nose. "You guys and your rules." He opened an envelope and dumped out cash. He counted out a large stack and put some back into his pocket. "Hundred large," he said to Stanton, who gave a dark look to Keller but began counting out chips for the boy.

The two new players looked at each other and silently decided to make an exception to their general rule about juveniles in poker games.

"Okay, the game is five-card draw," Keller said. "Minimum bet fifty, ante is twenty-five."

Piemonte won the cut and they began.

The hands were pretty even for the first hour, then Keller began pulling ahead slowly. Tony kept his head above water, the second winner—but only because, it seemed, the other players were getting bad hands; the boy was still hopeless when it came to calculating the odds of drawing. In a half-dozen instances he'd draw a single card and then fold—which meant he was trying for a straight or a flush, the odds of doing that were just 1 in 20. Either he should've discarded three cards, which gave him good odds of improving his hand, or gone with a heavy bluff after drawing a solo card, in which case he probably would've taken the pot a couple of times.

Confident that he'd nailed the boy's technique, Keller now began to lose intentionally when Tony seemed to have good cards—to boost his confidence. Soon the kid had doubled his money and had close to $200,000 in front of him.

Larry Stanton didn't seem happy with Keller's plan to take the boy but he didn't say anything and continued to play his cautious, old-man's game, slowly losing to the other players.

The voice of conscience . . .

As the night wore on, Lasky finally dropped out, having lost close to eighty thousand bucks. "Fuck, gotta raise the price for ding-pulling," he joked, heading for the door. He glanced at the duo from Chicago. "When you gentlemen leave, could you bang inta some parked cars on the way to the expressway?" A nod toward Keller. "An' if you wanta fuck up the front end of *his* Merc, I wouldn't mind one bit."

Piemonte smiled at this; Rothstein glanced up as if the body-shop man were speaking Japanese or Swahili and turned back to his cards to try to coax a winning hand out of them.

Grandpa too soon bailed. He still had stacks of chips left on the table—but another rule in poker was that a player can walk away at any time. He now cashed in and pushed his chair back glumly to sip coffee and to watch the remaining players.

Ten minutes later Rothstein lost his remaining stake to Tony in a tense, and long, round of betting.

"Damn," he spat out. "Tapped out. Never lost to a boy before—not like this."

Tony kept a straight face but there was a knowing look in his eye that said, And you didn't lose to one now—I'm not a boy.

The game continued for a half hour, with big pots trading hands.

Most poker games don't end with dramatic last hands. Usually players just run out of money or, like Grandpa, get cold feet and slip away with their tails between their legs.

But sometimes there *are* climactic moments.

And that's what happened now.

Tony shuffled and then offered the cut to Keller, who divided the deck into thirds. The boy reassembled the cards and began dealing.

Piemonte gathered his and, like all good poker players, didn't move them (rearranging cards can telegraph a lot of information about your hand).

Keller picked up his and was pleased to see that he'd received a good one: two pairs—queens and sixes. A very winnable one in a game this size.

Tony gathered his five cards and examined them, not revealing any reaction. "Bet?" he asked Piemonte, who passed.

To open the betting in draw poker a player needs a pair of jacks or better. Passing meant that either Piemonte didn't have that good a hand or that he did but was sandbagging—choosing not to bet to make the other players believe he had weak cards.

Keller decided to take a chance. Even though he had the two pairs, and *could* open, he too passed, which would make Tony think his hand was poor.

A tense moment followed. If Tony didn't bet, they'd surrender their cards and start over; Keller would swallow a solid hand.

But Tony glanced at his own cards and bet ten thousand.

Keller's eyes flickered in concern, which a bluffer would do, but in his heart he was ecstatic. The hook was set.

"See you," Piemonte said, pushing his chips in.

So, Keller reflected, the man from Chicago'd probably been sandbagging too.

Keller, his face blank, pushed out the ten thousand, then another stack of chips. "See your ten and raise you twenty-five."

Tony saw the new bet and raised again. Piemonte hesitated but stayed with it and Keller matched Tony's new bet. As dealer, he now "burned" the top card on the deck—set it facedown in front of him. Then he turned to Piemonte. "How many?"

"Two."

Tony slipped him the two replacement cards from the top of the deck.

Keller's mind automatically began to calculate the odds. The chances of getting three of a kind in the initial deal were very low so it was likely that Piemonte had a pair and a "kicker," an unmatched card of a high rank, probably a face card. The odds of his two new cards giving him a powerful full house were only 1 in 119. And if, by chance, he *had* been dealt a rare three of a kind at first, the odds of his getting a pair, to make that full house, were still long: 1 in 15.

Filing this information away, Keller himself asked for one card, suggesting to the other players that he was going for either a full house or a straight or flush—or bluffing. He picked up the card and placed it in his deck. Keller's mouth remained motionless but his heart slammed in his chest when he saw he'd got a full house—and a good one, three queens.

Tony himself took three cards.

Okay, Keller told himself, run the numbers. By taking three cards the boy signaled that he'd been dealt only one pair. So in order to beat Keller he'd have to end up with a straight flush, four of a kind or a full house of kings or aces. Like a computer, Keller's mind went through the various odds of this happening.

Based on his calculations about the boy's and Piemonte's draws, Keller concluded that he probably had the winning hand at the table. Now his goal was to goose up the size of the pot.

The boy shoved his glasses up on his nose again and glanced at Piemonte. "Your bet."

With a cautious sigh, the player from Chicago shoved some chips out. "Twenty thousand."

Keller had sat in on some of the great games around the country—both as a player and an observer—and he'd spent hundreds of hours studying how bluffers behaved. The small things they did—mannerisms, looks, when they hesitated and when they blustered ahead, what they said, when they laughed. Now he summoned up all these memories and began to act in a way that'd make the other players believe that he had a bum hand and was going for a bluff. Which meant he began betting big.

After two rounds, Piemonte finally dropped out, reluctantly—he'd put in close to $60,000—and he probably had a decent hand. But he was convinced that Keller or Tony had a *great* hand and he wasn't going to throw good money after bad.

The bet came around to Keller once more. "See your twenty," he said to Tony. "Raise you twenty."

"Jesus," Stanton muttered. Keller shot him a dark look and the old man fell silent.

Tony sighed and looked again at his cards, as if they could tell him what to do. But they never could, of course. The only answers to winning poker were in your own heart and your mind.

The boy had only fifteen thousand dollars left on the table. He reached into his pocket and took out an envelope. A hesitation. Then he extracted the rest of his money. He counted it out. Thirty-eight thousand. Another pause as he stared at the cash.

Go for it, Keller prayed silently. Please . . .

"Chips," the boy finally said, eyes locked on Keller's, who looked back both defiant and nervous—a bluffer about to be called.

Stanton hesitated.

"Chips," the boy said firmly.

The old man reluctantly complied.

Tony took a deep breath and pushed the chips onto the table. "See your twenty. Raise you ten."

Keller pushed $10,000 forward—a bit dramatically, he reflected—and said, "See the ten." He glanced at all he had left. "Raise you fifteen." Pushed the remaining chips into the center of the table.

"Lord," Piemonte said.

Even gruff Rothstein was subdued, gazing hypnotically at the massive pot, which was about $450,000.

For a moment Keller *did* feel a slight pang of guilt. He'd set up his opponent psychologically, calculated the odds down to the last decimal point—in short, he'd done everything that the youngster was incapable of. Still, the boy claimed he wanted to be treated like a man. He'd brought this on himself.

"Call," Tony said in a whisper, easing most of his chips into the pot.

Stanton looked away, as if avoiding the sight of a roadside accident.

"Queens full," Keller said, flipping them over.

"Lookit that," Piemonte whispered.

Stanton sighed in disgust.

"Sorry, kid," Keller said, reaching forward for the pot. "Looks like you—"

Tony flipped over his cards, revealing a full house—three kings and a pair of sixes. "Looks like I win," he said calmly and raked the chips in.

Piemonte whispered, "Whoa. What a hand. . . . Glad I got out when I did."

Stanton barked a fast laugh and Rothstein offered to Tony, "That was some fine playing."

"Just luck," the boy said.

How the *hell* had that happened? Keller wondered, frantically replaying every moment of the hand. Of course, sometimes, no matter how you calculated the percentages, fate blindsided you completely. Still, he'd planned everything so perfectly.

"Time to call it a night," Piemonte said, handing his remaining chips to Stanton to cash out and added humorously, "Since I just gave most of my fucking money to a teenager." He turned to Rothstein. "From now on, we stick to that rule about kids, okay?"

Keller sat back and watched Tony start organizing the chips in the pile. But the odds, he kept thinking. . . . He'd calculated the odds so carefully. At least a hundred to one. Poker is mathematics and instinct—how had both of them failed him so completely?

Tony eased the chips toward Stanton for cashing out.

The sound of a train whistle filled the room again. Keller sighed, reflecting that *this* time it signified a loss—just the opposite of what the urgent howl had meant at the game with the Frenchmen.

The wail grew louder. Only . . . focusing on the sound, Keller realized that there was something different about it this time. He glanced up at the old man and the two players from Chicago. They were frowning, staring at each other.

Why? Was something wrong?

Tony froze, his hands on the piles of his chips.

Shit, Keller thought. The sound wasn't a train whistle; it was a siren.

Keller pushed back from the table just as the front and back doors crashed open simultaneously, strewing splinters of wood around the back room. Two uniformed police officers, their guns drawn, pushed inside. "On the floor, now, now, now!"

"No," Tony muttered, standing and turning to face the cop nearest him.

"Kid," Keller whispered sternly, raising his hands. "Nothing stupid. Do what they say."

The boy hesitated, looked at the black guns and lay down on the floor.

Stanton slowly got down on his knees.

"Move it, old man," one of the cops muttered.

"Doing the best I can here."

Finally on their bellies and cuffed, the gamblers were eased into sitting positions by the cops.

"So what'd we catch?" asked a voice from the alley as a balding man in his late fifties, wearing a gray suit, walked inside.

Detective Fanelli, Keller noted. Hell, not him. The cop had been Jesus Mary and Joseph enthusiastic to purify the sinful burgh of Ellridge for years. He scared a lot of the small players into not even opening games and managed to bust about one or two big ones a year. Looked like Keller was the flavor of the week this time.

Stanton sighed with resignation, his expression matching the faces of the pro players from Chicago. The boy, though, looked horrified. Keller knew it wasn't the arrest; it was that the state confiscated gambling proceeds.

Fanelli squinted as he looked at Rothstein's and Piemonte's driver's licenses. "All the way from Chicago to get arrested. That's a pain in the ass, huh, boys?"

"I was just watching," Rothstein protested. He nodded at the table, where he'd been sitting. "No chips, no money."

"That just means you're a loser." The detective then glanced at Piemonte.

The man said a meek "I want to see a lawyer."

"And I'm sure a lawyer's gonna wanta see you. Considering how big his fee's gonna be to try and save your ass. Which he ain't gonna do, by the way. . . . Ah, Keller." He shook his head. "This's pretty sweet. I been after you for a long time. You really oughta move to Vegas. I don't know if you follow the news much but I hear gambling's actually legal there. . . . And who's this?" He glanced at Stanton. He took Stanton's wallet from one of the uniformed cops and looked at his license. "What the hell're you doing in Ellridge when you could be playing mahjong in Tampa with the ladies?"

"Can't afford the stakes down there."

"The old guy's a wise ass," the skinny detective muttered to the other cops. He then looked over Tony. "And who're you?"

"I don't have to tell you anything."

"Yeah, you do. This ain't the army. That name rank and serial number crap doesn't cut it with me. How old're you?"

"Eighteen. And I want a lawyer too."

"Well, Mr. I-Want-a-Lawyer-Too," Fanelli mocked, "you only get one after you've been charged. And I haven't charged you yet."

"Who dimed me out?" Keller asked.

Fanelli said, "Wouldn't be polite to give you his name but let's just say you took the wrong guy to the cleaners last year. He wasn't too happy about it and gave me a call."

Keller grimaced. Took the wrong guy to the cleaners last year. . . . Well, that short list'd have about a hundred people on it.

Looking down at the stacks of chips in front of where Tony'd been sitting, Fanelli asked, "Pretty colors, red, blue, green. What're they worth?"

"The whites're worth ten matchsticks," Rothstein said. "The blues're—"

"Shut up." He looked around the room. "Where's the bank?"

Nobody said anything.

"Well, we *will* find it, you know. And I'm not going to start in here. I'm going to start out front and tear Sal's bar to fucking pieces. Then we'll do the same to his office. Break up every piece of furniture. Toss every drawer. . . . Now, come on, boys, Sal doesn't deserve that, does he?"

Keller sighed and nodded to Stanton, who nodded toward the cupboard above the coffee machine. One cop took out two cigar boxes.

"Jesus our Lord," Fanelli said, flipping through them. "There's gotta be close to a half million here."

He glanced at the table. "Those're your chips, huh?" he said to Tony. The boy didn't answer but Fanelli didn't seem to expect him to. He laughed and looked over the players. "And you call yourselves men—letting a boy whip your asses at poker."

"I'm not a boy."

"Yeah, yeah, yeah." The detective turned back to the boxes one more time. He walked over to the officers. They held a brief, whispered conference then they nodded and stepped out of the room.

"My boys need to check on a few things," Fanelli said. "They've got to go corroborate some testimony or something. That's a great word, isn't it? 'Corroborate.'" He laughed. "I love to say that." He paced through the room, stopped at the coffee pot and poured himself a cup. "Why the hell doesn't anybody ever drink booze at high-stakes games? Afraid you'll get a queen mixed up with a jack?"

"As a matter of fact," Keller said, "yeah."

The cop sipped the coffee and said in a low voice, "Listen up, assholes. You especially, junior." He pointed a finger at Tony and continued to pace. "This happened at a . . . let's say a difficult time for me. We're concerned about some serious crimes that happen to be going down in another part of town."

Serious crimes, Keller was thinking. Cops don't talk that way. What the hell's he getting at?

A smile. "So here's the deal. I don't want to spend time booking you right now. It'd take me away from those other cases, you know. Now, you've lost the money one way or the other. If I take you in and book you the cash goes into evidence and when you're convicted, which you *will* be, every penny goes to the state. But if . . . let's just say *if* there was no evidence, well, I'd have to let you off with a warning. But that'd work out okay for me because I could get on to the other cases. The important cases."

"That're being corroborated right now?" Tony asked.

"Shut up, punk," the detective muttered, echoing Keller's thought.

"So what do you say?"

The men looked at each other.

"Up to you," the cop said. "Now what's it going to be?"

Keller surveyed the faces of the others around him. He glanced at Tony, who grimaced and nodded in disgust. Keller said to the detective, "We'd be happy to help you out here, Fanelli. Do our part to help you clean up some—what'd you call it? Serious crimes?"

Stanton muttered, "We have to keep Ellridge the showplace that it is."

"And the citizens thank you for your efforts," Detective Fanelli said, stuffing the money into his suit pockets.

The detective unhooked the handcuffs, stuffed them in his pockets too and walked back out into the alley without another word.

The players exchanged looks of relief—all except Tony, of course, on whose face the expression was one of pure dismay. After all, he was the big loser in all this.

Keller shook his hand. "You played good tonight, kid. Sorry about that."

The boy nodded and, with an anemic wave to everyone, wandered out the back door.

The Chicago players chattered nervously for a few minutes then nodded farewells and left the smoky room. Stanton asked Keller if he wanted another beer but the gambler shook his head and the old man walked into the bar. Keller sat down at the table, absently picked up a deck of cards, shuffled them and began to play solitaire. The shock of the bust was virtually gone now; what bothered him was losing to the boy, an okay player but not a great one.

But after a few minutes of playing, his spirits improved and he reminded himself of another one of the Rules According to Keller: Smart always beats out luck in the end.

Well, the kid'd been lucky this once. But there'd be other games, other chances to make the odds work and to relieve Tony, or others like him, of their bankrolls.

There was an endless supply of cocky youngster to bleed dry, Keller reckoned, and placed the black ten on the red jack.

∎

Standing on the overpass, watching a train disappear into the night, Tony Stigler tried not to think about the money he'd just won—and then had stolen away from him.

Nearly a half million.

Papers and dust swirled along the roadbed behind the train. Tony watched it absently and replayed something that Keller had said to him.

It's knowing everything about the game—even the little shit—that separates the men from the boys in poker.

But that wasn't right, Tony reflected. You only had to know one thing. That no matter how good you are, poker's always a game of chance.

And that's not as good as a sure thing.

He looked around, making sure he was alone, then reached into his pocket and extracted the Starbucks cup lid. He lifted off the false plastic disk on the bottom and shut off a tiny switch. He then wrapped it carefully in a bubble-wrap envelope and replaced it in his pocket. The device was his own invention. A miniature camera in the sipping hole of the lid had scanned each card whenever Tony'd been dealing and the tiny processor had sent the suit and rank to the computer in Tony's car. All he had to do was tap the lid in a certain place to tell the computer how many people were in the game, so the program he'd written would know everyone's hand. It determined how many cards he should draw and whether to bet or fold on each round. The computer then broadcast its instructions to the earpiece of his glasses, which vibrated according to a code, and Tony acted accordingly.

"Cheating for Dummies," he called the program.

A perfect plan, perfectly executed—the only flaw being that he hadn't thought about the goddamn police stealing his winnings.

Tony looked at his watch. Nearly one a.m. No hurry to get back; his uncle was out of town on another one of his business trips. What to do? he wondered. Marconi Pizza was still open and he decided he'd stop by and see his buddy, the one who'd tipped him to Keller's game. Have a slice and a Coke.

Gritting footsteps sounded behind him and he turned, seeing Larry Stanton walking stiffly down the alley, heading for the bus stop.

"Hey," the old guy called, noticing him and walking over. "Licking your wounds? Or thinking of jumping?" He nodded toward the train tracks.

Tony gave a sour laugh. "Can you believe that? Fucking bad luck."

"Ah, raids're a part of the game, if you're playing illegal," Stanton said. "You got to build 'em into the equation."

"A half-million-dollar part of the equation?" Tony muttered.

"That part's gotta sting, true," Stanton said, nodding. "But it's better than a year in jail."

"I suppose."

The old man yawned. "Better get on home and pack. I'm going back to Florida tomorrow. Who'd spend the winter in Ellridge if they didn't have to?"

"You have anything left?" Tony asked.

"Money? . . . A little." A scowl. "But a hell of a lot less than I *did*, thanks to you and Keller."

"Hold on." The boy took out his wallet and handed the man a hundred dollars.

"I don't take charity."

"Call it a loan."

Stanton debated for a moment. Then, embarrassed, he took the bill and pocketed it.

"Thanks. . . . " He shoved the cash away fast. "Better get going. Buses stop running soon. Well, good playing with you, son. You've got potential. You'll go places."

Yeah, the boy thought, I sure as hell *will* go places. The smart ones, the innovators, the young . . . we'll always beat people like you and Keller in the end. It's the way of the world. He watched Grandpa limp away, old and broke. Pathetic, the boy thought. Shoot me before I become him.

Tony pulled his stocking cap on, stepped away from the railing and walked toward his car, his mind already thinking of who the next mark should be.

■

Twenty minutes later the gassy municipal bus vehicle eased to the curb and Larry Stanton climbed off.

He walked down the street until he came to a dark intersection, the yellow caution light blinking for traffic on the main street, the red blinking for that on the cross. He turned the corner and stopped. In front of him was a navy-blue Crown Victoria. On the trunk were the words: *Police Interceptor*.

And leaning against that trunk was the lean figure of Detective George Fanelli.

The cop pushed away from the car and walked up to Stanton. The two other officers from the bust early that night were standing nearby. Both Fanelli and Stanton looked around and then shook hands. The detective took an envelope out of his pocket. Handed it to Stanton. "Your half—two hundred and twenty-two thousand."

Stanton didn't bother to count it. He put the cash away.

"This was a good one," the cop said.

"That it was," Stanton agreed.

He and the vice cop ran one of these scams every year when Stanton was up from Florida. Stanton'd work his way into some-body's confidence, losing money in a couple of private games and then, on high-stakes night, tip the cops off ahead of time. Fanelli'd blame the bust on some anonymous snitch, take the bank as a bribe and release everybody; poker players were so happy to be able to stay out of jail and keep playing that they never complained.

As for Stanton, the gaff like this had always suited him better than gambling.

I play all right but the odds're still against you. Anything serious I do with money? I make sure the odds're on my side.

"Hey, Larry," one of the cops called to Stanton. "Didn't mean to be an asshole when I collared you. Just thought it'd be more, you know, realistic."

"Handled it just right, Moscawitz. You're a born actor."

Stanton and the detective walked past the unmarked squad car and continued down the dirty sidewalk. They'd known each other for years, ever since Stanton had worked as head of security at Midwest Metal Products.

"You okay?" Fanelli glanced down at Stanton's limp.

"I was racing somebody on a Jet Ski up at Lake Geneva. Hit a wake. It's nothing."

"So when're you going back to Tampa?"

"Tomorrow."

"You flying down?"

"Nope. Driving." He pulled keys out of his pocket and opened the door of a new BMW sports car.

Fanelli looked it over admiringly. "Sold the Lexus?"

"Decided to keep it." A nod toward the sleek silver wheels. "I just wanted something sexier, you know. The ladies in my golf club love a man in a sports car. Even if he's got knobby knees."

Fanelli shook his head. "Felt bad about that kid. Where'd he get the money to sit in on a high-stakes game?"

"Tuition money or something. He inherited it from his folks."

"You mean we just dipped an orphan? I'll be in confession for a month."

"He's an orphan who cheated the pants off Keller and everybody else."

"What?"

Stanton laughed. "Took me a while to tip to it. Finally figured it out. He must've had some kind of electronic shiner or camera or something in his coffee cup lid. He was always playing with it on the table, moving it close to the cards when he dealt—and the only time he won big was on the deal. Then after the bust I checked out his car—there was a computer and some kind of antenna in the backseat."

"Damn," Fanelli said. "That was stupid. He'll end up dead, he's not careful. I'm surprised Keller didn't spot it."

"Keller was too busy running his own scam, trying to take the kid." Stanton told him about the pro's setup of Tony.

The detective laughed. "He tried to take the boy, the boy tried to take the table, and it was us old guys who took 'em both. There's a lesson there someplace." The men shook hands in farewell. "See you next spring, my friend. Let's try Greenpoint. I hear they've got some good high-stakes games over there."

"We'll do that." Stanton nodded and fired up the sports car. He drove to the intersection, carefully checked for cross traffic and turned onto the main street that would take him to the expressway.

Ninety-eight Point Six

Suit jacket slung over his shoulder, the man trudged up the long walk to the bungalow, his lungs aching, breathless in the astonishing heat, which had persisted well after sundown.

Pausing on the sidewalk in front of the house, trying to catch his breath, he believed he heard troubled voices from inside. Still, he'd had no choice but to come here. This was the only house he'd seen along the highway.

He climbed the stairs to the unwelcomingly dark porch and rang the bell.

The voices ceased immediately.

There was a shuffle. Two or three words spoken.

He rang the bell again and finally the door opened.

Sloan observed that the three people inside gazed at him with different expressions on their faces.

The woman on the couch, in her fifties, wearing an overwashed sleeveless house dress, appeared relieved. The man sitting beside her—about the same age, rounding and bald—was wary.

And the man who'd opened the door and stood closest to Sloan had a grin on his face—a thick-lipped grin that really meant, What the hell do you want? He was about Sloan's own age—late thirties—and his tattooed arms were long. He gripped the side of the door defensively with a massive hand. His clothes were gray, stained dungarees and a torn work shirt. His shaved scalp glistened.

"Help you?" the tattooed man asked.

"I'm sorry to bother you," Sloan said. "My car broke down—it overheated. I need to call Triple A. You mind if I use your phone?"

"Phone company's having problems, I heard," the tattooed man replied. Nodding toward the dense, still night sky. "With the heat—those rolling brownouts or blackouts, whatever."

He didn't move out of the doorway.

But the woman said quickly, "No, please come in," with curious eagerness. "Our phone just rang a bit ago. I'm sure it's working fine."

"Please," echoed the older man, who was holding her hand.

The tattooed man looked Sloan over cautiously, as people often did. Unsmiling by nature, Sloan was a big man, and muscular—he'd worked out every day for the past three years—and at the moment he was a mess; tonight he'd trekked through the brush to take a shortcut to the lights of this house. And like anyone walking around on this overwhelmingly humid and hot night, every inch of his skin was slick with sweat.

Finally the tattooed man gestured him inside. Sloan noticed a bad scar across the back of his hand. It looked like a knife wound and it was recent.

The house was overly bright and painfully hot. A tiny air conditioner moaned but did nothing to cool the still air. He glanced at the walls, taking in fast vignettes of lives spent in a small bubble of the world. He deduced careers with Allstate Insurance and a high school library and nebulous involvement in the Rotary Club, church groups and parent-teacher organizations. Busmen's holidays of fishing trips to Saginaw or Minnesota. A vacation to Chicago memorialized in framed, yellowing snapshots.

Introductions were made. "I'm Dave Sloan."

Agnes and Bill Willis were the couple. Sloan observed immediately that they shared an ambiguous similarity of manner that characterized people long married. The tattooed man said nothing about himself. He tinkered with the air conditioner, turning the compressor knob up and down.

"I'm not interrupting supper, I hope."

There was a moment of silence. It was eight p.m. and Sloan could see no dirty dishes from the night's meal.

"No" was Agnes's soft reply.

"Nope, no food here," the tattooed man said with a cryptic edge to the comment. He looked angrily at the air conditioner as if he were going to kick it out the window but he controlled himself and walked back to the place he'd staked out for himself—an over-stuffed Naugahyde armchair that still glistened with the sweat that'd leached from his skin before he stood to answer the door.

"Phone's in there," Bill pointed.

Sloan thanked him and went into the kitchen. He made his call. As soon as he stepped back into the living room, Bill and the younger man, who'd been talking, fell silent fast.

Sloan looked at Bill and said, "They'll tow it to Hatfield. The truck should be here in twenty minutes. I can wait outside."

"No," Agnes said. Then seemed to decide she'd been too force-ful and glanced at the tattooed man with a squint, almost as if she was afraid of being hit.

"Too hot outside," Bill said.

"No hotter'n in here," the tattooed man replied caustically, with that grin back. His lips were bulbous and the top one was beaded with sweat—an image that made Sloan itch.

"Set yourself down," Bill said cautiously. Sloan looked around and found the only unoccupied piece of furniture, an uncomfort-able couch, covered in pink and green chintz, flowers every-where. The gaudy pattern, combined with the still heat in the room and the nervous fidgeting of the large tattooed man, set him on edge.

"Can I get you anything?" the woman asked.

"Maybe some water if it's not too much trouble." Sloan wiped his face with his hand.

The woman rose.

"Notice," the tattooed man said coolly, "they didn't introduce me."

"Well, I didn't mean—" Bill began.

The man waved him silent.

"My name's Greg." Another hesitation. "I'm their nephew. Just stopped by for a visit. Right, Bill? Aren't we having a high old time?"

Bill nodded, looking down at the frayed carpet. "High old time."

Sloan was suddenly aware of something—a curious noise. A scraping. A faint bang. No one else seemed to hear it. He looked up as Agnes returned. She handed Sloan the glass and he drank half of it down immediately.

She said, "I was thinking, maybe you could look at Mr. Sloan's car, Bill. Why don't you and Greg go take a look at it?"

"Dave," Sloan said, "Please. Call me Dave."

"Maybe save Dave some money."

"Sure—" Bill began.

Greg said, "Naw, we don't wanna do that. Too much work in this heat. 'Sides, Dave looks like he can afford a proper mechanic. He looks like he's rollin' in dough. How 'bout it, Dave? Whatta you do?"

"Sales."

"Whatcha sell?"

"Computers. Hardware and software."

"I don't trust computers. Bet I'm the only person in the country without email."

"No, a good eighty million people don't have it, I heard," Dave told him.

Bill piped up. "Children, for instance."

"Like me, huh? Me and the kiddies? Is that what you're saying?"

"Oh, no," Bill said quickly. "I just was talking. Didn't mean any offense."

"How about you, Greg?" Sloan asked. "What line're you in?"

He considered for a minute. "I work with my hands. . . . Want to know what Bill does?"

A dark look crossed Bill's face then it vanished. "I was in insurance. I'm between jobs right now."

"He'll be working someday soon, though, won't you, Bill?"

"I hope to be."

"I'm sure you will," Agnes said.

"We're *all* sure he will. Hey, Sloan, you think Bill could sell computers?"

"I don't know. All I know is I enjoy what I do."

"You good at it?"

"Oh, I'm very good at it."

"Why computers?"

"Because there's a market for what my company makes right now. But it doesn't matter to me. I'll can sell anything. Maybe next year it'll be radiators or a new kind of medical laser. If I can make money at it, I'll sell it."

"Why don't you tell us about your computers?" Greg asked.

Sloan shrugged dismissively. "It's real technical. You'd be bored."

"Well, we don't want to bore anybody now, especially us kiddies. Not if we're having such an enjoyable party, the family all together . . . family." Greg thumped the arm of the chair with his massive hands. "Don't you think family's important? I do. You have family, Dave?"

"They're dead. My immediate family, that is."

"All of 'em?" Greg asked curiously.

"My parents and sister."

"How'd they die?"

Agnes stirred at this blunt question. But Sloan didn't mind. "An accident."

"Accident?" Greg nodded. "My folks're gone too," he added emotionlessly.

Which meant that, because he was their nephew, Bill and Agnes had lost a sibling too. But Greg didn't acknowledge their portion of the loss.

The sound of the air conditioner seemed to vanish as the silence of three mute human beings filled the tiny, stifling room. Then Sloan heard a faint thumping. It seemed to come from behind a closed door off the hallway. No one else noticed. He heard it again then the sound ceased.

Greg rose and walked to a thermometer tacked up on the wall. A silver wire ran through a hole sloppily drilled through the window jamb. He tapped the circular dial with his finger. "Busted," he announced. Then he turned back to the threesome. "I heard the news? Before? And they said that it was ninety-eight degrees at sunset. That's a record 'round here, the newscaster said. I got to thinking. Ninety-eight point *six*—that's the temperature of a human body. And you know what occurred to me?"

Sloan examined the man's eerie, amused eyes. He said nothing. Neither did Bill or Agnes.

Greg continued, "I realized that there's no difference between life and death. Not a bit. Whatta you think about that?"

"No difference? I don't get it." Sloan shook his head.

"See, take a bad person. What sort of person should we use, Bill? Maybe a person who doesn't pay his debts. How's that? Okay, now what I'm saying is that it's not his *body*, it's his *soul* that's a welsher. When he dies, what hangs around? A welsher's soul. Same thing with a good man. There's a good soul hanging around after a good body goes. Or a murderer, for instance. When they execute a murderer, there's a killer's soul still walking around."

"That's an interesting thought, Greg."

"The way I see it," the intense man continued, "a body is just a soul warmed to ninety-eight point six degrees."

"I'd have to think about it."

"Okay, our folks are dead, yours and mine," Greg continued.

"True," Sloan replied.

"But even when they're gone," Greg said philosophically, "you can still have trouble because of them, right?" He sat back in the slick, stained chair and crossed his legs. He wore no socks and Sloan got a look at another tattoo—one that started on his ankle and went north. Sloan knew that tattoos on the ankle were among the most painful on the body, since the needle had to hit bone. A tattoo there was more than body painting; it was a defiant reminder that pain was nothing to the wearer.

"Trouble?"

"Your parents can cause you grief after they're dead."

Any psychiatrist'd tell you that, Sloan thought, but decided that this was a bit too clever for Greg.

The young man rubbed his massive hand over his glistening crew cut. That was quite a scar he had. Another one was on his opposite arm. "There was this thing happened a few years ago."

"What was that?" Bill asked.

Sloan noticed that Agnes had shredded the napkin she was holding.

"Well, I'm not inclined to go into specifics with strangers," he said, irritated.

"I'm sorry," Bill said quickly.

"I'm just making a point. Which is that somebody who was dead was still causing me problems. I could see it real clear. A bitch when she was alive, a bitch when she was dead. God gave her a troublemaker's soul. You believe in God, Sloan?"

"No."

Agnes stirred. Sloan glanced at three crucifixes on the wall.

"I believe in selling. That's about it."

"That's *your* soul then. Warmed to ninety-eight point six." A rubbery grin. "Since you're still alive."

"And what's your soul like, Greg? Good, bad?"

"Well, I'm not a welcher," he said coyly. "Beyond that, you'll have to guess. I don't give as much away as you do."

The lights dimmed. Another dip in the power.

"Look at that," Greg said. "Maybe it's the souls of some family hanging around here, playing with the lights. Whatta you think, Bill?"

"I don't know. Maybe."

"A family that died here," Greg mused. "Anybody die here that you know of, Bill?"

Agnes swallowed hard. Bill took a sip from a glass of what looked like flat soda. His hands shook.

The lights came back on full. Greg looked around the place. "Whatta you think this house's worth, Sloan?"

"I don't know," he answered calmly, growing tired of the baiting. "I sell computers, remember? Not houses."

"I'm thinking a cool two hundred thousand."

The noise again from behind the door. It was louder this time, audible over the moaning of the air conditioner. A scraping, a thud.

The three people in the room looked toward the door. Agnes and Bill were uneasy. Nobody said a word about the sound.

"Where've you been selling your computers?" Greg asked.

"I was in Durrant today. Now I'm heading east."

"Times're slow 'round here. People out of work, right, Bill?"

"Hard times."

"Hard times here, hard times everywhere." Greg seemed drunk but Sloan smelled no liquor and noticed that the only alcohol in sight was a corked bottle of New York State port and a cheap brandy, sitting safely behind a greasy-windowed breakfront. "Hard times for salesmen too, I'll bet. Even salesmen who can sell *anything*, like you."

Sloan calmly asked, "Something about me you don't like, Greg?"

"Why, no." But the man's steely eyes muttered the opposite. "Where'd you get that idea?"

"It's the heat," Agnes said quickly, playing mediator. "I was watching this show on the news. CNN. About what the heat's doing. Rioting in Detroit, forest fires up near Saginaw. It's making people act crazy."

"Crazy?" Greg asked. "Crazy?"

"I didn't mean you," she said fast.

Greg turned to Sloan. "Let's ask Mr. Salesman here if I'm acting crazy."

Sloan figured he could have the boy on his back in a stranglehold in four or five minutes, but there'd be some serious damage to the tacky nicknacks. And the police'd come and there'd be all sorts of complications.

"Well, how 'bout it?"

"Nope, you don't seem crazy to me."

"You're saying that 'cause you don't want a hassle. Maybe you *don't* have a salesman's soul. Maybe you've got a liar's soul . . ." He rubbed his face with both hands. "Damn, I've sweated a gallon."

Sloan sensed control leaving the man. He noticed a gun rack on the wall. There were two rifles in it. He judged how fast he could get there. Was Bill stupid enough to leave an unlocked, loaded gun on the rack? Probably.

"Let me tell you something—" Greg began ominously, tapping the sweaty arms of the chair with blunt fingers.

The doorbell rang.

No one moved for a moment. Then Greg rose and walked to it, opened the door.

A husky man with long hair stood in the doorway. "Somebody called for a tow?"

"That'd be me." Sloan stood and said to Agnes and Bill, "Thanks for the use of the phone."

"No problem."

"You're sure you don't want to stay. I can put some supper on. Please?" The poor woman was now clearly desperate.

"No. I have to be going."

"Yeah," Greg said, "Dave's got to be going."

"Damn," the tow operator said. "Hotter in there than it is outside."

You don't know the half of it, Sloan thought, and started down the steps to the idling flatbed.

■

The driver winched Sloan's disabled Chevy onto the bed, chained it down and then the two men climbed inside the cab of the truck. They pulled out onto the highway, heading east. The air conditioner roared and the cool air was a blessing.

The radio clattered. Sloan couldn't hear it clearly over the sound of the AC but the driver leaned forward and listened to what was apparently some important message. When the transmission was over, the driver said, "They still haven't caught that guy."

"What guy?" Sloan asked.

"The killer. The guy who escaped from that prison about thirty miles east of here."

"I didn't hear about that."

"I hope it makes it on *American's Most Wanted*. You ever watch that show?"

"No. I don't watch much TV," Sloan said.

"I do," the tow driver offered. "Can be educational."

"Who is this guy?"

"Sort of a psycho killer, one of those sorts. Like in *Silence of the Lambs*. How 'bout movies, you like movies?"

"Yeah," Sloan responded. "That was a good flick."

"Guy was in the state prison about twenty miles west of here."

"How'd he escape? That's a pretty high-security place, isn't it?"

"Sure is. My brother . . . uhm, my brother had a *friend* did time there for grand theft auto. Hard place. What they said on the news was that this killer was in the yard of that prison and, what with the heat, there was a power failure. I guess the backup didn't go on either or something and the lights and the electrified fence were down for, I dunno, almost an hour. But by the time they got it going again, he was gone."

Sloan shivered as the freezing air chilled his sweat-soaked clothes. He asked, "Say, you know that family where you picked me up? The Willises?"

"No sir. I don't get out this way much."

They continued driving for twenty minutes. Ahead, Sloan saw a band of flashing lights.

The driver said, "Roadblock. Probably searching for that escapee."

Sloan could see two police cars. Two uniformed officers were pulling people over.

The salesman said to the tow driver, "When you get up there, pull off to the side. I want to talk to one of the cops."

"Sure thing, mister."

When they pulled over, Sloan got out and told the driver, "I'll just be a minute." Sloan inhaled deeply but no air seemed to get into his lungs. His chest began to hurt again.

One of the officers glanced at Sloan. The big man, his tan shirt dark with sweat, approached. "Hold up there, sir. Can I help you?" He held his flashlight defensively as he walked toward Sloan, who introduced himself and handed over a business card. Sloan observed the man's name badge. Sheriff Mills. The law enforcer looked over the card and then Sloan's suit and, satisfied that he wasn't the man they were looking for, asked, "What can I do for you?"

"Is this about that fellow who escaped from the prison?" He nodded at the squad car.

"Yessir, it is. You seen anything that might help us find him?"

"Well, it might be nothing. But I thought I should mention it."

"Go ahead."

"What's the prisoner look like?"

"Just escaped about two hours ago. We don't have a picture yet. But he's in his mid-thirties, beard. Six feet, muscular build. Like yours, more or less."

"Shaved head?"

"No. But if I was him I mighta shaved it the minute I got out. Lost the beard too."

"Tattoo?"

"Don't know. Probably."

Sloan explained about his car's breaking down and about his stop at the Willises' house. "You think that prisoner would come this way?"

"If he had his wits about him, he would. To go west'd take him fifty miles through forest. This way, he's got a crack at stealing a car in town or hitching a ride on the interstate."

"And that'd take him right past the Willises'?"

"Yep. If he took Route 202. What're you getting at, Mr. Sloan?"

"I think that fellow might be at the Willises' house."

"What?"

"Do you know if they have a nephew?"

"I don't think they ever mentioned one."

"Well, there's a man there now—sort of fits the description of the killer. He claimed he was Bill's nephew, visiting them. But something didn't seem right. I mean, first of all, it was supper-time but they hadn't eaten and they weren't cooking anything and there were no dirty dishes in the kitchen. And anything Greg told them to do, they did. Like they were afraid to upset him."

The sheriff found a wad of paper towel in his pocket and wiped his face and head. "Anything else?"

"He was saying weird stuff—talking about death and about this experience he had that made him look at dying differently. Like it wasn't that bad a thing. . . . Spooked me. Oh, and another thing—he said he didn't want to mention something in front of strangers.

He might've meant me but then why'd he say 'strangers,' not 'a stranger'? It was like he meant Bill and Agnes too."

"Good point."

"He also had some bad scars. Like he'd been in a knife fight. And he mentioned somebody who died—a woman, who gave him as much grief after she was dead as before. I was thinking he meant trouble with the law for killing her."

"What'd their daughter say?"

"Daughter?"

"The Willises have a daughter. Sandy. Didn't you see her? She's home from college now. And she works the day shift at Taco Bell. She should've been home by now."

"Jesus," Sloan muttered. "I didn't see her. . . . But I remember something else. The door to one of the bedrooms was closed and there was a sound coming from inside it. Everybody there was real upset about it. You don't think she was, I don't know, tied up inside there?"

"Lord," the sheriff said, wiping his face, "that escapee—he was arrested for raping and murdering girls. College girls." He pulled out his radio, "All Hatfield police units. This's Mills. I have a lead on that prisoner. The perpetrator might be out at Bill Willis's place off 202. Leave one car each on the roadblocks but everybody else respond immediately. Silent roll up, with lights out. Stop on the road near the driveway but don't go in. Wait for me."

Replies came back.

The sheriff turned to Sloan. "We might need you as a witness, Mr. Sloan."

"Sure, whatever I can do."

The sheriff said, "Have the driver take you to the police station—it's on Elm Street. My girl's there, Clara's her name. Just tell her the same thing you told me. I'll call her and tell her to take your statement."

"Be happy to, Sheriff."

The sheriff ran back to his car and jumped in. His deputy climbed into the passenger seat and they skidded 180 degrees and sped off toward the Willises' house.

Sloan watched them vanish and climbed back in the truck, then said to the driver, "Never thought I'd end up in the middle of this."

"Most exciting call *I've* ever had," the man replied, "I'll tell you that."

The driver pulled back into the highway and the flatbed clattered down the asphalt toward a faint band of light radiated by the heat-soaked town of Hatfield, Michigan.

■

"I don't see anybody but the Willises," the deputy whispered.

He'd made some fast reconnaissance of the bungalow through a side window. "They're just sitting there talking, Bill and Agnes."

Three male officers and two women—five-eighths of the Hatfield constabulary—surrounded the house.

"He might be in the john. Let's go in fast."

"We knock?"

"No," the sheriff muttered, "we don't knock."

They burst through the front door so fast that Agnes dropped her soda on the couch and Bill made it two steps to the gun rack before he recognized the sheriff and his deputies.

"Lord of mercy, you scared us, Hal."

"What a fright," Agnes muttered. Then: "Don't blaspheme, Bill."

"Are you okay?"

"Sure, we're okay. Why?"

"And your daughter?"

"She's out with her friends. Is this about her? Is she all right?"

"No, it's not about her," Sheriff Mills slipped his gun away. "Where is he, Bill?"

"Who?"

"That fellow who was here?"

"The guy whose car broke down?" Agnes asked. "He left in the tow truck."

"No, not him. The guy calling himself Greg."

"Greg?" Agnes asked. "Well, he's gone too. What's this all about?"

"Who is he?" the sheriff asked.

"He's my late brother's son," Bill said.

"He really is your nephew?"

"Much as I hate to say it, yeah."

The sheriff put the gun away. "That Sloan, the man who called the tow truck from here—he had this idea that maybe Greg was that escapee. We thought he'd held you hostage."

"What escapee?"

"A killer from that prison west of here. A psychopath. He escaped a couple of hours ago."

"No!" Agnes said breathlessly. "We didn't have the news on tonight."

The sheriff told them what Sloan had mentioned about how odd Greg had behaved—and how the Willises clearly didn't want him there, were even afraid of him.

Agnes nodded. "See, we . . ."

Her voice faded and she glanced at her husband, who said, "It's okay, honey, you can tell him."

"When Bill lost his job last year, we didn't know what we were going to do. We only had a little savings and my job at the library, well, that wasn't bringing in much money. So we had to borrow some. The bank wouldn't even talk to us so we called Greg."

Clearly ashamed, Bill shook his head. "He's the richest one in the family."

"Him?" Sheriff Mills asked.

Agnes said, "Yep. He's a plumber . . . no, sorry, a 'plumbing contractor.' Makes money hand over fist. Has eight trucks. He inherited the business when Bill's brother died."

Her husband: "Well, he made me a loan. Insisted on a second mortgage on the house, of course. And plenty of interest too. More'n the banks woulda charged. Was real obnoxious about it, since we never really had him and his dad over when he was growing up—my brother and me didn't get along too good. But he wrote us a check and nobody else would. I thought I'd have another job by now but nothing came up. And unemployment ran out. When I couldn't make the payments to him I stopped returning his phone calls. I was so embarrassed. He finally drove over here tonight and stopped by unannounced. He gave us hell. Threatening to foreclose, drive us out in the street."

"That's when Mr. Sloan showed up. We were hoping he'd stay. It was a nightmare sitting here listening to him go on and on."

"Sloan said he was scarred. Like knife wounds."

"Accidents on the job, I guess," Bill said.

"What'd he mean about a woman who died a few years ago?"

Nodding, Bill said, "He wouldn't tell us exactly what he meant." He looked at Agnes. "I'd guess that must've been his girl-friend. She died in a car wreck and Greg sort of inherited her son for a few months. It was a mess—Greg's not the best father, as you can imagine. Finally, her sister took the boy."

The sheriff remembered something else that Sloan had said. "He said he heard something in the other room. It seemed suspicious to him."

Agnes blushed fiercely. "That was Sandy."

"Your daughter?"

A nod. The woman couldn't continue. Bill said, "She came home with her boyfriend. They went into her room so she could change out of her uniform before they went out. The next thing you know—well, you can figure it out. . . . I told her to respect us. I told her not to be with him when we were home. She doesn't care."

So it was all a misunderstanding, Sheriff Mills reflected.

Bill laughed faintly. "And you thought Greg was the killer? That's wild."

"Wasn't that far-fetched," the sheriff said. "Think about it. The guy escaped at five tonight. That'd be just enough time to steal a car and get to your place from Durrant in early evening."

"Guess that's right, " Bill said.

The sheriff returned to the door and started to open it.

Bill said, "Wait a minute, Hal. You said Durrant?"

"Right. That's where the prison is that guy escaped from."

Bill looked at Agnes. "Didn't that fellow Sloan say he'd just come here from Durrant?"

"Yeah, he did. I'm sure."

"Really?" the sheriff asked. He returned to the Willises. Then asked, "What else did you know about him?"

"Nothing much really. Just that he said he sold computers."

"Computers?" The sheriff frowned. "Around here?"

"That's what he said."

This was odd; Hatfield was hardly a high-tech area of the state. The closest retail computer store was fifteen miles south of here. "Anything else?"

"He was pretty evasive, now that I think about it. Didn't say much of anything. Except he did say his parents were dead."

"And he didn't seem very upset about it," Agnes offered.

The sheriff reflected: And Sloan was about the same age and build as the killer. Dark hair too.

Damn, he thought to himself: I didn't even look at his driver's license, only his business card. He might've killed the real Sloan and stolen his car.

"And that was another thing. He said his car overheated," Bill pointed out. "You'd think a salesman'd be in a new car. And you ever hear about cars overheating nowadays? Hardly ever happens. And at night?"

"Mary, Mother of God," Agnes said, crossing herself, apparently finding an exception to the rule about blasphemy. "He was right here, in our house."

But the sheriff's mind continued further along this troubling path. Sloan, he now understood, had known there'd be a roadblock. So he'd disabled his car himself, called Triple A and waltzed right though the roadblock. Hell, he even walked right up to me, ballsy as could be and spun that story about Greg—to lead the law off.

And we let him get away. He could be—

No!

And then he felt the punch in his gut. He'd sent Sloan to police headquarters. Where there was only one other person at the moment. Clara. Twenty-one years old. Beautiful.

And whom the sheriff referred to as "his girl" not out of any vestigial chauvinism but because she was, in fact, his daughter, working for him on summer vacation from college.

He grabbed the Willises' phone and called the station. There was no answer.

Sheriff Mills ran from the house, climbed into his car. "Oh, Lord, please no . . ."

The deputy with him offered a prayer too. But the sheriff didn't hear it. He dropped into the seat and slammed the door. Ten seconds later the Crown Vic hit sixty as it cut through the night air, hot as soup and dotted with the lights from a thousand edgy fireflies.

■

No reconnaissance this time.

On Elm Street downtown the sheriff skidded to a stop against a trash can, knocking it over and scattering the street with empty soda bottles and Good Humor sticks and wrappers.

His deputy was beside him, carting the stubby scattergun, a shell chambered and the safety off.

"What's the plan?" the deputy asked.

"This," Sheriff Mills snapped and slammed into the door with his shoulder, leveling the gun as he rushed inside, the deputy on his heels.

Both men stopped fast, staring at the two people in the room, caught in the act of sipping Arizona iced teas. Dave Sloan and the sheriff's daughter, both blinking in shock at the hostile entrance.

The officers lowered their weapons.

"Dad!"

"What's the matter, Sheriff?" Sloan asked.

"I—" he stammered. "Mr. Sloan, could I see some ID?"

Sloan showed his driver's license to the sheriff, who examined the picture—it was clearly Sloan. Then Mills shamefacedly told them what he'd suspected after his conversation with the Willises.

Sloan took the news good-naturedly. "Probably should've asked for that license up front, Sheriff."

"I probably should have. Right you are. It was just that things seemed a little suspicious. Like you told them that you'd just come from Durrant—"

"My company installs and services the prison computers. It's one of my big accounts." He fished in his jacket pocket and showed the sheriff a work order. "These blackouts from the heat are hell on computers. If you don't shut them down properly it causes all kinds of problems."

"Oh. I'm sorry, sir. You have to understand—"

"That you got a killer on the loose." Sloan laughed again. "So they thought I was the killer. . . . Only fair, I suppose, since *I* thought Greg was."

"I called before," the sheriff said to his daughter. "There was no answer. Where were you?"

"Oh, the AC went out. Mr. Sloan here and I went out back to see if we could get it going."

A moment later the fax machine began churning out a piece

of paper. It contained a picture of a young man, bearded, with trim, dark hair: the two-angle mug shot of the escapee.

The sheriff showed it to Sloan and Clara. He read from the prison's bulletin. "Name's Tony Windham. Rich kid from Ann Arbor. Worth millions, trust funds, prep school. Honors grad. But he's got something loose somewhere. Killed six women and never showed a gnat of regret at the trial. Well, he's not getting through Hatfield. Route 202 and 17're the only ways to the interstate and we're checking every car." He then said to the deputy, "Let's spell the boys on the roadblocks."

Outside, Sheriff Mills pointed Dave Sloan to the garage where his Chevy was being fixed and climbed into his squad car with his deputy. He wiped the sweat with a soggy paper towel and said good night to the salesman. "Stay cool."

Sloan laughed. "Like a snowball in hell. 'Night, Sheriff."

■

In Earl's Automotive, Sloan wandered up to the mechanic, who was as stained from sweat as he was from grease.

"Okay, she's fixed," the man told Sloan.

"What was wrong with it?"

"The cap'd come loose and your coolant shot out is all. Feel bad charging you."

"But you're going to anyway."

The man pulled his soggy baseball cap off and wiped his forehead with the crown. Replaced it. "I'd be home in a cold bath right now, it wasn't for your wheels."

"Fair enough."

"Only charged you twenty. Plus the tow, of course."

Any other time Sloan would have negotiated but he wanted to get back on the road. He paid and climbed into the car, fired it up and turned the AC on full. He pulled onto the main street and headed out of town.

Ten miles east of Hatfield, near the interstate, he turned into the parking lot of a Greyhound bus station. He stopped the car in a deserted part of the lot. He climbed out and popped the trunk.

Looking inside, he nodded to the young bearded man in prison overalls. The man blinked painfully at the brilliant light above them and gasped for air. He was curled up fetally.

"How you doing?" Sloan asked.

"Jesus," Tony Windham muttered, gasping, his head lolling around alarmingly. "Heat . . . dizzy. Cramps."

"Climb out slow."

Sloan helped the prisoner out of the car. Even with the beard and sweat-drenched hair he looked much more like a preppy banker than a serial killer—though those two activities weren't mutually exclusive, Sloan supposed.

"Sorry," the salesman said. "It took longer than I'd thought for the tow to come. Then I got stuck in the sheriff's office waiting for them to come back."

"I went through two quarts of that water," Windham said. "And I still don't need to pee."

Sloan looked around the deserted lot. "There's a bus on the hour going to Cleveland. There's a ticket in there and a fake driver's license," he added, handing Windham a gym bag, which also contained some toiletries and a change of clothes. The killer stepped into the shadow of a Dumpster and dressed in the jeans and T-shirt, which said "Rock and Roll Hall of Fame." Windham pitched his prison outfit into the Dumpster. Then he hunched over and shaved the beard off with Evian water and Edge gel, using his fingers to make certain he'd gotten all the whiskers. When he was finished he stuffed his hair under a baseball cap.

"How do I look?"

"Like a whole new man.

"Damn," the boy said. "You did it, Sloan. You're good."

The salesmen had met Tony Windham in the prison library a

month ago when he was supervising upgrades of the penitentiary computer systems. He found Windham charming and smart and empathic—the same skills that had catapulted Sloan to stardom as a salesman. The two hit it off. Finally, Windham made his offer for the one thing that Sloan could sell: freedom. There was no negotiation. Sloan set the price at three million, which the rich kid had arranged to have transferred into an anonymous overseas account.

Sloan's plan was to wait for one of the hottest days of the year then, pretending there'd been a momentary electric blackout, would shut down the power and security systems at the prison using the computers. This would give Windham a chance to climb over the fence. Sloan would then pick up the killer, who'd hide in the trunk, specially perforated with air holes and stocked with plenty of water.

Since he'd be coming from the prison, Sloan had assumed that every car would be searched at roadblocks so he'd stopped the car outside one of the few houses along Route 202 and left his coolant cap off so the car would overheat. He'd then asked to use the phone. He'd intended to learn a little about the homeowners so he could come up with a credible story about suspicious goings-on at the house and distract the cops, keep them from searching his car. But he'd never thought he'd find as good a false lead as the crazy plumber, Greg.

I realized that there's no difference between life and death. Not a bit. Whatta you think about that?

Sloan gave Tony Windham five hundred in cash.

The killer shook Sloan's hand. Then he frowned. "You're probably wondering, now that I'm out, am I going to clean up my act? If I'm going to, well, keep behaving like I was before. With the girls."

Sloan held up a hand to silence him. "I'll give you a lesson about my business, Tony. Once the deal closes, a good salesman never thinks about what the buyer does with the product."

The boy nodded and started for the station, the bag over his shoulder.

Sloan got back in his company car and started the engine. He opened his attache case and looked over the sales sheets for tomorrow. Some good prospects, he reflected happily. He turned the AC up full, pulled out of the parking lot and headed east, looking for a hotel where he could spend the night.

You believe in God, Sloan?

No. I believe in selling. That's about it.

That's your soul then.

Dave Sloan reflected, It sure is.

Warmed to ninety-eight point six.

A Nice Place to Visit

When you're a natural-born grifter, an operator, a player, you get this sixth sense for sniffing out opportunities, and that's what Ricky Kelleher was doing now, watching two guys in the front of the smoky bar, near a greasy window that still had a five-year-old bullet hole in it.

Whatever was going down, neither of them looked real happy.

Ricky kept watching. He'd seen one guy here in Hanny's a couple of times. He was wearing a suit and tie—it really made him stand out in this dive, the sore thumb thing. The other one, leather jacket and tight jeans, razor-cut bridge-and-tunnel hair, was some kind of Gambino wannabe, Ricky pegged him. Or Sopranos, more likely—yeah, he was the sort of prick who'd hock his wife for a big-screen TV. He was way pissed off, shaking his head at everything Mr. Suit was telling him. At one point he slammed his fist on the bar so hard glasses bounced. But nobody noticed. That was the kind of place Hanny's was.

Ricky was in the rear, at the short *L* of the bar, his regular throne. The bartender, a dusty old guy, maybe black, maybe white, you couldn't tell, kept an uneasy eye on the guys arguing. "It's cool," Ricky reassured him. "I'm on it."

Mr. Suit had a briefcase open. A bunch of papers were inside. Most of the business in this pungent, dark Hell's Kitchen bar, west of Midtown, involved trading bags of chopped up plants and cases of Johnnie Walker that'd fallen off the truck and were conducted in the men's room or alley out back. This was something different. Skinny five-foot-four Ricky couldn't tip to exactly what was going down but that magic sense, his player's eye, told him to pay attention.

"Well, fuck that," Wannabe said to Mr. Suit.

"Sorry." A shrug.

"Yeah, you said that before." Wannabe slid off the stool. "But you don't really *sound* that fucking sorry. And you know why? Because *I'm* the one out all the money."

"Bullshit. *I'm* losing my whole fucking business."

But Ricky'd learned that other people losing money doesn't take the sting out of *you* losing money. Way of the world.

Wannabe was getting more and more agitated. "Listen careful here, my friend. I'll make some phone calls. I got people I know down there. You don't want to fuck with these guys."

Mr. Suit tapped what looked like a newspaper article in the briefcase. "And what're they gonna do?" His voice lowered and he whispered something that made Wannabe's face screw up in disgust. "Now, just go on home, keep your head down and watch your back. And pray they can't—" Again, the lowered voice. Ricky couldn't hear what "they" might do.

Wannabe slammed his hand down on the bar again. "This isn't gonna fly, asshole. Now—"

"Hey, gentlemen," Ricky called. "Volume down, okay?"

"The fuck're you, little man?" Wannabe snapped. Mr. Suit touched his arm to quiet him but he pulled away and kept glaring.

Ricky slicked back his greasy dark-blond hair. Easing off the stool, he walked to the front of the bar, the heels of his boots tapping loudly on the scuffed floor. The guy had six inches and thirty pounds on him but Ricky had learned a long time ago that craziness scares people a fuck of a lot more than height or weight or muscle. And so he did what he always did when he was going one on one—threw a weird look into his eyes and got right up in the man's face. He screamed, "Who I am is the guy's gonna drag your ass into the alley and fuck you over a dozen different ways, you don't get the fuck out of here now."

The punk reared back and blinked. He fired off an automatic "Fuck you, asshole."

Ricky stayed right where he was, kind of grinning, kind of not, and let this poor bastard imagine what was going to happen now that he'd accidentally shot a little spit onto Ricky's forehead.

A few seconds passed.

Finally Wannabe drank down what was left of his beer with a shaking hand and, trying to hold on to a little dignity, he strolled out the door, laughing and muttering, "Prick." Like it was Ricky backing down.

"Sorry about that," Mr. Suit said, standing up, pulling out money for the drinks.

"No, you stay," Ricky ordered.

"Me?"

"Yeah, you."

The man hesitated and sat back down.

Ricky glanced into the briefcase, saw some pictures of nice-looking boats. "Just gotta keep things calm 'round here, you know. Keep the peace."

Mr. Suit slowly closed the case, looked around at the faded beer promotion cut-outs, the stained sports posters, the cobwebs. "This your place?"

The bartender was out of earshot. Ricky said, "More or less."

"Jersey." Mr. Suit nodded at the door that Wannabe was just walked out of. Like that explained it all.

Ricky's sister lived in Jersey and he wondered if maybe he should be pissed at the insult. He was a loyal guy. But then he decided loyalty didn't have anything to do with states or cities and shit like that. "So. He lost some money?"

"Business deal went bad."

"Uh-huh. How much?"

"I don't know."

"Buy him another beer," Ricky called to the bartender then turned back. "You're in business with him and you don't know how much money he lost?"

"What I don't know," the guy said, his dark eyes looking right into Ricky's, "is why I should fucking tell you."

This was the time when it could get ugly. There was a tough moment of silence. Then Ricky laughed. "No worries."

The beers arrived.

"Ricky Kelleher." He clinked glasses.

"Bob Gardino."

"I seen you before. You live around here?"

"Florida mostly. I come up here for business some. Delaware too. Baltimore, Jersey Shore, Maryland."

"Yeah? I got a summer place I go to a lot."

"Where?"

"Ocean City. Four bedrooms, on the water." Ricky didn't mention that it was T.G.'s, not his.

"Sweet." The man nodded, impressed.

"It's okay. I'm looking at some other places too."

"Man can never have too much real estate. Better than the stock market."

"I do okay on Wall Street," Ricky said. "You gotta know what to look for. You just can't buy some stock 'cause it's, you know, sexy." He'd heard this on some TV show.

"Truer words." Now Gardino tapped his glass into Ricky's.

"Those were some nice fucking boats." A nod toward the briefcase. "That your line?"

"Among other things. Whatta *you* do, Ricky?"

"I got my hand in a lot of stuff. Lot of businesses. All over the neighborhood here. Well, and other places too. Maryland, like I was saying. Good money to be made. For a man with a sharp eye."

"And you have a sharp eye?"

"I think I do. Wanta know what it's seeing right now?"

"What, your eye?"

"Yeah."

"What's it seeing?"

"A grifter."

"A—?"

"A scam artist."

"I know what a grifter is," Gardino said. "I meant why do you think that's what I am?"

"Well, for instance, you don't come into Hanny's—"

"Hanny's?"

"Here. Hanrahan's."

"Oh."

"—to sell some loser asshole a boat. So what really happened?"

Gardino chuckled but said nothing.

"Look," Ricky whispered, "I'm cool. Ask anybody on the street."

"There's nothing to tell. A deal went south is all. Happens."

"I'm not a cop, that's what you're thinking." Ricky looked around and reached into his pocket, and flashed a bag of hash he'd been carrying around for T.G. "I was, you think I'd have this on me?"

"Naw, I don't think you're a cop. And you seem like an okay guy. But I don't need to spill my guts to every okay guy I meet."

"I hear that. Only . . . I'm just wondering there's a chance we can do business together."

Gardino drank some more beer. "Again, why?"

"Tell me how your con works."

"It's not a con. I was going to sell him a boat. It didn't work out. End of story."

"But . . . see, here's what I'm thinking," Ricky said in his best player's voice. "I seen people pissed off 'cause they don't get a car they wanted, or a house, or some pussy. But that asshole, he wasn't pissed off about not getting a boat. He was pissed off about not getting his down payment back. So, how come he didn't?"

Gardino shrugged.

Ricky tried again. "How's about we play a game, you and me? I'll ask you something and you tell me if I'm right or if I'm full of shit. How's that?"

"Twenty questions."

"Whatever. Okay, try this on: You *borrow*"—he held up his fingers and made quotation marks—"a boat, sell it to some poor asshole but then on the way here it *sinks*—" again the quotation marks —"and there's nothing he can do about it. He loses his down payment. He's fucked. Too bad, but who's he going to complain to? It's stolen merch."

Gardino studied his beer. Son of a bitch still wasn't giving away squat.

Ricky added, "Only there never was any boat. You never steal a fucking thing. You just show him pictures you took on the dock and a fake police report or something."

The guy finally laughed. But nothing else.

"Your only risk is some asshole whaling on you when he loses the money. Not a bad grift."

"I sell boats," Gardino said. "That's it."

"Okay, you sell boats," Ricky eyed him carefully. He'd try a different approach. "So that means you're looking for buyers. How 'bout I find one for you?"

"You know somebody who's interested in boats?"

"There's a guy I know. He might be."

Gardino thought for a minute. "This a friend of yours we're talking?"

"I wouldn'ta brought him up, he was a friend."

The sunlight came through some clouds over Eighth Avenue and hit Gardino's beer. It cast a tint on the counter, the yellow of a sick man's eye. Finally he said to Ricky, "Pull your shirt up."

"My—?"

"Your shirt. Pull it up and turn around."

"You think I'm wired?"

"Or we just have our beers and bullshit about the Knicks and we go our separate ways. Up to you."

Self-conscious of his skinny build, Ricky hesitated. But then he slipped off the stool, pulled up his leather jacket and lifted his dirty T-shirt. He turned around.

"Okay. You do the same."

Gardino laughed. Ricky thought he was laughing at him more than he was laughing at the situation but he held on to his temper.

The con man pulled up his jacket and shirt. The bartender glanced at them but he was looking like nothing was weird. This was, after all, Hanny's.

The men sat down and Ricky called for more brews.

Gardino whispered, "Okay, I'll tell you what I'm up to. But listen. You get some idea that you're in the mood to snitch, I got two things to say: One, what I'm doing is not exactly legal, but it's not like I'm clipping anybody or selling crack to kids, got it? So even if you go to the cops, the best they can get me for is some bullshit misrepresentation claim. They'll laugh you out of the station."

"No, man, seriously—"

Gardino held up a finger. "And number two, you dime me out, I've got associates in Florida'll find you and make you bleed for days." He grinned. "We copacetic?"

Whatever the fuck that meant. But Ricky said, "No worries, mister. All I wanta do is make some money."

"Okay, here's how it works: Fuck down payments. The buyers pay everything right up front. A hundred, hundred fifty thousand."

"No shit."

"What I tell the buyer is my connections know where there're these confiscated boats. This really happens. They're towed off by the DEA for drugs or Coast Guard or State Police when the owner's busted for sailing 'em while drunk. They go up for auction. But, see, what happens is, in Florida, there's so many boats that it takes time to log 'em all in. I tell the buyers my partners break into the pound at three in the morning and tow a boat away before there's a record of it. We ship it to Delaware or Jersey, slap a new number on it, and, bang, for a hundred thousand you get a half-million-dollar boat.

"Then, after I get the money, I break the bad news. Like I just did with our friend from Jersey." He opened up his briefcase and pulled out a newspaper article. The headline was:

THREE ARRESTED IN COAST GUARD IMPOUND THEFTS

The article was about a series of thefts of confiscated boats from a federal government impound dock. It went on to add that security had been stepped up and the FBI and Florida police were looking into who might've bought the half dozen missing boats. They'd arrested the principals and recovered nearly a million dollars in cash from buyers on the East Coast.

Ricky looked over the article. "You, what? Printed it up yourself?"

"Word processor. Tore the edges to make it look like I ripped it out of the paper and then Xeroxed it."

"So you keep 'em scared shitless some cop's going to find their name or trace the money to them."

Now, just go on home, keep your head down and watch your back.

"Some of 'em make a stink for a day or two, but mostly they just disappear."

This warranted another clink of beer glasses. "Fucking brilliant."

"Thanks."

"So if I *was* to hook you up with a buyer? What's in it for me?"

Gardino debated. "Twenty-five percent."

"You give me fifty." Ricky fixed him with the famous mad-guy

Kelleher stare. Gardino held the gaze just fine. Which Ricky respected.

"I'll give you twenty-five percent, if the buyer pays a hundred Gs or less. Thirty, if it's more than that."

Ricky said, "Over one fifty, I want half."

Gardino debated. He finally said, "Deal. You really know somebody can get his hands on that kind of money?"

Ricky finished his beer and, without paying, started for the door. "That's what I'm going to go work on right now."

■

Ricky walked into Mack's bar.

It was pretty much like Hanrahan's, four blocks away, but was busier, since it was closer to the convention center, where hundreds of Teamsters and union electricians and carpenters would take fifteen-minute breaks that lasted two hours. The neighborhood surrounding Mack's was better too: redeveloped town houses and some new buildings, expensive as shit, and even a Starbucks. Way fucking different from the grim, hustling combat zone that Hell's Kitchen had been until the seventies.

T.G., a fat Irishman in his mid-thirties, was at the corner table with three, four buddies of his.

"It's the Lime Ricky man," T.G. shouted, not drunk, not sober—the way he usually seemed. Man used nicknames a lot, which he seemed to think was cute but always pissed off the person he was talking to mostly because of the way he said it, not so much the names themselves. Like, Ricky didn't even know what a Lime Ricky was, some drink or something, but the sneery tone in T.G.'s voice was a putdown. Still, you had to have major balls to say anything back to the big, psycho Irishman.

"Hey," Ricky offered, walking up to the corner table, which was like T.G.'s office.

"The fuck you been?" T.G. asked, dropping his cigarette on the floor and crushing it under his boot.

"Hanny's."

"Doing what, Lime Ricky Man?" Stretching out the nickname.

"Polishing me knob," Ricky responded in a phony brogue. A lot of times he said stuff like this, sort of putting himself down in front of T.G. and his crew. He didn't want to, didn't like it. It just happened. Always wondered why.

"You mean, polishing some *altar boy's* knob," T.G. roared. The more sober in the crew laughed.

Ricky got a Guinness. He really didn't like it but T.G. had once said that that and whiskey were the only things real men drank. And, since it was called stout, he figured it would make him fatter. All his life, trying to get bigger. Never succeeding.

Ricky sat down at the table, which was scarred with knife slashes and skid marks from cigarette burns. He nodded to T.G.'s crew, a half dozen losers who sorta worked the trades, sorta worked the warehouses, sorta hung out. One was so drunk he couldn't focus and kept trying to tell a joke, forgetting it halfway through. Ricky hoped the guy wouldn't puke before he made it to the john, like yesterday.

T.G. was rambling on, insulting some of the people at the table in his cheerful-mean way and threatening guys who weren't here.

Ricky just sat at the table, eating peanuts and sucking down his licorice-flavored stout, and took the insults when they were aimed at him. Mostly he was thinking about Gardino and the boats.

T.G. rubbed his round, craggy face and his curly red-brown hair. He spat out, "And, fuck me, the nigger got away."

Ricky was wondering which nigger? He thought he'd been paying attention, but sometimes T.G.'s train of thought took its own route and left you behind.

He could see T.G. was upset, though, and so Ricky muttered a sympathetic "That asshole."

"Man, I see him, I will take that cocksucker out so fast." He clapped his palms together in a loud slap that made a couple of the crew blink. The drunk one stood up and staggered toward the men's room. Looked like he was going to make it this time.

"He been around?" Ricky asked.

T.G. snapped, "His black ass's up in Buffalo. I just told you that. The fuck you asking if he's here?"

"No, I don't mean here," Ricky said fast. "I mean, you know, *around*."

"Oh, yeah," T.G. said, nodding, as if he caught some other meaning. "Sure. But that don't help me any. I see him, he's one dead nigger."

"Buffalo," Ricky said, shaking his head. "Christ." He tried to listen more carefully, but what mostly he was thinking about was the boat scam. Yeah, that Gardino'd come up with a good one. And man, making a hundred thousand in a single grift (he and T.G.'d never come close to that before).

Ricky shook his head again. He sighed. "Got half a mind to go to Buffalo and take his black ass out myself."

"You the man, Lime Ricky. You the fucking man." And T.G. started rambling once again.

Nodding, staring at T.G.'s not-drunk, not-sober eyes, Ricky was wondering: How much would it take to get the fuck out of Hell's Kitchen? Get away from the bitching ex-wives, the bratty kid, away from T.G. and all the asshole losers like him. Maybe go to Florida, where Gardino was from. Maybe that'd be the place for him. From the various scams he and T.G. put together, he'd saved up about thirty thousand in cash. Nothing shabby there. But, man, if he conned just two or three guys in the boat deal, he could walk away with five times that.

Wouldn't set him for good, but it'd be a start. Hell, Florida was full of rich, old people, most of 'em stupid, just waiting to give their money to a player had the right grift.

A fist colliding with his arm shattered the daydream. He bit the inside of his cheek and winced. He glared at T.G., who just laughed. "So, Lime Ricky, you going to Leon's, ain't you? On Saturday."

"I don't know."

The door swung open and some out-of-towner wandered in. An older guy, in his fifties, dressed in beltless tan slacks, a white shirt and a blue blazer, a cord around his neck holding a convention badge, AOFM, whatever that was.

Association of . . . Ricky squinted. Association of Obese Ferret Molesters.

He laughed at his own joke. Nobody noticed. Ricky eyed the tourist. This never used to happen, seeing geeks in a bar around here. But then the convention center went in a few blocks south and, after that, Times Square got its balls cut off and turned into Disneyland. Suddenly Hell's Kitchen was White Plains and Paramus, and the fucking yuppies and tourists took over.

The man blinked, eyes getting used to the dark. He ordered wine—T.G. snickered, wine in this place?—and drank down half right away. The guy had to've had money. He was wearing a Rolex and his clothes were designer shit. The man looked around slowly, and it reminded Ricky sort of the way people at the zoo look at the animals. He got pissed and enjoyed a brief fantasy of dragging the guy's ass outside and pounding him till he gave up the watch and wallet.

But, of course, he wouldn't. T.G. and Ricky weren't that way; they steered clear of busting heads. Oh, a few times somebody got fucked up bad—they'd pounded a college kid when he'd taken a swing at T.G. during a scam, and Ricky'd slashed the face of some spic who'd skimmed a thousand bucks of their money. But the rule wasn't you didn't make people bleed if you could avoid it. If a mark lost only money, a lot of times he'd keep quiet about it, rather than go public and look like a fucking idiot. But if they got hurt, more times than not he'd go to the cops.

"You with me, Lime Ricky?" T.G. snapped "You're off in your own fucking world."

"Just thinking."

"Ah, thinking. Good. He's thinking. 'Bout your altar bitch?"

Ricky mimicked jerking off. Putting himself down again. Wondered why he did that. He glanced at the tourist again. The man was whispering to the bartender, who caught Ricky's eye and lifted his head. Ricky pushed back from T.G.'s table and walked to the bar, his boots making loud clonks on the wooden floor.

"Whassup?"

"This guy's from out of town."

The tourist looked at Ricky once then down at the floor.

"No shit." Ricky rolled his eyes at the bartender.

"Iowa," the man said.

Where the fuck was Iowa? Ricky'd come close to finishing high school and had done okay in some subjects but geography had bored him crazy and he never paid any attention in class.

The bartender said, "He was telling me he's in town for a conference at Javits."

Him and the ferret molesters . . .

"And . . ." the bartender's voice faded as he glanced at the tourist. "Well, why don't *you* tell him?"

The man took another gulp of his wine. Ricky looked at his hand. Not only a Rolex, but a gold pinkie ring with a big honking diamond in it.

"Yeah, why don't you tell me?"

The tourist did—in a halting whisper.

Ricky listened to his words. When the old guy was through, Ricky smiled and said, "This is your lucky day, mister."

Thinking: Mine too.

■

A half hour later, Ricky and the tourist from Iowa were standing in the grimy lobby of the Bradford Arms, next to a warehouse at Eleventh Avenue and Fiftieth Street.

Ricky was making introductions. "This's Darla."

"Hello, Darla."

A gold tooth shone like a star out of Darla's big smile. "How you doing, honey? What's yo' name?"

"Uhm, Jack."

Ricky sensed he'd nearly made up "John" instead, which would've been pretty funny, under the circumstances.

"Nice to meet you, Jack." Darla, whose real name was Sha'quette Greeley, was six feet tall, beautiful and built like a runway model. She'd also been a man until three years ago. The tourist from Iowa didn't catch on to this, or maybe he did and it turned him on. Anyway, his gaze was lapping her body like a tongue.

Jack checked them in, paying for three hours in advance.

Three hours? thought Ricky. An old fart like this? God bless him.

"Y'all have fun now," Ricky said, falling into a redneck accent. He'd decided that Iowa was probably somewhere in the South.

■

Detective Robert Schaeffer could've been the host on one of those Fox or A&E cop shows. He was tall, silver-haired, good-looking, maybe a bit long in the face. He'd been an NYPD detective for nearly twenty years.

Schaeffer and his partner were walking down a filthy hallway that stank of sweat and Lysol. The partner pointed to a door, whispering, "That's it." He pulled out what looked like an electronic stethoscope and played the sensor over the scabby wood.

"Hear anything?" Schaeffer asked, also in a soft voice.

Joey Bernbaum, the partner, nodded slowly, holding up a finger. Meaning wait.

And then a nod. "Go."

Schaeffer pulled a master key out of his pocket, and drawing his gun, unlocked the door then pushed inside.

"Police! Nobody move!"

Bernbaum followed, his own automatic in hand.

The faces of the two people inside registered identical expressions of shock at the abrupt entry, though it was only in the face of the pudgy middle-aged white man, sitting shirtless on the bed, that the shock turned instantly to horror and dismay. He had a Marine Corps tattoo on his fat upper arm and had probably been pretty tough in his day but now his narrow, pale shoulders slumped and he looked like he was going to cry. "No, no, no . . ."

"Oh, fuck," Darla said.

"Stay right where you are, sweetheart. Be quiet."

"How the fuck you find me? That little prick downstair at the desk, he dime me? I know it. I'ma pee on that boy next time I see him. I'ma—"

"You're not going to do anything but shut up," Bernbaum snapped. In a ghetto accent he added a sarcastic, "Yo, got that, girlfriend?"

"Man oh man." Darla tried to wither him with a gaze. He just laughed and cuffed her.

Schaeffer put his gun away and said to the man, "Let me see some ID."

"Oh, please, Officer, look, I didn't—"

"Some ID?" Schaeffer said. He was polite, like always. When you had a badge in your pocket and a big fucking pistol on your hip you could afford to be civil.

The man dug his thick wallet out of his slacks and handed it to the officer, who read the license. "Mr. Shelby, this your current address? In Des Moines?"

In a quivering voice, he said, "Yessir."

"All right, well, you're under arrest for solicitation of prostitution." He took his cuffs out of their holder.

"I didn't do anything illegal, really. It was just . . . it was only a date."

"Really? Then what's this?" The detective picked up a stack of money sitting on the cockeyed nightstand. Four hundred bucks.

"I—I just thought . . ."

The old guy's mind was working fast, that was obvious. Schaeffer wondered what excuse he'd come up with. He'd heard them all.

"Just to get some food and something to drink."

That was a new one. Schaeffer tried not to laugh. You spend four hundred bucks on food and booze in this neighborhood, you could afford a block party big enough for fifty Darlas.

"He pay you to have sex?" Schaeffer asked Darla.

She grimaced.

"You lie, baby, you know what'll happen to you. You're honest with me, I'll put in a word."

"You a prick too," she snapped. "All right, he pay me to do a 'round the world."

"No . . ." Shelby protested for a moment but then he gave up and slumped even lower. "Oh, Christ, what'm I gonna do? This'll kill my wife . . . and my kids . . ." He looked up with panicked eyes. "Will I have to go to jail?"

"That's up to the prosecutor and the judge."

"Why the hell'd I do this?" he moaned.

Schaeffer looked him over carefully. After a long moment he said, "Take her downstairs."

Darla snapped, "Yo, you fat fuck, keep yo' motherfuckin' hands offa me."

Bernbaum laughed again. "This mean you ain't my girlfriend no more?" He gripped her by the arm and led her outside. The door swung shut.

"Look, Detective, it's not like I robbed anybody. It was harmless. You know, victimless."

"It's still a crime. And don't you know about AIDS, hepatitis?"

Shelby looked down again. He nodded. "Yessir," he whispered.

Still holding the cuffs, Schaeffer eyed the man carefully. He sat down on a creaky chair. "How often you get to town?"

"To New York?"

"Yeah."

"Once a year, if I've got a conference or meeting. I always enjoy it. You know what they say, 'It's a nice place to visit.'" His voice faded, maybe thinking that the rest of that old saw—"but you wouldn't want to live there"—would insult the cop.

Schaeffer asked, "So, you got a conference now?" He pulled the badge out of the man's pocket, read it.

"Yessir, it's our annual trade show. At the Javits. Outdoor furniture manufacturers."

"That's your line?"

"I have a wholesale business in Iowa."

"Yeah? Successful?"

"Number one in the state. Actually in the whole region." He said this sadly, not proudly, probably thinking of how many customers he'd lose when word got out about his arrest.

Schaeffer nodded slowly. Finally he put the handcuffs away.

Shelby's eyes narrowed, watching this.

"You ever done anything like this before?"

A hesitation. He decided not to lie. "I have. Yessir."

"But I get a feeling you're not going to again."

"Never. I promise you. I've learned my lesson."

There was a long pause.

"Stand up."

Shelby blinked then did what he was told. He frowned as the cop patted down his trousers and jacket. With the guy not wearing a shirt, Schaeffer was 99 percent sure the man was legit, but had to make absolutely certain there were no wires.

The detective nodded toward the chair and Shelby sat down. The businessman's eyes revealed that he now had an inkling of what was happening.

"I have a proposition for you," Schaeffer said.

"Proposition?"

The cop nodded. "Okay. I'm convinced you're not going to do this again."

"Never."

"I could let you go with a warning. But the problem is the situation got called in."

"Called in?"

"A vice cop on the street happened to see you go into the hotel with Darla—we know all about her. He reported it and they sent me out. There's paperwork on the incident."

"My name?"

"No, just a John Doe at this point. But there *is* a report. I could make it go away but it'd take some work and it'd be a risk."

Shelby sighed, nodding with a grimace, and opened the bidding.

It wasn't much of an auction. Shelby kept throwing out numbers and Schaeffer kept lifting his thumb, more, more. . . . Finally, when the shaken man hit $150,000, Schaeffer nodded.

"Christ."

When T.G. and Ricky Kelleher had called to say that he'd found a tourist to scam, Ricky told him the mark could go six figures. That was so far out of those stupid micks' league that Schaeffer had to laugh. But, sure enough, he had to give the punk credit for picking out a mark with big bucks.

In a defeated voice Shelby asked, "Can I give you a check?"

Schaeffer laughed.

"Okay, okay . . . but I'll need a few hours."

"Tonight. Eight." They arranged a place to meet. "I'll keep your driver's license. And the evidence." He picked up the cash on the table. "You try to skip, I'll put out an arrest warrant and send that to Des Moines too. They'll extradite you and *then* it'll be a serious felony. You'll do real time."

"Oh, no, sir. I'll get the money. Every penny." Shelby hurriedly dressed.

"Go out by the service door in back. I don't know where the vice cop is."

The tourist nodded and scurried out of the room.

In the lobby by the elevator the detective found Bernbaum and Darla sharing a smoke.

"Where my money?" the hooker demanded.

Schaeffer handed her the two hundred of the confiscated cash. He and Bernbaum split the rest, a hundred fifty for Schaeffer, fifty for his partner.

"You gonna take the afternoon off, girlfriend?" Bernbaum asked Darla.

"Me? Hell, no, I gots to work." She glanced at the money Schaeffer'd given her. "Least till you assholes start paying me fo' not fuckin' same as I make *fo'* fuckin'."

■

Schaeffer pushed into Mack's bar, an abrupt entrance that changed the course of at least half the conversations going on inside real fast. He was a crooked cop, sure, but he was still a cop, and the talk immediately shifted from deals and scams and drugs to sports, women and jobs. Schaeffer laughed and strode across the room. He dropped into an empty chair at the scarred table, muttered to T.G., "Get me a beer." Schaeffer being about the only one in the universe who could get away with that.

When the brew came he tipped the glass to Ricky. "You caught us a good one. He agreed to a hundred fifty."

"No shit," T.G. said, cocking a red eyebrow. (The split was Schaeffer got half and then Ricky and T.G. divided the rest equally.)

T.G. asked, "Where's he getting it from?"

"I dunno. His problem."

Ricky squinted. "Wait. I want the watch too."

"Watch?"

"The old guy. He had a Rolex. I want it."

At home Schaeffer had a dozen Rolexes he'd taken off marks and suspects over the years. He didn't need another one. "You want the watch, he'll give up the watch. All he cares about is making sure his wife and his cornpone customers don't find out what he was up to."

"What's cornpone?" Ricky asked.

"Hold on," T.G. snarled. "Anybody gets the watch, it's me."

"No way. I saw it first. It was me who picked him."

"My watch," the fat Irishman interrupted. "Maybe he's got a money clip or something you can have. But I get the fucking Rolex."

"Nobody has money clips," Ricky argued. "I don't even want a fucking money clip."

"Listen, little Lime Ricky," T.G. muttered. "It's mine. Read my lips."

"Jesus, you two are like kids," Schaeffer said, swilling the beer. "He'll meet us across the street from Pier Forty-six at eight tonight." The three men had done this same scam or variations on it for a couple of years now but still didn't trust each other. The deal was they all went together to collect the payoff.

Schaeffer drained the beer. "See you boys then."

After the detective was gone they watched the game for a few minutes, with T.G. bullying some guys to place bets, even though it was in the fourth quarter and there was no way Chicago could come back. Finally, Ricky said, "I'm going out for a while."

"What, now I'm your fucking babysitter? You want to go, go." Though he still made it sound like Ricky was a complete idiot for missing the end of a game that only had eight minutes to run.

Just as Ricky got to the door, T.G. called in a loud voice, "Hey, Lime Ricky, my Rolex? Is it gold?"

Just to be a prick.

■

Bob Schaeffer had walked a beat in his youth. He'd investigated a hundred felonies, he'd run a thousand scams in Manhattan and Brooklyn. All of which meant that he'd learned how to stay alive on the streets.

Now, he sensed a threat.

He was on his way to score some coke from a kid who operated out of a newsstand at Ninth and Fifty-fifth and he realized he'd been hearing the same footsteps for the past five or six minutes. A weird scraping. Somebody was tailing him. He paused to light a cigarette in a doorway and checked out the reflection in a storefront window. Sure enough, he saw a man in a cheap gray suit, wearing gloves, about thirty feet behind him. The guy paused for a moment and pretended to look into a store window.

Schaeffer didn't recognize the guy. He'd made a lot of enemies over the years. The fact he was a cop gave him some protection—it's risky to gun down even a crooked one—but there were plenty of nut jobs out there.

Walking on. The owner of the scraping shoes continue his tail. A glance in the rearview mirror of a car parked nearby told him the man was getting closer, but his hands were at his side, not going for a weapon. Schaeffer pulled out his cell phone and pretended to make a call, to give himself an excuse to slow up and not make the guy suspicious. His other hand slipped inside his jacket and touched the grip of his chrome-plated SIG-Sauer 9mm automatic pistol.

This time the guy didn't slow up.

Schaeffer started to draw.

Then: "Detective, could you hang up the phone, please?"

Schaeffer turned, blinked. The pursuer was holding up a gold NYPD shield.

The fuck is this? Schaeffer thought. He relaxed, but not

much. Snapped the phone closed and dropped it into his pocket. Let go of his weapon.

"Who're you?"

The man, eyeing Schaeffer coldly, let him get a look at the ID card next to the shield.

Schaeffer thought: Fuck me. The guy was from the department's Internal Affairs Division—the boys that tracked down corrupt cops.

Still Schaeffer kept on the offensive. "What're you doing following me?"

"I'd like to ask you a few questions."

"What's this all about?"

"An investigation we're conducting."

"Hello," Schaeffer said sarcastically. "I sort of figured that out. Give me some fucking details."

"We're looking into your connection with certain individuals."

"'Certain individuals.' You know, not all cops have to talk like cops."

No response.

Schaeffer shrugged. "I have 'connections' with a lotta people. Maybe you're thinking of my snitches. I hang with 'em. They feed me good information."

"Yeah, well, we're thinking there might be other things they feed you. Some *valuable* things." He glanced at Schaeffer's hip. "I'm going to ask you for your weapon."

"Fuck that."

"I'm trying to keep it low key. But you don't cooperate, I'll call it in and we'll take you downtown. Then everything'll all be public."

Finally Schaeffer understood. It was a shakedown—only this time he was on the receiving end. And he was getting scammed by Internal Affairs, no less. This was almost fucking funny, IAD on the take too.

Schaeffer gave up his gun.

"Let's go talk in private."

How much was this going to cost him? he wondered.

The IAD cop nodded toward the Hudson River. "That way."

"Talk to me," Schaeffer said. "I got a right to know what this's all about. If somebody told you I'm on the take, that's bullshit. Whoever said it's working some angle." He wasn't as hot as he sounded; this was all part of the negotiating.

The IAD cop said only, "Keep walking. Up there." He pulled out a cigarette and lit it. Offered one to Schaeffer. He took it and the guy lit it for him.

Then Schaeffer froze. He blinked in shock, staring at the matches. The name on them was *McDougall's Tavern*. The official name of Mack's—T.G.'s hangout. He glanced at the guy's eyes, which went wide at his mistake. Christ, he was no cop. The ID and badge were fake. He was a hit man working for T.G., who was going to clip him and collect the whole hundred fifty Gs from the tourist.

"Fuck," the phony cop muttered. He yanked a revolver out of his pocket, then shoved Schaeffer into a nearby alley.

"Listen, buddy," Schaeffer whispered, "I've got some good bucks. Whatever you're being paid, I'll—"

"Shut up." In his gloved hands, the guy exchanged his gun for Schaeffer's own pistol and pushed the big chrome piece into the detective's neck. Then the fake cop pulled a piece of paper out of his pocket and stuffed it into the detective's jacket. He leaned forward and whispered, "Here's the message, asshole: For two years T.G.'s been setting up everything, doing all the work and you take half the money. You've fucked with the wrong man."

"That's bullshit," Schaeffer cried desperately. "He needs me! He couldn't do it without a cop! Please—"

"So long—" He lifted the gun to Schaeffer's temple.

"Don't do it! Please, man, no!"

A scream sounded from the mouth of the alley. "Oh my god." A middle-aged woman stood twenty feet away, staring at the man with the pistol. Her hands were to her mouth. "Somebody, call the police!"

The hit man's attention was on the woman. Schaeffer shoved him into a brick wall. Before he could recover and shoot, the detective sprinted fast down the alley.

He heard the man shout, "Goddamn it!" and start after him. But Hell's Kitchen was Bob Schaeffer's hunting grounds, and in five minutes the detective had raced through dozens of alleys and side streets and lost the killer. Once again on the street he paused and pulled his backup gun off his ankle holster, slipped it into his pocket. He felt the crinkle of paper—what the guy had planted on him. It was a fake suicide note, Schaeffer confessing that he'd been on the take for years and he couldn't take the guilt anymore. He had to end it all.

Well, he thought, that was partly right.

One thing was fucking well about to end.

■

Smoking, staying in the shadows of an alley, Schaeffer had to wait outside Mack's for fifteen minutes before T.G. Reilly emerged. The big man, moving like a lumbering bear, was by himself. He looked around, not seeing the cop, and turned west.

Schaeffer gave him half a block and then followed.

He kept his distance but when the street was deserted he pulled on gloves then fished into his pocket for the pistol he'd just gotten from his desk. He'd bought it on the street years ago—a cold gun, one with no registration number stamped on the frame. Gripping the weapon, he moved up fast behind the big Irishman.

The mistake a lot of shooters make during a clip is they feel they've gotta talk to their vic. Schaeffer remembered some old Western where this kid tracks down the gunslinger who killed his father. The kid's holding a gun on him and explaining why he's about to die, you killed my father, yadda, yadda, yadda, and the gunslinger gets this bored look on his face, pulls out a hidden gun and blows the kid away. He looks down at the body and says, "You gonna talk, talk. You gonna shoot, shoot."

Which is just what Robert Schaeffer did now.

T.G. must've heard something. He started to turn. But before he even caught sight of the detective, Schaeffer parked two rounds in the back of the fat man's head. He dropped like a bag of sand. He tossed the gun on the sidewalk—he'd never touched it with his bare hands—and, keeping his head down, and walked right past him, hit Tenth Avenue and turned north.

You gonna shoot, shoot.

Amen . . .

■

It took only one glance.

Looking into Ricky Kelleher's eyes, Schaeffer decided he wasn't in on the attempted hit.

The small, goofy guy, with dirty hair and a cocky face, strode up to the spot where Schaeffer was leaning against a wall, hand inside his coat, near his new automatic. But the loser didn't blink, didn't show the least surprise that the cop was still alive. The detective had interviewed suspects for years and he now concluded that the asshole knew nothing about T.G.'s attempted hit.

Ricky nodded. "Hey." Looking around, he asked, "So where's T.G.? He said he'd be here early."

Frowning, Schaeffer asked, "Didn't you hear?"

"Hear what?"

"Damn, you didn't. Somebody clipped him."

"T.G.?"

"Yep."

Ricky just stared and shook his head. "No fucking way. I didn't hear shit about it."

"Just happened."

"Christ almighty," the little man whispered. "Who did it?"

"Nobody knows yet."

"Maybe that nigger."

"Who?"

"Nigger from Buffalo. Or Albany. I don't know." Ricky then whispered, "Dead. I can't believe it. Anybody else in the crew?"

"Just him, I think."

Schaeffer studied the scrawny guy. Well, yeah, he *did* look like he couldn't believe it. But, truth was, he didn't look *upset*. Which made sense. T.G. was hardly Ricky's buddy; he was a drunk loser bully.

Besides, in Hell's Kitchen the living tended to forget about the dead before their bodies were cold.

Like he was proving this point, Ricky said, "So how's this going to affect our, you know, arrangement?"

"Not at all, far as I'm concerned."

"I'm going to want more."

"I can go a third."

"Fuck a third. I want half."

"No can do. It's riskier for me now."

"Riskier? Why?"

"There'll be an investigation. Somebody might turn up something at T.G.'s with my name on it. I'll have to grease more palms." Schaeffer shrugged. "Or you can find yourself another cop to work with."

As if the Yellow Pages had a section, "Cops, Corrupt."

The detective added, "Give it a few months, after things calm down, I can go up a few more points then."

"To forty?"

"Yeah, to forty."

The little man asked, "Can I have the Rolex?"

"The guy's? Tonight?"

"Yeah."

"You really want it?"

"Yeah."

"Okay, it's yours."

Ricky looked out over the river. It seemed to Schaeffer that a faint smile crossed his face.

They stood in silence for a few minutes and, right on time, the tourist, Shelby, showed up. He was looking terrified and hurt and angry, which is a fucking tricky combination to get into your face all at one time.

"I've got it," he whispered. There was nothing in his hands—no briefcase or bag—but Schaeffer had been taking kickbacks and bribes for so long that he knew a lot of money can fit into a very small envelope.

Which is just what Shelby now produced. The grim-faced tourist slipped it to Schaeffer, who counted the bills carefully.

"The watch too." Ricky pointed eagerly to the man's wrist.

"My watch?" Shelby hesitated and, grimacing, handed it to the skinny man.

Schaeffer gave the tourist his driver's license back. He pocketed it fast then hurried east, undoubtedly looking for a taxi that'd take him straight to the airport.

The detective laughed to himself. So, maybe New York ain't such a nice place to visit, after all.

The men split the money. Ricky slipped the Rolex on his wrist but the metal band was too big and it dangled comically. "I'll get it adjusted," he said, putting the watch into his pocket. "They can shorten the bands, you know. It's no big deal."

They decided to have a drink to celebrate and Ricky suggested Hanny's since he had to meet somebody over there.

As they walked along the avenue, blue-gray in the evening light, Ricky glanced at the placid Hudson River. "Check it out."

A large yacht eased south in the dark water.

"Sweet," Schaeffer said, admiring the beautiful lines of the vessel.

Ricky asked, "So how come you didn't want in?"

"In?"

"The boat deal."

"Huh?"

"That T.G. told you about. He said you were going to pass."

"What the fuck're you talking about?"

"The boat thing. With that guy from Florida."

"He never said anything to me about it."

"That prick." Ricky shook his head. "Was a few days ago. This guy hangs at Hanny's? He's who I'm gonna meet. He's got connections down in Florida. His crew perps these confiscated boats before they get logged in at the impound dock."

"DEA?"

"Yeah. And Coast Guard."

Schaeffer nodded, impressed at the plan. "They disappear *before* they're logged. That's some smart shit."

"I'm thinking about getting one. He tells me I pay him, like, twenty Gs and I end up with a boat worth three times that. I thought you'd be interested."

"Yeah, I'd be interested." Bob Schaeffer had a couple of small boats. Had always wanted a really nice one. He asked, "He got anything bigger?"

"Think he just sold a fifty-footer. I seen it down in Battery Park. It was sweet."

"Fifty feet? That's a million-dollar boat."

"He said it only cost his guy two hundred or something like that."

"Jesus. That asshole, T.G. He never said a word to me." Schaeffer at least felt some consolation that the punk wouldn't be saying *anything* to *anyone* from now on.

They walked into Hanrahan's. Like usual, the place was nearly deserted. Ricky was looking around. The boat guy apparently wasn't here yet.

They ordered boilermakers. Clinked glasses, drank.

Ricky was telling the old bartender about T.G. getting killed, when Schaeffer's cell phone rang.

"Schaeffer here."

"This's Malone from Homicide. You heard about the T.G. Reilly hit?"

"Yeah. What's up with it? Any leads?" Heart pounding fast, Schaeffer lowered his head and listened real carefully.

"Not many. But we heard something and we're hoping you can help us out. You know the neighborhood, right?"

"Pretty good."

"Looks like one of T.G.'s boys was running a scam. Involved some tall paper. Six figures. We don't know if it had anything to do with the clip, but we want to talk to him. Name of Ricky Kelleher. You know him?"

Schaeffer glanced at Ricky, five feet away. He said into the phone, "Not sure. What's the scam?"

"This Kelleher was working with somebody from Florida. They came up with a pretty slick plan. They sell some loser a confiscated boat, only what happens is, there is no boat. It's all a setup. Then when it's time to deliver, they tell the poor asshole that the feds just raided 'em. He better forget about his money, shut up and go to ground."

That little fucking prick. . . . Schaeffer's hand began shaking with anger as he stared at Ricky. He told the Homicide cop, "Haven't seen him for a while. But I'll ask around."

"Thanks."

He disconnected and walked up to Ricky, who was working on his second beer.

"You know when that guy's going to get here?" Schaeffer asked casually. "The boat guy?"

"Should be any time," the punk said.

Schaeffer nodded, drank some of his own beer. Then he lowered his head, whispered, "That call I just got? Don't know if you're interested but it was my supplier. He just got a shipment from Mexico. He's gonna meet me in the alley in a few minutes. It's some really fine shit. He'll give it to us for cost. You interested?"

"Fuck yes," the little man said.

The men pushed out the back door into the alley. Letting Ricky precede him, Schaeffer reminded himself that after he'd strangled the punk to death, he'd have to be sure to take the rest of the bribe money out of his pocket.

Oh, and the watch too. The detective decided that you really couldn't have too many Rolexes after all.

■

Detective Robert Schaeffer was enjoying a grande mocha outside the Starbucks on Ninth Avenue. He was sitting in a metal chair, none too comfortable, and he wondered if it was the type that outdoor furniture king Shelby distributed to his fellow hicks.

"Hey there," a man's voice said to him.

Schaeffer glanced over at a man sitting down at the table next to him. He was vaguely familiar and, even though the cop didn't exactly recognize him, he smiled a greeting.

Then the realization hit him like ice water and he gasped. It was the fake Internal Affairs detective, the guy T.G. and Ricky had hired to clip him.

Christ!

The man's right hand was inside a paper bag, where there'd be a pistol, of course.

Schaeffer froze.

"Relax," the guy said, laughing at the cop's expression. "Everything's cool." He extracted his hand from the bag. No gun. He was holding a raisin scone. He took a bite. "I'm not who you think I am."

"Then who the fuck are you?"

"You don't need my name. I'm a private eye. That'll do. Now listen, we've got a business proposition for you." The PI looked up and waved. To Schaeffer he said, "I want to introduce you to some folks."

A middle-aged couple, also carrying coffee, walked outside. In shock, Schaeffer realized that the man was Shelby, the tourist they'd scammed a few days ago. The woman with him seemed familiar too. But he couldn't place her.

"Detective," the man said with a cold smile.

The woman's gaze was chilly too, but no smile was involved.

"Whatta you want?" the cop snapped to the private eye.

"I'll let them explain that." He took a large bite of scone.

Shelby's eyes locked onto Schaeffer's face with a ballsy confidence that was a lot different from the timid, defeated look he'd had in the cheap hotel, sitting next to Darla, the used-to-be-a-guy hooker. "Detective, here's the deal: A few months ago my son was on vacation here with some friends from college. He was dancing in a club near Broadway and your associates T.G. Reilly and Ricky Kelleher slipped some drugs into his pocket. Then you came in and busted him for possession. Just like with me, you set him up and told him you'd let him go if he paid you off. Only Michael decided you weren't going to get away with it. He took a swing at you and was going to call nine-one-one. But you and T.G. Reilly dragged him into the alley and beat him so badly he's got permanent brain damage and is going to be in therapy for years."

Schaeffer remembered the college kid, yeah. It'd been a bad beating. But he said, "I don't know what you're—"

"Shhhhh," the private eye said. "The Shelbys hired me to find out what happened to their son. I've spent two months in Hell's Kitchen, learning everything there is to know about you and those two pricks you worked with." A nod toward the tourist. "Back to you." The PI ate some more scone.

The husband said, "We decided you were going to pay for what you did. Only we couldn't go to the police—who knew how many of them were working with you? So my wife and I and our other son—Michael's brother—came up with an idea. We decided to let you assholes do the work for us; you were going to double-cross each other."

"This is bullshit. You—"

The woman snapped, "Shut up and listen." She explained: They set up a sting in Hanny's bar. The private eye pretended to be a scam artist from Florida selling stolen boats and their older son played a young guy from Jersey who'd been duped out of his money. This got Ricky's attention, and he talked his way into the phony boat scam. Staring at Schaeffer, she said, "We knew you liked boats, so it made sense that Ricky'd try to set you up."

The husband added, "Only we needed some serious cash on the table, a bunch of it—to give you losers some real incentive to betray each other."

So he went to T.G.'s hangout and asked about a hooker, figuring that the three of them would set up an extortion scam.

He chuckled. "I kept *hoping* you'd keep raising the bidding when you were blackmailing me. I wanted at least six figures in the pot."

T.G. was their first target. That afternoon the private eye pretended to be a hit man hired by T.G. to kill Schaeffer so he'd get all the money.

"You!" the detective whispered, staring at the wife. "You're the woman who screamed."

Shelby said, "We needed to give you the chance to escape—so you'd go straight to T.G.'s place and take care of him."

Oh, Lord. The hit, the fake Internal Affairs cop. . . It was all a setup!

"Then Ricky took you to Hanrahan's, where he was going to introduce you to the boat dealer from Florida."

The private eye wiped his mouth and leaned forward. "Hello," he said in a deeper voice. "This's Malone from Homicide."

"Oh, fuck," Schaeffer spat out. "You let me know that Ricky'd set me up. So . . ." His voice faded.

The PI whispered, "You'd take care of him too."

The cold smile on his face again, Shelby said, "Two perps down. Now, we just have the last one. You."

"What're you going to do?" the cop whispered.

The wife said, "Our son's got to have years of therapy. He'll never recover completely."

Schaeffer shook his head. "You've got evidence, right?"

"Oh, you bet. Our older son was outside of Mack's waiting for you when you went there to get T.G. We've got real nice footage of you shooting him. Two in the head. Real nasty."

"And the sequel," the private eye said. "In the alley behind Hanrahan's. Where you strangled Ricky." He added, "Oh, and we've got the license number of the truck that came to get Ricky's body in the Dumpster. We followed it to Jersey. We can implicate a bunch of very unpleasant people, who aren't going to be happy they've been fingered because of you."

"And, in case you haven't guessed, " Shelby said, "we made three copies of the tape and they're sitting in three different lawyers' office safes. Anything happens to any one of us, and off they go to Police Plaza."

"You're as good as murderers yourself," Schaeffer muttered. "You used me to kill two people."

Shelby laughed. "*Semper Fi* . . . I'm a former Marine and I've been in two wars. Killing vermin like you doesn't bother me one bit."

"All right," the cop said in a disgusted grumble, "what do you want?"

"You've got the vacation house on Fire Island, you've got two boats moored in Oyster Bay, you've got—"

"I don't need a fucking inventory. I need a number."

"Basically your entire net worth. Eight hundred sixty thousand dollars. Plus my hundred fifty back. . . . And I want it in the next week. Oh, and you pay his bill too." Shelby nodded toward the private eye.

"I'm good," the man said. "But very expensive." He finished the scone and brushed the crumbs onto the sidewalk.

Shelby leaned forward. "One more thing: my watch."

Schaeffer stripped off the Rolex and tossed it to Shelby.

The couple rose. "So long, Detective," the tourist said.

"Love to stay and talk," Mrs. Shelby said, "but we're going to see some sights. And then we're going for a carriage ride in Central Park before dinner." She paused and looked down at the cop. "I just love it here. It's true what they say, you know. New York really *is* a nice place to visit."

Afterword to "Afraid"

I'd like to put on my professor's tweed jacket for a moment and welcome you to Fear 101, also known as "How to scare the socks off your readers in a few easy lessons." I'm going to offer some brief comments on how I incorporate fear into my writing.

I'm a suspense writer, not a philosopher or a psychiatrist. I'm concerned with fear only as it relates to storytelling. I've written "Afraid" to illustrate five essential fears that I regularly work into my writing. I'll also share several rules that enhance the effects of those fears in my audience.

The first of the five is our fear of the unknown. Throughout the story "Afraid" Marissa never knows exactly what's going to happen (and neither do we readers). At the beginning Antonio says, "It's a surprise," and I sustain the uncertainty established by that sentence for as long as I can. Marissa didn't know where they were going, what the old woman meant, who Lucia really was, what Antonio was doing at the house in Florence, what was in the wine cellar. . . . In fact, she realizes—too late—that she didn't really know Antonio at all.

Second is the fear we experience when others are in control of our lives—that is, we fear being vulnerable. Marissa is a shrewd businesswoman, intelligent and strong, and yet I've taken away all her resources. In "Afraid" Antonio is the driver and Marissa is solely a passenger, both literally and figuratively. At the end of the story, she's nearly naked, in a remote country home, without a cell phone or weapon, trapped in a sealed cell, at the complete mercy of a madman with a knife, and nobody even knows where she is. Can you be any more vulnerable than that?

The third fear is others' lacking control of themselves. When people play by society's rules, we are less afraid of them. When they don't, we are more. Psychopaths like Antonio have no control over their behavior so we can't reason with them, and they're not governed by laws and ethics. The fear is greatest when the lack of control is within someone we're close to. A random murderer or other criminal is bad enough but when people we know and are intimate with start acting strange and in threatening ways, we are particularly terrified. That's why I made my two characters lovers.

The fourth fear I use in my writing is our own lack of self-control. I mention the inexplicable drive to throw ourselves off a bridge or cliff—an urge that we've all experienced in one form or another. Marissa fears giving in to this specific impulse but in my story I use the impulse as a metaphor for a broader fear: of her loss of self-control with regard to Antonio. I also ply Marissa with drugs to further weaken her self-restraint.

The fifth fear is actually a broad category, which I call the icons of terror. These are the images (often clichés) that make us afraid either because they're imprinted into our brains or because we have learned to fear them. Some of the icons I used in this story are:

- The harbinger of evil (in Florence, the old woman with the jaundiced eyes, and the twin boys).
- The religious motifs and violent imagery in the tapestry Marissa was looking at when they met.
- The poison ring that Antonio bought for Marissa.
- The echos of evil associated with a particular locale (the Monster of Florence—a real serial killer, by the way—and the fictional torture/killings on the highway between Florence and Siena).
- The dead boy.

- Dolls. (Sorry, Madame Alexander, but they can be just plain creepy.)
- The isolated, gothic setting of the vacation house.
- The windowless cell.
- Blood.
- Various phobias (Marissa's claustrophobia, for instance).
- Darkness.
- The occult (the flowers and cross left by the stream).

These are just a few of the hundreds of icons of terror that can be used to jangle readers' nerves.

Finally I wish to mention two more rules I keep in mind when creating fear.

One, I enhance the experience of horror by making sure that my characters (and therefore my readers) stand to lose something important if the threatened calamity comes to pass. This means the people in my stories—the good characters and the bad—must be fleshed out and must themselves care about losing their lives or about suffering some loss. Marissa wouldn't be afraid if she didn't care about living or dying, and readers wouldn't be afraid for her if they didn't care about her as a character.

Two, I always remember that my job as a suspense writer is to make my audience afraid but never disgusted or repulsed, as happens when there's graphic gore or violence against, say, children or animals. The emotion that fear engenders in thriller fiction should be cathartic and exhilarating. Yes, make your readers' palms sweat, and make them hesitate to shut the lights out at night—but at the end of the ride make sure they climb off the roller coaster unharmed.

About the Author

A former journalist, folksinger and attorney, Jeffery Deaver is an international number-one best-selling author. His novels have appeared on a number of best-seller lists around the world, including *The New York Times*, the *Times* of London and the *Los Angeles Times*. His books are sold in 150 countries and translated into 25 languages. The author of twenty-two novels, he's been awarded the Steel Dagger and Short Story Dagger by the British Crime Writers' Association, is a three-time recipient of the Ellery Queen Reader's Award for Best Short Story of the Year and is a winner of the British Thumping Good Read Award. He's been nominated for six Edgar Awards from the Mystery Writers of America, an Anthony Award and a Gumshoe Award. His book *A Maiden's Grave* was made into the HBO movie *Dead Silence* starring James Garner and Marlee Matlin, and his novel *The Bone Collector* was a feature release from Universal Pictures, starring Denzel Washington and Angelina Jolie. His most recent books are *The Cold Moon*, *The Twelfth Card*, *Garden of Beasts* and *Twisted: Collected Stories*.

His next novel will be *The Sleeping Doll*, published in 2007.

And, yes, the rumors are true, he did appear as a corrupt reporter on his favorite soap opera, *As the World Turns*. Readers can visit his website at www.jefferydeaver.com.